QUILT
STORIES

QUILT
STORIES

Cecilia Macheski

Editor

THE UNIVERSITY PRESS OF KENTUCKY

Permissions for reprinting copyrighted materials
are indicated on pages 286-287.

Copyright © 1994 by The University Press of Kentucky

Scholarly publisher for the Commonwealth,
serving Bellarmine College, Berea College, Centre
College of Kentucky, Eastern Kentucky University,
The Filson Club, Georgetown College, Kentucky
Historical Society, Kentucky State University,
Morehead State University, Murray State University,
Northern Kentucky University, Transylvania University,
University of Kentucky, University of Louisville,
and Western Kentucky University.

Editorial and Sales Offices: Lexington, Kentucky 40508-4008

Library of Congress Cataloging-in-Publication Data

Quilt stories / Cecilia Macheski, editor.
    p.   cm.
    Includes bibliographical references (p.).
    ISBN 0-8131-1849-2 (alk. paper). —ISBN 0-8131-0821-7 (pbk.   :
alk. paper)
    1. Quilting—Literary collection.   2. Quilts—Literary
collections.   3. American literature.   I. Macheski, Cecilia, 1951–.
PS509.Q55Q55   1994
810.8'0355—dc20   93-33292

For my mother,
who taught me to sew,
and for
all the New Zealand Quilters

Contents

IV. WHEEL OF MYSTERY
Stories of Murder and Mystery

V. OLD MAID'S RAMBLE
Stories of Age and Wisdom

Acknowledgments

Quilt Stories emerged, in part, from my research for a forthcoming book, *Penelope's Daughters: Needlework and Women's Writing.* These sister projects have had support from friends, family, and colleagues over many years, for which I remain grateful. Special thanks are due to my colleagues in the English Department at LaGuardia Community College, The City University of New York, particularly Sandra Sellers Hanson, Leonard Vogt, Danny and Clellie Lynch, and Marian Arkin. I also wish to thank Dorothy Cozart for help in locating Alice Mac-Gowan's story and the American Quilt Study Group for their bibliographic support.

I am likewise very grateful to the New Zealand-United States Educational Foundation for sponsoring me on two Fulbright grants as a Senior Scholar to New Zealand, where I had the opportunity to tell quilting stories at Victoria University in Wellington, the University of Waikato in Hamilton, the University of Canterbury in Christchurch, and Otago University in Dunedin. Mr. Laurie Cox, executive director of the foundation, generously supported my research and travels, while patient and generous colleagues indulged my quilt obsession and plied me with hospitality. Particular thanks to the Women's Studies Department at Victoria: Jacqui Matthews, Phillida Bunkle, Alison Laurie, Janey Beddgood, and the students. At Waikato: Jan Pilditch, Marshall Walker, Alan Riach, Stuart and Stephanie Murray, and Margaret Thomson, who made quilts behind her computer. Elsewhere in New Zealand, thanks to Jeanette and Colin Gibson, Jocelyn Harris, Janet Wilson, and the staff at the American Embassy in Wellington. And, as always, I acknowledge the kiwi-Celtic hospitality from Maureen Montgomery and Rodney Foster.

Closer to home, the friendship quilt covers Mary Anne Schofield, Byrne Fone, Cathy Stern, Jeremiah Rusconi, and Mark, John, and Annie Speyer. To the Macheskis—Helen, Sylvia, Art, and Dianne—and to the memory of Andrew and Daniel, much love.

Introduction

*"There seemed to be every pattern
that the ingenuity of woman could devise and the
industry of woman could put together."*

So speaks the narrator in *Aunt Jane of Kentucky* when she stares in amazement at the piles of quilts Aunt Jane has brought out to air. The same might be said of the stories, poems, plays, song lyrics, autobiographies, and novels written by women from the mid-nineteenth century to the present that celebrate quilts and women's lives.

Quilt Stories brings together over twenty-five literary "blocks" to form a quilt of words. The works gathered here represent only a small portion of the literature about quilts and quiltmaking written in the last 150 years and while this is not a definitive collection, it does offer a wide range of the available literature. The majority of the pieces are written by women from the United States; others come from Canada and the United Kingdom. One is by a man writing in 1849 for the famous American women's magazine *Godey's Lady's Book*. The works are assembled into five thematic groups to emphasize the remarkable similarity of interests that exist within chronological and stylistic diversity. By placing the nineteenth- and twentieth-century writers side by side, *Quilt Stories* pieces together a sort of literary album quilt composed of the unique blocks created and signed by the writers.

The similarity of themes within the diversity of forms creates an argument for women's literary history as a continuous strand. The repetition and variation of patterns might be taken as evidence of the intricate, deliberate, and often subversive networks women created as they told one another stories. Often rejected by the mainstream literary world, women began publishing in popular magazines or writing in genres like the mystery novel. Ironically, the mass market through which they found a voice allowed them to reach more readers than the more traditional outlets. At the same time, the modern writers who have achieved mainstream literary recognition suggest by their use of quilts that they still claim kinship with their nineteenth-century sisters.

In the imagery of the quilt women writers found the literary model they needed. Renouncing the competitiveness of the patriarchal world they chose instead a model of cooperative and supportive creativity, one that gave voice not only to their individual talents but also to the experiences of women who had earlier stitched instead of penned their histories. Thus the five "blocks" of Quilt Stories are named for traditional quilting patterns, and the stories and poems are grouped by common themes rather than chronology.

In the first section of Quilt Stories each literary block shares with the others a reading of the quilt as a memory device. The writers, all women, envision the quilt as a cherished storehouse of women's experiences, memories, dreams, power, and pride. Denying the commonplace notion that quilts are "just scraps" or rags, each story and poem urges the reader to see not only the fragments but the whole, to learn to understand the code each quilter used as she planned and stitched her pattern. Through the metaphor of the quilt, the writers ask us to go beyond merely recognizing the artistic beauty of the designs; they insist we read the whole fabric to find the thread of women's history stitching the shapes together. In this way they are the templates for the stories in the rest of the book.

"Memory Blocks" is an intricate geometric pattern, where rectangles are imposed on squares and triangles rebel against corners and poke their sharp edges into the rectilinear space of the square, like memory invading and defining the present moment. There is no neat geometric pattern to memory, no regularity or predictability. The shape of childhood in our personal memory blocks may seem to have the crisp edges of a corner until our space is pieced into the family fabric; our triangles don't always fit someone else's squares, and we learn to overlap the patterns.

"The Patchwork Quilt," excerpted from The Lowell Offering, was written in 1845 by one of the young women who left her rural New England home to work in the cloth mills of Lowell, Massachusetts. The mill girls lived in dormitories on the factory site and were encouraged to write pieces for the Offering to ease the homesickness so many felt. Under the pseudonym of "Annette" this writer calls her quilt "a precious reliquary of past treasures." Like a book, the quilt is a "bound volume of hieroglyphics, each of which is a key to some painful or pleasant remembrance."

The subsequent poems are more volumes in the library of quilt stories. In an excerpt from *Natural Resources*, Adrienne Rich reminds us of how the unwritten history of women is often hidden among the objects of daily life, including scraps and stitches. Robin Morgan, in "Quilts," examines the quilting processes, the finding of the pattern, the solitary work, the ripping-out and resewing, comparing these steps to women's self-discovery. Joyce Carol Oates and Marge Piercy not only suggest the shared interest in the quilt as a memory device but argue for a thread connecting women's lives and experiences, a tradition passed on and preserved, a well-defined women's literary tradition. Their use of quilts has a warmth and familiarity so similar to that of the nineteenth-century women whose stories come later in the book that we are encouraged to see women's literary history as a giant, timeless quilting bee, where the writers gather around a frame and trade stories, gossip, and love. The last selection, by Canadian Paulette Jiles, continues the themes of the earlier selections, expanding the quilt-as-memory motif in a story-poem that recalls the author's childhood through the names of quilt patterns, which become "found poems" by the vividness of their imagery: Ohio Star, Bear Paw, Delectable Mountains, Rocky Road to California, Sister's Choice.

From quilts of memory we turn to those of celebration and to the ritual of the quilting bee where women came together to fabricate their patterns. Among the popular products of such a gathering is the Double Wedding Ring quilt. This lively design uses tiny colorful pieces to form mosaic circles that overlap and intertwine to symbolize the marriage bond. If placed against a dark background, the rings seem to dance and frolic, much as did the quilters and the men who joined them when the quilting frame was removed at the end of the afternoon and the fiddler came in to play reels.

The nineteenth-century American stories in this section look at the quilting bee that drew together groups of women to create the quilts so cherished by the modern writers. The earliest appeared in *Godey's Lady's Book* in 1849, the first important women's magazine; the latest appeared fifty years later. "The Quilting Party" is a sentimental tale written by a man, T.S. Arthur, who offers us insight into how the gathering of women can look to an outsider. Subsequent writers bring us into the quilters' circle. Harriet Beecher Stowe and Mary Eleanor Wilkins Freeman both remain well-known and in print today, while Marietta Holley and the anonymous playwright who created *Aunt Jerusha's Quilting Party* have been almost forgotten. Perhaps the strong, positive sense of women's identity that informs Freeman's and Stowe's work explains their survival, whereas the reliance of the others on often unpleasant stereotypes of older women accounts for their neglect. Jane Wilson Joyce's poem "Whitework, or Bride's Quilt" offers a modern reading of the quilting bee and its marriage traditions. Finally, an excerpt from Patricia Wendorf's novel *Double Wedding Ring*, published in 1989, uses the voice of its pioneer heroine to narrate a charming tale of courtship and marriage that unfolds through the device of traditional quilting bees and the wedding pattern. Presented as a diary of the main character, Rhoda Greypaull Salter, the narrative uses colloquial language and erratic spelling to reflect the lack of formal education that propels Rhoda to communicate through her quilt.

Read separately, one of the stories might seem again a mere "scrap," but read against the others, it creates part of a pattern. The repetition and variation of themes and motifs in the stories, as in the quilts, reveals an active women's literary network, a metaphorical sewing circle where women's words were pieced together into texts. Quilting bees likewise created women's communities in their use of oral rather than written words to initiate young women into courtship and marriage. The domestic ritual of the bee helps us appreciate the importance of both the quilts and the stories tied into them.

"Radical Rose," according to quilt legend, was a name given to a traditional rose pattern by a quilter sympathetic with the abolition movement before the Civil War. To express her rage in a society that denied her a vote, she stitched a black circle into the center of the rose, a glaring symbol of the slavery despoiling the nation. Each of the stories in this third section echoes the political spirit of some of the nineteenth- and twentieth-century quilters and features the experience of African American women and their quilts. Linking the struggle for justice and freedom with spiritual power and Gospel stories, each writer finds in her quilt a vehicle for breaking the silence imposed on women by oppression, disenfranchisement, and illiteracy.

Rebecca Cox Jackson was a spiritual leader, a Shaker Eldress, and an African American who found that despite her title and her religious community, she was treated with inequality by her "sisters." Her parable of washing quilts is an enigmatic but powerful response to injustice. "Gospel Quilt" and the excerpt from the novel *Black April* are tales that present African American experience through dialect that, to modern ears, may sound as outmoded and politically incorrect as Al Jolson in burnt cork. While no biographical information is available on Alice MacGowan, we know Julia Peterkin was a plantation owner's wife in Georgia. She wanted to record the daily life she saw around her and published a novel without a single white character. Presumably, both authors were white. Like T.S. Arthur in the previous section, they offer an outsider's view of a world they saw vanishing. Like him, too, Mac-Gowan leans toward a sentimental and stereotypical view reminiscent of the portrayal of the gossipy women in Aunt Jerusha's parlor. Nevertheless, the picture Peterkin provides of Southern life is invaluable for its record of domestic details, as the chapter called "The Quilting" demonstrates. Alice Walker's modern story "Everyday Use" balances *Black April* with an insider's view of the value placed on quilts by African American women as she argues for the quilt to be kept on the bed and off the museum wall, for the quilt to be read in context of its use, its womanist context, not flattened out and seen merely as an abstract design void of stories. Jane Wilson Joyce's poem "Bible Quilt, circa 1900" and Otto Whitney's recent *How To Make an American Quilt* take a similar position. Based in part on the story of Harriet Powers, maker of the magnificent Gospel quilt now owned by the Boston Museum of Fine Arts, Whitney's novel retells the tragic story of Powers's surrender of her cherished quilt to a white woman in order to make a few dollars to buy food during the Depression, but alters the ending, creating a modern daughter who reclaims the quilt from the woman who "bought" it. The daughter asserts her right to the fabled quilt because she knows the stories that must accompany the pictures; without the stories, the quilt is meaningless, a wall hanging without history or context. Like *Quilt Stories*, Whitney's reimagining of Powers's tale argues for a reunification of text and textile, of story and quilt.

"Wheel of Mystery" continues to represent the political and social themes writers find in the quilt with tales by twentieth-century women who write murder stories. Through the popular form of the whodunit, these writers use quilts to explore the insidious presence of violence in American society. Jane Wilson Joyce's "Rose of Sharon" introduces the theme of reading quilts for the secret knowledge they contain. Susan Glaspell's play *Trifles* makes a transition from the political stories in "Radical Rose" as she presents two women who conspire to protect a neighbor who is suspected of strangling her husband to death. The log cabin quilt square they discover in her workbox is a "trifle" to the sheriff and his partner (who happen to be the husbands of the two women), but to the women's more sympathetic eyes the quilt square is a biography recording a life of domestic violence from which the suspect escaped by committing murder. Their re-evaluation of the word "evidence" sets a literary and social precedent for modern criticism that looks for women's history in the personal and material culture of our society as well as in the official record. Sharyn McCrumb's *The Hangman's Beautiful Daughter* likewise challenges traditional ways of gathering evidence, by centering on Nora Bonesteel, a Tennessee quilter and knitter who has "the sight," an ability to see the future but not to change it. The excerpt here shows Nora explaining an unusual quilt, designed with cemetery and grave-stones, to the newly arrived Laura Bruce, wife of the local minister who is serving as military chaplain in the Saudi desert. Quilt historians are familiar with such mourning quilts, further examples of the remembrance motif and emblems of grief and death. (Readers will find another example in Bobbie Ann Mason's story "Love Life," in the final section of *Quilt Stories*.) The selection from Mari Sandoz is what she calls an allegorical tale of a young man who collects scraps for a blanket and finds himself an unwilling witness to a murder. Experimental in approach, Sandoz's tale leaves us to ponder the meaning of American violence.

The "Wheel of Mystery" pattern is a variant of Winding Ways, a cousin to the more familiar Robbing Peter to Pay Paul. A single block fails to suggest the visual intricacy the pattern creates when multiple blocks are assembled into a bedcover. The viewer's eye is carried from seemingly straight lines into circles; from small bow-tie shapes the eye travels into curving arches that reach across the design. Add the variant of color and we have a precursor of Op Art, a metaphor of the mysterious, tricky plots of the well-crafted crime novels. The quilter who can see both the part and the whole, the compass point and the extended curve, surpasses the police official as a sleuth because her special skills at perception exceed those of the patriarchal lawman.

"Old Maid's Ramble" concludes *Quilt Stories* with celebrations of growing old. "An Honest Soul" and *Aunt Jane of Kentucky* are early stories that enshrine the honesty and dignity of women for whom quilts are livelihood and life itself. Mary Eleanor Wilkins Freeman's heroine refuses to do shoddy work, even when she is tired and hungry. Aunt Jane fills her clothesline with quilts as other women display family photos.

Dorothy Canfield's "The Bedquilt" is a triumphant story of another spinster who rises from her place as "a little mouselike creature" by the creation of a quilt that wins first prize at the county fair. The family who supports Aunt Mehetabel reassesses her when she is herself transformed by her creative work. The quilt, an original design, comes to her in a kind of dream vision, and her execution of it brings pride and self-esteem: "As it hung before her eyes she saw the glory that shone around the creation of her hand and brain. She struggled for words." When she tries to borrow words from the prayer book, she worries first that this would be sacrilegious and then dismisses those hallowed words as "not being nearly striking enough" to describe her glorious quilt. The last story, "Love Life" by Bobbie Ann Mason, introduces us to yet another "ancient" figure, but this one has shelved her quilts in favor of watching MTV and sipping Coke spiked with peppermint schnapps. Opal, we learn, who "never cared for stories," passes the unfinished quilt on to her niece Jenny, for whom it becomes a talisman. The story title is both descriptive, if read as "her love life," and a command by which Opal lives—to love life at all costs.

"Old Maid's Ramble" is a variant of the Flying Geese pattern, a geometric design of triangles set together to make rectangles, then extended into long kite tales that are abstract renditions of geese in flight. This design variation creates an X by laying one strip across the other, suggesting perhaps that old maids go off in too many directions at once, instead of flying in the neat, straight rows of convention dictated by younger pilots. Read another way, the pattern creates a strong center block from which energy radiates to the very edges, pulsing with color and demonstrating its own logic.

In the triangles and squares, the colors and patterns, the words and symbols of the quilts and the stories, then, we can find ourselves, like Aunt Jane's visitor, in amazement. But, like her, we should stop to listen to the stories that accompany the quilts.

I
MEMORY BLOCKS

Stories of Remembrance and Meaning

The Patchwork Quilt

Annette (pseud.)

THERE IT IS! in the inner sanctum of my "old-maid's hall"—as cosy a little room as any lady need wish to see attached to her *boudoir*, and gloomy only from the name attached to it—for there is *much in a name*; and the merriest peal of laughter, if echoed from an "old-maid's hall," seems like the knell of girlhood's hopes.

Yes, there is the PATCHWORK QUILT! looking to the uninterested observer like a miscellaneous collection of odd bits and ends of calico, but to me it is a precious reliquary of past treasures; a storehouse of valuables, almost destitute of intrinsic worth; a herbarium of withered flowers; a bound volume of hieroglyphics, each of which is a key to some painful or pleasant remembrance, a symbol of—but, ah, I am poetizing and spiritualizing over my "patchwork quilt." Gentle friends! it contains a piece of each of my childhood's calico gowns, and of my mother's and sisters'; and that is not all. I must tell you, and then you will not wonder that I have chosen for this entertainment my *patchwork quilt*.

It is one of my earliest recollections, and that of the memorable period when I emerged from babyhood to childhood—the commencement of this patchwork quilt. I was learning to sew! O, the exultations, the aspirations, the hopes, the fears, the mortifications, the perseverance—in short, all moral emotions and valuable qualities and powers, were brought out in this grand achievement—the union of some little shreds of calico. And can I ever forget the long-suffering, patience and forbearance of my kind mother?—her smiles and words of encouragement and sympathy; her generosity in the donation of calico bits; her marvellous ingenuity in joining together pieces of all shapes, so that they would result in a perfect square! Parents, never purchase for your children mathematical puzzles—you can teach them and amuse them by making patchwork.

Nor must I forget the beautiful brass thimble that my father gave me, with the assurance that if I never would lose it he would one day give me one of silver! Nor the present of the kind old lady who expressed her gratification over my small stitches by a red broadcloth strawberry, which was introduced to me as an emery-bag. An emery-bag! its office and functions were all to be learned! How much there was that I did not know. But when I had so far learned to sew that five minutes' interval of rest and triumph did not occur between every two stitches, the strenuous application, by which I drove the perspiration from every pore of the hand, soon taught me the value of the emery-bag. O what a heroine was I in driving the stitches! What a martyr under the pricks and inflictions of the needle, which often sent the blood from my fingers but could not force a tear from my eyes! These were the first lessons in heroism and fortitude. How much, too, I learned of the world's generosity in rewarding the efforts of the industrious and enterprising. How many pieces in that quilt were presented because I "could sew," and *did sew*, and was such an adept in sewing. What predictions that I should be a noted sempstress; that I should soon be able to make shirts for my father, sheets for my mother, and nobody knows what not for little brothers and sisters. What legends were told me of little girls who had learned patchwork at three years of age, and could put a shirt together at six. What magical words were *gusset, felling, buttonhole-stitch*, and so forth, each a Sesame, opening into an arcana of workmanship—through and beyond which I could see embroidery, hem-stitch, open-work, tambour, and a host of magical beauties. What predictions that I could some day earn my living by my needle—predictions, alas! that have most signally failed.

Here, also, are the remembrances of another memorable period—the days when the child emerged into girlhood!—when the mind expanded beyond the influence of calico patchwork, and it was laid aside for more important occupations. O what a change was there! Once there could have been nothing more important—now the patchwork was almost beneath my notice. But there was another change. Muslin and lace, with cloths of more common texture, had long occupied my attention when my thoughts and efforts were returned to my patchwork quilt. Well do I remember the boy who waited upon me home from singing-school "six times running." I do not mean that he *waited* "*running*," but that he escorted me home six times in succession. What girl would not, under such circumstances, have resumed her patchwork quilt? but how stealthily it was done. Hitherto the patchwork joys had been enhanced by the sympathy, praises and assistance of others; but now they were cherished "in secrecy and silence." But the patchwork quilt bears witness to one of the first lessons upon the vanity of youthful hopes—the mutability of earthly wishes; and—and—any body might accompany me home six hundred times now, and such attentions would never be succeeded by a renewal of those patchwork hopes. Well do I remember the blushes of painful consciousness with which I met my sister's eye, when she broke into my sanctuary, and discovered my employment. By these alone might my secret have been discovered.

But how many passages of my life seem to be epitomized in this patchwork quilt. Here is the piece intended for the centre; a *star* as I called it; the rays of which are remnants of that bright copperplate cushion which graced my mother's easy chair. And here is a piece of that radiant cotton gingham dress which was purchased to wear to the dancing school. I have not forgotten the almost supernatural exertions by which I attempted to finish it in due season for the first night; nor how my mantua-maker, with pious horror, endeavored as strenuously to disappoint me; but spite of her it was finished, and she was guiltless—finished, all but the neck-binding, and I covered that with my little embroidered cape.

Here is a piece of the first dress I ever saw, cut with what were called "mutton-leg" sleeves. It was my sister's, and what a marvellous fine fashion we all thought that was. Here, too, is a remnant of the first "bishop sleeve" my mother wore; and here is a fragment of the first gown that was ever cut for me with a bodice waist. Was there ever so graceful beautiful pointed a fashion for ladies' waists before? Never, in my estimation. By this fragment I remember the gown with wings on the shoulders, in which I supposed myself to look truly angelic; and, oh, down in this corner a piece of that in which I first felt myself a woman—that is, when I first discarded pantalettes.

Here is a fragment of the beautiful gingham of which I had so scanty a pattern, and thus taxed my dress-maker's wits; and here a piece of that of which mother and all my sisters had one with me. Wonderful coincidence of taste, and opportunity to gratify it! Here is a piece of that mourning dress in which I thought my mother looked so graceful; and here one of that which should have been warranted "not to wash," or to wash all white. Here is a fragment of the pink apron which I ornamented so tastefully with "tape trimming;" and here a piece of that which was pointed all around. Here is a token of kindness in the shape of a square of the old brocade-looking calico, presented by a venerable friend; and here a piece given by the naughty little girl with whom I broke friendship, and then wished to take it out of its place, an act of vengeance opposed by my then forbearing mother—on this occasion I thought too forbearing. Here is a fragment of the first dress which baby brother wore when he left off long clothes; and here are relics of the long clothes themselves. Here a piece of that pink gingham frock, which for him was so splendidly decked with pearl buttons; and here a piece of that for which he was so unthankful, for he thought he was big enough to wear something more substantial than calico frocks. Here is a piece of that calico which so admirably imitated vesting, and my mother—economical from necessity—bought it to make "waistcoats" for the boys. Here are pieces of that I thought so bright and beautiful to set off my quilt with, and bought strips of it by the cent's worth—strips more in accordance with the good dealer's benevolence than her usual price for the calico. Here is a piece of the first dress which was ever earned by my own exertions! What a feeling of exultation, of self-dependence, of *self-reliance*, was created by this effort. What expansion of mind!—what awakening of dormant powers! Wellington was not prouder, when he gained the field of Waterloo, than I was with that gown. The belle, who purchases her dresses with the purse her father has always filled, knows not of the triumphant beatings of my heart upon this occasion. And I might now select the richest silk without that honest heart-felt joy. To do for myself—to earn my own living—to meet my daily expenses by my own daily toil, is now a task quite deprived of its novelty, and Time has robbed it of some of its pleasure. And here are patterns presented by kind friends, and illustrative of their tastes; but enough for you.

Then was another era in the history of my quilt. My sister—three years younger than myself—was in want of patchwork, while mine lay undisturbed, with no prospect of being ever called from its repository. Yes, she was to be married; and I not spoken for! She was to be taken, and I left. I gave her the patchwork. It seemed like a transference of girlish hopes and aspirations, or rather a finale to them all. Girlhood had gone, and I was a woman. I felt this more than I had ever felt it before, for my baby sister was to be a wife. We arranged it into a quilt. Those were pleasant hours in which I sympathized so strongly in all her hopes that I made them mine. Then came the quilting; a party not soon to be forgotten, with its jokes and merriment. Here is the memento of a mischievous brother, who was determined to assist, otherwise than by his legitimate occupation of rolling up the quilt as it was finished, snapping the chalkline, passing thread, wax and scissors, and shaking hands across the quilt for all girls with short arms. He must take the thread and needle. Well, we gave him white thread, and appointed him to a very dark piece of calico, so that we might pick it out the easier; but there! to spite us, he did it so nicely that it still remains, a memento of his skill with the needle—there in that corner of the patchwork quilt.

And why did the young bride exchange her snowy counterpane for the patchwork quilt? These dark stains at the top of it will tell—stains left by the night medicines, taken in silence and darkness, as though to let another know of her pains and remedies would make her sickness more real. As though Disease would stay his hand if met so quietly, and repulsed so gently. The patchwork quilt rose and fell with the heavings of her breast as she sighed in the still night over the departing joys of youth, of health, of newly wedded life. Through the bridal chamber rang the knell-like cough, which told us all that we must prepare for her an early grave. The patchwork quilt shrouded her wasted form as she sweetly resigned herself to the arms of Death, and fell with the last low sigh which breathed forth her gentle spirit. Then settled upon the lovely form, now stiffening, cold and lifeless.

And back to me, with all its memories of childhood, youth, and maturer years; its associations of joy, and sorrow, of smiles and tears; of life and death, has returned to me THE PATCHWORK QUILT.

Natural Resources

Adrienne Rich

12.

THESE THINGS by women saved
are all we have of them

or of those dear to them
these ribboned letters, snapshots

faithfully glued for years
onto the scrapbook page

these scraps, turned into patchwork,
doll-gowns, clean white rags

for stanching blood
the bride's tea-yellow handkerchief

the child's height penciled on the cellar door
In this cold barn we dream

a universe of humble things—
and without these, no memory

no faithfulness, no purpose for the future
no honor to the past

Quilts

Robin Morgan

FRUGALITY is not the point. Nor waste.
It's just that very little is discarded
in any honest spending of the self,
and what remains is used and used
again, worn thin by use, softened
to the pliancy and the translucence
of old linen, patched, mended, reinforced,
and saved. So I discover how
I am rejoicing slowly into a woman
who grows older daring to write
the same poem over and over, not merely
rearranged, revised, reworded, but one poem
hundreds of times anew.

The gaudy anniversaries.
The strips of colorless days gone unexamined.
This piece of watered silk almost as shot with light
as a glance he gave me once. This sturdy
canvas shred of humor. That fragment of pearl velvet,
a particular snowstorm. Assorted samples of anger—
in oilcloth, in taffeta, in tufted chenille,
in every imaginable synthetic and ready-to-wear.
This diamond of tie-dyed flannel baby blanket.
The texture of deception, its heavy embroidery.
A segment of bleached muslin still crisp with indifference.
That torn veil of chiffon, pewter as the rain
we wept through one entire July. These brightly printed

squares across which different familiar figures
walk through parks or juggle intricate abstract designs.

Two butterflies of yellow organdy my mother cut
when I was four years old. A mango cross-grain ribbon
fading toward peach. The corner of an old batik
showing one small window that looked out on—what?
A series of simple cotton triangles in primary colors.
And this octagonal oddment: a sunburst or mandala or pinwheel
radiating rainbow stripes against what turns out
upon inspection to be a densely flowered background.
It's striking enough to be a centerpiece.

Once I thought, this work could be less solitary.
Many of us, I imagined, would range ourselves
along the edges of some pattern we would all agree on
well beforehand, talking quietly while we worked
each with her unique stitch inward to the shared center.

This can still be done of course, but some designs
emerge before they can be planned, much less agreed on,
demand an entire life's work, and are best viewed upon
completion.
And then, so many designers bore too easily
to work out the same theme over and over, with only
the subtlest adjustments, like changing
your thread from brown to gray.

Still the doorbell tolls in the visitors, some of whom
slash rents across the section just perfected—all
        without meaning to,
and some of whom admire the quality
of scraps—but rarely notice the order, which is
the only thing you control. Some do contribute:
a quarter yard of paisley, or a length of gauze
fine enough for bandages. Once somebody left behind
an entire packet of gold lamé all by itself.
The challenge is to use it in such a way

that the tarnished griefs she stuffed it with
to lend it shape need no longer be hidden.

Throwing a piece away is not the answer. Nor
has hoarding anything to do with this.
And anybody really hazards piecework in the expectation
that someday all these fragments might inevitably fit
into a gentle billow of warmth, to comfort
the longest winter sleep.
Not even that,
It's just the pleasure of rescuing some particle
into meaning. For a while.

Of course, this means that you yourself
are placed where you risk being
all the more severely worn
into translucency
held up toward the light.

Looking at Quilts

Marge Piercy

Who DECIDED what is useful in its beauty
means less than what has no function besides beauty
(except its weight in money)?
Art without frames: it held parched corn,
it covered the table where soup misted savor,
it covered the bed where the body knit
to self and other and the
dark wool of dreams

The love of the ordinary blazes out: the backyard
miracle: Ohio Sunflower,
                    Snail's Track,
                              Sweet Gum Leaf,
              Moon over the Mountain.

In the pattern Tulip and Peony the sense
of design masters the essence of what sprawled
in the afternoon: called conventionalized
to render out the intelligence, the graphic wit.

Some have a wistful faded posy yearning:
                              Star of the Four Winds,
              Star of the West,
                        Queen Charlotte's Crown.
In a crabbed humor as far from pompous
as a rolling pin, you can trace wrinkles
from smiling under a scorching grasshopper sun:

Monkey Wrench
        The Drunkard's Path
                Fool's Puzzle,
        Puss in the Corner
                Robbing Peter to Pay Paul,
and the deflating
                Hearts and Gizzards.

Pieced quilts, patchwork from best gowns,
winter woolens, linens, blankets, worked jigsaw
of the memories of braided lives, precious
scraps: women were buried but their clothing wore on.

Out of death from childbirth at sixteen, hard
work at forty, out of love for the trumpet vine
and the melon, they issue to us:
                Rocky Road to Kansas,
        Job's Troubles,
                Crazy Ann,
                        The Double Irish Chain,
        The Tree of Life:
                this quilt might be
the only artifact a woman
would ever see, yet she did not doubt
what we had forgotten, that out of her
potatoes and colic, sawdust and blood
she could create: together, alone,
she seized her time and made new.

Celestial Timepiece

Joyce Carol Oates

By squares, by inches, hour after hour,
the great quilts grew.
Serendipity and *Felicity* and *All-Hallows-Eve*
and *Wonder-Working Providence* and *Milky Way*
and *Celestial Timepiece*—plants, suns, fireballs, moons—
covering half a wall
like a conqueror's map.

The men, the husbands, drew up such maps.
Their strategy has always been maps.

Look at these massive wool-and-feather-lined quilts,
recording square by square these wondrous years—
1784, 1806, 1848—
Glass Garden survives though frayed, and *Fools* and *Poppies*,
and *Gyroscope* all aflame, of 1864.

Soldiers are always passing along the roads.
Soldiers, the dead, prisoners in churches.
A hospital in a churchyard, the women's fingers working,
1865, 1876, conquerors on horseback along the roads,
Butterflies and *Christmas Eve* and *Jesus Our Savior.*

Square by square, spilling to the floor.
Winter days when the sun was a brief parenthesis overhead.
Spring days when no letters came. No news.
Calla lillies for the dead, gowns for the infants,

sunflowers bawdy as the first day of Creation.
Years. Decades. Centuries. Rags
torn from sheets, torn from dresses and trousers,
here is the resurrection of the body!—in the quilt's soiled squares.

The men's maps too are tearing,
so often folded.
The soldiers, the dead.
The conquerors on horseback.

She takes your hand, *Feel this, feel each square*, she says,
do you understand?
So many textures, a Babel of textures—coarse wool, fine silk,
satin, lace, burlap, cotton, brocade, hemp, fussy pleats—
you close your eyes, *Can your read it?* she asks, *Do you understand?*

Here, an entire world stitched to perfection.
By squares, by inches. You are the child-witness.
Your fingers read it like Braille.

My Grandmother's Quilt

Paulette Jiles

THE OLD HUFFMAN HOUSE outside New Lebanon, Missouri, is small, made of board-and-batten; it has a fireplace for cooking, three rooms downstairs and an attic with a small window. In the 1880's there was still a great deal of original timber on the rolling hills; not all of it has been cleared. The farms of the area are small, because the soil is good, and are mostly self-sufficient. The Missouri, Kansas and Texas Railroad takes the surplus to market out of Otterville, the nearest town. Jesse James is hiding out 150 miles away in St. Joseph, and the most profitable recent crop is mules, to be sold to the U.S. Army. The Lamine River floods out the valley once a year, but it hasn't yet come as far as the Huffman house. The more affluent town ladies in Otterville and Boonville are wearing bustles, would never appear in the street without a hat, and are not concerned so much with getting the vote as getting a cookstove, and wallpaper and a mangle. But these are luxury items and Margaret Johanna Burnett Huffman is a poor widow. Samuel Huffman, who came from Virginia by ox-cart in 1853 and convinced her to come with him, was a fiddlefoot, a storyteller, and a man with no feck whatever. He resisted joining the New Lebanon church because he had been raised in the German Reformed Church of Virginia and was proud of it. The whole community regarded him as standoffish. Maggie Jo had come with him mostly because her Burnett relatives were already out there in Missouri, and there were uncles and aunts to meet her. And now, even though she has seen her children grown and married, she has two more to care for.

LULA BELLE

The mouth is the place that thoughts leap out of; it is the starting gate of our hearts, where words race out like horses, the words of preachers, whispered

conversations, stories told sitting on the rails of the salt springs, the words of
fortune tellers. My whole life has been made up out of other people's stories.

The congregation of the New Lebanon church is gathered in the
graveyard, under the big pine, to bury Nanni King. Brother Ewing is
saying the last words as the red dirt flies.

"Our sister Nancy Elizabeth King leaves behind with us, brothers
and sisters, leaves unto our care, two little girls and a grieving husband.
The affliction she bore with Christian patience has reached its end, and
the soul of Nanni King has gone to dwell in Heaven with Our Lord, who
in His infinite mercy gave it, and in His unscrutable wisdom has taken it
away. So it is said by the prophet Malachi, chapter four, verses five and
six, 'Behold! I shall send you Elijah the Prophet before the coming of the
Great and Dreadful Day of the Lord, and he shall turn the hearts of the
fathers unto the children, and the hearts of the children unto their fathers, lest I come and smite the earth with a curse.' So here we have the
father and the children left to look out after each other, and I know
brother King need not fear that warning."

Brother Ewing gives a stiff look at William Nelson King, who is
standing there with his hat off, and the two girls clinging to his britches,
and the wind up his back. Brother Ewing turns back to the grave and says
of his cousin: "And we commend Nanni King's body to the earth, and
her spirit will dwell with the Lord."

The congregation sings an old hymn called "Higher Ground," and
the wind is still galloping down the Lamine River Valley, snatching at
rain and leaves by the handfuls:

> *Lord, lift me up and let me stand*
> *by Faith in Heaven's table-land . . .*

And the shovels are dispatching dirt onto the coffin and, in the
distance, the sound of pigs grunting. Somebody calls out in a desperate
stage whisper:

"Chesley Burnett's pigs are out!!"

But the congregation keeps on singing:

> *A higher plane than I have found*
> *Lord, plant my feet on higher ground . . .*

This is bad news: pigs are known to root up graves, if they can get at
them. Maybe they are checking it out; maybe Nanni won't be able to
rest in peace.

"Get them damn pigs outa here," says Henry T. Ewing.

"Them's Chesley Burnett's pigs!" says another man.

Somebody slips quietly away from the mourning and hymn singing and then there is a shot and a squeal and then no more pig sounds.

"Well, Burnett's going to be short one spotted pig, I tell you what."

LULA BELLE
A-women
A-men!
Shot at a rooster and
Killed a hen!

At Maggie Jo's house after the funeral, the girls and their father have come to sink into chairs and commune in broken sentences with one another, stunned as stones. November is a terrible time to lose a wife, a mother, a daughter, and then there were those terrible spying sinister pigs at the funeral. Maggie Jo rocks to the sound of Samuel Huffman's Virginia clock that has a sun and a moon on it and the picture of a lady and a gentleman spooning under a willow.

"Here I am seventy-two years old and still a-living," says Maggie Jo.

"What's that, Mrs. Huffman?" asks William looking up.

"I don't know why it wasn't me that was took," says Maggie Jo, looking up at the Virginia clock. "It's a full moon."

"Well, if anything should happen while I'm gone, go get Chesley and get him to telegraph me on the Katy," says William, trying to think ahead. He knows he has to leave the girls with their grandmother and take up his brakeman's lantern to supply the money to support this household. Or at least he intends to. "Go to Otterville and send a telegram, Mrs. Huffman."

"What's the Katy, Poppa?" asks Dale.

"That's the Missouri, Kansas and Texas Railroad, honey," says William. "That's where daddy works."

"If anything was to happen, I'd send Dale running over to Whitlow's and tell him," says Maggie Jo, making herself stop dwelling on the pigs and the full moon.

"I'd keep them if I could, Mrs. Huffman," says William, "but you know I won't be home but every three days."

"Grandma? Do I have to run through Whitlow's hog field?" says Dale. She is now permanently afraid of pigs.

"No, honey, run through the horse field," says Maggie Jo.

"That's just if anything was to happen, Dale," says William. "Like you broke a leg or something. And I'd come home right away. Right away. Now, Mrs. Huffman, Brother Ewing is farming your creek land, and Henry T. Ewing will be cutting your timber . . ."

"Well, she's with the angels now," says Maggie Jo.

"Yes, she is," says William.

"Yes, that's where Mama's at," says Dale, wanting to believe it.

"Where's Mama at?" asks Lula Belle, age four.

"With the angels, Lula Belle," says William.

"Mama is gone with the angels, sister," says Dale, as she suddenly becomes a little mother. It will be a permanent condition.

"Well, when's she coming back?"

"Oh God, children, we do not know when the Grim Reaper will arrive to take us to our final abode!" says William, starting to cry. "A month ago, one night she took all the pins out of her hair and said to me, as I am standing here, she said, 'Mr. King, they say long hair means long life!' Just as I am sitting here. She was beautiful and healthy and . . . (he thinks of the words from the newspaper) . . . accomplished in all the womanly arts, and now she's alaying in the graveyard. And here's two motherless children. Mrs. Huffman, I am stabbed to the heart."

"Mr. King, take hold of yourself," says Maggie Jo, also starting to cry. "And her out doing a washing in the yard not two weeks ago, a-wringing out everybody's underdrawers."

"Maggie Johanna, Mrs. Huffman, I am going to drive out now. I'm going to Mr. Hanlin's. He will want to hear about the funeral."

"But Poppa," says Dale, jumping up to catch him, "You left your pipe!"

"So I did," says William.

"Poppa, don't go over there," says Dale. "You're just going over there to drink some liquor. Everything in this whole house wants fixin'!"

"Don't tell me what I'm going to do, Dale. My grief is more than I can bear at this particular time."

Old man Hanlin lives on Hess Creek. Chickens roost on his bedstead. He keeps a still and a liquor shop. This is a man's world, over there on Hess Creek; the infamous Lost Corners.

There is rain and distant thunder. It is the spring of 1885. In places, it rains through the old Huffman house. At night the girls lie in their bed up in the attic room and whisper. They have pried up the mill sidings used as finish boards in two places, to keep their small treasures dry, and Lula Belle has discovered that the board-and-battens are a cover over the older house—a log cabin with walnut logs. There is a family of field mice in the old clay chinking. They become her audience, attentive, bright-eyed, rivetted by her scattered thoughts.

LULA BELLE

Me and Dale were born a little while apart. We used to wonder where we came from. We could have been waiting in the clouds of heaven to get born. But then me and Dale started arguing about what kinds of clouds.

A crack of thunder rattles the panes.

I said they would have been thunderclouds, big men-o-war clouds with blazing edges sailing away towards Tennessee. And when the rains come down, it's very tall, like long pieces of jewelry, we could have been wearing the rain for baby clothes, we could have rained on mama in spirits. I mean, our spirits. But Dale said:

And the family of field mice all turn to Dale:

DALE

No, it's the clouds like laundry, we could have been washed out of the Holy Washtubs up there!

LULU BELLE

This is big thinking. Me and Dale like Big Thinking, but we only talk it betwixt ourselves, at night, or when we walk down by Hess Creek.

The audience of field mice in the log chinking are suddenly joined, she thinks, by an audience of spotted pigs out in the field. Don't pigs go to sleep at night? She thinks of something else:

We'll be angels after, me and Dale. She says Mama is an angel now.

Maggie Jo looks over at the Virginia Clock. The gentleman and lady, forever fastidiously in love, look down at hands that say ten-thirty.

"Time you girls went to sleep now," says Maggie Jo. "And burn the cobwebs off from over your bed with that candle! But don't you dare burn a spider! That'll mean a death is coming."

Maggie Jo goes back to piecing the "Kaleidoscope" quilt by candle-

light. The storm is moving towards them, but slowly. The wind blows up
the scent of new leaves and sap rising in the sassafras.

LULA BELLE

*I hear mama at night; she taps at the window of Maggie Jo's house, and all the
windows of all the houses we be sent to stay at. I remember the time we came
down sick. Mama and me had brain fever, we had pneumonia, we swelled up
and tossed back and forth in our beds, we lay in a swoon, they cooled our
fevered brows and prayed over us both day and night. Mama died, and my
mind hasn't been the same as other people's minds since then.*

The chorus is made up of Cumberland Presbyterians, a Frenchman
in knee-britches with his sword and pistol by his side, a fortune-telling
woman, Lucifer, Lula Belle's dear departed mother, sinister pigs, and
darling mice:

CHORUS

*This unfortunate child Lula Belle King is never going to be right in the head,
brothers and sisters, from the outcome and the effects of brain fever, so let her
hear what she hears, let her see what she sees. She is not playing with a full
deck, she is one brick short of a load. Go to sleep now girls.*

"Go to sleep now, girls," says Maggie Jo.
"Goodnight, Dale."
"Goodnight, Lou."
"God bless you, Dale."
"God bless you, Lou."

LULA BELLE

*When I first looked at my reader in school, the letters took fire, they swelled up
and crossed each other, I got everything backwards. At night there was only
one candle on the table, but sometimes I could see two of them, or everybody
had holy angel haloes around their heads. I kind of liked it. And I didn't want
to learn to read anyhow.*

"Now Lou, listen to me," says Dale.
"What?"
"See, this here is an A. See there? It sticks up just like a woodpile."
"A like a woodpile."
"And this here is a B," says Dale. "Like a pair of big old pillows. Like
Aunt Lizzy's bosoms!"

"Like Aunt Lizzy's bosoms!"

"Well, ain't it?" says Dale, drawing another B.

"Yes, and A goes 'aaaahhh' and B goes Buh! Buh! Ah—BUH! Ah-buh! We did that already."

Dale pushes the paper in front of Lula Belle and writes the letters again, B first and then A.

"So, if I write them this way . . . say the sounds. . . . I'll give you a hint. What does Maggie Leona's nanny goat say?"

"Baaaaaaaaaaaaa!" shouts Lula Belle.

Dale writes the letters again.

"I just wrote that down!" says Dale. "Now read it."

"Abuh," says Lula Belle, squinting at the letters. "It says Abuh. What's a Abuh?"

"How come you're reading it backwards??!!"

"Well," says Lula Belle, after a long pause. "Ain't that how it's writ?"

"Grandma Maggie Jo! Come over here and whup this child!" shouts Dale, reaching for Lou.

"Don't you touch me a lick!" says Lula Belle, jumping up. "I'll snatch you bald-headed!"

Maggie Jo leaves off carding cotton and comes to settle things.

"Now Dale," she says. "Sometimes Lula Belle sees things backwards. I've noticed her doing that. But, Lula Belle, see this pattern here? On this quilt?" says Maggie Jo, pointing to the quilt covering her bed over in the corner.

"Double Irish Chain, Grandma," says Lula Belle.

"And that one over there on the trunk?"

"The Drunkard's Path. Ha. Goes from here all the way to Old Man Hanlin's."

"You're walking on thin ice, sister," says Dale, primly.

Maggie Jo goes back to the cotton and pulls a wad loose; picks up more between the carding batts.

"Well, she can read quilt patterns, Dale."

"You little hussy," says Dale, furious that all her efforts have gone nowhere.

"But you can see them all at once," says Lula Belle, looking over at the quilt on the bed.

"Let it go, Dale. Her mind was affected," says Maggie Jo, carding with practiced strokes.

"My mind was affected," smirks Lula Belle.

"If you don't learn to read, they'll take you to the county poorhouse, Lula Belle King."

"Hear what she says, Lula Belle," says Maggie Jo. "Just keep on trying. I never learned to read, and I'm just about in the poorhouse."

"Oh, Grandma," says Dale, "nobody would ever let you go to the poorhouse! Grandma, don't say that. If my mama was here . . . if my mama was here. . . ."

"Hush, Dale," says Maggie Jo. "Tomorrow after school you all go catch crawdads. I don't think studying's too good for your eyes."

CHORUS

> Ah-buh! Ah-buh! Ah-buh! Ah-buh!
> Old Joe Clark was a preacher man,
> he preached all over the plain,
> and the only Bible he ever knew
> was Ace High, Jack, and the Game.
>
> Old Joe Clark had a yellow cat,
> it could neither sing nor pray,
> stuck his head in the buttermilk jar
> and washed his sins away.
>
> A rig-dum bottom-mitchi-kimbo!
> Ah-buh, ah-buh, ah-buh . . .

Lula Belle and Dale and a cousin, Denver Huffman, have gone to wade in Hess Creek, and balance on the logs that stick out over it, and wonder what they would see if they followed Hess Creek all the way up to Lost Corners.

Denver and Lula Belle are in the shallows, ankle-deep, splashing after crawdads. Lula Belle has on a long dress with her bonnet hanging by its strings, her hair coming out of its braids.

"Put your hand behind him, Lula!" says Denver. "Behind him! They scoot backwards, watch it!"

"I got him, I got him!" says Lula Belle as she fists it up tight in her hand and feels it wiggle and pinch. "Oh, ick, I don't want him. Here Denver, you take him."

Dale watches from the edge, holding his school shoes. The giant willows and sycamore trees brace up a blue sky, grapevines snake down from their branches.

"Eat him, go on Lula," dares Dale. "Crunch him up."

"Eat him, Lula, go on," says Denver. "Crawdads are good."

"I'll eat it, I don't care," says Lula Belle, standing there with the crawdad in her fist, staring defiantly at Denver.

"Go on, Lula, I dare you," says Denver.

"I'll eat it, I don't care."

"Sure, you had brain fever and everything," he says. "You don't know no better."

So she eats it, making crunching noises, pretending to enjoy it. Dale runs out in the creek and tries to open Lula Belle's mouth to pry it out.

"As God is my witness! She ate it!" says Denver, and begins to imitate Brother Ewing. He addresses a congregation of sycamores:

"Brothers and sisters, cast your eyes upon this afflicted woman! Yes! Afflicted with eatin' things! She's eat things ever since she was a baby! Be healed, woman! Rise up and eat no more!"

"Well, now that I done that, I'm going swimming," says Lula Belle, spitting out pieces of crawdad and splashing water into her mouth. "I'm going to take off my dress and swim."

"Over my dead body you are going to take off your dress," says Dale.

"But Grandma won't find out!"

"I'm just going wading," says Dale. "I don't want people talking about me."

Denver knows neither one of them are going to take off anything. He wants to get rid of them so he can.

"Hey, look—a snake!"

"What? What is it?" says Dale.

"A cottonmouth!" says Denver.

Dale and Lula Belle splash out of the creek screaming and run, then walk, towards home. They wring their hems out, bitching at each other. Lula knows she'll never get to swim naked, not ever, and so she doesn't think about it anymore. Their dresses are uncomfortable, heavy and wet, as they are still wearing homespun, even though almost every other girl in the county now has dresses of machine-woven calico or other cotton. They walk and drip and sigh, pick up Dale's books from a stump beside the road, and go home.

At Grandma Maggie Jo's. Lula Belle is still poking at paper with a pencil now and then, dyslexic, unable to make sense of the scrambled print.

She sits beside Dale and cuts out pieces for the "Kaleidoscope," one of the most difficult patterns to fit.

LULA BELLE

Well, Dale reads pretty good now, but I don't read. She reads the Bunceton Eagle out loud to me, which tells all the news around this part of the country, and who got married or born or died or robbed. She saved the paper with mama's obituary on it, which is eight years old.

Dale lays aside her schoolbook and picks up the huge, leatherbound King Family Bible. In Revelations, chapter ten, is a newspaper clipping. Dale reads:

"In the death of Nancy Elizabeth King, which occurred at the family abode as the result of brain fever, near New Lebanon Church, there passed away one of Cooper County's best-loved citizens. By a life of self-sacrificing motherly devotion, Mrs. King always endeavoured to set an example before those who were careless and indifferent to their soul's best interests. The attractive and beautiful Mrs. King was accomplished in all the womanly arts and led an exemplary Christian life, leaving two small girls, Dale Burnett King and Lula Belle King, ages four and six, and a grieving husband, William Nelson King. Mrs. King was twenty-eight."

Lula Belle looks at the familiar clipping and asks, "Was she beautiful or was the newspaper just saying that out of habit?"

Dale holds the newspaper clipping as if it were Holy Writ, between her two hands, but she is looking into the fire.

"She had brown eyes, she had a big heavy head of hair that come out of its pins and fell down to the seat of the chair she was sitting on. She had a looking-glass of silver where she could see how pretty she was, and she used to sing 'Wayfaring Stranger.' Do you like that song, Lou? I like 'Motherless Children' better. It makes me cry."

"Sometimes I like crying," says Lula Belle.

"Me too."

"Sometimes I like just getting right down and howling and bawling," says Lula Belle.

"I like sitting on the sycamore down at the creek and weeping and pining," says Dale.

"Me too. And now, read me 'Jim Drew, Worthless Otterville Negro.'"

Dale groans to herself. She turns the clipping over to the other side and reads: "Alright. 'Jim Drew, Worthless Otterville Negro, Gets Ready For Another Trip To The Penitentiary. When Ester Lacy, a colored boy from near Belle Aire, came to Otterville Tuesday night, he tied his horse, a three-year-old bay mare, to the hitchrack of Ollie Jones' store. After transacting some business, he returned to find his mount gone. Upon inquiry, he found that Jim Drew was also missing. Now, when Jim Drew gets some bad whisky in him, the first thing he thinks about is getting his hands on something loose. Sheriff Lambert . . .' And here's where it's torn."

Lula Belle knows that's where it ends but pretends to be disappointed.

"Lou, this paper is eight years old," says Dale.

"You know what?" says Lula Belle. "If everybody in the world wanted it to be 1873, it would be 1873."

Dale thinks about it, and gives up. She says, instead: "Where do you come up with these notions? That's demented."

"That Jim Drew, was that the colored man they took out and hung?"

"Where'd you hear that!!??"

"I hear anything I want to," says Lula Belle, satisfied and sly. "I had brain fever. Nobody pays any attention to me."

"I don't know whether it was him or not," says Dale, turning the clipping over again. "That happened on November 19th, 1876, was what I heard."

"So it's not in that paper?"

"It's not in any paper."

Lula Belle takes up the scissors and cuts carefully into an old dress that had been given them by the church.

"You know what?" she says. "I'm going to make a quilt myself, and make it out of old patches from everybody's clothes so that you can see all the stories in it."

"Well, some stories you'd better keep quiet about," says Dale, reluctantly putting the clipping away. It seems another small loss to put it back in chapter ten, and close the heavy bible on it. Lula Belle is off on "that" subject however, and won't quit.

"A bunch of men got drunk and went out and did that. Down by Chouteau Creek. Drunk on Old Man Hanlin's whisky. And where was Daddy, pray tell?"

Dale goes back to her schoolbook.

"Why . . . why he was off in Otterville, that's where. Look for some nicer stories, Lula."

Lula Belle shakes out the dress she is cutting up. Small bits of hay fall out; timothy seeds.

"Uh-huh!" says Lula Belle. "Maybe here, look, this is one of those Speece girls' dresses, and there's hay in it! She's been up in their hayloft with that jigger-face Eleazar Ewing!"

"I SAID LOOK FOR SOME NICER STORIES, LULA!"

So Lula Belle says, "Will you get married, Dale?"

"Oh, I reckon. Maggie said we had to go to bed at ten. That's half an hour." Dale puts the Bible back on the shelf over the trunk and reaches a book out from behind and then sits again at the table with it.

"Maggie Jo will be home from Chesley's any time now," says Dale. "You better go on up and get ready for bed." She leafs through the book.

"What's that book you got there?"

"Nothing."

"It's a romance novel!" says Lula Belle, seeing an illustration. "You ain't supposed to be reading those!"

"Oh, ain't I?" snorts Dale. "Don't you tell!" She knows Maggie Jo can't read, and so she feels relatively safe. However, the illustrations, copperplate engravings full of dainty women with round chins and feet the size of pie-wedges, massive dresses and pencil-thin waists, and men with great chests and swords, are a dead giveaway.

"Let me look at it," says Lula Belle, crowding up.

Dale decides the secret is more delicious if it is shared. It becomes a conspiracy.

"Look at these illustrations here! Look at that dress. It's en feston with alternate flounces and muslin undersleeves. Wouldn't Tom Bodine take a second look at me if I had a dress like that?"

Lula Belle looks carefully: "What's the name of it?"

"*The Enemy Conquered*, or *Love Triumphant*. 'Her heart yielded to no feeling but the love of Captain Armstrong, on whom she gazed with intense delight.'"

"Read some. Read some more," says Lula Belle, for once paying attention to a book.

"I will when you get some sense," says Dale, closing the book. "Now we got to go up to sleep."

Up the narrow stairs, almost a ladder, into the attic, tired and formal in their great flannel nightgowns.

"Goodnight, Dale."

"Goodnight, Lou."

"God bless you, Dale."
"God bless you, Lou."

At Grandma Maggie Jo's. It is late summer or maybe very early fall and
they are making hominy to can for the winter. The corn kernels are
being stirred in the big cast-iron pot in a solution of lye and water to slip
the hulls. Maggie Jo has put Lula Belle at peeling apples for applesauce.
There is a haze all up and down the valley from burning brush-piles, and
other kettles in other farmyards.

LULA BELLE
*Dale says if we don't get married, we must be old maids in somebody else's
kitchen and work for nothing all our lives. Dale says that this is life: we bind
ourselves to foolish men, fiddlefoots, gandy-dancers, men who are in love with
the racetrack, with the railroad, a jug or a bottle, in love with the last idea they
had, the one yesterday, the one the day before; we must entwine our hands
beneath the willow and become as one. Gaze on somebody with intense delight. Then you have a home of your own. Right now our dresses is made of
cotton domestic and our shoes wouldn't hold walnuts without leaking. From
what they all say, this is where our fortune lies—in* Love Triumphant *or* The
Enemy Conquered.

"Now when you peel them apples, Lula Belle," calls out Maggie Jo,
"keep a continual peel falling and it will fall on the ground and compose
the initials of the man you marry."

"Wherever you go," Aunt Lizzy calls from the porch, where she too
is peeling apples, "count the white horses that you see, and when you
have counted forty, the first man you see in a red shirt will be the man
you marry. And you can't count any of them twice!"

"Oh, I don't believe that!" laughs Dale over the steaming hominy
kettle like a little witch.

"And don't look at the new moon over your left shoulder or you'll be
an old maid!" adds Maggie Jo.

"Catch me being an old maid!" says Dale, thinking of Captain
Armstrong.

LULA BELLE
*I've been gathering a bag of quilt pieces from here, there and yonder, and they
each have a story in them because they were what people were wearing when
something happened. The stories are complicated and sometimes secret. But I*

have to start back at the beginning of the world. Our family all came from Virginia, a beautiful fair land where they fought the English King a long time ago. This was because he was bothering people and he wouldn't let them make whisky.

Dale is fed up with Lula's mooning over apple peels. "Lula, are you going to come on and help here?"

"Lula, are you going to watch that lye water for the hominy or what, girl?"

Lula Belle continues inventing the history of the Thirteen Colonies:

I could have told the English King never to get between a man and his whisky, but nobody ever listens to me. It's a fact of life. They come by generations out of Virginia, through Tennessee and Kentucky, and some got lost on the way and others were et by things. The Kings and the Burnses, the Burnetts and Huffmans and Hanlins and Speeces and Ewings. The Cumberland Presbyterian preachers come after their erring flocks, which was always a-erring and a-erring. And here we are and we marry our fourth cousins and pull our own teeth and make our own whisky and vote Democrat. The men go off to all the wars that's offered. They like the noise. It's the noise that draws them.

"Lula, come over here and stir this corn!" says Dale. "The hulls are slippin and MY ARM'S TIRED!!"

"Well, give me the stir pole," says Lula Belle as she drifts over to the kettle. "I'll just stir and think."

"Don't put that lid on too tight when you're done," says Dale. "It's boilin', it'll blow up."

Lula Belle goes on to the causes of international conflicts:

They like the bullets and the noise. I have pieces of old uniforms I found, Union ones, because all the Huffman's and the King fought for the Union and that caused a lot of trouble around here, because of that. And then my Uncle Samuel D. Burnett went to fight in the Mexican War in 1846 just to get him a new uniform, and by the time they got to St. Louis to join up, the captain said, "Why boy, the war's over. We won." He was so mad he missed it, he got drunk down on the levee and they had to throw him in jail and then send him home on the War Eagle. Old man Laird Burns, he fought at the battle of New Orleans. He still talks about it even though he's nearly ninety, he says, "Ah, my gurrl, there was martial music and the thrillin' report of the cannon, and our shootin' pieces got so hot they blew up in our faces!"

And she has walked off and left the lid on too tight, there is the thrillin' report of a small explosion, and now there is a kettle-full of

hulled corn all over the yard and in the Devil's Trumpet vine. The big
Barred Rocks come dashing for the corn, rolling from side to side and
squawking.

"Lula," shouts Dale, "I told you not to put that lid on too tight!"

"There's hominy all over the yard," says Maggie Jo, dropping the
apple-butter funnel.

"Oh, those chickens just love it!" laughs Lula Belle.

Maggie Jo takes up a stick and goes after the Barred Rocks. "Girl, I
don't know how you're going to make your way in life if you don't learn
your work right."

The neighbor women have come to help Maggie Jo and the girls finish
the "Kaleidoscope" quilt. It is a ladies sewing circle, later in the fall,
after the fruit and corn and beans have been put up, gardens harvested,
threshers fed, hogs butchered and lard rendered down, the cotton picked
and packed up in sacks for carding into quilt batts, and a thousand other
jobs we can hardly think of from this distance in time and culture. Now
there is time to sew.

LULA BELLE
*When Dale reads of an evening on that romantic novel, you can see her by
the new lamp we got; her eyes move back and forth in jerks like quilting
needles . . .*

There is a low hum as the women talk and stitch.

LULA BELLE
*Stitching up words and sentences. But you can see a quilt pattern all at once,
which is important for the roundness of your brain.*

Dale and two other women are going over an old quilt, looking at
the pieces of dresses, at the stitches, the prairie-point edging.

"Look here at this quilt piece!" says Dale. "This here is from my
dress when I was five years old! Mama sewed it for me. I recall I fell into
the salt spring in it! We were visiting with that old Jacob Kendall . . ."

"Oh, look at this piece, this lavender one with the daisies," says
Aunt Lizzy. "That was grandma Mary's dress. She was a Lionberger from
the Shenandoah. That was the one she tore up for bandages that time,
when his guts was all hanging out."

"Where?" asks Maggie Jo. "I can't hardly see good anymore, Lizzy."

"There, grandma," says Dale, pointing.

"You all seen my Virginia quilt?" says Maggie Jo. "The 'Ladies Fan?'"
Lizzy is going to get bored. "I thought it was Tumbling Blocks."
"It's a Ladies Fan or I'm a Chinaman. Go get it for me, Dale."
Lizzy whispers to Aunt Missouri Abigail, "Did you see what I saw?"
Missouri Abigail leans closer. "What?"

Maggie Jo and Dale have been rooting around in the old trunk and
have come up with the Ladies Fan. "See that piece?" says Maggie Jo.
"That's the old homespun, that was from one of the Lionberger girls'
dresses."

"Wasn't there one of them girls got kilt by Indians?" says Lizzy. "Or
et by hogs? No . . . no . . . it was they drank opium."

Maggie Jo remembers the stories much better. Her deceased husband's mother was a Lionberger. "No, you're thinking of Sally Louisa,
she was in love with Thomas Giles Speece, and he up and married her
sister, and so she poured coal-oil over herself and set herself afire. Her
mother was a Burnett. Or was she a Boulware? Well, they said it was a
regular barbecue, I tell you what."

Lizzy turns back to whispering to Missouri Abigail. "Abigail, I saw
. . . an insect of a kind that is unmentionable foraging about in Lula
Belle's braids!"

"Well, God have mercy!" whispers Abigail. "And her dresses is too
short. She's eleven and her ankles is still showing about up to her knees!"

"Maggie Johanna is just too old to keep them anymore," whispers
Lizzy.

And Abigail whispers back, "Well, where they going to go?"

"Dale, let's make some coffee for these folks," says Maggie Jo, putting the quilt away.

Dale hesitates. "Grandma, we're out of coffee."

"Oh Maggie Johanna," says Abigail, looking up from whispering, "I
don't care for any. Not for me."

"Oh, me neither!" says Lizzy. "Why it makes me as jumpy as a cat
with nine kittens. I don't know which way to run."

Abigail returns quickly to the stories. "Well how come she wanted to
marry a Speece so bad? I wouldn't marry a Speece, they're great big terrible
villainous people, they're always investing money in peculiar things . . ."

Lula Belle has drifted away.

I can't get any material from dream figures, or from folks who have passed
away and gone to their reward; all I can get is material from people now for my

quilt, except for great-aunt Sally Louisa, who left some quilt pieces before she spontaneously combusted.

The ladies have left, and the Kaleidoscope is now basted onto the batt and the backing. Maggie Jo goes to the dark window, looks out into the moonlight, with her hands around her face.

"Girls, is that your daddy I see a-coming down the road?" she says.

Lula Belle's heart leaps wildly, but she stays within her own world.

LULA BELLE

You could see the daylight between the boards and battens of the old Huffman house, and I loved my old grandmother so much I wanted to make her float up high as the turkey vultures when you see them on the string of the wind like kites.

The deer are slipping back into the harvested gardens to glean.

"Lula!" shouts Dale. "Come a-running'! It's Poppa!"

LULA BELLE

Oh, they have hymns up there in the great churches of clouds. They see this whole earth like a patchwork quilt, the creeks bordering around, Chouteau Creek, Loutre Creek, Bonne Femme Creek, Hess Creek, Hungry Mother Creek and Short Rations Branch. And these are the quilt patterns the earth appears in, the names of our luck, our habits, and our destinies.

> The Ohio Star
> Log Cabin
> Cathedral Windows
> Ladies Fan
> Card Trick
> Broken Dishes
> Courthouse Steps and
> Alabama Belle. There is
> The Road To California
> Double Irish Chain
> Kaleidoscope
> Wedding Ring and
> the Drunkard's Path.

"Is he sober, Grandma?" asks Dale, running out to stand beside Maggie Jo.

"If he ain't, I'll take a stick of kindling to him."

LULA BELLE

I would like to see my grandmother fly high like a turkey vulture, riding the updrafts, but you have to learn to work hard in this life. And the hymn that the turkey vultures sing is "Higher Ground."

CHORUS

> *Lord lift me up, and let me stand*
> *By faith on Heaven's table-land . . .*

Lula Belle hears heavenly voices. She is caught up in her flight and can't come down and maybe fears to come down; after all, Poppa might not be sober and she loves him so much and it might be safer, all told, up in heaven. It's her seventh fit—a lucky number.

William sits by her bed. "Are you waking up, daughter?"

"Poppa?"

"Well, darlin', you shouldn't get yourself so overworked and excited."

"I saw you coming down the road; I guess I got too excited."

"Do you know what day it is?"

"I was in another land from this. I was very high up. I saw where all the creeks go, and the river."

"Do you want some tea with sugar in it?"

"We ain't got no sugar."

"Lula Belle, I brought ten pounds of it," he says, patting her hand. "And oh, just lots of things."

"There's lights around here," says Lula Belle.

"There is? Where, Lou?"

The girls stand uneasily around the kitchen table, where Maggie Jo has called them for a talk.

LULA BELLE

After a while Maggie Jo couldn't keep us, as she was such an old lady and there was nobody there but us to help, with daddy being gone all the time, and me dropping down in a fit from time to time, although I must insist I was peaceful about it. But Grandma couldn't see one way or the other if we was dressed proper in the mornings or stark naiket, or our hair was sticking out like wild men off of Borneo or if we was clean bald or what.

"Well girls, I guess you'd better pack your traps."

"How come, Grandma?" asks Dale.

"Where we going?" asks Lula Belle.

"I guess I'm too old to look after you-all. I can't see to fix your-alls hair. Lizzy come with Chesley and said your-alls hair wasn't fixed right. They said there was things in your hair. I can't see too good anymore, honey."

"But I washed Lula's hair in coal-oil!" says Dale.

"I love you-all. But my hands is begun to shake so bad and I can't see to fix your-alls hair nor dresses. Lizzy is going to make you some pretty dresses."

"But Grandma," says Dale, crying, "Why can't we just stay with them a little while and then come back and look after you?"

Maggie Jo disengages Dale's hands from her sleeve.

"I'm just glad Samuel died before me," she says. "Samuel wasn't capable anymore. I reckon I'll die here sometime before you-all is big enough to come back and do for me. They say you-all have something in your hair but Lizzy won't say what."

Lula Belle whispers fiercely to Dale; "Oh, I do wish Aunt Lizzy would blow it out her drawers!"

Dale whispers back, "Hush up your mouth, or I'll smack you upside the head such a whack . . ."

"When I hear the train at night now," says Maggie Jo, "I get up and go out looking, because I think somebody's making a noise. Sounds like somebody cryin' for help."

Lula Belle is crying too, looking wildly for a solution. "Can't you go back to Virginia? We could all go back to Virginia."

"I'll go back to Virginia when I die, honey," says Maggie Jo. "Now, when you-all get all your things in those sugar sacks, I want you to take these here dishes with you over to Lizzy and Chesley. These here are Virginia dishes, from the Lionbergers. It's weeping willow pattern. I got just these two pieces left, just these here two. Now, you girls is going to have to walk over there because Chesley's gone off to Boonville for a week with the wagon. It's fifteen mile. Sleep over at Jacob Kendall's house. You pack them dishes careful and Lizzy will have them to pass down to people."

It is nighttime and the girls are walking down the dirt road that runs along the Lamine River, going north. They are carrying their sugar sacks which contain their few articles of clothing, and the *Love Triumphant* book with the newspaper clipping safely stuck in Chapter 24; Maggie Jo will look after the King family Bible for a while. It is too precious to go walking down a dirt road with. They are carrying the two Virginia dishes—a gravy boat and a plate—as an offering to the Burnett's, something to bring into the household of value besides two hungry mouths. They have their combs and ribbons and two quilts. They are walking the fifteen miles up valley to Chesley and Lizzy's because there is nobody to take them, or maybe Maggie Jo is too proud to ask; but, after all, they are young and strong. They started early in the morning but they have dawdled, throwing rocks off the Hess Creek bridge and looking into a cave at the foot of the bluffs. It's late. They don't want to sleep over at Jacob Kendall's house. They've always known there is something Bad about Jacob Kendall, even if Maggie Jo doesn't. He lives alone and he's got a big yellow dog and screaming guinea-hens sitting on his yard rails. They will pretend they can't make it by nightfall.

The moon is one-quarter and setting. It has on a nightgown of flannely mist, spangled with stars. Sometimes hard dry leaves fall from the sycamores in the woods alongside them, and drop into the buckbrush with stiff crashes. Maybe they just like wandering along the roads like gypsies, away from society and all its hopeless rules; rules they will never quite be able to obey.

"See, she was talking about going back to Virginia," says Lula Belle. "That's where mama went when she died."

"It was a manner of speaking, Lou."

"They have honeysuckle parties there. Everybody plays the banjo."

"A honeysuckle party?" Dale snorts. "We ain't going to make it to Kendall's tonight, Lou."

"I wonder how she met Grandpa Samuel? They come from Page County, Virginia. I bet she met him underneath the willow. She gazed upon Samuel Huffman with intense delight and they entwined their hands and became as one."

Dale laughs. "How come you to know this?"

Lula Belle pulls something out of her dress pocket. "Look here, this is her handkerchief. She brought it with her from the Shenandoah. I'm going to put it in my quilt. I have to remember everything she said so that we remember. She said she got up when she heard the train at night to help people, and she said they come over the Cumberland Gap with oxes."

"I wish you'd get things right, Lula," says Dale, trudging on.

"But I am! I am! What else have we got in the world but stories? And listen, listen. She said a long time ago our people were old Scotsmen that come to Virginia before there was a United States to get away from the English King because he wouldn't let them pray unless they prayed like heathens. And they come to a town called Luray. And Samuel's father was John, and before him was James, and before him was Ambrose, and before him was Daniel . . ."

Dale is tired of ancestors. She sees they are coming near the salt springs, and says "Ain't you tired of walking along in the dead of night carrying a bunch of dishes and saying the Begats?"

". . . and before him was George, and before him was John, and then two more Johns, and one of them come in 1690 or something."

Dale forges ahead. "Here's the salt springs, Lula, just up ahead."

Lula Belle veers instantly to the Salt Spring Subject and keeps on either inventing or patching bits together. "And you know what? There's a dead Frenchman down there in that salt spring, pickled like a ham! With his French uniform on and his sword and pistol by his side. Yessir. That's the truth."

Dale has heard this too. "No, Lou, they found that old body over near Cobb Springs in 1809 in a cave."

"I tell you what, cross my heart, Dale, he fell down in that salt spring when they was exploring this country, and he reached down to get him a handful of that salty clay and a great perishing SNAKE!! grabbed him by that gold lace on his wrist and kind of snatched him down there and I swear he's there yet . . ."

They stop by the grassy flat uphill of the salt springs.

"Let's rest," says Dale. "Let's just rest here. There ain't no Frenchman, Lou. We're just going to have to sleep out under that quilt top of yours."

The girls are wrapped up in their quilts, with the book and the Virginia dishes safely wrapped in the dresses inside the sugar sacks. They sleep with their heads on their coats. The stars are winding down towards midnight.

"How come we have to keep going, Dale? How come we can't just lay down here and make Jesus do all the work?"

"It'll be better over at Chesley and Lizzy's, Lou," sighs Dale. "Really it will. Things will get a whole lot better. They got a wagon, and lath-and-plaster on the walls, and a china cabinet. They got sugar all the time, and Lizzy makes cornbread with milk, is what I heard."

"What about Grandma Maggie Jo?" asks Lula Belle.

"Daddy will come and do for her, and Ewings rents the fields."

Lula Belle thinks a moment and says: "Daddy is sad all the time, like something was bothering his immortal soul."

"Goodnight, Lou."

"Goodnight, Dale."

"God bless you, Lou."

"Dale, what if something comes up in the night and eats us?"

Dale looks up and finds the Big Dipper, a generous cauldron of star-milk. She says, "Mama is looking down on us from heaven."

"No she ain't," says Lula Belle, grimly. "She's gone to Virginia."

Dale groans. "We said God bless you so you have to go to sleep."

Lula Belle closes her eyes and whispers, "Goodnight, Dale."

"Goodnight, Frenchman," giggles Dale.

And long after they have gone to sleep, a spectral voice from the salt spring says, "Goodnight, leetle girls . . ."

The next evening. Chesley and Lizzy's farm is backed up against the ridge under Rattlesnake Hill (upon which no one has ever seen a rattlesnake, but there are generous amounts of copperheads), a farm with acres of good bottom-lands and a spring and good timber. The house is a small balloon-frame, with a cookstove chimney and no fireplace.

LULA BELLE

Dale says I don't remember when Mama died, but I remember. When she died, she come to me in a dream to say goodbye. She said, Oh how I hate to leave my baby girls. She said, So long, darlings. She said, Bury me beneath the willows. She said, Oh fare thee well, sweetheart, Captain William, I'm off over the mountains, and then she flew away back to the Shenandoah Valley, which is very sweet and very fair. The whippoorwills all go to the Shenandoah in the winter and then come to Missouri every spring. And mama isn't really buried anywhere; you can hear her singing . . .

CHORUS

> *I'm going there to see my mother*
> *She said she'd meet me when I come*
> *I'm only going over Jordan*
> *I'm only going over home . . .*

LULA BELLE

You learn that there are people who will take in the stranger at the door and those who will not. You learn to be subtle and sly, judging the quality of the refreshments or the accommodations, you learn to hide.

Chesley escorts the girls upstairs to the attic and says, "Now, Lula Belle and Dale, we're going to put you up here by the chimney and you'll be warm all winter."

"Lula, there ain't no heat up here," says Dale in a fierce whisper.

"Well, we got to put up with it," says Lula Belle.

"We're going to have to sleep upside the chimney to keep warm."

"You take one side and I'll take the other," says Lula.

Later that night, Lizzy and Chesley are talking downstairs in the kitchen. Chesley says, "Elizabeth, you are not charged with admonishing the erring."

"It was fifteen men from around here that took that black man out and hung him," says Lizzy.

Chesley would like sometimes to run out the door and leave the county but says, "Dixie Kendall had a black baby and everybody knew who the father was! It was a known thing that he forced her! That he caught her in the barn and forced his attentions upon her! That outrages were visited upon that woman by a nigger! I want you to ponder that."

"Old man Kendall kept those girls locked up like they was in jail," says Lizzy, keeping at it. "How come their mother ran off? She run off and disappeared and then he chased off every young man that come to call. And so Dixie and the black hired man met in the barn and consorted together. Why, he as good as threw them together! Do you understand what was going on, Chesley? And who's to say they didn't, well, love one another?"

Chesley feels like several of his hairs are turning white as he stands there, one hand on the kitchen pump handle.

"Love one another!! Why, you should talk about cattle and swine loving one another! The Lord God made us separate and we are transgressing his laws when we interbreed, and anyway, I had nothing to do with it!"

Lizzy picks up something from the woodbox she has been keeping for years, and why she has chosen this moment, nobody knows but her. "Then what's this shirt here, Chesley? This blue shirt that was in the barn all those years, smelling like sweat and dying? Why'd you bring it home and keep it, if you didn't want me to ask? And who else was there?"

Dale is rigidly awake and the quarter-moon shines in at the dormer window. It is hours later. Dale sits up as she feels Lula come back to bed.

"Lula, you was at the head of the stairs listening."

"Yes."

"What's that you got?"

Lula Belle holds something up to the weak moonlight. "A piece of that black man's shirt. They went to bed and I went down and snuck it."

"You're going to put that in your quilt."

"Jesus knows even when a sparrow falls," says Lula Belle. "Though it don't do the sparrow no good. And fifteen men went and took that black man out and hung him."

Dale had the piece of cloth in her hand—she drops it. "That's a black man's! and he went and died in it! It's prolly got cooties!"

"So did we," says Lula Belle . . . "Dale, do you think Daddy might have been one of those men?"

"Oh never! He'd never!" says Dale in an angry whisper as she thrashes around in the covers. "Sometimes he don't know what he's doing when he's drinking, but he don't ever fight. He just gets drunk and falls down."

"Yes, he don't ever fight," agrees Lula Belle, relieved.

"What a terrible story, Lou. Did Dixie Kendall really have a black baby?"

"That's what they say. But I don't know, I never seen her, she went to Illinois. Lizzy said old man Kendall kept the two of them locked in the barn all day and all night so that they consorted together. Is it consorting that gives you a baby?"

"I think so."

"Is consorting a word like drawers? You ain't supposed to say drawers."

"No," decides Dale, "you can say consort."

"It will be the thing to keep him in remembrance," says Lula Belle, full of the sense of power that storytellers are often charged with. "If ever that baby grows up, I'll say to it someday, see this here piece of blue workshirt, in my Wedding Ring quilt? This was your daddy that they hung."

Dale likes this thought. "It will be the consorting piece."

"Yes, the consorting piece."

"Goodnight, Lou."

"Goodnight, Dale."

"God bless you, Lou."
"God bless you, Dale."

Lula Belle sits on the rails of the salt spring communing with the Frenchman. He is wearing knee britches, his sword and pistol by his side.

LULA BELLE
*One night I got very lonesome for my father, for him to protect me against the
world and all its snares and traps, that I walked away from the Burnetts one
night to go down to the railroad tracks to see if I could see him coming by.*

She can hear a whistle in the distance.
The Frenchman leads the chorus:

> *Someone's in the kitchen with Dinah*
> *Someone's in the kitchen I know*
> *Strumming on the old banjo*
> *and that's just how it goes, you know?*
> *It was astonishing, it was amusing.*

LULA BELLE
*They said I'd taken a fit. And so here we are. But I know Daddy wants us to
grow up in a home with lath-and-plaster on the walls and a china cabinet. He
worked all up and down the Katy line, swinging his red bull's eye lantern in the
night, to tell the trains how to keep on the tracks, and with his big long face and
the light shining up, it looks like he's saying:*
                              THIS WAY TO HELL!
*He'll go off some night like a shooting star and end up in Oklahoma. He needs
somebody to take care of him, that's what it is.*

At William Nelson's house near Otterville. This is the house he inherited
from his father, and where the family had lived before Nanni died. It has a
second story added on to a large log cabin and then sided over. He stays
there when he is not travelling as a brakeman. He is a bachelor without
comforts, except for old man Hanlin's whisky.
   "William Nelson, I heard you were to home," says Lucifer.

LULA BELLE
*That's why me and Dale can't go live with him, really. Because you ever know
when Lucifer comes to visit him and he and the devil have to have a drink
together.*

"How did you come to know that?" says William.

"Why, I stopped at Lost Corners to inquire for you and the man who keeps that dissolute and sordid whisky-shop told me you would be at home looking after your hangover. He said you were very merry, he said you had retired quite late."

"Well, the horse brought me home, I guess."

Lucifer's statements leak flaming into the room. He wears knee britches and gold lace, and he has a sword and pistol by his side. "We should have a drink together to keep off the delirium tremens."

"I wasn't planning on having any delirium tremens," says William.

"Of course you are. I am them," says Lucifer.

William remembers something practical he ought to do, "I was going into Otterville to get my hair cut."

"You couldn't even get them harness buckles done up if you were going to take the buggy. Got anything in the pie safe, here? Or, if you were going to ride, I doubt if you could catch that contrary horse of yours."

"I think I have an allergy to whisky, you know. I should never drink it," says William, as he watches Lucifer rummage around in the pie safe. "I'm a Cumberland Presbyterian, you know."

"I have more Cumberland Presbyterians down in hellfire than any other denomination, I assure you. It's because everything going is a sin for a Presbyterian. I didn't invent sin, you know. People make up sin for themselves. If they say card-playing and cosmetics is sinful, why, I am amiable, come on down to the Lakes Of Fire! I have no objections. And then they pass over in silence the times they took out and hung people down in the draw of Chouteau Creek in the dead of night. Ah, here's that whisky."

"I had nothing to do with taking out and hanging people!" says William, jumping up. "Nothing at all in this world."

"And if you didn't, could you have stopped it? Saying here, or allowing, just for the conversation, that you didn't."

"I said I was going into town to get my hair cut, and I'm going if I never cock another gun."

"Have one first," says Lucifer, pouring out two glasses of brimstone and sulphur. "Where's them two girls of yours?"

"They've gone to live with relatives up in Buffalo Prairie. I couldn't keep them after their mother died."

Lucifer nods. "You couldn't take care of them before, either."

"No sir, not in the least is that the truth! It was after their mother died that I took to drinking. After the funeral I drank so much I wasn't fit to be with for two weeks. I ended up in a house next to Lost Corners. I don't recall how I got there. But I know how I left—laying in a democrat."

"It is said there are disreputable women in that house," says Lucifer, drinking up his own glass. "A woman who drinks opium, and another who tells fortunes with cards and a crystal ball—the sort of women no gentleman would speak their name in the family abode."

"We didn't have no family abode by that time."

"Your oldest daughter is coming of age," says Lucifer. "She's been visiting over at Bodine's farm. There is a young man there as you might know. Tom Bodine is now twenty-one. He's broken a hundred acres of upland all his own. And when Old Man Bodine dies—my goodness, dear fellow! All that bottomland!"

"Visiting Tom Bodine?" shouts William. "Over my dead body! Over my dead body she'll go walking disorderly about this valley with some young buck that don't know how to keep his pecker in his pants!"

"And Lula Belle is fourteen," says Lucifer. "You've been careless and indifferent about their soul's best interests. You must see to the cultivation of their Christian characters."

"I'm going to get you drunk, sir," says William, jumping up. "And then I'm going to set this house on fire and burn you down with it."

"This house is already on fire," agrees Lucifer. "I already burnt down with it. I fell out of the bottom end of heaven and burnt my wings. I am life's other side. I am the Son of the Morning when the darkest hour is just before dawn, and I came with you all out of Virginia. I've burnt down your houses many times."

William Nelson King takes the bottle from Lucifer and throws it into the woodstove, and the lamp turns over and the oil runs and the pie safe catches fire and everything catches fire.

"All you Speeces were great big villainous people," says William.

At Chesley and Lizzy's farm under Rattlesnake Hill. Dale sits in a rocking chair. She looks across the Burnett bottomland to the line of trees along the Lamine River, the bluffs and chimney rock on the other side, at the turkey vultures riding the updrafts. Lula Belle comes out.

"Dale, what are you doing sitting out here on the porch?"

"Nothing."

"You're reading that book."

"What of it?" says Dale, shutting the book. "Go away and give me some peace."

"Dale, what if we never did get married? When you're married you can't own anything; Uncle Chesley told me your husband owns everything."

Dale clutches *Love Triumphant*. "I said go away, Lula, and give me some peace."

Lula Belle walks down the front porch steps toward the pear tree. "Well, alright then."

Dale takes up the book and reads: "Her lofty beauty, seen by the glimmering of the chandelier, filled his heart with rapture. 'Lady Ambulinia,' said he, trembling, 'I have long desired a moment like this. I dare not let it escape.' Lady Ambulinia's countenance showed uncommon vivacity, with a resolute spirit. 'Captain Armstrong,' said she . . .'" Dale shuts the book. "Well, I'll just run off with him then, if Poppa won't let me get married."

Chesley is in the buggy, pulling up to the train station in Otterville. He ties the horses and walks in, up to the telegraph operator in the operations room.

"Here, you," says Chesley, leaning across the counter, "I want you to send this to William Nelson King at the roundhouse in Jefferson City. He's a brakeman on the Katy."

The operator doesn't know Chesley, but he knows William. "You bet."

"Send this. 'Your eldest daughter about to run off with Tom Bodine, return Otterville next train, suggest marriage be planned this spring. Girls to move to Abigail and Henry T.'s.'"

The operator happily takes the paper out of Chesley's hand. "Why, that scoundrel," he says.

"Who?"

"Tom Bodine."

Chesley waits for the gravity of the situation to sink in. "I don't feel you should concern yourself with this, and if you do, you'll soon be wearing that instrument around your neck. Now send that."

"Yes, sir."

We are at the graveyard across from New Lebanon Church, near the big pine.

LULA BELLE

They said the best sermon over Maggie Jo. It was March, and there was a rainstorm. Her whole name was Margaret Johanna Burnett Huffman, she was nearly eighty-nine years old. She taught me to work hard in life, and how to get along without no sugar and how to make hominy corn and about salt and spiders and the new moon. She taught me how to endure what is hard in life. She taught me all the quilt patterns there ever was. And her own pattern was the Ladies Fan, because she always kept the air a-stirring around her, and her mind was very fanciful. Dale was all tore up because Grandma wouldn't get to see her wedding this June, and she cried into her hands all during the funeral, it sounded like a train, it sounded like somebody crying for help.

The Chorus is made up of many ancestors buried here, there, yonder, and in Virginia.

And in the final days, the clouds openeth and the grandmothers rain down upon us.

"Oh, Lula," whispers Dale, "nobody said that!"

CHORUS

Yea, it is said, children and fools speak the truth and this seems to mean that wise people and grownups prevaricate. Yes, the secrets and the lies are manifold; many are called by grace, but few answer, and if they do, they give the wrong name.

"Oh, Lula," snuffles Dale, "if you're going to repeat the sermon, do get it straight!"

CHORUS

Cross the Lamine River, the Blackwater River, cross thou Hess Creek, Loutre Creek, Chouteau Creek, Hungry Mother Creek and Short Rations Branch, walk even beyond the salt springs, which welleth up like the bullets of desperadoes and the tears of the dispossessed, the young fresh tears of motherless children.

A solo voice sings "The Darkest Hour Is Just Before Dawn" or "Life's Other Side."

CHORUS

Fear not! Thy grandmothers shall give thee Virginia dishes of the best willowware and thou shalt break them. Thy grandmother shall give thee all the tall jewelry of the Shenandoah, and thou shalt lose it, but the quilts thou shalt lose not.

"Lou, you just hear what you want to hear," says Dale. "You make it up. Now don't cry. They're going to shovel in the dirt."

CHORUS
The quilts break not and they are too big to fall down cracks. Thy grandmothers are sending thee into the next century with rags and the design of rags and these shall defend thee against all manner of ee-vell.

"Oh, Lou!" says Dale, beginning to quietly shake with laughter.

CHORUS
Of the rags and tatters of the poor, the humble, the dispossessed and the hanged one, thou shalt make quilts, and these will tell their stories time without end, and protect thee with stories, even though the earth shall burn and the heavens be rolled up like a scroll. Amen!

In Aunt Missouri Abigail's Kitchen. The girls are now living with Aunt Missouri Abigail and Uncle Henry T.

LULA BELLE
After awhile Chesley and Lizzy said we had to go live with Aunt Missouri Abigail and Uncle Henry T., because Chesley didn't want to be responsible in case Dale ran off with Tom Bodine, and we was so contrary. So we packed our things, the quilts and the Virginia dishes, as we decided not to let Lizzy have them, and we moved again. Dale said it was all a trouble and a trial, but she would soon be married and have a home of her own.

The girls are washing dishes. They have taken out the two Virginia pieces as well; the willow patterns are dusty.

"How do you fortell the future, Dale? Can you go to a witch-woman?"

"I reckon. . . . There's an astrologer, like a kind of fortune-telling woman at the county fair."

Lula Belle squashes lye soap into the washpan. "Maybe it's sinful," she says. "Like when King Saul called up the Witch of Endor to see what the dead people were doing down there."

"Well," says Dale, "her name is Madame Perrigo, but just don't let anybody find out. Especially Aunt Missouri Abigail her very own self, alright?"

Lula Belle is happy with this answer, and starts singing: "Frog went a-courtin' and he did ride . . ."

"A *rig-dom-bottom-mitch-i kimbo!*"

"A sword and pistol by his side . . ." sings Lula Belle.

A rig-dom-bottom-mitch-i kimbo!
Keemo-kimo, haro-jaro, hey catch a rat trap pennywinkle flammadoodle,
A-rig-dom-bottom-mitchi-i kimbo!

Lula is jumping to the singing and drops a dish.

"Oh, Dale! Grandma's dish!!"

"That was Grandma's *Virginia* dish!"

"I killed it," says Lula Belle, holding up the blue-willow pieces.

"I ain't never see such a dead dish," says Dale, as she starts sweeping it up. They start to giggle.

"I went and broke my grandma's dish . . ." sings Lula.

And Dale joins in: *A rig-dom-bottom-mitchi-i kimbo!*

"And I really do not give a piss . . ." contributes Dale.

"So hang me for a Methodist!" says Lula Belle.

Keemo-kimo, haro-jaro, hey catch a rat trap pennywinkle flammadoodle,
a rig-dom-bottom-mitchi-i kimbo!

They toss up the broken pieces.

"My daddy's house went and burnt down . . ." adds Lula.

"And now he's living in a tavern in the town!" sings Dale.

They are becoming hysterical with laughter.

"He'd drink more liquor but he can't get it down!" adds Lula Belle.

Keemo-kimo, haro-jaro, hey catch a rat trap pennywinkle flammadoodle,
yellowbug, a rig-dom-bottom-mitchi-i kimbo!

Dale listens a moment and then cries, "Oh, no, Aunt Abigail's coming! She heard us! I'm leaving!" and flees the scene. As she runs she bumps into the kitchen table; a crash.

"Godalmighty, Dale!! You went and broke the *other* one!" cries Lula Belle, holding the fragments.

Aunt Abigail sails into the room, redheaded and full of power. "*What* did I hear you say, Lula Belle King?"

"I said piss and I said Godalmighty," says Lula Belle, and stares back at her.

"There are words I will not allow to be said in my house and you say them at your peril. I will put you and your sister out on the road. You will go to the poorhouse."

"My daddy will come and get us!"

"That desperate and intemperate drunkard will never come and get anybody. I want an apology."

"I'm sorry, Aunt Abigail," says Lula Belle, giving in.

"Well, there are some things that just cannot be apologized for. You think you can use language like that in my house and then just apologize . . ."

Lula Belle starts backing out of the kitchen.

". . . and then everything's alright; well, you can think twice, sister . . ."

The only response to Aunt Missouri Abigail's self-righteous superiority is flight. Lula Belle runs out of the house, past the pear tree, and pauses by the washhouse.

"Dale! Are you back here?"

"I'm in the woodshed," whispers Dale.

The woodshed is musty and spidery; it smells like cedar and lye. They clang into froes and saws.

"What're we going to do?" says Lula Belle.

"I don't *know*. I don't *want* to live with relatives no more. I'm too big! Too big to be hollered at like that. And I ain't got no stockings, even."

"She made me apologize and then she said . . ."

"I know. She always does that. She makes people apologize and then says an apology ain't good enough. Thank God I'm going to be married. Nobody will fool with me then."

"I'm going to put a piece of her *drawers* in my quilt and say to everybody, that was from my Aunt Missouri Abigail, the HORSE'S ASS!!" says Lula Belle.

"Drawers! Drawers!" laughs Dale.

"Piss! Testicles! Organs!" shouts Lula Belle, becoming intemperate.

"Damn! Hell! Male Organs!!" cries Dale.

"Female organs!! Buttocks!"

"Penises! Shit! Damnation and Faust!!" shouts Dale.

And then they sing, together and in harmony:

And it was from Aunt Dinah's quilting party,
he was seeing Nellie home . . .

At Aunt Abigail and Henry T.'s place. It is Dale's wedding. The yard is full of wagons and the women have been pressing dresses and crinolines for days with the old sad irons, family silver has come out of the silver cases, and cream for the whipping is being kept cool in the springhouse. Aunt Missouri Abigail has baked three layers of cake in her new "Prosperous" cookstove, and Uncle Henry T. has brought ice from Otterville, packed in sawdust in the wagon. All of these efforts say they are sorry they made Dale go without stockings and do all the hand-mangling jobs like shelling field corn—but now they will be rid of their obligation. Her husband will buy her stockings. She will be "married off," and this shows they are generous people after all, aren't they? Dale and Thomas Sheridan Bodine have been through the marriage ceremony at the church, made promises to the community and God and each other, and have returned to Aunt Abigail's and Henry T.'s for the wedding party.

LULA BELLE

A week before Dale's wedding I had come down with a fainting fit again, and had called out the names of lost and departed ones, and I was visited by the Frenchman who lives in the salt springs, who was very well-connected, he said, in the other world, and for a week after I saw lights around things, and so it was lovely and amusing at Dale's wedding, and there were so many lamps. I bet it was like that in Virginia, I reckon they had beautiful dresses, and gentlemen, and a hundred fiddlers at every wedding . . .

Dale and Lula Belle, aunts, cousins and friends are in the back room getting themselves ready. Dale's dress is a vast green and lavender plaid taffeta.

"Oh, Dale, it's very fetching and smart," says Caledonia.

"Daddy brought me the taffeta. It's en feston with alternate flounces."

"Dale, you're so young, honey," says Lizzy. "Now don't go wading in the creek with it."

"Oh, I thought I'd go slop Chesley's hogs with it," says Dale. "Them hogs have made it to every funeral and wedding that I know of."

"Well, they're here all right," says Lizzy. "On a plate. Maybe you want some lemons and salt, Dale, you look faint."

Dale is putting tiny white bloodroot flowers in her corona of braids. "Oh, I'm alright," says Dale. "Give me that fan there, that Jesus fan. Well, at least he ain't a Baptist."

"Who are you referring to?" sniffs Aunt Abigail. "Jesus?"

The other women burst out laughing.

"I fail to see what's funny," says Abigail, sternly.

Two women cousins fall to snorting. "She fails to see . . .!" And then the fiddle starts up "Here Come The Bride!"

"This is you, Dale, go on," says Lizzy.

There is a tearing sound as Dale tears a flounce off her dress.

"Lula Belle, here's a piece of my wedding dress to put in that quilt of yours, darlin'."

"Dale!! You tore a flounce of your dress!"

"And you tell the story of how I nearly had to run off with Tom Bodine before Daddy would take any notice at all," says Dale, kissing Lula on the cheek. "Is that a big enough piece?"

"I will treasure it with all my heart and put it right in the middle," says Lula Belle, stashing it in the sleeve of her new dress.

Applause as Dale enters the living room. The furniture has all been moved to the barn to make room for the dance.

Thomas Sheridan, stiff in a five-button cutaway, turns to Dale. "Mrs. Bodine, I thought you were going to keep me waiting forever."

"Ladies and gentlemen, form up for the Virginia Reel," calls out the fiddler, a big villainous Speece. "Just form up there; you all going to dance or what?"

"I'll have the first dance with my daughter, Mr. Bodine," says William.

A man in the crowd whispers loudly: "He's gone and bought a pony keg of whisky and I'll be goddamned if he didn't drink the greater part of it himself . . . excuse my language."

"Mr. King, remove yourself from the dance," says the fiddler. "You're a bit too merry."

"Shut your mouth, George Speece!" says William. "Son of a bitch, fifteen years ago it would have been as much as your life was worth . . ."

"Mr. King," insists the fiddler, "leave the premises."

"Oh, poppa, please . . ." pleads Dale.

"To tell me to remove *my* premises! You Confederate son-of-a-bitch!" shouts William.

"William!"

"Mr. King!"

"How'd I miss you at Wilson's Creek is what I want to know!" says William, suddenly possessed by memories of the battle of Wilson's Creek, with him on one side and the Speece brothers on the other. "I should have blowed your head off when it was legal!"

"I will remove you myself, then!" yells the fiddler.

"Well, who's a-henderin' you?" says William, as he takes off his coat. Lula Belle runs out and grabs his arm. "Daddy, dance with me."

"Get out of here, Lula, Go on. Go away. Daddy wants to fight."

The fiddler thinks better of it and begins playing instead. The guitar and mandolin follow.

"Dance with Lula, Daddy, and come on now . . ." says Dale, as she joins her sister.

Outside at night: guests are leaving, wagons creak off, people have had a good time anyway. That's what they came for, by God.

"Well, sister," says Dale, and leans out of the wagon, "we'll be off now."

The two of them hold hands.

"Soon as we get back from Jeff City you'll come and visit, Lula," says Tom. "Don't worry! You'll come and stay with us! Now, where's your dad?"

"I put him to sleep in the upstairs," says Lula. "Well . . ."

"Goodnight, Dale."

"Goodnight, Lou."

"God bless you, Dale."

"God bless you, Lou."

Lula Belle and her father are crossing the valley by wagon. Lula Belle is moving back to Lizzy and Chesley's again. Now, instead of a sugar sack she has a small carpet bag, and a few things left to her by Maggie Jo. She has the King Family Bible with the clipping in it.

LULA BELLE

The last time I moved anyplace was back again with Uncle Chesley and Aunt Lizzy, because me and Aunt Missouri Abigail couldn't stand each other. And my daddy took me over there in the wagon. We come down the long road through the valley.

And as they ride along, they silently note who is planting what, and how the small patches of cotton are growing, and the wheat. The sun is shining on Chimney Rock and on the ridges around them.

LULA BELLE

We came down the long road through the valley, at evening, through Buffalo Prairie, in September, and the moon was coming up on one side of the world

*and the sun was going down on the other. And turkey buzzards were uplifting
on the air drafts like ashes flying in the heat of the sunset fire, and I think one
of them was carrying the soul of my grandmother on his back. The road was
still hot from the day, but the air was cool, and it made a heavy mist in the
valley of the Lamine River and the hollows of the creeks, liquid and white,
Chouteau Creek and Loutre Creek, Hess Creek and Hungry Mother Creek
and Short Rations branch. And daddy took the opportunity to tell me he was
quitting the railroad and going out west to the Indian Nation. He said that
railroad men tempted him to drink and his oldest daughter was married and
gone, and there was only me to be married yet. So he might as well go on out
and drive a combine team in the harvest season. There were Cherokees out
there, he said, and Chickasaws, and Wyandottes. And oh, how the fields of
the valley did shine along beside us, it was rich and very blue, with the heads of
sorghum sticking up like soldier's plumes, and every hollow filled with our
people and all our stories, the good and the bad of them all, places where people
had a good time and places where they died. Driving past all these stories was
like running a stick down a picket fence in your mind. And so me and Daddy
talked at last and said all that was in our hearts. Well, that's not altogether
true. Dale says I have to be more rigorous with myself about reporting conversations. I guess I asked him about his life and he told me. That's how it was,
yes, I'm sure that's pretty well accurate.*

"Well, poppa, did you ever kill a man?"

"I did," says William, after a long thought.

"When did you do that?"

William sighs and looks out over Jacob Kendall's fields. "I wish I had
a son I could tell this to."

"I was just asking," says Lula Belle, and pulls up her tapestry shawl,
her good one.

·"Well, it was in the War."

"What happened?"

"It was at Lexington; the Battle of Lexington up there on the Missouri River. The Confederates come over the breastworks—they were
cotton bales we'd pitched up—and we were out of ammunition, you see,
and hadn't had a drink of water in two days; we were dying of thirst—
and then they set fire to the cotton bales. There was many a man died
there in the smoke of it. . . . And they made a charge, and a fellow
come over the top of them cotton bales and since I didn't have any
bullets I stuck the ramrod down the barrel of my musket and poured in a

load of black powder and shot him through the breast. Transfixed him. I'm sorry I did it. He was a young fellow. So was I. I was a young fellow too. We hadn't any water for so many days. . . . I saw men drinking the bloody water the surgeons was going to throw out. I guess I cultivated a permanent thirst, there. Been thirsty ever since then."

"Who was it?" asks Lula Belle.

"Who was what?" says William, looking at her.

"The fellow you transfixed."

"Why, I don't know," says William, shaking his head. "He wasn't from around here. I think he was with a Tennessee Regiment."

"Who was you with?"

"The 49th Missouri Volunteers, Company C. Now, let's not talk about the War ever again. Most of your uncles went to the Confederacy and we must cease any discussion of it from this time forth."

"Yes, daddy. But you know, I can't rest until I know something."

"What?" sighs William.

"Well, that black man they took out and hung, was that 'Jim Drew, Worthless Otterville Negro?'"

"Well, I'll be goddamned," says William, muttering to himself. 'Lulu, the things you get your mind around . . . well, I guess you can't help it. . . . Yes. But listen. He wasn't worthless. No man is worthless. God accepts everybody, and I ought to know. Believe me, I ought to know. Now hush up about it."

"Daddy . . ."

"What, darlin'?"

"Where you going this time?"

"To Oklahoma, to the Indian Nation."

"How come?"

"Well, daughter, if I go out there and work in the hayfields, there's not . . . they don't have any whisky out there, on account of the Indians. So there won't be any for me to be tempted by. And then . . . well, I'll be making a lot of money, you know. I'm good with a team. And I'll send you taffeta silk for your wedding dress, and . . . what else would you want?"

"What else would I want? Well, I really don't know . . ."

"Well . . ." laughs Lula Belle.

William is happy to get away from war and murder and onto beaux. He doesn't want to make the same mistake he did with Dale.

"You can tell your daddy."

"No, poppa, really I don't have any in mind. But . . . send me the silk taffeta *anyway*."

"It's a promise, Lula."

Going to the Cooper County Fair. The Burnetts will take her now that there is only one of them. It's a long trip: nearly thirty miles and they will stay overnight.

LULA BELLE

And so I went to the Cooper County Fair in Boonville, with Aunt Lizzy and Uncle Chesley, and I took with me the anxieties and fears that I held in my heart. For I didn't know what was to become of me in the world, and I didn't know what to do with myself. And so I decided to go to Madame Perrigo with a dollar that daddy had sent me from the Indian Nation.

South of the fairgrounds the wagons are parked, with awnings stretched from the wagonboxes to poles, and under the awnings quilts and straw mattresses are laid out. The men are in knots talking carefully about their cattle. Sometimes women, too, have hogs or sheep or cattle to sell and so they stand at the edge of these discussions. This is the local economy of Cooper County. It is dominated by white men who are Baptists, vote Democrat and have pianos in the parlours. Lizzy is entering a lace tablecloth and Grandma Maggie Jo's Kaleidoscope quilt. Altho Lizzy has finished the quilt herself, she wants to enter it under Maggie Jo's name. She is worried about whether this will be allowed or not. Chesley has brought nothing to show but he might buy; he heads directly toward a group of men he knows who are dealing in the new Herefords. They said there was to be a Hereford bull at the fair.

LULA BELLE

There were so many things at the Cooper County Fair! People that had a lot of hair, and a woman with a mustache, and vegetables being judged for moisture and tint, animals and their progeny, a boar pig the size of a woodshed, it was tumultuous, it was amusing. You could eat cotton candy and lose your entire face in it, they had fetching little kewpie dolls as adorable as candy hearts, and the horses that came to show! I never expect to sit on a horse like that, and Aunt Lizzy said . . .

"Well, Lula, maybe you'll marry a man that likes horses," says Lizzy as she bustles along to the Home Arts building, grasping the quilt and the lace tablecloth.

Lula Belle talks Lizzy into letting her go by herself to the Poultry building, but instead heads for the Midway.

LULA BELLE

And so I took my dollar and I went to see the fortune teller, Madame Perrigo, as soon as I could cut loose from Lizzy and Chesley.

"She reveals secrets no mortal ever knew!" says the barker. "She restores happiness to those who, from doleful events, catastrophes, crosses in love, loss of relatives, money or friends, have become despondent! Gives you the name, likeness, and characteristics of the one you will marry! From the stars we see in the firmament, she deducts the future destiny of man! Go in through there, young lady.

"Thank you, sir," says Lula Belle, and walks into the sinfully brilliant calico curtains, into a place whose decorations and furnishings scream "Mystery!!" instead of "Propriety." It is lit by a coal-oil lamp and there is a small crystal ball.

Madame Perrigo is satisfyingly gypsy: scarves, rings, deep eyes and rouge and an accent.

"Well, you're only about as big as a minute, honey. I don't know if you're big enough to have a future yet. Save yourself a dollar and wait a few years."

"I'm fourteen," says Lula Belle. "and I have two very important questions."

"Of course," nods Madame Perrigo and shuffles her cards. "Of course."

LULA BELLE

Oh, she was beautiful. She had fringes and crystal shade weights hanging off all over her, she had a deck of cards that was all pictures, and earrings on either side of her head that looked like advertisements for ears. Her hair was unnaturally black and she had a voice that reached backwards into time and forwards into the future.

"Now, here are the cards laid out. And what are your questions?"

"One question is, who will I marry, and the other is of great import."

"Aha. One has to meditate and empty one's mind of any knowledge connected to the subject. . . . Now, I will read. In the position of your past, I see a boneyard. You got two dead people back there."

"One of them was my mother when I was little."

Madame Perrigo nods in agreement. "The cards never lie," she says. "Now, in your immediate future, I see a journey where you will meet your intended. Probably a long voyage in the next county."

"Oh, I would like that!"

"And here in your house of family and relations, there are absent ones."

"Yes," says Lula Belle. "You see, my momma died when I was young and then my daddy had to go away to work in the Indian Nation. And also I had brain fever when my momma died so I have visions."

Perrigo looks up, suddenly cautious, and her earrings flash. "You have *visions*?"

"Yes," says Lula Belle. "Now, do I *have* to get married?"

Perrigo stares at her, wondering if the girl is pregnant. "Do you have to . . . well, what else are you going to do? And you with visions!"

"I don't know. I can't read or write at all. Look there—what's that card?"

"That's Temperance," says Perrigo, looking down. This isn't going right; this fourteen-year-old has taken over the reading.

"Read that card," says Lula Belle.

"Well, Temperance is a good card, balance and harmony. You see there, she's pouring something out of a jug. That's in your house of distant future."

"That's my daddy."

"He knocks back a few, does your daddy?"

"He's trying *not* to."

"Good for your daddy," says Perrigo. And this here . . ."

"It's the hanged man!!" says Lula Belle, jumping up. "That's what I wanted to ask you about!"

". . . this here is about your future intended," says Perrigo, quickly shifting the subject. "You'll get married all right."

"Well, what about you, have you been married?"

"Repeatedly."

"Maybe I could tell fortunes?" asks Lula Belle.

"Honey," says Perrigo, shaking her head, "they'd run you out of whatever church you go to on Sunday and, besides, it's an occult art. Now settle down and listen here to this about your intended."

"No, no, I want to hear about the Hanged Man. That was my other question. There was a man, a black man that they took out and hung on

November 29th, 1876, down by the draw of Chouteau Creek, and I want
to know if my daddy, who is William Nelson King and who is at present
residing in the Indian Territory at no fixed address, if he was in on it,
when that man perished, and I can't go on with life until I know."

"My dear!! The cards don't tell that kind of thing! Ain't that a matter for the sheriff?"

"It was seven years ago," says Lula Belle.

Madame Perrigo decides to take it because her knowledge of the
incident is secular and not divine.

"I see. November 29th, 1876. William Nelson King. Yes. Bill King."

"Do you know him?" asks Lula Belle.

"Well, in a way."

"Then what does the Hanged Man say?"

"Alright. Though it may be perilous to enquire of matters that are
occult and dark, and in the past, I shall enquire. Spirits, come! Speak!
Ahhhh. . . . Indeed, the card says your daddy on the night in question
was disporting himself in a house in Lost Corners and he was so merry
he was incapacitated and couldn't have hung anybody if he tried. Now
that information is tendered you in secret and if you ever reveal it your
daddy will have your hide, and life would become somewhat uncomfortable for me. Don't you ever tell you come to see Madame Perrigo, my
dear."

"Cross my heart and hope to die, stick a thousand needles in my
eye."

"Good, good. Whew. Now, for your intended . . . you'll marry a
Baptist."

"What!!" says Lula Belle, shoving the cards away. "I ain't going to
marry no Baptist!"

"That's the breaks, kid. And you will have a hard life."

"I *already* had a hard life," says Lula Belle.

"You'll have *more* hard life," says Perrigo, gathering up the cards.
"Ah . . . you are doing something in secret, are you not?"

"Yes . . . yes, I'm making a quilt with patches from everybody's
clothes in them, to remember the stories that are told, and what happened to people."

"Ah," says Perrigo, smiling a little doubtfully, "that's lovely."

"And they're just like your cards there. I mean, there's the Hanged
Man, and there's Temperance with her jug, and people falling from the

burning tower, that's when my daddy fought at Lexington, and what's this one, the man stepping out over the cliff, with the dog and the rose?"

"That's the Fool card, honey. He's going to step out over that cliff and *fly*."

"Then that's my grandma, Maggie Jo!"

"Well," says Perrigo, returning to the reading, "here's the final outcome. Yes . . . hmmm . . . your life will be hard but your quilts will become a precious heirloom, and none of your stories will ever be forgotten, because they are so fetching and so strange. It'll be just like one of them romance novels, where, you know, where people cry over the last pages, and sigh to themselves, and just can't put it down, and wish it would start again."

"I know what you mean. *Love Triumphant,* or *The Enemy Conquered.*"

"That is very so. Your daddy is a very good looking man, girl, and he's been through the midnight fire, and he means the best for you. Now run along, run along, your cards have been told."

"Thank you, Madame Perrigo! Thank you. Goodbye."

LULA BELLE

The mouth is the place that thoughts leap out of, it is the starting-gate of our hearts. The words of preachers, whispered conversations, stories told sitting on the rails of the salt spring, newspaper talk, the words of fortune tellers. I never looked at the new moon over my left shoulder, and he was the first man I saw after I counted forty white horses. Daddy sent me a dress length of silk taffeta in pale green that he bought in St. Louis, and he is coming home any day now from the Indian Nation. He no longer goes walking disorderly about the county with Lucifer because Lucifer can't locate him. I won't get my quilt finished in time for my wedding, and it won't be finished for years. It is something to amuse myself with, it will be something to give my children. And, oh, one story I forgot was the rose baby that Grandma Huffman saved when she was a midwife, and you know something else? I forgot to tell about how Sylvania Speece and the Hanlin girl sold all Old Man Hanlin's hogs at the fair when he was drunk and run off with the money to . . .

II

DOUBLE WEDDING RING

Stories of Community and Courtship

The Quilting Party

T.S. Arthur

O̲U̲R̲ ̲Y̲O̲U̲N̲G̲ ̲L̲A̲D̲I̲E̲S̲ of the present generation know little of the mysteries of "Irish chain," "rising star," "block work," or "Job's trouble," and would be as likely to mistake a set of quilting frames for clothes as for anything else. It was different in our younger days. Half a dozen handsome patchwork quilts were as indispensable then as a marriage portion; quite as much so as a piano or guitar is at present. And the quilting party was equally indicative of the coming-out and being "in the market," as the fashionable gatherings together of the times that be.

As for the difference in the custom, we are not disposed to sigh over it as indicative of social deterioration. We do not belong to the class who believe that society is retrograding, because everything is not as it was in the earlier days of our life history. And yet—it may be a weakness; but early associations exercise a powerful influence over us. We have never enjoyed ourselves with the keen zest and heartiness, in any company, that we have experienced in the old fashioned quilting party. But we were young then, and every sense perfect in its power to receive enjoyment. No care weighed down the spirit; no grief was in the heart; no mistakes had occurred to sober the feelings with unavailing regrets. Life was in the beauty and freshness of its spring time; in the odor of its lovely blossoms. We had but to open our eyes—to touch, to taste—to feel an exquisite delight. Of the world we knew nothing beyond the quiet village; and there we found enough to fill the measure of our capacity. In a wider sphere we have not found greater social pleasures; though in a more extended usefulness there has come a different source of enjoyment—purer, and more elevating to the heart.

But this is all too grave for our subject. It is not the frame of mind in which to enjoy a quilting party. And yet, who can look back upon early times without a browner hue upon his feelings?

There was one quilting party—can we ever forget it? Twenty years have passed since the time. We were young then, and had not tarried long at Jericho! Twenty years! It seems but yesterday. With the freshness of the present it is all before us now.

In our village there dwelt a sweet young girl, who was the favorite of all. When the invitations to a quilting party at Mrs. Willing's came, you may be sure there was a flutter of delight all around. The quilting party was Amy's, of course, and Amy Willing was to be the bright, particular star in the social firmament. It was to be Amy's first quilting, moreover; and the sign that she was looking forward to the matrimonial goal, was hailed with a peculiar pleasure by more than one of the village swains, who had worshiped the dawning beauty at a respectful distance.

We had been to many quilting parties up to this time; but more as a boy than as a man. Our enjoyment had always been unembarrassed by any peculiar feelings. We could play at blind man's bluff, hunt the slipper, and pawns, and not only clasp the little hands of our fair playfellows, but even touch their warm lips with our own, and not experience a heart-emotion deeper than the ripple made on the smooth water by a playful breeze. But there had come a change. There was something in the eyes of our young companions, as we looked at them, that had a different meaning from the old expression, and particularly was this true with Amy. Into her eyes we could no longer gaze steadily. As to the reason we were ignorant; yet so it was.

The invitation to attend her quilting was an era; for it produced emotions of so marked a character, that they were never forgotten. There was an uneasy fluttering of the heart as the time drew near, and a pressure upon the feelings that a deep, sighing breath failed to remove. The more we thought about the quilting, the more restless did we grow, and the more conscious that the part we were about to play would be one of peculiar embarrassment.

At last the evening came. We have never shrunk from going alone into any company before. But now we felt that it was necessary to be sustained from without; and such sustentation we sought in the company of the good-natured, self-composed bachelor of the village, who went anywhere and everywhere freely, and without apparent emotion.

"You're going to Amy Willing's quilting?" said we to L——, on the day before the party.

"Certainly," was his reply.

"Will you wait until we call for you?"

"Oh yes," was as good-naturedly answered.

"So much gained," thought we, when alone.

In the shadow of his presence we would be able to make our debut with little embarrassment. What would we not have then given for L——'s self-possession and easy confidence!

When the time came we called, as had been arranged, upon L——. To our surprise, we found no less than four others, as bashful as we, waiting his convoy. L—— very good-humoredly—he never did an ill-natured thing in his life—assumed the escort, and we all set off for the cottage of Mrs. Willing. How the rest felt, we know not, but as for our own heart, it throbbed slower and heavier at each step, until, by the time the cottage was reached, the pulses in our ears were beating audibly. We could not understand this. It had never been so before.

The sun still lingered above the horizon when we came in sight of the cottage—fashionable hours were earlier then than now. On arriving at the door, L—— entered first, as a matter of course, and we all followed close in his rear, in order to secure the benefit of his countenance. The room was full of girls, who were busy in binding Amy's quilt, which was already out of the frame, and getting all ready for the evening's sport. There was no one equal to L—— for taking the wire edge from off the feelings of a promiscuous company, and giving a free and easy tone to the social intercourse, that would otherwise have been constrained and awkward. In a little while the different parties, who had entered under his protection, began to feel at home among the merry girls, it was not long before another and another came in, until the old-fashioned parlor, with its old-fashioned furniture, was filled, and the but half-bound quilt was forcibly taken from the hands of the laughing seamstresses, and put "out of sight and out of mind."

The bright, particular star of that evening was Amy Willing—gentle, quiet, loving Amy Willing. Here was a warmer glow upon her cheeks, and a deeper tenderness in her beautiful eyes, than they had ever worn before. In gazing upon her, how the heart moved from its very depths! No long time passed before we were by the side of Amy, and our eyes resting in hers with an earnestness of expression that caused them to droop to the floor. When the time for redeeming pawns came, and it was our turn to call out from the circle of beauty a fair partner, the name of Amy fell from our lips, which were soon pressed, glowing, upon those of the blushing maiden. It was the first warm kiss of love. How it thrilled, exquisitely, to the very heart! Our lips had often met before—kissing was then a fashionable amusement—but never as at this time. Soon it became Amy's place to take the floor. She must "kiss the one she loved the best." What a moment of suspense! Stealthily her eyes wandered around the room; and then her long, dark lashes lay quivering on her beautiful cheeks.

"Kiss the one you love best," was repeated by the holder of the pawns.

The fringed lids were again raised, and again her eyes went searching around the room. We could see that her bosom was rising and falling more rapidly than before. Our name at length came, in an undertone, from her smiling lips. What a happy moment! The envied kiss was ours, and we led the maiden in triumph from the floor.

And, to us, the whole evening was a series of triumphs. Somehow or other, Amy was by our side, and Amy's hand in ours oftenest of any. It was our first, sweet dream of love. But we knew little then of human nature, and less of woman's human nature. And as little of all this knew a certain young man, who was present, and who, more sober and silent than any, joined in the sports of the evening, but with no apparent zest. Amy never called him over when she was on the floor; nor did he mention her name when the privilege of touching some maiden's lips with his own was assigned him.

He was first to retire; and then we noticed a change in Amy. Her voice was lower, her manner more subdued, and there was a thoughtful, absent expression in her face.

A few weeks later, and this was all explained. Edward Martin was announced in the village as Amy's accepted lover. We did not, we could not, we would not, accredit the fact. It was impossible! Had she not called us out at the quilting party, as the one "loved best?" Had not her hand been oftenest in ours, and our lips oftenest upon hers? It could not be! Yet time proved the truth of the rumor;—ere another twelvemonth went by, Amy Willing was a bride. We were at the wedding; but as silent and sober as was Edward Martin at the quilting. The tables were turned against us, and hopelessly turned.

Ah, well! More than twenty years have passed since then. The quiltings, the corn-huskings, the merry-makings in the village of M—— are not forgotten. Nor is Amy Willing and *the* party forgotten, as this brief sketch assuredly testifies. Twenty years. How many changes have come in that period! And Amy, where is she? When last at M—— we saw a sweet young maiden, just in the dawn of womanhood, and, for the moment, it seemed as if we were back again in the old time—the intervening space but a dream. Her name was Amy. It was not *our* Amy. She had passed away, leaving a bud of beauty to bloom in her place.

Our sketch of a merry-making has turned out graver than was intended. But it is difficult for the mind to go back in reminisence, and not take a sober hue. We will not attempt to write it over again, for, in that case, it might be graver still.

The Minister's Wooing

Harriet Beecher Stowe

By six o'clock in the morning, Miss Prissy came out of the best room to the breakfast-table, with the air of a general who has arranged a campaign,—her face glowing with satisfaction. All sat down together to their morning meal. The outside door was open into the green, turfy yard, and the apple-tree, now nursing stores of fine yellow jeannetons, looked in at the window. Every once in a while, as a breeze shook the leaves, a fully ripe apple might be heard falling to the ground, at which Miss Prissy would bustle up from the table and rush to secure the treasure.

As the meal waned to its close, the rattling of wheels was heard at the gate, and Candace was discerned, seated aloft in the one-horse wagon, with her usual complement of baskets and bags.

"Well, now, dear me! if there isn't Candace!" said Miss Prissy; "I do believe Miss Marvyn has sent her with something for the quilting!" and out she flew as nimble as a humming-bird, while those in the house heard various exclamations of admiration, as Candace, with stately dignity, disinterred from the wagon one basket after another, and exhibited to Miss Prissy's enraptured eyes sly peeps under the white napkins with which they were covered. And then, hanging a large basket on either arm, she rolled majestically towards the house, like a heavy-laden India-man, coming in after a fast voyage.

"Good-mornin', Miss Scudder! good-mornin', Doctor!" she said, dropping her curtsy on the door-step; "good-mornin', Miss Mary! Ye see our folks was stirrin' pootty early dis mornin', an' Miss Marvyn sent me down wid two or tree little tings."

Setting down her baskets on the floor, and seating herself between them, she proceeded to develop their contents with ill-concealed triumph. One basket was devoted to cakes of every species, from the great

Mont-Blanc loaf-cake, with its snowy glaciers of frosting, to the twisted cruller and puffy doughnut. In the other basket lay pots of golden butter curiously stamped, reposing on a bed of fresh, green leaves,—while currants, red and white, and delicious cherries and raspberries, gave a final finish to the picture. From a basket which Miss Prissy brought in from the rear appeared cold fowl and tongue delicately prepared, and shaded with feathers of parsley. Candace, whose rollicking delight in the good things of this life was conspicuous in every emotion, might have furnished to a painter, as she sat in her brilliant turban, an idea for an African Genius of Plenty.

"Why, really, Candace," said Mrs. Scudder, "you are overwhelming us!"

"Ho! ho! ho!" said Candace, "I's tellin' Miss Marvyn folks don't git married but once in der lives, (gin'ally speakin', dat is,) an' den dey oughter hab plenty to do it wid."

"Well, I must say," said Miss Prissy, taking out the loaf-cake with busy assiduity,—"I must say, Candace, this does beat all!"

"I should rader tink it oughter," said Candace, bridling herself with proud consciousness; "ef it don't, 'ta'n't 'cause ole Candace ha'n't put enough into it. I tell ye, I didn't do nothin' all day yisterday but jes' make dat ar cake. Cato, when he got up, he begun to talk someh'n' 'bout his shirtbuttons, an' I jes' shet him right up. Says I, 'Cato, when I's r'ally got cake to make for a great 'casion, I wants my mind *jest* as quiet an' *jest* as serene as ef I was a-goin' to de sacrament. I don't want no 'arthly cares on't. Now,' says I, 'Cato, de ole Doctor's gwine to be married, an' dis yer's his quiltin'-cake,—an' Miss Mary, she's gwine to be married, an' dis yer's *her* quiltin'-cake. An' dar'll be eberybody to dat ar quiltin'; an' ef de cake a'n't' right, why, 'twould be puttin' a candle under a bushel. An' so,' says I, 'Cato, your buttons mus' wait.' An' Cato, he sees de 'priety ob it, 'cause, dough he can't make cake like me, he's a 'mazin' good judge on't, an' is dre'ful tickles when I slips out a little loaf for his supper."

"How is Mrs. Marvyn?" said Mrs. Scudder.

"Kinder thin and shimmery; but she's about,—habin' her eyes eberywar 'n' lookin' into eberyting. She jes' touches tings wid de tips ob her fingers an' dey seem to go like. She'll be down to de quiltin' dis arternoon. But she tole me to take de tings an' come down an' spen' de day here; for Miss Marvyn an' I both knows how many steps mus' be taken sech times, an' we agreed you oughter favor yourselves all you could."

"Well, now," said Miss Prissy, lifting up her hands, "if that a'n't what 'tis to have friends! Why, that was one of the things I was thinking of, as I lay awake last night; because, you know, at times like these, people run their feet off before the time begins, and then they are all limpsey and lop-sided when the time comes. Now, I say, Candace, all Miss Scudder and Mary have to do is to give everything up to us, and we'll put it through straight."

"Dat's what we will!" said Candace. "Jes' show me what's to be done, an' I'll do it."

Candace and Miss Prissy soon disappeared together into the pantry with the baskets, whose contents they began busily to arrange. Candace shut the door, that no sound might escape, and began a confidential outpouring to Miss Prissy.

"Ye see," she said, "I's *feelin's* all de while for Miss Marvyn; 'cause, ye see, she was expectin', ef eber Mary was married,—well—dat 'twould be to somebody else, ye know."

Miss Prissy responded with a sympathetic groan.

"Well," said Candace, "ef 't had ben anybody but de Doctor, *I* wouldn't 'a' been resigned. But arter all he has done for my color, dar a'n't nothin' I could find it in my heart to grudge him. But den I was tellin' Cato t'oder day, says I, 'Cato, I dunno 'bout de rest o' de world, but I ha'n't neber felt it in my bones dat mass'r James is r'ally dead, for sartin.' Now I feels tings *gin'ally*, but *some* tings I feels *in my bones*, and dem allers comes true. And dat ar's a feelin' I ha'n't had 'bout Mass'r Jim yit, an' dat ar's what I'm waitin' for 'fore I clar make up my mind. Though I know, 'cordin' to all white folks' way o' tinkin', dar a'n't no hope, 'cause Squire Marvyn he had dat ar Jeduth Pettibone up to his house, a-questionin' on him, off an' on, nigh about tree hours. An' r'ally I didn't see no hope no way, 'xcept jes' dis yer, as I was tellin' Cato,—*I can't feel it in my bones.*"

Candace was not versed enough in the wisdom of the world to know that she belonged to a large and respectable school of philosophers in this particular mode of testing evidence, which, after all, the reader will perceive has its conveniences.

"Anoder ting," said Candace, "as much as a dozen times, dis yer last year, when I's been a-scourin' knives, a fork has fell an' stuck straight up in de floor; an' de las' time I pinted it out to Miss Marvyn, an' she on'y jes' said, 'Why, what o' dat, Candace?'"

"Well," said Miss Prissy, "I don't believe in *signs*, but then strange things do happen. Now about dogs howling under windows,—why, I don't believe in it a bit, but I never knew it fail that there was a death in the house after."

"Ah, I tell ye what," said Candace, looking mysterious, "dogs knows a heap more'n dey likes to tell!"

"Jes' so," said Miss Prissy. "Now I remember, one night, when I was watching with Miss Colonel Andrews, after Marthy Ann was born, that we heard the *mournfulest* howling that ever you did hear. It seemed to come from right under the front stoop; and Miss Andrews she just dropped the spoon in her gruel, and says she, 'Miss Prissy, do, for pity's sake, just go down and see what that noise is.' And I went down and lifted up one of the loose boards of the stoop, and what should I see there but their Newfoundland pup?—there that creature had dug a grave and was a-sitting by it, crying!"

Candace drew near to Miss Prissy, dark with expressive interest, as her voice, in this awful narration, sank to a whisper.

"Well," said Candace, after Miss Prissy had made something of a pause.

"Well, I told Miss Andrews I didn't think there was anything in it," said Miss Prissy; "but," she added, impressively, "she lost a very dear brother, six months after, and I laid him out with my own hands,—yes, laid him out in white flannel."

"Some folks say," said Candace, "dat dreamin' 'bout white horses is a sartin sign. Jinny Styles is berry strong 'bout dat. Now she come down one mornin' cryin', 'cause she'd been dreamin' 'bout white horses, an' she was sure she should hear some friend was dead. An' sure enough, a man come in dat bery day an' tole her her son was drownded out in de harbor. An' Jinny said, 'Dar! she was sure dat sign neber would fail.' But den, ye see, dat night he come home. Jinny wa'n't r'ally disappinted, but she allers insisted he was *as good as drownded*, any way, 'cause he sunk tree times."

"Well, I tell you," said Miss Prissy, "there are a great many more things in this world than folks know about."

"So dey are," said Candace. "Now, I ha'n't neber opened my mind to nobody; but dar's a dream I's had, tree mornin's runnin', lately. I dreamed I see Jim Marvyn a-sinkin' in de water, an' stretchin' up his hands. An' den I dreamed I see de Lord Jesus come a-walkin' on de water an' take hold ob his hand, an' says he, 'O thou of little faith, wherfore didst thou doubt?' An' den he lifted him right out. An' I ha'n't said nothin' to nobody, 'cause, you know, de Doctor, he says people mus'n't mind nothin' 'bout der dreams, 'cause dreams belongs to de ole 'spensation."

"Well, well, well!" said Miss Prissy, "I am sure I don't know what to think. What time in the morning was it that you dreamed it?"

"Why," said Candace, "it was jest arter birdpeep. I kinder allers wakes myself den, an' turns ober, an' what comes arter dat is apt to run clar."

"Well, well, well!" said Miss Prissy, "I don't know what to think. You see, it may have reference to the state of his soul."

"I know dat," said Candace; "but as nigh as I could judge in my dream," she added, sinking her voice and looking mysterious, "as nigh as I can judge, *dat boy's soul was in his body!*"

"Why, how do you know?" said Miss Prissy, looking astonished at the confidence with which Candace expressed her opinion.

"Well, ye see," said Candace, rather mysteriously, "de Doctor, he don't like to hab us talk much 'bout dese yer tings, 'cause he tinks it's kind o' heathenish. But den, folks as is used to seein' sech tings knows de look ob a sperit *out* o' de body from de look ob a sperit *in* de body, jest as easy as you can tell Mary from de Doctor."

At this moment Mrs. Scudder opened the pantry-door and put an end to this mysterious conversation, which had already so affected Miss Prissy, that, in the eagerness of her interest, she had rubbed up her cap border and ribbon into rather an elfin and goblin style, as if they had been ruffled up by a breeze from the land of spirits; and she flew around for a few moments in a state of great nervous agitation, upsetting dishes, knocking down plates, and huddling up contrary suggestions as to what ought to be done first, in such impossible relations that Mrs. Katy Scudder stood in dignified surprise at this strange freak of conduct in the wise woman of the parish.

A dim consciousness of something not quite canny in herself seemed to strike her, for she made a vigorous effort to appear composed; and facing Mrs. Scudder, with an air of dignified suavity, inquired if it would not be best to put Jim Marvyn in the oven now, while Candace was getting the pies ready,—meaning, of course, a large turkey which was to be the first in an indefinite series to be baked that morning; and discovering, by Mrs. Scudder's dazed expression and a vigorous pinch from

Candace, that somehow she had not improved matters, she rubbed her spectacles into a diagonal position across her eyes, and stood glaring, half through, half over them, with a helpless expression, which in a less judicious person might have suggested the idea of a state of slight intoxication.

But the exigencies of an immediate temporal dispensation put an end to Miss Prissy's unwonted vagaries, and she was soon to be seen flying round like a meteor, dusting, shaking curtains, counting napkins, wiping and sorting china, all with such rapidity as to give rise to the notion that she actually existed in forty places at once.

Candace, whom the limits of her corporeal frame restricted to an altogether different style of locomotion, often rolled the whites of her eyes after her and gave vent to her views of her proceedings in sententious expressions.

"Do you know why *dat ar* neber was married?" she said to Mary, as she stood looking after her. Miss Prissy had made one of those rapid transits through the apartment.

"No," answered Mary, innocently. "Why wasn't she?"

"'Cause neber was a man could run fast enough to cotch her," said Candace; and then her portly person shook with the impulse of her own wit.

By two o'clock a goodly company began to assemble. Mrs. Deacon Twitchel arrived, soft, pillowy, and plaintive as ever, accompanied by Cerinthy Ann, a comely damsel, tall and trim, with a bright black eye, and a most vigorous and determined style of movement. Good Mrs. Jones, broad, expansive, and solid, having vegetated tranquilly on in the cabbage-garden of the virtues since three years ago, when she graced our tea-party, was now as well preserved as ever, and brought some fresh butter, a tin pail of cream, and a loaf of cake made after a new Philadelphia receipt. The tall, spare, angular figure of Mrs. Simeon Brown alone was wanting; but she patronized Mrs. Scudder no more, and tossed her head with a becoming pride when her name was mentioned.

The quilt-pattern was gloriously drawn in oak-leaves, done in indigo; and soon all the company, young and old, were passing busy fingers over it and conversation went on briskly.

Madame de Frontignac, we must not forget to say, had entered with hearty *abandon* into the spirit of the day. She had dressed the tall china vases on the mantel-pieces, and, departing from the usual rule of an equal mixture of roses and asparagus-bushes, had constructed two quaint and graceful bouquets, where garden-flowers were mingled with dropping grasses and trailing wild vines, forming a graceful combination which excited the surprise of all who saw it.

"It's the very first time in my life that I ever saw grass put into a flower-pot," said Miss Prissy; "but I must say it looks as handsome as a picture. Mary, I must say," she added, in an aside, "I think that Madame de Frongenac is the sweetest dressing and appearing creature I ever saw; she don't dress up nor put on airs, but she seems to see in a minute how things ought to go; and if it's only a bit of grass, or leaf, or wild vine, that she puts in her hair, why, it seems to come just right. I should like to make her a dress, for I know she would understand my fit; do speak to her, Mary, in case she should want a dress fitted here, to let me try it."

At the quilting, Madame de Frontignac would have her seat, and soon won the respect of the party by the dexterity with which she used her needle; though, when it was whispered that she learned to quilt among the nuns, some of the elderly ladies exhibited a slight uneasiness, as being rather doubtful whether they might not be encouraging Papistical opinions by allowing her an equal share in the work of getting up their minister's bed-quilt; but the younger part of the company were quite captivated by her foreign air, and the pretty manner in which she lisped her English; and Cerinthy Ann even went so far as to horrify her mother by saying that she wished she'd been educated in a convent herself,—a declaration which arose less from native depravity than from a certain vigorous disposition, which often shows itself in young people, to shock the current opinions of their elders and betters. Of course, the conversation took a general turn, somewhat in unison with the spirit of the occasion; and whenever it flagged, some allusion to a forthcoming wedding, or some sly hint at the future young Madame of the parish, was sufficient to awaken the dormant animation of the company.

Cerinthy Ann contrived to produce an agreeable electric shock by declaring, that, for her part, she never could see into it, how any girl could marry a minister,—that she should as soon think of setting up housekeeping in a meeting-house.

"Oh, Cerinthy Ann!" exclaimed her mother, "how can you go on so?"

"It's a fact," said the adventurous damsel; "now other men let you have some peace,—but a minister's always round under your feet."

"So you think, the less you see of a husband, the better?" said one of the ladies.

"Just my views," said Cerinthy, giving a decided snip to her thread with her scissors; "I like the Nantucketers, that go off on four-years' voyages, and leave their wives a clear field. If ever I get married, I'm going up to have one of those fellows."

It is to be remarked, in passing, that Miss Cerinthy Ann was at this very time receiving surreptitious visits from a consumptive-looking, conscientious, young theological candidate, who came occasionally to preach in the vicinity, and put up at the house of the Deacon, her father. This good young man, being violently attacked on the doctrine of Election by Miss Cerinthy, had been drawn on to illustrate it in a most practical manner, to her comprehension; and it was the consciousness of the weak and tottering state of the internal garrison that added vigor to the young lady's tones. As Mary had been the chosen confidante of the progress of this affair, she was quietly amused at the demonstration.

"You'd better take care, Cerinthy Ann," said her mother; "they say that 'those who sing before breakfast will cry before supper.' Girls talk about getting married," she said, relapsing into a gentle didactic melancholy, "without realizing its awful responsibilities."

"Oh, as to that," said Cerinthy, "I've been practising on my pudding now these six years, and I shouldn't be afraid to throw one up chimney with any girl."

This speech was founded on a tradition, current in those times, that no young lady was fit to be married till she could construct a boiled Indian-pudding of such consistency that it could be thrown up chimney and come down on the ground, outside, without breaking; and the consequence of Cerinthy Ann's sally was a general laugh.

"Girls a'n't what they used to be in my day," sententiously remarked an elderly lady. "I remember my mother told me when she was thirteen she could knit a long cotton stocking in a day."

"I haven't much faith in these stories of old times,—have you, girls?" said Cerinthy, appealing to the younger members at the frame.

"At any rate," said Mrs. Twitchel, "our minister's wife will be a pattern; I don't know anybody that goes beyond her either in spinning or fine stitching."

Mary sat as placid and disengaged as the new moon, and listened to the chatter of old and young with the easy quietness of a young heart that has early outlived life, and looks on everything in the world from some gentle, restful eminence far on towards a better home. She smiled at everybody's work, had a quick eye for everybody's wants, and was ready with thimble, scissors, or thread, whenever any one needed them; but once, when there was a pause in the conversation, she and Mrs. Marvyn were both discovered to have stolen away. They were seated on the bed in Mary's little room, with their arms around each other, communing in low and gentle tones.

"Mary, my dear child," said her friend, "this event is very pleasant to me, because it places you permanently near me. I did not know but eventually this sweet face might lead to my losing you, who are in some respects the dearest friend I have."

"You might be sure," said Mary, "I never would have married, except that my mother's happiness and the happiness of so good a friend seemed to depend on it. When we renounce self in anything, we have reason to hope for God's blessing; and so I feel assured of a peaceful life in the course I have taken. You will always be as a mother to me," she added, laying her head on her friend's shoulder.

"Yes," said Mrs. Marvyn; "and I must not let myself think a moment how dear it might have been to have you *more* my own. If you feel really, truly happy,—if you can enter on this life without any misgivings——"

"I can," said Mary, firmly.

At this instant, very strangely, the string which confined a wreath of sea-shells around her glass, having been long undermined by moths, suddenly broke and fell down, scattering the shells upon the floor.

Both women started, for the string of shells had been placed there by James; and though neither was superstitious, this was one of those odd coincidences that make hearts throb.

"Dear boy!" said Mary, gathering the shells up tenderly; "wherever he is, I shall never cease to love him. It makes me feel sad to see this come down; but it is only an accident; nothing of him will ever fail out of my heart."

Mrs. Marvyn clasped Mary closer to her, with tears in her eyes.

"I'll tell you what, Mary; it must have been the moths did that," said Miss Prissy, who had been standing, unobserved, at the door for a moment back; "moths will eat away strings just so. Last week Miss Vernon's great family-picture fell down because the moths eat through the cord; people ought to use twine or cotton string always. But I came to tell you that the supper is all set, and the Doctor out of his study, and all the people are wondering where you are."

Mary and Mrs. Marvyn gave a hasty glance at themselves in the glass, to be assured of their good keeping, and went into the great kitchen, where a long table stood exhibiting all that plenitude of provision which the immortal description of Washington Irving has saved us the trouble of recapitulating in detail.

The husbands, brothers, and lovers had come in, and the scene was redolent of gayety. When Mary made her appearance, there was a moment's pause, till she was conducted to the side of the Doctor; when, raising his hand, he invoked a grace upon the loaded board.

Unrestrained gayeties followed. Groups of young men and maidens chatted together, and all the gallantries of the times were enacted. Serious matrons commented on the cake, and told each other high and particular secrets in the culinary art, which they drew from remote family-archives. One might have learned in that instructive assembly how best to keep moths out of blankets,—how to make fritters of Indian corn undistinguishable from oysters,—how to bring up babies by hand,—how to mend a cracked teapot,—how to take out grease from a brocade,—how to reconcile absolute decrees with free will, how to make five yards of cloth answer the purpose of six,—and how to put down the Democratic party. All were busy, earnest, and certain,—just as a swarm of men and women, old and young, are in 1859.

Miss Prissy was in her glory; every bow of her best cap was alive with excitement, and she presented to the eyes of the astonished Newport gentry an animated receipt-book. Some of the information she communicated, indeed, was so valuable and important that she could not trust the air with it, but whispered the most important portions in a confidential tone. Among the crowd, Cerinthy Ann's theological admirer was observed in deeply reflective attitude; and that high-spirited young lady added further to his convictions of the total depravity of the species by vexing and discomposing him in those thousand ways in which a lively, ill-conditioned young woman will put to rout a serious, well-disposed young man,—comforting herself with the reflection, that by-and-by she would repent of all her sins in a lump together.

Vain, transitory splendors! Even this evening, so glorious, so heart-cheering, so fruitful in instruction and amusement, could not last forever. Gradually the company broke up; the matrons mounted soberly on horseback behind their spouses; and Cerinthy consoled her clerical friend by giving him an opportunity to read her a lecture on the way home, if he found the courage to do so.

Mr. and Mrs. Marvyn and Candace wound their way soberly home-ward; the Doctor returned to his study for nightly devotions; and before long, sleep settled down on the brown cottage.

"I'll tell you what, Cato," said Candace, before composing herself to sleep, "I can't feel it in my bones dat dis yer weddin's gwine to come off yit."

Miss Jones' Quilting

Marietta Holley

OUR MINISTER was merried a year ago, and we hev been piecing him a bed-quilt; and last week we quilted it. I always make a pint of going to quiltings, for you can't be backbited to your face, that's a moral sertenty. I know wimmen jest like a book, for I hev been one a good while. I always stand up for my own sect, still I know sertin effects follow sertin causes, to wit, and namely, if two bricks are sot up side by side, if one tumbles over on to the other one, the other one can't stand, it ain't natur'. If a toper holds a glass of liker to his mouth, he can't help swallerin', it ain't natur'. If a young man goes a slay-riding with a pretty girl, and the buffelo robe slips off, he can't help holdin' it round her, it ain't natur'. I might go on illustratin', but enuff; quiltin' jest sets wimmen to slanderin' as easy and beautiful as enything you ever see. So I went. There wasn't anybody there when I got there. For reason, I always go early.

I hadn't been there long before Miss Deacon Graves came, and then the Widder Tubbs, and then Squire Edwardses wife, and Maggie Snow, and then the Dobbs girls (we call 'em *girls*, though it would be jest as proper to call mutton lamb, for forty summers hev gilded their heads if one has gilt 'em). They was the last that come, for Miss Brown's baby had the mumps, and otherwise couldn't leave; and the Ripleys had unexpected company. But with Miss Jones, where the quiltin' was held, and her girls, Mary Ann and Alzina, we made as many as could set round the quilt comfortable.

The quilt was made of different kinds of calico; all the wimmen round had pieced a block or two, and we took up a collection to get the batten and linin', and the cloth to set it together with, which was turkey red, and come to quilt it it looked well; we quilted it herrin'-bone, and a runnin' vine round the border. After the path-master was demoralized, the school-mistress tore to pieces, the party to Ripleys scandelized, Miss Brown's baby voted a unquestionable idiot, and the rest of the unrepresented neighborhood dealt with, Lucinder Dobbs spoke up, and sez she:

"I hope the minister will like the bed-quilt" (Lucinder is the one that studies mathematics to disipline her mind, and has the Romen nose).

"It ain't noways likely he will," sez her sister Ophelia (she is the one that has her hair frizzled on top, and wears spectacles). "It ain't noways like likely he will—he is a cold man, a stone statute."

Now, you see, I set my eyes by the minister, he is always doin' good to somebody, besides preachin' more like a angel than a human bein'. I can't never forget—nor I don't want to—how he took hold of my hand, and how his voice trembled and the tears stood in his eyes, when my little Joe died; pretty little lamb, he was in his infant class, and he loved him; you see such things cut deep, and there is some lines you can't rub out, if you try ever so hard. And I wasn't goin' to set still and hear him run down; you see it riled up the old Smith blood, and when that is riled, Josiah says he always takes his hat and leaves till it settles. And I spoke up, and sez I:

"Lucky for him he was made of stone before he was married, for common flesh and blood," sez I, "would have gin out a hundred times, chaste round by the girls as he was" (you see it was the town's talk how Ophelia Dobbs acted before he was married, and she almost went into a decline, and took heaps of mother-wort and fetty).

"I don't know what you mean, Miss Allen," sez she, turning red as a brick. "I never heard of his bein' chaste; I know I never could bear the sight of him."

"The distant sight," sez Mary Ann Jones.

Ophelia looked so mad at that, that I don't know but she would have pricked her with her quiltin' needle, if old Miss Graves hadn't spoke up. She is a fat old lady with a double chin, "mild and lovely" as Mount Vernen's sister. She always agrees with everybody; Thomas Jefferson, Josiah's boy by his first wife, calls her "Woollen Aprons," for one day he sez he heard her say to a neighbor, "I don't like woollen aprons, do you?" "Why, yes, Miss Graves, I do." "Wall, so do I." But good old soul, if we was all such peacemakers as she is, we should be pretty sure of heaven, though Thomas J. said that if Saten should ask her to go the other way, she would go rather than hurt his feelings; I jest told him to shet up his weekedness, and he shet up.

As I said, she looked mildly up over her spectacles and nodded her purple cap ribbons two or three times, and said, "Yes," "Jest so," to both of us; and then she was so afraid that we wouldn't think she was jinein' with both of us, sez she, "Yes, Miss Allen," "Jest so, Ophelia." And then to change the subject, sez she, "Has the minister's wife got home yet?"

"I think not," said Maggie Snow. "I was to the village day before yesterday, and she had not come then."

"I suppose her mother is well off," sez the Widder Tubbs, "and as long as she stays there she saves the minister five dollars a week. I should think she would stay all summer."

The widder is about as savin' a woman as belongs to the meetin'-house.

"It don't look well for her to be gone so long," sez Lucinder Dobbs; "I am very much afraid it will make talk."

"Mebby it will save the minister five dollars a week," sez Ophelia, "as extravagant as she is in dress—as many as four silk dresses she has got, and folks as good as she is in the congregation hain't got but one, and a certain person *full* as good as she is, that hain't got any" (Ophelia's best dress is poplin), "it won't take her long to run out the minister's salery."

"She had her silk dresses before she was married, and her folks was wealthy," said Miss Squire Edwards.

"As much as we have done and are still doing for them, it seems ungrateful in her," sez Lucinder, "to wear such a bonnet as she wore all last summer—a plain white straw with a little bit of white ribbon on it; it looked so scrimped and stingy. I have thought she wore it on purpose to mortify us before the Baptists, jest as if we couldn't afford to dress our minister's wife as good as they did theirs."

Maggie Snow's cheeks was gettin' red as fire, and her eyes begun to shine jest as they did that day we found some boys stonin' her cat. You see she and the minister's wife are the greatest friends that ever was. And I see she couldn't hold in much longer; she was jest openin' her mouth to speak, when the door opened, and in walked Betsy Bobbet.

"Why, it seems to me you are late, Betsy," said Miss Jones; "but walk rite into the spare bedroom and take off your things."

"Things!" said Betsy, "who cares for things?" And she dropped into the nearest rockin'-chair and commenced rockin' violently.

Betsy Bobbet was a humbly critter. But we hadn't no time to meditate on her, for as Miss Jones asked her agin to take off her things, she
broke out:

"Would that I had died when I was an infant babe!"

"Amen!" whispered Mary Ann Jones to Maggie Snow.

"Do tell us what is the matter, Betsy," said Miss Jones.

"Yes, do," said Miss Deacon Graves.

"Matter enuff!" sez she; "no wonder there is earthquakes and jars! I
heard the news jest before I started, and it made me weak as a cat; I had
to stop to every house on the way down to rest, and not a soul had heard
of it till I told 'em. Such a turn as it give me, I sha'n't get over it for a
week; but it is jest as I always told you; I always said the minister's wife
wasn't any *too good*. It didn't surprise me—not a bit."

"You can't tell me one word against Mary Linden that I will believe,"
said Maggie Snow.

"You will admit that the minister went North last Tuesday, won't
you?"

Seven wimmen spoke up to once, and said, "Yes, his mother was
took sick, and they telegraphted for him."

"So he said," sneered Betsy Bobbet; "so he said; I believe it's for
good."

"Oh, dear!" shrieked Ophelia Dobbs, "I shall faint away; ketch hold
of me, somebody."

"Ketch hold of yourself," said I severely, and then sez I to Betsy, "I
don't believe he's run away any more than I believe I am the next President of the United States."

"Well, if he hain't he'll wish he had," sez she. "His wife came night
before last on the cars."

Four wimmen said, "Did she?" two said, "Do tell?" and three
opened their mouths and looked at her speechless; amongst the last was
Miss Deacon Graves. I spoke in a kolected manner, and sez I, "What of
it?"

"Yes, what of it?" said she. "I believe the poor man mistrusted it all
out, and run away from trouble and disgrace."

"How dare you!" sez Maggie Snow, "speak the word disgrace in connection with Mary Linden?"

"How dare I," sez Betsy Bobbet. "Ask Jake Coleman, as it happened
I got it from his own mouth, it didn't come through two or three."

"Get what?" sez I. "If you can speak the English language, Betsy Bobbet, and have got sense enuff to tell a straight story, tell it and be done with it," sez I.

"Well, jest as I come out the gate to our house," sez she, "Jake Coleman came along, and sez he, 'Betsy, I have got something to tell you,' sez he, 'I want to tell somebody that can keep it; it ought to be kept,' sez he, and then he went on and told; sez he, 'Miss Linden has got home, and she didn't come alone, neither.' Sez I, 'What do you mean?' He looked as mysterious as a ghost, and sez he, 'I mean what I say,' sez he; 'I drove the carriage home from the depot,' and sez he, 'as sure as my name is Jack Coleman, I heard her talking to somebody she called Hugh (you know her husband's name is Charles); I heard her tell this Hugh that she loved him, loved him better than the whole world.' And then he made me promise not to tell; but he said he heard not only one kiss, but fourteen or fifteen. Now," sez Betsy, "what do you think of the minister's wife?"

"Good heavens!" cried Ophelia Dobbs, "am I deceived? is this a phantagory of the brain, or have I got ears? Have I got ears?' she kontinude, wildly glaring at me.

"You can feel and see," said I, shortly.

"Will he live with the wretched creature?" kontinude Ophelia. "No, he will get a divorcement from her; such a tender-hearted man as he is too. If ever a man wanted a comforter in a tryin' time he is the man, and to-morrow I will go and comfort him."

"I guess you will find him, first," said Betsy Bobbet. "And I guess if he was found there is a certain person he would be as glad to see as he would another certain person."

"There is some mistake," said Maggie Snow. "Jake Coleman is always joking."

"It was a male," said Lucinder Dobbs, "else why did she call him Hugh? You have all heard the minister say his wife hadn't a relative on earth except her mother and a maiden aunt; it couldn't have been her mother, and it couldn't have been the maiden aunt, for her name was Martha instead of Hugh. Besides," she kontinude, for she had so hardened her mind with mathematics, that she could grapple the hardest fact and floor it, so to speak. "Besides," sez she, "the maiden aunt died a year and a half ago; that settles the matter conclusively it was not the maiden aunt."

"I have thought something was on the minister's mind all the spring," said the Widder Tubbs, "I have spoken to sister Ann about it a number of times." Then she kinder rolled up her eyes, jest as she does in class-meetin', and sez she, "It is an awful dispensation, but I hope he'll turn it into a means of grace; I hope his speritooil strength will be renewed. But," sez she, "I have borryed a good deal of trouble about his bein' so handsome; I have noticed that handsome ministers don't turn out well, they most always have somethin' happen to 'em sooner or later; but I hope he'll be led."

"Well, I never thought that Miss Linden was any too good," said Betsy Bobbet.

"Neither did I," said Lucinder Dobbs.

"She has turned out jest as I always thought she would," said Ophelia, "and I have just as good an opinion of her as I have for them that stand up for her."

Maggie Snow spoke up then; just as clear as a bell her voice sounded; she ain't afraid of anybody, for she is Lawyer Snow's only child, and has been to Boston to school. Sez she, "Aunt Allen," (she is a little related to me on her mother's side) "Aunt Allen, why is it that, as a general rule, the very worst folks are the first ones to suspect other folks of being bad?"

Sez I, "Maggie, they draw their pictures from memory." And sez I, "They want to pull down other folkses reputations, for they feel as if their own goodness is in a totterin' condition, and if they fall, they want somebody to fall on, so as to come down easier like."

Maggie Snow laughed, and so did Miss Edwards, and the Joneses, but Betsy Bobbet and the Dobbs' girls looked as black as Erobious. And sez Betsy Bobbet to me, sez she: "I shouldn't think, Josiah Allen's wife, that you would countenance such conduct."

"I will first know there is wrong conduct," sez I. Sez I, "Miss Linden's face is jest as innocent as a baby's, and I ain't a-goin' to mistrust any evil out of them pretty brown eyes till I am obleeged to."

Jest at this minute the hired girl came in and said supper was ready, and we all went out to eat it. Miss Jones said there wasn't anything on the table fit to eat, and she was afraid we couldn't make out, but we did have a splendid supper, good enough for the zero of Rushy.

We hadn't more'n got up from the supper table and got back into the parlor, when we heard a knock onto the front door. Miss Jones went and

opened it, and who, of all the live world, should walk in but the minister! The faces of the wimmen as he entered would have been a study for
Michael Angelico, or any of the old painters. Miss Jones was so flus-
trated that she asked him the first thing to take his bonnet off, then she
bethought herself, and sez she, "How's your mother?" before she had sot
him a chair or anything. But he looked jest as pleasant and composed as
ever, though his eyes kinder laughed. And he thanked her and told her
he left his mother, the day before, a good deal better; and then he turned
to Maggie Snow, and sez he:

"I have come after you, Miss Maggie," sez he. "My wife came home
night before last, and wanted to see you so bad, that I told her as I had
business past your house I would call for you as I went home, and your
mother told me you was here. I think I know," sez he, "why she wants
to see you so very much now, she is so proud of our boy she can't wait
till—"

"Your boy!" gasped nine wimmen to once.

"Yes," sez he, smilin' more pleasant than I ever see him. "I know you
will all wish me joy. We have a nice little boy, little Hugh, for my wife
has named him already for her father. He is a fine, healthy little fellow—
almost two months old."

"It wouldn't have done any good for Michael Angelico to have been
there then, nor Mr. Ruben, nor none of the rest of them we read of, for
if they had their palates and easelses all ready they never could have
done any justice to the faces of Betsy Bobbet and the Dobbs girls, and as
for Miss Deacon Graves, her spectacles fell off unnoticed, and she
opened her mouth so wide that it was very doubtful to me if she could
ever shet it agin. And, as for me, I was truly happy enuff to sing the Te
Deus.

Maggie Snow flew out of the room to put on her bonnet, with her face
shinin' like a cherubin, and; as I lived half a mile on the road they was
goin', and the quilt was most off, and he had two horses, and insisted, I
rode with 'em, and I haint seen none of the quilters sense.

A Quilting Bee
in Our Village

Mary Eleanor Wilkins Freeman

ONE SOMETIMES WONDERS whether it will ever be possible in our village to attain absolute rest and completion with regard to quilts. One thinks after a week fairly swarming with quilting bees, "Now every housewife in the place must be well supplied; there will be no need to make more quilts for six months at least." Then, the next morning a nice little becurled girl in a clean pinafore knocks at the door and repeats demurely her well-conned lesson: "Mother sends her compliments, and would be happy to have you come to her quilting bee this afternoon."

One also wonders if quilts, like flowers, have their seasons of fuller production. On general principles it seems as if the winter might be more favorable to their gay complexities of bloom. In the winter there are longer evenings for merriment after the task of needlework is finished and the young men arrive; there are better opportunities for roasted apples, and chestnuts and flip, also for social games. It is easier, too, as well as pleasanter, to slip over the long miles between some of our farmhouses in a sleigh if it is only a lover and his lass, or a wood-sled if a party of neighbors or a whole family.

However, so many of our young women become betrothed in the spring, and wedded in the autumn, that the bees flourish in the hottest afternoons and evenings of midsummer.

For instance, Brama Lincoln White was engaged to William French, from Somerset, George Henry French's son, the first Sunday in July, and the very next week her mother, Mrs. Harrison White, sent out invitations to a quilting bee.

The heat during all that week was something to be remembered. It was so warm that only the very youngest and giddiest of the village people went to the Fourth of July picnic. Cyrus Emmett had a sunstroke

out in the hayfield, and Mrs. Deacon Stockwell's mother, who was over
ninety, was overcome by the heat and died. Mrs. Stockwell could not go
to the quilting, because her mother was buried the day before. It was a
misfortune to Mrs. White and Brama Lincoln, for Mrs. Stockwell is one
of the fastest quilters who ever lived, but it was no especial deprivation
to Mrs. Stockwell. Hardly any woman who was invited to that quilting
was anxious to go. The bee was on Thursday, which was the hottest day
of all that hot week. The earth seemed to give out heat like a stove, and
the sky was like the lid of a fiery pot. The hot air steamed up in our faces
from the ground and beat down on the tops of our heads from the sky.
There was not a cool place anywhere. The village women arose before
dawn, aired their rooms, then shut the windows, drew the curtains and
closed blinds and shutters, excluding all the sunlight, but in an hour the
heat penetrated.

Mrs. Harrison White's parlor faced southwest, and the blinds would
have to be opened in order to have light enough; it seemed a hard ordeal
to undergo. Lurinda Snell told Mrs. Wheelock that it did seem as if
Brama Lincoln might have got ready to be married in better weather,
after waiting as long as she had done. Brama was not very young, but
Lurinda was older and had given up being married at all years ago. Mrs.
Wheelock thought she was a little bitter, but she only pitied her for
that. Lydia Wheelock is always pitying people for their sins and short-
comings instead of blaming them. She pacified Lurinda, and told her to
wear her old muslin and carry her umbrella and her palm-leaf fan, and
the wind was from the southwest, so there would be a breeze in Mrs.
White's parlor even if it was sunny.

The women went early to the quilting; they were expected to be
there at one o'clock, to secure a long afternoon for work. Eight were
invited to quilt: Lurinda and Mrs. Wheelock, the young widow, Lottie
Green, and five other women, some of them quite young, but master
hands at such work.

Brama and her mother were not going to quilt; they had the supper
to prepare. Brama's intended husband was coming over from Somerset to
supper, and a number of men from our village were invited.

A few minutes before one o'clock the quilters went down the street,
with their umbrellas bobbing over their heads. Mrs. Harrison White
lives on the South Side in the great house where her husband keeps
store. She opened the door when she saw her guests coming. She is a

stout woman, and she wore a large plaid gingham dress, open at her creasy throat. Her hair clung in wet strings to her temples and her face was blazing. She had just come from the kitchen where she was baking cake. The whole house was sweet and spicy with the odor of it.

She ushered her guests into the parlor, where the great quilting-frame was stretched. It occupied nearly the entire room. There was just enough space for the quilters to file around and seat themselves four on a side. The sheet of patchwork was tied firmly to the pegs on the quilting-frame. The pattern was intricate, representing the rising sun, the number of pieces almost beyond belief; the calicoes comprising it were of the finest and brightest.

"Most all the pieces are new, an' I don't believe but what Mis' White cut them right off goods in the store," Lurinda Snell whispered to Mrs. Wheelock when the hostess had withdrawn and they had begun their labors.

They further agreed among themselves that Mrs. White and Brama must have secretly prepared the patchwork in view of some sudden and wholly uncertain matrimonial contingency.

"I don't believe but what this quilt has been pieced ever since Brama Lincoln was sixteen years old," whispered Lurinda Snell, so loud that all the women could hear her. Then suddenly she pounced forward and pointed with her sharp forefinger at a piece of green and white calico in the middle of the quilt. "There, I knew it," said she. "I remember that piece of calico in a square I saw Brama Lincoln piecing over to our house before Francis was married." Lurinda Snell has a wonderful memory.

"That's a good many years ago," said Lottie Green.

"Yes," whispered Lurinda Snell. When she whispers her s's always hiss so that they make one's ears ache, and she is very apt to whisper. "Used to be hangin' round Francis considerable before he was married," she whispered in addition, and then she thought that she heard Mrs. White coming, and said, keeping up very loud, in such a pleasant voice, "How comfortable it is in this room for all it is such a hot afternoon." But her cunning was quite needless, for Mrs. White was not coming.

The women chalked cords and marked the patchwork in a diamond pattern for quilting. Two women held the ends of a chalked cord, stretching it tightly across the patchwork, and a third snapped it. That made a plain chalk line for the needle to follow. When a space as far as they could reach had been chalked they quilted it. When that was finished they rolled the quilt up and marked another space.

Brama Lincoln's quilt was very large; it did seem impossible to finish it that afternoon, though the women worked like beavers in the exceeding heat. They feared that Brama Lincoln would be disappointed and think they had not worked as hard as they might when she and her mother had been at so much trouble to prepare tea for them.

Nobody saw Brama Lincoln or Mrs. White again that afternoon, but they could be heard stepping out in the kitchen and sitting-room, and at five o'clock the china dishes and silver spoons began to clink.

At a quarter before six the men came. There were only three elderly ones in the company: Mr. Harrison White, of course, and Mrs. Wheelock's husband, and Mr. Lucius Downey, whose wife had died the year before. All the others were young, and considered beaus in the village.

The women had just finished the quilt and rolled it up, and taken down the frame, when Lurinda Snell spied Mr. Lucious Downey coming, and screamed out and ran, and all the girls after her. They had brought silk bags with extra finery, such as laces and ribbons and combs, to put on in the evening, and they all raced upstairs to the spare chamber.

When they came down with their ribbons gayly flying, and some of them with their hair freshly curled, all the men had arrived, and Mrs. White asked them to walk out to tea.

Poor Mrs. White had put on her purple silk dress, but her face looked as if the blood would burst through it, and her hair as if it were gummed to her forehead. Brama Lincoln looked very well; her front hair was curled, and Lurinda thought she had kept it in papers all day. She wore a pink muslin gown, all ruffled to the waist, and sat next to her beau at the table.

Lurinda Snell sat on one side of Mr. Lucius Downey and Lottie Green on the other, and they saw to it that his plate was well filled. Once somebody nudged me to look, and there were five slices of cake and three pieces of pie on his plate. However, they all disappeared—Mr. Downey had a very good appetite.

Mrs. White had a tea which will go into the history of the village. Everybody wondered how she and Brama had managed to do so much in that terrible heat. There were seven kinds of cake, besides doughnuts, cookies and short gingerbread; there were five kinds of pie, and cup custards, hot biscuits, cold bread, preserves, cold ham and tongue. No woman in the village had ever given a better quilting supper than Mrs. Harrison White and Brama.

After supper the men went into the parlor and sat in a row against the wall, while the women all assisted in clearing away and washing the dishes.

Then the women, all except Mrs. Wheelock, who went home to take care of Lottie Green's children, joined the men in the parlor, and the evening entertainment began. Mrs. White tried to have everything as usual in spite of the heat. She had even got the Slocum boy to come with his fiddle that the company might dance.

First they played games—copenhagen, and post-office, roll the cover, and the rest. Young and old played, except Brama Lincoln and her beau; they sat on the sofa and were suspected of holding each other's hands under cover of her pink flounces. Many thought it very silly in them, but when Lurinda Snell told Mrs. Wheelock of it next day she said that she thought there were many worse things to be ashamed of than love.

Lurinda Snell played the games with great enjoyment; she is very small and wiry, and could jump for the rolling cover like a cricket. Lurinda, in spite of her bitterness over her lonely estate, and her evident leaning toward Mr. Lucius Downey, is really very maidenly in some respects. She always caught the cover before it stopped rolling, and withdrew her hands before they were slapped in copenhagen, whereas Lottie Green almost invariably failed to do so, and was, in consequence, kissed so many times by Mr. Downey that nearly everybody was smiling and tittering about it.

However, Lurinda Snell was exceedingly fidgety when post-office was played, and Lucius Downey had so many letters for Lottie Green, and finally she succeeded in putting a stop to the game. The post-office was in the front entry, and of course the parlor door was closed during the delivery of the letters, and Lurinda objected to that. She said the room was so warm with the entry door shut that she began to feel a buzzing in her head, which was always dangerous in her family. Her grandfather had been overheated, been seized with a buzzing in his head, and immediately dropped dead, and so had her father. When she said that, people looked anxiously at Lurinda; her face was flushed, and the post-office was given up and the entry door opened.

Next Lottie Green was called upon to sing, as she always is in company, she has such a sweet voice. She stood up in the middle of the floor, and sang "Annie Laurie" without any accompaniment, because the Slocum boy, who is not an expert musician, did not know how to play that tune, but Lurinda was taken with hiccoughs. Nobody doubted that she really had hiccoughs, but it was considered justly that she might have smothered them in her handkerchief, or at least have left the room, instead of spoiling Lottie Green's beautiful song, which she did completely. If the Slocum boy could have played the tune on his fiddle it would not have been so disastrous, but "Annie Laurie" with no accompaniment but that of hiccoughs was a failure. Brama Lincoln tiptoed out into the kitchen, and got some water for Lurinda to take nine swallows without stopping, but it did not cure her. Lurinda hiccoughed until the song was finished.

The Slocum boy tuned his fiddle then and the dancing began, but it was not a success—partly because of Lurinda and partly because of the heat. Lurinda would not dance after the first; she said her head buzzed again, but people thought—it may have been unjustly—that she was hurt because Lucius Downey had not invited her to dance. That spoiled the set, but aside from that the room was growing insufferably warm. The windows were all wide open, but the night air came in like puffs of dark, hot steam, and swarms of mosquitoes and moths with it. The dancers were all brushing away mosquitoes and wiping their foreheads. Their faces were blazing with the heat, and even the pretty girls had a wilted and stringy look from their hair out of curl and their limp muslins.

When Lurinda refused to dance Brama Lincoln at once said that she thought it would be much pleasanter out-of-doors, and took William French by the arm and led the way. The rest of the quilting bee was held in Harrison White's front yard. The folks sat there until quite late, telling stories and singing hymns and songs. Lottie Green would not sing alone; she said it would make her too conspicuous. The front yard is next to the store, and there was a row of men on the piazza settee, besides others coming and going. The yard was light from the store windows. Brama Lincoln and William French sat as far back in the shadow as they could.

Mr. Lucius Downey sat on the door-step, out of the dampness; he considers himself delicate. Lottie Green sat on one side of him and Lurinda Snell on the other.

There was much covert curiosity as to which of the two he would escort home. Some thought he would choose Lottie, some Lurinda. The problem was solved in a most unexpected manner.

   Lottie Green lives nearly a mile out of his way, in one direction,
Lurinda half a mile in another. When the quilting bee disbanded, Lottie,
after lingering and looking back with sweetly-pleading eyes from under her
pretty white rigolette, went down the road with Lydia Wheelock's husband; Lurinda slipped forlornly up the road in the wake of a fond young
couple, keeping close behind them for protection against the dangers of
the night, and Mr. Lucius Downey went home by himself.

Aunt Jerusha's Quilting Party

Anonymous

CHARACTERS

JERUSHA DOW
HEPZIBAH SPOONER, *deaf*
HANNAH PIKE, *old maid*
JOHANNA HINES, *widow*
RACHEL GRAY, *quakeress*
PATIENCE PEABODY, *old maid*
MRS. SIMEON STUBBS, *gossip*
DRUCILLA THOMPKINS, *lecturer*

CHARITY COOPER, *old maid*
MRS. DEACON SIMPKINS
MRS. AARON PRIDE
PHOEBE MIRANDA PRIDE
JOHN DOW
DEACON SIMPKINS
SQUIRE PRIDE
PREACHER LOVEJOY

COSTUMES—ECCENTRIC

LADIES. Old-fashioned gowns and aprons. Hair dressed plainly with old-fashioned shell combs. PHOEBE wears her hair in curls hanging loose.

GENTLEMEN. PREACHER LOVEJOY wears a black suit, trousers rather short, silk hat, old-fashioned collar and necktie. DEACON SIMPKINS, SQUIRE PRIDE and JOHN DOW wear suits of course material, colored shirts and leather boots. DEACON SIMPKINS wears a black wig and SQUIRE PRIDE a partly bald gray wig.

SCENE

Old-fashioned sitting-room. Patchwork quilt on frames, resting on four chairs at side of stage. JERUSHA *stands beside quilt with chalk and string in hand.*

JERUSHA. There! I've got it all marked. I hope the ladies'll come early and I hope they'll quilt as fast as they'll talk. I had to invite more than I needed to jist to quilt, 'cause of hurtin' folks feelin's, but I've got some patchwork on hand so I'll set part of 'em to piecin'. I shall have to manage to keep Widder Hines away from the quilt, 'cause she don't know nothin' bout quiltin'. She thinks she does, though. [*Rap at door.*] Some one's come now. [*Opens door. Enter* PATIENCE PEABODY.] Why, how d'ye do, Patience?

PATIENCE [*surprised*]. Am I *first*? Ye see, Aunt Jerusha, my nerves are in an awful condition—jist what time is it? [*Looks at clock.*] Yes, yes, I see it ain't quite time for my pill. It's a dreadful thing to be so nervous. I never——

JERUSHA. Take off your things, Patience, and set down.

PATIENCE [*removing hat*]. I presume I shall have to send for Doctor Brown to-night if I quilt any, but I wasn't goin' to treat you so mean as to stay away. I couldn't begin to tell ye, Aunt Jerusha, what I've suffered with my nerves. Ye wouldn't believe——

JERUSHA. Shan't I unpin your shawl for ye? Ye oughter set down and rest ye.

PATIENCE [*unpinning shawl*]. Why Aunt Jerusha, it's a miracle that I'm alive and able to come to your quiltin'. [*Looks at clock.*] There! It's two minutes past time for my pill. It'll be three by the time I get it down. [*Takes pill. Rap at door.*]

[*Enter* RACHEL GRAY *and* MRS. DEACON SIMPKINS.]

RACHEL [*curtsying*]. How is thee, Aunt Jerusha? Isn't it too much for thee to be having a quilting party?

JERUSHA. O, no, I'm feeling first-rate these days. How be you?

RACHEL. I'm free from all the ills that flesh is heir to.

PATIENCE. O, that I could say that, too.

MRS. SIMPKINS. Well, I never felt better nor more like quilting than I do this very minute. Can't we begin right away, Aunt Jerusha?

JERUSHA. Certainly. Ye can sit jist where ye want to. [*The four take seats at quilt.*]

[*Enter* MRS. AARON PRIDE *and* PHOEBE.]

MRS. PRIDE. I didn't stop to rap 'cause I thought we's late. Don't get up, Aunt Jerusha, we'll help ourselves. It took Pheeb such an everlastin' while to curl her hair, I thought we'd never get here. It was awful nice of you to ask her over. Pheeb can't quilt but if you've got some patchwork she can do that.

JERUSHA. I'm glad ye could come, Phoebe. How be ye to-day?

PHOEBE. O, just lovely, Aunt Jerusha.

JERUSHA. Set jist where ye want to, Sister Pride, and I'll get some patchwork for Phoebe.

[*Takes pieces from table and shows* PHOEBE *how to put them together.*
MRS. PRIDE *takes seat at quilt.*]

MRS. PRIDE. How are ye, ladies? [*Lowering her voice.*] Who's all been
invited this afternoon, do ye know?

MRS. SIMPKINS. I know that the Widow Hines has and she don't know
any more 'bout quilting than a goose does. She's coming now. I saw
her pass the window. [*Louder.*] Aunt Jerusha, you better fix some
patchwork for the Widow Hines. She's coming and we don't want her
here.

MRS. PRIDE. You're right we don't. Head her off Aunt Jerusha.

JERUSHA [*opening door*]. Walk right in, ladies, I seen ye comin'.

[*Enter* JOHANNA HINES, HANNAH PIKE, *and* HEPZIBAH SPOONER.]

JOHANNA. Is Mrs. Simpkins here? Oh yes, I see she is. You're a purty
woman to run off and leave me. Ye needn't expect me to call fir you
again.

MRS. SIMPKINS. I didn't know you said anything about calling for me. [*To
ladies at quilt.*] She's always snapping me up for something. If she's
going to quilt I'm going to piece blocks. That woman is enough to kill
a saint. I don't wonder her husband died. Why if here ain't Hanner
Pike. How d' ye do, Hanner? Seems to me you look kinder peaked.

PHOEBE [*aside*]. Pike's Peak.

JERUSHA. Hanner, you set right down here by Mrs. Simpkins. [HANNAH
takes seat at quilt.]

HEPZIBAH [*laying hand on* PHOEBE's *shoulder*]. What ye doin', little gal?

PHOEBE. I ain't little. [*Raising her voice.*] I'm piecin' blocks.

HEPZIBAH. Twistin' your locks, be ye?

[*Lays hand on* PHOEBE's *curls.* PHOEBE *looks cross and jerks her head
away.*]

PHOEBE [*louder*]. I'm piecin' the lover's chain.

HEPZIBAH. Havin' an awful pain?

PHOEBE [*impatiently*]. Aunt Jerusha, do set Mrs. Spooner to quilting.

JERUSHA [*putting mouth close to* HEPZIBAH's *ear*]. Do ye feel like quiltin'
this afternoon?

HEPZIBAH. Yes, yes, Jerusha, that's what I came for.

JOHANNA. She needn't set down there. I'm going to set there myself as
soon as I find my darnin' needle.

MRS. SIMPKINS. A darnin' needle!

HANNAH. What be ye goin' to do with a darnin' needle?

JOHANNA. Quilt with it, of course. What do ye's suppose?

MRS. PRIDE. If that's what ye want it for it won't make any difference whether ye find it or not.

RACHEL. Thee needs a small, short needle to quilt with, Johanna.

MRS. SIMPKINS. You can get along faster to use a long needle.

JOHANNA. I won't use a long needle, anyhow.

JERUSHA. Seein' ye can't find your darnin' needle, would ye like to piece some blocks?

PHOEBE [aside]. She shan't sit by me.

[JERUSHA takes pieces from tables to hand to JOHANNA.]

JOHANNA. Thank ye, I brought along some blocks of my own to piece. [Sits down.]

MRS. SIMPKINS. I s'pose you'll be having a quilting party next.

JOHANNA. I know who I'll invite if I do.

MRS. PRIDE. How ye getting on, Pheeb, with your piecing?

PHOEBE. I pricked my finger and had to do it up.

MRS. PRIDE. How many seams have you sewed?

PHOEBE. One. [Aside.] That was one too many.

[Enter CHARITY COOPER and DRUSCILLA THOMPKINS.]

DRUSCILLA. We thought we'd walk right in, Aunt Jerusha, and not make you any trouble. Got the quilt most done?

JERUSHA. O, no, there's plenty to do yet.

DRUSCILLA. I'm sorry I'm late but I had to finish writing a lecture.

CHARITY [taking seat at quilt]. "Better late than never."

RACHEL. What subject does thee take, Druscilla?

DRUSCILLA. Woman's sphere, of course. There never has been and never will be so great a subject as that.

HANNAH. I think your sphere for the present is to quilt a while. Woman's sphere is well enough, but what I don't like is bein' a hemisphere.

DRUSCILLA. I see, ladies, you are inclined to make light of serious matters. If you realised the vastness of the subject, as I do, you'd not let a moment pass without talking or writing about it. Man was made a little lower than the angels, but woman was made on a higher plane. Woman is endowed with soul-inspiring gifts. She was made to be the head of the house——

HEPZIBAH [excitedly]. A mouse! Where is it?

PHOEBE [screams and stands on chair, drawing her skirts closely around her ankles]. Kill it, Aunt Jerusha, kill it.

JERUSHA. There ain't any mouse in the room, Phoebe. Hepzibah didn't hear straight.

HANNAH. Stop your lecturin', Druscilla, and go to quiltin'. You're gettin' too noisy.

CHARITY. "Empty casks make the most noise."

DRUSCILLA. When, O when will woman come to a proper understanding and appreciation of her sphere?

> [*Takes seat at quilt. Part of the ladies talk among themselves, the rest joining in, until all are talking and laughing at the same time. After a few moments* MRS. SIMPKINS *raps on the quilt frame with her shears to get the attention of the ladies.*]

MRS. SIMPKINS. I think it's time this quilt was rolled.

RACHEL. Thee is right, sister.

HANNAH. My arms feel as if it ought to be. How is it with you, Patience?

PATIENCE [*sighing*]. I guess I've reached too far. O, my nerves! My hands and arms are numb. O, my poor nerves!

MRS. PRIDE. Get a fan, Patience is fainting.

RACHEL. Has thee any spruce gum in the house, Aunt Jerusha? That's the best thing for nervousness.

MRS. PRIDE. Pheeb's got some. Pass it over, Pheeb.

PHOEBE. I hain't through chewing it yet.

MRS. PRIDE. Phoebe Miranda Pride! Shame on ye.

PHOEBE. She can have a piece of it. [*Gives a piece to* PATIENCE.]

HANNAH. Take a pinch of snuff, that'll revive ye.

> [PATIENCE *takes a pinch from* HANNAH'S *snuff-box.*]

JERUSHA. Ye better git into a rockin'-chair and not quilt any more this afternoon. I'm sorry if you have overdone.

> [PATIENCE *leaves quilt and takes rocking-chair.*]

MRS. SIMPKINS [*to ladies at quilt*]. It's the hypo that ails her. She needs a good scolding to get her out of it. Who's going to help me roll?

HANNAH. I will.

MRS. PRIDE. I'll help Rachel with the other side. [*They roll quilt.*]

JERUSHA. Do any of ye know whether Mrs. Stubbs [*enter* MRS. STUBBS *unobserved*] is sick or gone away? She said she'd surely be here this afternoon.

HANNAH. She's out collectin' news, most likely.

MRS. STUBBS. She's right here, if you please, and I'd like to have ye know that Mrs. Stubbs never gossips.

PHOEBE [*aside*]. What a story!

MRS. STUBBS [*removing bonnet and shawl*]. Do ye know what has happened to your neighbors, Mrs. Simpkins?

MRS. SIMPKINS. I'm not attending to my neighbors' business.

MRS. STUBBS [*takes chair and rocks vigorously*]. I can't help it if you ain't, it's true all the same that Dan Smith and his wife have parted. Dan says that Mary Ann is so bossy he can't stand it any longer.

CHARITY. "It is a sad house where the hen crows louder than the cock."
    [*After quilt is rolled*, MRS. SIMPKINS, MRS. PRIDE, HANNAH, HEPZI-BAH, DRUSCILLA *and* RACHEL *take seats at quilt. The rest, except* PATIENCE *and* MRS. STUBBS, *piece blocks.*]

MRS. STUBBS. Say, Hanner, Billy Jones is married.

HANNAH. What do I care if he is.

MRS. STUBBS. I guess 'most anybody'd marry him if they thought he'd die the next day and leave 'em his hundred thousand dollars.

MRS. SIMPKINS. When was he married?

MRS. STUBBS. It must have been last night, 'cause I saw the preacher drive into Sally Tinker's yard all dressed up. Mrs. Brown came in jist then in a big hurry for some sour milk and took me from the winder or I should seen more.

MRS. PRIDE. Did ye see Billy around anywhere?

MRS. STUBBS. No, but most likely he went into the house while I was gettin' the sour milk. Say, Pheeb, I heerd that Sammy'd gone back on ye.

PHOEBE. What do I care for Sammy Tucker? He's the meanest boy in town, if he is your relation.

MRS. SIMPKINS. Phoebe'd rather have the new preacher.

PHOEBE. You bet I had. Preacher Lovejoy is just lovely. He's my Sunday-school teacher, and I know he thinks Phoebe's the prettiest name he ever heard.

PATIENCE. Exceptin' Patience.

CHARITY. Exceptin' Charity.

JOHANNA. Ye needn't think there's any chance for you three with Preacher Lovejoy. He's too old for you, Pheeb, and too young for Charity and Patience.

PHOEBE. And you're too stingy for him.

MRS. PRIDE. Pheeb, you mustn't talk so.

PHOEBE. You say I must always tell the truth.

RACHEL. Thee better not set thy affection on Preacher Lovejoy. He may have a sweetheart in some other town.

CHARITY. "Love without charity is like a rose without scent." [*Ladies laugh.*]

MRS. SIMPKINS. Pretty good, Charity.

MRS. STUBBS. Say, ladies, did ye know there was an awful poor fam'ly over on Jake Smith's place?

JERUSHA. How poor be they?

MRS. STUBBS. Wal, my man went over there last night and he said there was four slices of bread and a pint of milk on the table for seven of 'em. There's five small children. One of 'em's sick in bed and the mother looks as if she oughter be there, too. They jist moved in last week. They say there's two older gals a-workin' over in Clayton that don't help their folks any, 'cause they put all their money on their backs.

CHARITY. "Silks and satins put out the kitchen fire."

MRS. PRIDE. What about the old man?

MRS. STUBBS. Wal, Sim says if he ever had any ambition he must have lost it or left it behind.

JERUSHA. Here's a chance, ladies, to do good. Mrs. Simpkins, you're the president of the sewing society, what do you think will be the best thing to do?

MRS. SIMPKINS. The sewing society will meet with me a week from to-day, and I'll ask Mrs. Pride, Hanner Pike and Rachel Gray to find out what is needed in the way of clothing so that we can sew for them that day. I think the first thing we ought to do for them is to feed them. How many of the ladies will donate provisions?

RACHEL. Thee may depend upon me for a bushel of potatoes.

MRS. STUBBS. I sent 'em over a quart of carrots by my man this mornin'.

JERUSHA. I'll bake 'em some bread and pies.

PATIENCE. If my nerves get stronger I'll take 'em a chunk of pork.

JERUSHA. Hepzibah, what would you like to take to a poor fam'ly in the way of eatables?

HEPZIBAH. Hey?

JERUSHA. There's a very poor fam'ly in town. What would ye like to take 'em?

HEPZIBAH. I could let 'em have some soft soap.

JERUSHA. It's somethin' to eat they need.

HEPZIBAH. O, somethin' to eat. [*Shaking her head.*] I shall have to ask Jonathan 'bout that.

DRUSCILLA [*indignantly*]. Ask Jonathan about that! There it is again, ladies. Do you know of any one that works any harder than Hepzibah Spooner? Jonathan handles all the money just as if Hepzibah hadn't any mind of her own. O, ladies, such is not woman's sphere. Rouse yourselves and help to put the evil down. Think about it, write about it, talk about it. Use every weapon you can to fight against it. Work night and day, if need be, until woman is brought higher and higher——

HEPZIBAH. Where's the fire? [*Jumps up knocking quilt off chairs.*]

JERUSHA. There isn't any fire, Hepzibah.

HEPZIBAH. Land a massy, I's sure some one hollered fire.

HANNAH. Do stop your lecturin', Druscilla, and finish that block.

DRUSCILLA. That block, Hanner Pike, is nothing but a trifle compared to woman's sphere.

MRS. SIMPKINS. Attention, ladies. Johanner Hines, what will you take to the poor folks?

JOHANNA. If the old man is so lazy he won't work and the girls put all their money on their backs, I won't give 'em anything.

RACHEL. Thee ought not to let six go hungry to spite three.

MRS. PRIDE. I'll send 'em some fried cakes and apple butter.

MRS. SIMPKINS. Charity, what will you donate?

CHARITY. Dried apples.

MRS. SIMPKINS. Hanner, do you want to send something?

HANNAH. Of course I do. I'll take 'em over some thoroughwort and sage. That'll be as good as anything if some of 'em's sick.

MRS. SIMPKINS. Druscilla, they've all said what they'd do but you and me.

DRUSCILLA [*firmly*]. Well, I intend to lecture the old man for my part. I'll give him a piece of my mind. He ought to earn his own bread and butter.

CHARITY. "He that will eat the kernel must crack the shell."

DRUSCILLA. You've hit it right, Charity.

MRS. SIMPKINS. I'll make my donation a sack of flour.

    [*Conversation again becomes general for a few moments. The ladies laugh and talk.*]

HANNAH [*rapping on frame with shears*]. This quilt ought to be rolled again.

RACHEL. I agree with thee.

HANNAH. There ain't more than half an hour's work to do on it. [*Roll quilt.*]

JERUSHA. You've worked fast, ladies, and done it beautifully, too.

MRS. STUBBS. The preacher's a-comin', as sure as ye live.

JERUSHA. Ye don't mean it.

MRS. STUBBS. Yes, I do. I seen him pass the winder.

PHOEBE. Don't let him in, Aunt Jerusha, till I fix my curls.
[*Rises and arranges curls before mirror.* CHARITY *rises and looks over* PHOEBE's *shoulder in mirror.*]

CHARITY. "Charity is the chief and most charming beauty."
[PATIENCE *rises and looks in mirror.*]

PHOEBE [*pushing* CHARITY *and* PATIENCE *away*]. You just keep away till I'm through. I got here first.

MRS. PRIDE. Hurry up. Pheeb, or the preacher'll catch ye a-prinkin'.

JERUSHA. Brother Lovejoy never stops to rap; he always walks right in.
[PHOEBE, CHARITY *and* PATIENCE *take seats. Enter* PREACHER LOVEJOY.]
Why how d' ye do, Brother Lovejoy?

LOVEJOY [*rubbing his hands*]. Ahem! I didn't know you were having a quilting party, Sister Dow.

JERUSHA. That don't matter. We're awful glad to see ye. Take a chair.

LOVEJOY [*bowing*]. I'm please to meet you sisters. You seem to be very industrious. [*Sits down.*]

CHARITY. "Industry is fortune's right hand."

LOVEJOY. True, very true. How is the Deacon to-day, Sister Simpkins?

MRS. SIMPKINS. All right, I guess; I left him chopping wood.

LOVEJOY. Ah, I see that Sister Spooner is here. [*Crosses stage.*] How is your health, Sister Spooner?

HEPZIBAH. Hey?

LOVEJOY. How is your health to-day?

HEPZIBAH. Very good. How is your ma?

LOVEJOY. She is well. How is Brother Spooner?

HEPZIBAH. He felt purty well till he fell in the well, but he hain't felt well since.

RACHEL. Doesn't thee think this is a handsome quilt?

LOVEJOY. Very fine indeed. [PHOEBE *moves* LOVEJOY's *chair near hers.* PATIENCE *pulls it away but* PHOEBE *gets it again.*] What are you making, Sister Phoebe? [*Sits down by* PHOEBE.]

PHOEBE. It's the lover's chain. I think it would be prettier if it was made of just two pieces, don't you?

LOVEJOY. Perhaps so, but "variety is the spice of life," Sister Phoebe. [*Turning to* PATIENCE.] Seems to me you are not looking very strong, Sister Patience.

PATIENCE. O, it's my nerves. The doctor thinks if I had some strong, healthy person to cling to, I'd be all right. He thinks I lead too lonely a life.

LOVEJOY. Ahem! The sickness of the body may prove the strength of the soul, Sister Patience.

HANNAH. Let us hope so.

MRS. STUBBS. Ye want to be careful, Brother Lovejoy, or you'll get caught in a trap. Say, have ye called on that poor fam'ly over in Jake Smith's house? If ye hain't ye better right away.

JERUSHA. Don't hurry Brother Lovejoy off. We'd like to have him stay the rest of the afternoon.

PHOEBE. Of course we would.

PATIENCE [*aside*]. I think my nerves would feel better.

HANNAH. Did your ma get that bag of thoroughwort I sent her?

LOVEJOY. Really, Sister Pike, I'm sorry to say that she did, for I've had to drink the stuff ever since to please her.

HANNAH. It's good for ye. It'll make ye preach better sermons.

MRS. SIMPKINS. There! I've taken the last stitch of the quilting. Now we'll take the quilt off and bind it.

> [RACHEL, HANNAH, DRUSCILLA *and* MRS. SIMPKINS *take quilt off frames.* MRS. SIMPKINS *shakes it and throws it over* PHOEBE *and* LOVE-JOY. CHARITY *and* PATIENCE *try to get under the quilt. Ladies laugh.* PREACHER LOVEJOY *throws quilt off and smooths his hair looking disgusted.*]

MRS. STUBBS. I told ye they'd be gettin' ye in a trap if ye didn't look out. Ye look as if ye didn't know what they meant by throwin' that quilt over your head. It's a sign ye'll be married 'fore the year's up.

LOVEJOY. I'm exceedingly shocked, sisters. The dignity of my vocation restrains me from seeing anything funny whatever in such a proceeding.

HANNAH. Did Pheeb kiss ye?

LOVEJOY. Worse and worse. Where's my hat, Sister Dow?

JERUSHA. Look a here, Brother Lovejoy, you might as well attempt to lock up the winds, or chain the fury of the waves as to expect to get

into a sewing society or a quilting party and not have some joke
played on ye.

LOVEJOY. This experience, sisters, will last me a lifetime. It shall be my
first duty before making any calls to inquire if there is a sewing society
or a quilting party at the place.

RACHEL. If thee would be a successful preacher thee must not be so dignified that thee cannot enjoy innocent fun and amusements.

MRS. SIMPKINS. I s'pose I'm to blame for it but instead of making an
apology I'd rather do the same thing again.

PHOEBE. O, do, I wish you would.

JOHANNA. Charity and Patience would prob'ly get under the quilt first
the next time.

PHOEBE. I bet they wouldn't.

LOVEJOY. You do not piece blocks it seems, Sister Stubbs.

JOHANNA. It takes all of her time to tell the news.

MRS. STUBBS. You see, Brother Lovejoy, if it hadn't been for me the
sisters wouldn't known 'bout the poor fam'ly in Jake Smith's house.
Now we're goin' to sew for 'em at our next sewin' society.

JOHANNA [*sarcastically*]. Yes, *we* are goin' to sew for 'em.

MRS. STUBBS. And we're goin' to take 'em somethin' to eat too.

LOVEJOY. That's right, that's right. You will be acting the part of the
good Samaritan. It is very gratifying to know that the sisters are so
forward in good works. It is a good thing to have charity.

CHARITY. "Sweetest charity not pride should walk forever by thy side."

PATIENCE. Charity is well enough but to have patience is better.

MRS. STUBBS. Remember what I said 'bout the trap.

LOVEJOY [*rising*]. I've made quite a call, sisters, I trust it has not inter-
fered with your work.

PHOEBE. O, don't go.

JERUSHA. We'd like to have you stay to tea.

LOVEJOY. That would be impossible, Sister Dow, as I have a number of
important calls to make. I trust that I may have charity and patience
to do my work well. Good-afternoon. [*Exit.*]

MRS. STUBBS. I don't see how he can have ye both, Charity and Patience, unless he moves to Utah.

MRS. PRIDE. How many blocks have you pieced, Pheeb?

PHOEBE. You don't s'pose I'd work while the preacher was here, do ye?

MRS. SIMPKINS. I noticed that you didn't. [*Ladies laugh.*]

PHOEBE. I know my manners better than that.

MRS. PRIDE. I'd like to change works with some of ye. I'd rather piece blocks awhile.

JOHANNA. I'll change with ye. [MRS. PRIDE *and* JOHANNA *change places.*]

JERUSHA. I shall have to ask the sisters to move a little so I can set the table.

HANNAH. Certainly, certainly, Jerusha, we won't object to that.

    [*Ladies binding quilt move to opposite side of stage.*]

PHOEBE. Let me help ye, Aunt Jerusha.

JERUSHA. You're very kind, Phoebe. If you'll come with me I'll get you an apron.

    [*Exeunt* JERUSHA *and* PHOEBE.]

MRS. SIMPKINS. I wonder if this wouldn't be a good time to take orders for the aprons we are going to make in the society.

RACHEL. I think thee has spoken well, Sister Simpkins. I'll take one.

    [*Enter* JERUSHA *and* PHOEBE. *They set the table which consists of two tables placed together.* PHOEBE *eats on the sly while she helps. Lighted candles are brought in.*]

MRS. SIMPKINS. Hanner, you'll want one, won't ye?

HANNAH. No, I've got a whole drawer full now.

MRS. PRIDE. I'll take one.

MRS. STUBBS. I'll take a fifteen center.

MRS. SIMPKINS. The aprons are all worth a quarter.

MRS. STUBBS. I'll wait awhile then. I don't believe in throwin' money away.

MRS. SIMPKINS. Hepzibah, would you like to buy an apron of the sewing society?

HEPZIBAH. I'll have to ask Jonathan first. If he's willin', I'm willin'.

DRUSCILLA. Have to ask Jonathan! It's a shame that Hepzibah has to lead such a life! And to think, ladies, of the many, many women all over the world that have to bow down to the men just as Hepzibah does. Woman *must* demand her rights and assume her proper sphere.

    [*Enter* PHOEBE *with a plate of doughnuts. She trips and falls and doughnuts roll around on the floor.*]

MRS. PRIDE. Phoebe Miranda Pride! What would the preacher say to see you do such an awkward thing as that?

HANNAH. He'd prob'ly say pride had had a fall.

PHOEBE. Most likely he'd a picked me up.

[Picks up plate and doughnuts and sets them on table. Exit.]

MRS. SIMPKINS. Well, Johanner, how many aprons will you buy?

JOHANNA. Not any.

MRS. SIMPKINS. Won't ye take one?

JOHANNA. No, not *one*. It's cheaper to make' em myself.

RACHEL. Thee hasn't the right idea of it, Johanner. Just so much money has to be raised by the society, and making aprons is one way that we take to raise it. Thee ought to be willing to do thy part.

MRS. SIMPKINS. There's two yards and a half in every apron and the cloth is good. Patience, don't you want one?

PATIENCE. When my nerves get stronger I'll think about it.

CHARITY. "Never put off until to-morrow what you can do to-day."

MRS. SIMPKINS. Charity, you ought to have one.

CHARITY *[shaking her head]*. "It's the littles that drains the purse."

MRS. SIMPKINS. Druscilla, you are the last one. Jerusha ordered an apron a few days ago.

DRUSCILLA. I'd like to know what the sisters are thinking about. What do we meet to make aprons for? It isn't to sell them to members of other societies for they have their own to dispose of. I think it's the duty of every sister to buy an apron. I'll take one.

RACHEL. Thee is right, Sister Druscilla.

MRS. STUBBS. Say, did ye know that Abigal Hill's baby is worse? It won't live, I know it won't, for Abigal broke a lookin'-glass a few days ago and that's a sure sign of a death in the fam'ly.

RACHEL. Thee doesn't believe in signs, does thee?

MRS. STUBBS. Of course I do. I always shake hands with a friend if my right hand itches, and it never fails to storm if the cat sets with his back to the stove, and I always have comp'ny if a rooster crows on the door-step, and when my nose itches——

[Enter JERUSHA and PHOEBE.]

PHOEBE. You scratch it, don't you?

JERUSHA. Lay aside your work, ladies, tea is all ready.

HANNAH. And we've just finished the quilt. *[Folds quilt.]*

JERUSHA. Take seats jest where ye choose.

[Ladies take seats at table.]

MRS. SIMPKINS. Land sakes, Jerusha, you've got so many good things we'll all be sick.

CHARITY. "Suppers will kill more than the greatest doctors ever cured."

JERUSHA. There ain't enough here to hurt anybody. Jist help yourselves
to the victuals and pass 'em around. [JERUSHA *pours tea.*]

HANNAH. Quiltin' parties make me so hungry, don't they you, Patience?

PATIENCE. I never eat much. I hain't any appetite. I s'pose it's all owin' to
my nerves. [*Puts two large spoonfuls of apple butter on her plate.*]

PHOEBE. Don't take it all, Patience. [*Lowering her voice.*] That's all the
apple butter Aunt Jerusha's got. I had to scrape the crock to get that.

JERUSHA. Hepzibah, how do ye take your tea?

HEPZIBAH. Hey?

JERUSHA [*louder*]. How do ye take your tea?

HEPZIBAH. Without any trimmin's, Jerusha.

MRS. STUBBS. Brother Lovejoy don't drink tea, he drinks hot water.

PHOEBE. I'll take hot water, Aunt Jerusha. No, I won't either. I'll take
tea, 'cause I want Hanner to tell my fortune.

MRS. PRIDE. Phoebe Miranda Pride! You've spilled my tea all over me.
What would the preacher say?

PHOEBE. He'd tell ye to drink hot water, most likely.

RACHEL. Sister Patience, thee ought to eat lots of beans; they are said to
be a very good food for the nerves.

JOHANNA. My man eat beans three times a day for fifteen years and died
of nervous prostration.

CHARITY. "What's one man's meat is another man's poison."
[*Ladies eat, and talk among themselves for a few moments.* PHOEBE
chokes while drinking her tea.]

MRS. PRIDE. Don't drink so fast, Pheeb. What would the preacher say?
[*Pats* PHOEBE *on back.*]

PHOEBE. I want Hanner to tell my fortune first.

JERUSHA. Are ye sick, Phoebe? Ye hain't eat nothin' scarcely. Don't ye
want a tart?

PHOEBE. No ma'am.

HANNAH. Ye oughter have Pheeb drink thoroughwort. That'll give her
an appetite.

MRS. PRIDE. I should know what ailed her if we's at home 'cause she
always eats when she sets the table. [*Taking* PHOEBE's *cup and turning it
around.*]

HANNAH. Wal, Pheeb, there's lots of things in your cup. I see a letter, a
pile of money and a couple bein' married. The gal has curly hair and
the man is dark complected.

MRS. SIMPKINS. That must be the preacher, Pheeb.

DRUSCILLA. Preachers don't have piles of money.

MRS. STUBBS. I guess it must be Sammy.

PHOEBE [*taking cup and looking in it*]. It ain't, neither. Sammy Tucker's bow-legged and this one in the cup ain't.

HANNAH. Patience, let me see your cup.

PATIENCE. What's your hurry, my tea ain't out yet.

HANNAH. I thought you hadn't any appetite. Ye must have found it by the way you're holdin' on.

PATIENCE [*drinking tea and handing cup to* HANNAH]. There! Take it if you're in such an awful hurry. Nervous people shouldn't be hurried.

HANNAH [*taking cup and turning it around*]. There ain't a man to be seen. [PATIENCE *sighs*.] There's nothin' here but an old maid settin' all alone a weepin'.

DRUSCILLA. That must be you, Patience, having a nervous spell.

HANNAH. Charity, let me look in your cup. I'll tell ye jist as it is.

CHARITY [*shaking her head*]. "Truth and roses have thorns about them."

JOHANNA. Charity's 'fraid there won't be a man in her cup. What's in yours, Hanner?

HANNAH. There ain't nothin'. My future can't be read.

MRS. STUBBS. What do ye see in my cup? [*Hands cup to* HANNAH.]

HANNAH. I see sorrow and tribulation. I see a fun'ral, a sick child, a one-legged man, a dead horse, a sick cow, a heap of dead chickens, and a ——

MRS. STUBBS. There, there! Stop, Hanner! Don't tell any more or I'll have the nightmare to-night.

RACHEL. We hope thee won't have all that trouble at once.

JERUSHA. I'm 'fraid ye hain't had enough to eat, ladies.

MRS. SIMPKINS. It's our fault then, not yours, for the table was loaded and you told us to help ourselves.

JERUSHA [*rising*]. Jist take it easy and visit while I clear the table.

MRS. SIMPKINS. Let's all take hold and help.

PATIENCE. I'd help if it wasn't for my nerves. [*Takes rocking-chair.*]

CHARITY. "Where the will is ready the feet are light."

RACHEL. Of course we will help thee.

PHOEBE. I helped set the table, ma, now you can help unset it.

MRS. PRIDE. Then you must finish that block you've started. You ought to be ashamed not to piece *one*.

PHOEBE. I hate to piece blocks. It'll take me all night to finish it.

> [*Sits down and begins to sew. Ladies talk and laugh while cleaning the table. They move tables to back of stage and sit down.*]

MRS. STUBBS. I'm awful sorry, Aunt Jerusha, but I'll have to go home. Sim wouldn't put the twins to bed if I stayed all night.

JERUSHA. That's too bad, Sister Stubbs.

DRUSCILLA. O, the horrid men!

PHOEBE. Preacher Lovejoy ain't horrid.

> [MRS. STUBBS *puts on wraps. Exits.*]

JERUSHA. Sister Pride, did ye tell the Squire to bring his violin this evening?

MRS. PRIDE. Yes, I told him, but he said he'd forgotten 'bout everything he used to play. [*Enter* JOHN DOW *and* SQUIRE PRIDE.] Here he is now.

SQUIRE PRIDE. How'd ye do, Jerusha, and all the rest of ye. This is John Dow, ladies, I don't s'pose he's showed himself before to-day. We men don't figger much at quiltin' parties.

JERUSHA. John always plans to work in the woods when I'm goin' to have a quiltin' party [*Ladies laugh.*]

JOHN DOW. You see, ladies, if I do it then I know Jerusha ain't alone.

> [SQUIRE PRIDE *and* JOHN DOW *sit down. The* SQUIRE *draws his chair close to* HEPZIBAH.]

SQUIRE. What's Brother Spooner doin' these days?

HEPZIBAH. Hey?

SQUIRE. What's Jonathan doin' to-day?

HEPZIBAH. Yes, yes, I know. I'm gray but I ain't bald yet.

SQUIRE [*louder*]. I said what is Jonathan at?

HEPZIBAH. Yes, yes, I know I'm fat but I can't help it.

SQUIRE. Ye don't understand me. What is Jonathan doin'?

HEPZIBAH. Laws a me I ain't a chewin'. What's the matter with ye, Squire?

SQUIRE. I'll give it up. [*Rap at door;* JERUSHA *opens door. Enter* DEACON SIMPKINS.] Hello there, Deacon, I'm glad you've come. John and me won't feel so much like cats in a strange garret.

JERUSHA. It never seems to trouble ye very much, Squire.

DEACON SIMPKINS. No, it never seems to make much difference where the Squire is, he's the same old feller.

SQUIRE. I saw the Deacon once when he didn't look like the same old feller. It was when he's a chasin' his pig and lost his wig. [*Laughs.*]

DEACON. There, there, Squire, your mem'ry's too good. [*Moves chair close to* HEPZIBAH.] Is Brother Spooner in the woods to-day?

    [*Exit* JOHN DOW.]

HEPZIBAH. Hey?

DEACON. Is Jonathan sawin' wood? *

HEPZIBAH. O, yes, I'm feelin' quite good. How be you, Deacon?

DEACON. Ye might jist as well talk to a stone.

JERUSHA. You men don't know how to talk to Hepzibah. [JERUSHA *puts her mouth close to* HEPZIBAH's *ear.*] What is Jonathan doin' to-day?

HEPZIBAH. Sawin' wood.

SQUIRE. I'm glad that's settled.

DEACON. I'm glad I ain't Jonathan.

    [*Enter* JOHN DOW *with a pan of apples which he passes around.*]

SQUIRE. Say, Deacon, speakin' 'bout my mem'ry bein' good, do ye remember that Sunday night I got the start of ye and went home with the gal you's a waitin' for?

DEACON. I reckon I do, Squire. I didn't feel so calm over it then as I do now. But do ye remember how I paid ye back? [*Laughs.*]

SQUIRE. That was a mean trick, Deacon. I never felt quite even with ye.

DEACON. You see, ladies, the Squire had made his plans to go home with Saray Green from the spellin' bee and I was bound to pay him back so I hid his hat. The best part of it was the Squire had tucked a bag of candy in his hat, so I jist shelled it out to Saray as if it was mine and we had a jolly time.

JERUSHA. I expect ye grew fat on that, Deacon.

DEACON. I gained right along till Saray mittened me.

JOHN DOW. I remember the lickin' ye got, Deacon.

DEACON. Wal, I have a faint recollection of it, too. I tried to have the teacher whip me on the Italian system, the up strokes heavy and the light ones down, but she wouldn't do it.

SQUIRE. Do ye remember that sleigh-ride party at Delilah Hartshorn's where we got the preacher to playin' snap up?

MRS. SIMPKINS. I remember it, Squire, for the preacher liked it so well he wouldn't play anything else. He kissed all the girls a dozen times that night.

JERUSHA. We had jolly good times those days.

SQUIRE. I shouldn't mind havin' a game of snap up now.

DEACON. Guess we're most too old for that, Squire; but we might have

some singin'. The most of ye used to sing in the choir years ago. Sister
Pride used to pipe it up lively and Hanner Pike wan't any behind.

JERUSHA. Sing somethin' that'll take us back to the good old days we've
been talkin' 'bout.

MRS. SIMPKINS. I enjoy talking over the good old times once in a while.
Come, Sister Pride and Hanner give us a song.

MRS. PRIDE. Land sakes, I'm all out of practice but if Hanner'll sing, too,
I'll try it. I guess that song "Inside the Old Church Door" 'll suit
Jerusha.

[MRS. SIMPKINS and HANNAH sing "Inside the Old Church Door."]

MRS. SIMPKINS. Now, Squire, it's your turn to furnish some music.

[The SQUIRE takes his violin and plays a lively selection. The DEACON
keeps time to the music with his feet.]

DEACON. I declare, if that music don't take me back to my dancin' days. I
used to love to dance.

SQUIRE [aside]. We'll have him a dancin' yet.

[Plays "Money Musk"; the DEACON keeping time with his feet. After
a strain or two PHOEBE jumps up and begins to dance. She takes hold
of the DEACON's arm and he dances with her. Ladies look horrified.
MRS. SIMPKINS tries to get hold of the DEACON's coat.]

MRS. PRIDE. What would the preacher say?

[Enter LOVEJOY. Music and dancing stop. PHOEBE tries to get out of
sight of the preacher.]

LOVEJOY [gravely]. Deacon Simpkins, I'm astonished!

DEACON [humbly]. I declare for it I be, too. I don't see how it happened.
I guess the Squire's music made me clean forget myself. If I'm forgiven
this time I'll never do it again.

SQUIRE [aside]. I guess I'm even with the Deacon now.

LOVEJOY. I suppose we will have to overlook it this time on your promise
to never do it again. This should be a striking lesson to us all to
constantly watch ourselves lest we be overcome by sudden tempta-
tions. I advise you to keep perfectly quite about this matter. Let nothing be said to any one.

DEACON [leaning head on hand]. Amen! Amen!

MRS. SIMPKINS. Thank goodness, Mrs. Stubbs ain't here.

PATIENCE [aside]. I guess Pheeb won't get the preacher now.

MRS. PRIDE. I think we'd better be goin' home.

MRS. SIMPKINS. I think so, too. Come on, Deacon.

JERUSHA. Don't hurry, it ain't late.

SQUIRE. Let's have some more singin' 'fore we go and everybody jine in. [*All rise and form a semicircle.* PHOEBE *and* PATIENCE *stand beside the preacher. All sing the following words to the tune "Seeing Nelly Home."*]

> Though the years may come and leave us
> In our hearts will ring this chime.
> It was at Aunt Jerusha's quilting party
> That we had a good old time.

> [*Chorus.*]

> That we had a good old time,
> That we had a good old time.
> It was at Aunt Jerusha's quilting party
> That we had a good old time.

CURTAIN

Whitework, or Bride's Quilt

Jane Wilson Joyce

IN THIS
colorless, exacting
work
the last
quilt of girlhood
the nub and chafe
of hours spent
tell how skill
unwinds a dozen spools
of cotton, threads
the needle seven
hundred times
stitches the pattern of
promise
drawn from memory
freehand
the pattern
dazzlehidden
that only angle or
shadow
unveils

At the center, one
white rose
petals open
White grapes
cluster, ghostly

tendrils trailing
Heliotropes
at the four
corners turn
bleached heads
blindly
seeking the sun
Winding all around
vines feather
heavy with
hearts bled
white

She set a saucer of
talc on the table
faithfully wore
her mother's gold thimble
folded a handkerchief
into her bodice, should
her needle sow
this virgin snow-
field with a single
seed, blood
red

Excerpt from

Double Wedding Ring

Patricia Wendorf

Wendorf's novel is told in the form of the diary of Rhoda Greypaull Salter. A pioneer woman with limited education, Rhoda is determined to keep a diary of her journey from Somerset, England, to the United States after her first marriage. Her spelling is often irregular, as she writes "qwilt" for "quilt," but her voice is compelling nonetheless. In this excerpt, she tells of her courtship with her second husband, Captain James Kerr Black, a Civil War veteran and now a successful farmer who commissions her to make her own wedding quilt.

December 7

The first blizzard of the winter strikes and we are isolated. Overnight, great drifts pile up around the house, covering the lower windows. I say to the children: "We are on our own now. It is up to us to show that we can manage."

They all speak up bravely, but I see that they are ankshus. Rosa brings all our thickest clothes into the kitchen. Georgie has had the forethought to bring shovels into the house so that we are eqwipped to dig our way out and to the cow barn.

I say to Jon: "Better you bide in the warm kitchen. George will see to your chores." But he runs to the place where his boots are kept. He pulls them on, and looks for his cap and mackinaw. His little face is streaked with tears.

"Jon come too," he cries. "Jon's chickens all dead!"

I see that there is nothing for it but to take him with us.

We are a long time shovelling our way out to the barn. By the time we reach them my poor Holsteins are in great discomfort. Rosa and I set to about the milking, while Jon contents himself that his preshus flock has survived the night. George feeds the hogs. He builds a fire, fills pans with snow and melts it so that we have water for the stock and dairy. He cleans the sheds, puts down fresh straw, cuts hay, chops wood and carries it back into the house. I say to Rosa: "One year ago and he could hardly swing the axe. I am so proud of him, the way he buckles down just lately."

She says: "He is trying to show you something, Mama."

"Show me what?"

"That *he* is all the man you will ever need about this farm."

My girl bends her head towards the pan of milk; her hand is not qwite steady as she skims the cream.

"Why Rosa," I cry, "whatever do you mean?"

Her cheeks are flushed. "Oh nothing! I just thought—perhaps Uncle Robert or Johnnie or Willum won't be able to get through to us."

It is not what she meant and we both know it. I turn to find Georgie standing at my shoulder. He sets down two pails of water. He says: "Have no fear, Mama! I guess your brave Captain friend will be shovelling his way over before the day is out, even if the drifts should stand at twenty feet."

I wheel qwickly to outface him, but Georgie shows me such a sweet smile that there is nothing I can say.

December 9

Snow now lying four feet deep on level ground. Robert and his boys break through to us this forenoon, they being ankshus as to our situashun in this, our first taste of a farming winter in the northwoods. They are pleased to find us all safe and cheerful, our stock fed and watered and all in order. Robert says: "You have a good son in George. It can't have been easy for him this past year, growing-up like he did in the city, knowing nothing about farm life."

"Oh yes," say I, "I qwite rely on him these days. Whatever should I do without him!"

My brother-in-law looks me foursquare in the eyes. "Maybe," says he, "you should not always be so dependent on your boy for help about the place. From what he says to Chas, young George would like to go on with his butchering apprenticeship. After all, it was what his poor father wanted for him."

For no reason that comes to mind I feel a blush upon my face.

I say in some haste: "I shall never hold him here if he is set on leaving! As you say, the butchering is his proper trade. I might hire a man to do the heavy chores." We are standing on the stoop, the Vickery one-horse sleigh (which I am told is called a cutter hereabouts) stands waiting on the cleared path. Robert looks across to where a plume of smoke curls up from the chimney of the Black Farm.

"Now there," says he, "lives one of the finest men in this whole territory. A real good guy if ever I saw one! He sure does hold you in high regard, Rhoda!"

I am all at once nervous. I pull my shawl close about me. I have such a wish to change the subject of his thoughts.

I say in a high tone: "Why Robert, how American your speech is become!"

He goes on as if I had not spoken. "This blizzard is but the start of a hard long winter. You'd do well to think about your future, Rhoda! A woman alone has a tough life in these parts!"

He climbs into the cutter, his two sons beside him. They wave, and I wave back, my head in such confushon! I stand until the sound of sleigh bells fades away. I call out, too late: "But I am not alone here, Robert," and my cry is lost upon the wind. I turn back into the house. In the kitchen the children make ready to go out again into the bitter weather. They laugh and joke together, but there are dark marks about the eyes of Rosa and Georgie; I feel the droop of weariness in my own shoulders.

Jon says: "How long snow stay, Mama?"

"Until April," I tell him. As I speak a great loneliness comes upon me. Jim Black has not come thru' the drifts to see us. I recall our last meeting and am not too surprised!

December 20

Johnnie Vickery brings his mother over to us in the cutter. Never was the sound of sleigh-bells sweeter or more welcome. Elizabeth and I have much catching up to do. It is three whole weeks since last we were together. She remarks that I look weary, what is small wonder! She offers to send Willum to me to help out.

"It is such a kind thought," say I, "but my Georgie is so set on proving himself. He would be mortally hurt if Willum came here. He is touchy at present over any outside aid."

Elizabeth looks troubled. She begins to talk of the three English-men who lately came to Suamico. Their house and barn, she says, was finished just before the deep snows fell, what is fortunate for them. "Altho," says my sister, "there can be very little homeliness and comfort in a place where three men 'bach' together. Mr. Goodman," she adds, "is a poor-looking specimen and never likely to get wed. Mr. Sutton, on the other hand, is qwite presentable while Mr. Hopkins is downright handsome, having all his own teeth, and a full head of hair even tho' he is middle-aged."

"Perhaps," I say, "they do not wish to get wed. In fact, it is my belief that if a man is still unmarried at the age of forty then he is a lost cause and best left by himself. Such men become set in their bachelor ways, they grow selfish and self-opiniated."

Elizabeth gives me a keen look and begins to speak of other matters.

For some time past it would seem that Suamico folk have wished to build a church where the Episcopalians might worship in comfort. The women of the congregation have formed a society to raise money. Jim Black is their Treasurer. He himself, says Elizabeth, has already made a contribushun of five hundred dollars.

"He does not," say I, "give the impreshun of being so well-off."

"Oh," says Eliizabeth, "Jim is not the man for outside show. But remember, Rhoda, he is a foreman-logger. Such men command high wages in the lumber camps. When the season ends, Jim never goes on a drinking spree with the other 'jacks' into Green Bay. He comes home straightaway to his farm, and saves his money." She nods. "Yes, yes! Jim Black is prudent. He is probably among the best-off of all the farmers hereabouts."

"It is easy," I say, "for a non-drinking bachelor to hoard his gold. How else should he spend it? He certainly wastes little on clothing and home comforts!"

Elizabeth smiles. "Perhaps he has never had the chance—yet? Perhaps he is longing to spoil some lucky woman?"

I make no answer.

My sister asks how long it is since I have done any qwilting. Not for some time, I tell her. She says what a pity, since I am qwick and skilful at the task.

"We had hoped," she says, "to hold a Qwilting Bee. A fine patchwork qwilt will fetch as much as fifty dollars. It would help a good deal towards the funds for our new church. But in weather such as this it will be months before a group of us can meet together. I hesitate to ask when you are so hard-pressed in the yard and dairy . . .?"

"But I would love to make a qwilt!" say I. "It is a soothing occupashun on a winter's evening." I point out our tablecloth and cushions.

"These are all the work of Rosa. As you know, I learned plain qwilting in
England. But Rosa is very skilled in the American fashun of patchwork."

My sister says: "I have a customer in mind, Rhoda. One who will pay
a good price for a fine qwilt.

I laugh. "Do not tell me who it is. The Suamico ladies are such
skilled needlewomen. To know her name would make me nervous."

Rosa comes into the room and we tell her of the project. She runs to
find our scraps bag. We spend a happy hour sorting thru' the pieces.

December 22

The dairy work is long and hard in these low temperatures, but a log
barn is cosier than I would have once believed. How interested my father
would have been in this American way of building. My Holsteins seem
content; they still milk-down at a good rate. Our butter is as sweet and
rich as any I have ever tasted, and no trouble as to storage of it in this
bitter cold. In fact, Georgie and I need to set up a small stove in the
dairy since the cream will not rise in frosty air.

Smoke flies every morning from the chimney of the Black Farm.
The fields that lie between my house and his are deep in snow, tho' the
main trails now opened up. He could visit me if he so wished.

December 23

Elizabeth comes with news that the doctor is calling once again at the
Black Farm. Jim Black, she says, now has his hands full, what with
caring for his sick brother, and all the chores of house and yard. "It
would," she says, "be a Christian act on your part, Rhoda, to go across
and see them."

When evening comes, I fill a satchel with jars of my preserves, and
some cakes fresh-baked by Rosa. I bid Georgie to take them to Matthew
Black. On his return, my son's report causes me to worry. Matt has
developed a deep and wracking cough and is most unwell. Furthermore,
snow begins to fall as Georgie makes his way home. I am wakeful in the
small hours. From my window I see that a lamp burns night-long over at
the Black Farm. The wind gets up and I am fearful of a blizzard.

December 24

It is my birthday! I am forty-four years old, but no time to ponder on it!
Once again we awaken to drifted snow and blocked trails. We are obliged

to dig our way out towards the cow barn. We go about our tasks with heavy hearts. There is no doubt that we are once more qwite cut-off from all our dear ones. The storm rages round the house and barn, the path being blocked almost as fast as we can clear it. By evening we are all worn-out, even Jon, who is beside himself with worry for his feathered flock, and so must come with us where 'ere we go! As I pen these words my little boy falls fast to sleep across the bearskin rug before the fireplace. Georgie carries him to bed.

Christmas Day 1874
The storm is over. We awaken to clear skies and starshine, tho' the frost still deep. We gather in the kitchen where Georgie has already fired the stove and has coffee boiling. He has a glum look. "First time," he says, "that I was ever sent out to work on a Christmas Day!"

"Well I'm sorry, Georgie," I tell him, "but unfortunately our Holsteins take no heed of the Season."

Rosa is also low in spirit.

"I was so looking forward to dinner at Aunt Elizabeth's. It's so much nicer being with them. They're still a proper family." She sends me an apologetic look. "Well, you know what I mean, Mama. They still have a father."

Oh yes, I do indeed know what she means. At this time of year, more than any other, I remember George and our first years together, when Eddie was a small boy, and all our lives seemed to stretch out before us. I recall my dear husband's premonition that his would be a short span; and poor Ed, cut down in the flower of his young manhood. Tears come to my eyes. The children see this and are contrite. Georgie begins to help Jon put on his many layers of warm clothes. Rosa clears away the breakfast dishes. She says in a bright voice: "I know what we can do! We'll begin to make that qwilt, Mama! We'll start this very evening!"

We say a short prayer together before setting out upon our chores.

The path between house and barn has stayed clear overnight. But the half-mile of trail between us and Elizabeth, and to James Black, is still blocked by deep drifts.

The thought of the qwilt qwite lifts our spirits. We talk it over thru' the milking. I say: "Better I think if we stick to the sort of sewing I know best."

"Oh no," she cries, "this customer will want bright colours and a bold pattern. After all, Mama, if a person is willing to pay fifty dollars into the church fund, then we must come up with something more romantic than your plain qwilting."

"I had never," say I, "thought of qwilts and romance both together."

"In American families," my girl tells me, "a qwilt is so much more than a warm covering in winter. It is a symbol. There are engagement qwilts and bridal qwilts, and each has its own speshul pattern."

"You seem to know a lot about it."

"Oh, indeed I do, Mama! You recall when we first came to this house and I made throws and cushions? It was Aunt Elizabeth's friends who showed me how to piece the patterns, and each one has its own name. There's Grandmother's Flower Garden and Courthouse Steps, Barn Raising and Log Cabin, Drunkards Path and Cathedral Window, and, oh, a whole heap more! Some of the designs," says Rosa, "have *hidden meanings*."

We finish the milking and go to the dairy. Georgie comes into the barn. He is ready to clean up and put down fresh straw. He hears our talk. He says: "There's an old qwilting-frame up in the attic. I'll get it down for you when we're all through with chores."

We almost forget that it is Christmas Day, and that we are isolated by the snow. The work goes with a will! After supper is done with, Georgie brings to us the frame. Rosa cleans it with a damp cloth. It is in perfect order. Already, Jon has sorted out our scraps bag. He makes heaps of each separate colour, but Rosa says we are far short of what is needed. We go each one to our highboy drawers and cupboards, and find odd garments, rarely worn. I have a few bolts of plain calico, bought in Green Bay when we first came here. All together, says my girl, it should be suffishent!

We sit around the kitchen table, the frame beside us. Now comes the great decishun. What pattern should we follow?

"I am in your hands," I say to Rosa. "It is you who knows all about this American fashun of patchwork."

"Well," says she, "there is a *most romantic qwilt*, always in demand. It's not the easiest to make, but oh, it looks so fine when finished!"

Georgie sends his sister a very *hard* look, and I think he is about to speak, but then he would seem to bite back on the words. Rosa's cheeks are flushed, her eyes a-sparkle, her dark curls shining in the lamplight. I see how pretty she has grown.

"Since we don't know," she goes on, "who our customer will be, it may be safer to choose a tradishunal qwilt. The one I have in mind is called Double Wedding Ring. It's a repitishun of linked circles made of patterned fabrics against a plain background. Oh, Mama, it looks so elegant, do say that we can do it!"

I am doubtful, but do not wish to spoil her pleashur. I say: "If you are sure about this?"

She turns to face her brother. "You'll help us, won't you, George? The Vickery boys help Aunt Elizabeth with *her* qwilts on winter evenings, and it's all in a *good cause*."

December 27

More snow falls. We turn to our new evening occupashun, thankful for the interest. I pay Jon two bits for one night's needle-threading. He is kept busy with three of us to thread for. Georgie, after some small struggle, takes up a needle. He is slow but neat. We decide, in the end, on a background of lilac-coloured calico, with the rings of the pattern worked in pieces of flowered and checkered cotton. To my surprise I find this American patchwork a most calming occupashun.

January 1

Robert and Elizabeth get through to us this forenoon! They are concerned that we spent Christmas by ourselves but I tell them we were not too low in spirit. Rosa shows them our qwilt and they are full of praise. We spend two happy hours together. They say that, as they came, a party of neighbours were clearing the trail up to the Black Farm.

January 4

No more snow. The cleared trails stay open. My conshunce troubles me on behalf of Matthew, tho' truth to tell we could not have reached him until now.

Our morning chores once done, I say to Rosa: "We *must* go over to the Black Farm." I pack a basket. We take soup and cakes, and a batch of my fresh muffins, with a crock of our new butter to be melted on them. George bides to home with Jon.

The door of the loghouse is opened to us by Captain Black. I am shocked at his appearance. He has grown so gaunt in these past weeks. More still am I alarmed at Matthew. I go into the rear room to find that he has taken to his bed again and looks mortal sick. I say to Jim Black: "Whatever happened? I thought your brother to be almost recovered when I last came here. He was sitting out and on the mend."

Captain Black is very low, has quite lost his old style of command and is so humbled in his spirit that I am driven to comfort him.

"I am sure it was not your fault that he had a set-back. Your care of him is so devoted. But he does not seem at all well."

"It was the blizzard, Mrs. Salter. Matt said that he was better. He would come out to help me with the yard work tho' I said he shouldn't."

Even as we speak, a bout of coughing wracks poor Matthew. We rush to help him.

I say to Captain Black: "This is bronchitis! We need to get moisture into the air to ease his breathing! You *must* keep a kettle boiling on the stove at all times."

I look around me. The little house is in a sad state, the sink piled-up with unwashed dishes, the floors unswept, and Matthew's bed all rumpled-up and needing clean sheets.

"Bring me fresh linen," I say, "and lift your brother for a moment while I put it beneath him." I remake the poor man's bed, for which he thanks me. As I do so, I notice the poorness of his blankets, which are heavy but give little warmth. "It is a qwilt you really need," I tell him.

"Our mother made qwilts when we were children back in Kingston," says Matthew. "Oh my, but they were nice and cosy."

Jim Black grins at his brother. "And you shall have a qwilt again right soon! Elizabeth tells me that Mrs. Salter here has gotten started on my order."

He turns to me. "I shall pay my fifty dollars to the church fund just as soon as you have put the last stitch in, ma'am!"

By this time I am toasting muffins at the fire. A burning colour floods my face, what I pray he will put down to my occupashun.

I am too mortified to answer. I recall the qwilt design of the Double Wedding Ring. Such patterns, my daughter says, are meant to carry hidden meanings. It is an American tradishun. Well the message of *my* qwilt cannot possibly be clearer, can it? For a widow to stitch such a pattern for a batchelor's bed surely is unheard of?

I say in a faint voice: "My sister said she had a customer waiting. I did not guess that it was you sir." My anger drives me to be busy. I set about me with broom and duster. I wash up dishes while Rosa feeds Matt from a tray of soup and buttered muffins.

I say to Jim Black: "Better that you go outside and chop-up wood, sir! You are such a *large* man. You all but fill this little cabin."

January 6
Our work on the qwilt now has an urjent feel about it. What is very silly, since only yesterday I took three of my own plain old qwilts across to the Black Farm for Matthew's use.

It is Jim Black who harps on about the new one I am making. He has, so he says, a superstitious feel about it. That it alone will see the turning-point for Matthew.

"What nonsense!" say I. "It is good medicine your poor brother needs!" I pick up the doctor's bottle of red-coloured liquid, and sniff at it.

"This is of little use to a man in Matt's condishun. It will only serve to irritate his damaged stomach. Now I have a remedy, Captain Black, what will sooth his cough, and put new life back in him." (Truth to tell, I needs must turn the conversashun since talk of qwilts now sends the colour burning to my face.)

"What we really need," I go on, "is a number of lemons. Since we have none then a quart of Elizabeth's apple-cider will do just as well. To the cider you add glycerine and honey in the qwantities that I will show you. This mixture to be used as needed, one or two teaspoons at a time. The honey has life-giving qwalities and will not harm Matt's stomach."

I see by his baffled look that the cabin holds neither glycerine nor honey.

"Oh, never mind," I cry. "I will make the linctus for you, and send Georgie over with it!"

January 8
Was again today over to the Black Farm. Matt takes his new medicine, he says it tastes much nicer than the old one, tho' his cough not yet much improved. I fear the bronchitis will turn to pleurisy. I say to Jim Black: "We shall need to take sterner meashurs if we are to cure your brother."

"Anything!" says he. "We are in your capable hands, ma'am."

The concern shows in his face, and I am moved to see it. Perhaps I have somewhat misjudged him? On reflectshun, it might even be that I have been at fault? I have sometimes, I know, goaded him to argument on farming matters; but in normal times he has such a big and *commanding* presence, that I am driven to take issue with him.

I say: "There is another remedy, long known of in my family. It reqwires a chamois vest and a qwantity of black tar, but I have neither."

Jim Black smiles. "But we have tar, ma'am! A whole barrelful out in the barn. We have a piece of chamois too."

"Then, " say I, "there is yet hope for Matthew."

It turns out to be a slow and pungent operashun. The smell of warm tar fills the cabin, bringing tears to all our eyes. I spread the stuff on Matthew's chest and back, then sew the vest of chamois on him tightly, so that he is all encased from neck to waist. It takes some time, and all the while Jim must needs support his brother, so weak has Matt become. As we labour around our paishunt, Jim's fingers touch my own, but it is accidental. He says, when we are finished, and Matthew resting qwietly: "Ah, Rhoda, whatever should Matthew and I do without you!"

January 10

Jim comes across each morning to help me with the milking and churning, while Rosa goes over to minister to Matthew and give him breakfast. There is no doubt that a man's strong arm makes all the difference on a farmstead. Find myself less tired by evening, and so able to work longer on our qwilt.

Jim turns out to be a first rate dairyman. I was not sure at first if we could work together, but so far all is harmonious between us. He points out that I am running short of winter fodder, but forbears to menshun that this lack is due to my own wilful wish to grow clover rather than corn. He loads up his cutter with sacks of flour and grain, grown in his own fields, suffishent to see me thru' until harvest comes around again.

*   *   *

Private conversation was difficult to come by. Georgie longed to talk to Rosa but Mama was ever present. They had become a family which worked and ate together, and even when their outside chores were done they gathered close around the quilting frame each evening. Opportunity came on Sunday afternoon when Mama, having sent her daughter on an errand to the Vickery farmstead, grew alarmed at darkening skies and begged George to go at once and bring his sister home.

The track which lay between the farmsteads was narrowed by snow heaped-up on either side. Small flakes, soft as feathers, began to fall from a yellow sky. Rosa started to walk faster, but he deliberately slowed his pace.

She said: "Don't dawdle, Georgie," but in an abstracted way as if her thoughts were elsewhere. He looked down at the untroubled face underneath her bonnet brim. He studied the neatness of her, the precise way in which she placed one foot before the other on the uneven ground. He fell behind a further half-dozen paces. Her composure angered him, so that the question he had intended should be subtle burst from him in a great roar.

"What's going on between Mama and Jim Black?"

Rosa turned very slowly round to face him. He moved towards her, looked down on her from his superior height.

She said in the high and careful voice that sounded so exactly like the English tones of their Mama: "Why—whatever can you mean, George?"

He should have been warned by the clipped consonants and short vowels, but the fire in his brain, held so long in check, now flared up, consuming all discretion.

"Don't pretend with me, Rosa Salter! Don't treat me like I'm stupid or something!"

She came so close that he could see the glints in her blue eyes. Two small, gloved fingers tapped the thickness of his jacket.

"You are *so* stupid, Georgie Salter. The whole trouble is that *nothing's* going on between them."

Shock held him fast so that he could neither speak nor move. The sweet voice went on, without emphasis or passion: "Mama's in love with Captain Black. Pity is that she's the only one who doesn't know it."

His voice seemed to come from a great distance. He heard himself say: "Well I didn't know it!"

"Oh you! You never see what's underneath your long nose. Why, Signa Peterson's been mad about you ever since the sugaring-off. Now tell me that you haven't noticed her!"

He said: "I haven't noticed her."

Rosa said: "What *do* you think about, George? You look so keen and smart, but I often wonder what goes on inside your head."

He considered.

"I think about Chicago. Often. I remember Ed and me, and all the plans we had. We never did manage to get that pony. I think about Papa, and all the dreams he had. He did so want us to be George Hodder Salter and Sons, Meat-Packers of Chicago."

Rosa took his gloved hand and patted it. "You could still do that, George."

"How could I? My apprenticeship is only half-through. Looks like I'm doomed to be a farmer all my life."

They began to walk again, but very slowly.

He said: "I don't want another father. I want things to stay the way they are."

"Do you really, Georgie?" Her voice was soft in the way he most distrusted. "Think about it, why don't you? If things stay as they are, you'll never get back to Chicago, will you? You'll never finish your apprenticeship. You said it yourself. Looks like you're doomed to be a farmer all your life. Now if we had the Captain for a father then you'd be free to do whatever you choose."

"I thought," he burst out, "I thought you loved our Pa the same as I did!"

"But I do, George. I miss him all the time, and so does Mama. But she's lonesome, too. All the burden falls on her now, and there's always Jon. He'll never be able to manage on his own. Mama never could bear to be alone, not in all her life. She needs a husband."

They walked on together through the thickening snow. She gazed anxiously up into his face.

"Promise me," she said, "that you will at least think on what I've said. You were meant for a businessman, George—it's what Papa wanted for you."

*   *   *

January 15

Today my George is seventeen years old. We make the house festive with paper-chains and green boughs. After all, we have missed Christmas! Between the morning and evening milking I take an hour or two to look at my appearance. My gown of crimson silk with the narrow bodice and deep-frilled skirt, still lies in tissue-paper. Rosa irons it for me while I wash my hair. She is critical lately.

She says: "Why must you always dress your hair so severely, Mama? It would wave so nicely if only you would not scrape it back behind your ears." She seizes the comb and begins to braid, but loosely. She coils the braid and pins it high upon my head. I look in the mirror. It is not a fashun I am used to, but the result is not displeasing. The hair indeed waves softly round my face giving me a *younger* look. Even Jon has noticed. When I am dressed in the crimson silk he says: "You look real pretty, Mama!"

The road is open between the three farmsteads. The whole Vickery family comes over, even little Robert who soon falls to sleep, and is laid in Rosa's bed. Poor Matthew, tho' still too weak to leave his bed, *incists* that Jim shall join us. We are a merry party! We drink my boy's health in apple-cider. Our table groans beneath the food set out upon it. I look around the dear faces of my relatives and friends, and know that life is *good*.

"Another toast!" I cry. "Let us drink to this great land of America, and especially to the State of Wisconsin where we have all found such a welcome, and a good home."

My eyes are drawn often towards Jim, who is looking uncommon fine. He wears trousers of a tight cut in dark-green plaid, with a short jacket of black velvet trimmed with silver buttons. His shirt is of silk with a frilled and lace-edged jabot. His shoes black-patent with silver buckles. I whisper to Elizabeth: "What is that outfit?"

She says: "It is the tradishunal Scottish. He wears it only on very *speshul occashuns*."

We sit long at table. The men ask if they may smoke. Cigars are lit and there is the rich smell of good tobacco. The talk winds around to the time when we older folk were also seventeen.

Georgie says: "And what were you doing, Captain, when you were my age?"

"Why," says Jim, "that's just the age when I left the home farm and started lumbering. My father died when Matt and I were children. Years later, when Mother passed away there was nothing to hold us—we just lit out with our few belongings—Matt and me." He grinned. "That's when we came to America and met up with you folks."

Robert says: "That must have been a hard life."

"I was a young man in a young country. At the age of eighteen I was riding the log-rafts down the Ottowa River."

Georgie leans forward in his chair, his interest caught: "I've heard about life in the logging-camps. Is it really as tough as it's made out?"

"It's a mite more civilised in these days, but I guess it's not all that different. Being snow-locked is the worse thing, when mail and extra supplies can't get through. That's when a foreman needs to be real strict."

"How," I ask, "does a man come to be a logger?"

"Well it's not always voluntary. It's like this—the company agents mostly set up shop in a saloon. When recruiting starts there's a brisk flow of free whisky. There's many a youngster who comes in looking for his buddy, or just to warm himself before the fire—and he wakes up hours later in a sleigh on the backroads to the pineries—and with a thundering headache!"

Rosa says: "Did that happen to you?"

"No. I went of my own free will. I'd watched the men who ride the log-jams in the spring. It looked to me like a fine adventure. But such men are part of a skilled crew. I had first of all to learn to be a logger, before I could be a white-water man." Jim grinned at Georgie. "The camp life is pretty dull. You get up in darkness, and you come back in darkness. There's no home comforts. Fifty, maybe sixty, men to every bunkhouse, a couple of box stoves with wet socks and other garments hung on lines above 'em. There's always a card game going on, but never for money. Gambling stirs up hard feelings in the men, likewise alcohol makes 'em slow and stupid. There's always one who can play the flute or the harmonica, so we sometimes have a sing-song. Sundays is for letter-writing and mending ripped clothes. Nobody shaves. Most men sleep all Sunday through, only waking up when the cookhouse gong sounds."

I say: "What kind of food is served in such condishuns?"

He smiles at me. "Why nothing so excellent, ma'am, as the meal you've given us this evening. But the camp food is good and a decent cook is worth gold. There's always salt pork and beef, potatoes and baked beans. Pies and cake are favourite—washed down with strong tea. Sometimes the cook will barter sugar with the Indians for a few pails of blueberries or cranberries."

Georgie says: "Tell us more about the log-drive."

"That's the most dangerous time of all," says Jim. "First of all you have to get your logs down to the river. I send a couple of men out overnight to sprinkle water on the track, so that the sleighs will pull well on the icy surface. We calk the horses shoes—ah but that's a fearsome sight, to see the great horse-drawn sleighs loaded up with timber! Then we wait for warmer weather. When the snow melts the river level rises. The stacked-up logs are rolled down to the water, and that's a risky job too. A log-jam is the worst of all. There's many a young man lost his life working to free a jam."

"How long," I ask, "does it take to get the logs down to the mills?"

"Why, several weeks, ma'am. The cookshack goes with us. We sleep in tents along the river-bank as we move downstream. Those nights are awful cold, and a man gets pretty well soaked through working on the river. I've known mornings in the early spring when my clothes were frozen solid to my body. There's no time to stop and dry things. Just got to keep moving every day."

I say: "It's a wonder you're still here to tell your story!"

"It's a job for strong men," says he, "who are not afraid of hard work."

"What happens," asks George, "when the drive is over?"

Jim draws on his cigar. His dark eyes twinkle. "You've been hearing talk, I don't doubt, about the binges that occur when the lumbermen hit Green Bay and Escanaba, with six-months pay burning in their pockets? Well, I'll tell you. The most of them stories are true! Oh I won't mislead you folks. Matt and I went on a binge or two when we were young blades. But I've been Mr. Tremble's foreman for a good few years now, and I've learned some sense along the way. Put it down to my Presbyterian upbringing, or that I come from Scottish stock—but I'm real careful with my dollars these days!"

He looks at me across the table. He says: "Guess I'm as respectable and qwiet a man as any gently-brought-up lady could ever want?"

The colour rises in my face so that my cheeks match the crimson of my gown. They are all watching me. I say, to change the subject, and because it is the first thing that comes into my head: "Perhaps you would like to see the qwilt, sir? It is more than half-way finished."

He says in a most *seerious* tone: "Show it to me, Rhoda, when you have it all done."

February 10

No entry made since George's birthday. We work every evening on the qwilt. I go to visit Matthew most days. He improves, but slowly. George now talks admiringly of Jim, as does Rosa. Indeed, I also see him in a different light since learning more about him. To know is to understand. Allowance can be made for the roughness of a man's appearance when the cause is hard work and condishuns. How I regret my high words about his beard when he came back from last spring's log-drive! It was after all, a very fine beard, black and curling. Jim is altogether a most imposing figure of a man, and qwite the strongest I have ever known.

Watching him when he helps out around my yard and cowbarn I am *amazed* at the ease with which he lifts bales and sacks. The work goes twice as fast with Jim's help. The little I can do for Matthew seems small return for so much kindness. I must go now to take my place at the qwilting-frame. Rosa is already sewing. Georgie grows speedy with the qwilting needle, and Jon kept busy threading for us all.

My Double Wedding Ring qwilt is almost finished.

February 17

Elizabeth comes over in the cutter, bringing little Robert with her. Jon and he play well together. My sister, being skilled at the American patchwork, helps to put the final touches to our qwilt. We spread it out across the kitchen table. The linked rings are in shades of blue with here and there a touch of red and yellow, flowered and striped patches, matched carefully by Rosa who is the *artist* among us. The rings show up fine and bold against the lilac-coloured background. Elizabeth looks at me with meaning. She says:

"Oh my, but Jim will surely love this qwilt!"

I say: "It is meant to bring good health to Matthew. Jim has this fanciful noshun about it. That it will be for a turning-point."

Elizabeth smiles in that secretive way of hers that tells me she has *prior* knowledge. "Oh I don't doubt but it'll be a turning-point for somebody!" says she.

I begin to talk fast about my butter. "When the weather eases," I tell her, "I intend to sell my whole stock in the Green Bay butter market where the price is better."

My sister lays her hand upon my forearm; she pats the finished qwilt. "You were ever good at hiding your true feelings, Rhoda; but do be wary of hiding them too well! The men of this country are simple and direct. Without encouragement of some kind a suitor might well become faint-hearted and give up the chase. Espeshully if he should be a bachelor of mature years, and not used to women's ways."

I gather up the tea-cups. I say: "How nice it is for Jon to have your little boy to play with. I fear he is too much with us older folk."

Elizabeth shakes her head, gathers up her child, and drives away.

February 19

It is in these candle-hours that I am lonesome. The wind roars tonight about the house, the children are long a-bed, and here sit I, my accounting Ledgers spread out upon the kitchen table. But I have no heart for adding figures. I am lower in spirit than I have been since we left Chicago.

Jim comes over to help George put new roofing shingles on the hog-house. When he is all done he comes into the kitchen. I show him the completed qwilt.

I say: "Well, here it is—and I hope it is what you wanted."

I can see he is impressed. He stands back a pace. "Mag-nificent," he cries.

I wait, but it seems that the one word is all that is to pass his lips. I say, in a *desperate* fashun: "It is the Double Wedding Ring design. It is not easy to do." I try to make the words sound offhand, as if the whole matter means nothing to me. After all I still have some pride left.

"It is a Bridal Qwilt," I say. I think he must surely take heart from all of this, but he stands tall and broad and mute.

The silence between us is *awful*. I cannot bear it. I begin to bundle the qwilt fast together. I push it into his hands.

I say, rather coldly, "Well, I hope it looks well on Matthew's bed."

Jim turns and walks away.

As he goes I cry out: "Now, don't forget, will you? You owe the sum of fifty dollars to our church building fund!"

February 22

Meetings between myself and Captain Black grow more awkward by the day. He loses all his former boldness and is now as tongue-tied as my George gets when Rosa's friends come calling. It is very *vexashus* since *I* am now more than a little fond of *him*.

February 23

I know that he wants me. It is in his voice, his look, whether or not he will *admit* it. He just cannot seem to broach the subject. Oh, whatever shall I do? It is up to me to bring him to the *point*. But how best to do it without loss of face, or seeming *forward*?

February 28

Trails are now open between all farmsteads, altho' snow still lying deep in fields and on the backroads. The raising of funds for our new Episco-pal church is becoming urjent. Young couples who have planned to wed at Eastertide must go all the way to Green Bay if they would marry in their family faith. A "Basket Soshul" is to be held by the ladies of our congregashun. This is a very pleasant and *romantic* American means of raising funds for a good cause. The habit is for the ladies and girls to each one decorate a box or basket and fill it with refreshments for *two*. On a certain evening the community assembles in the school room, and each box or basket is auctshuned-off with the men and boys bidding on them. Of course, no one is allowed to know the owner of these lovely boxes, since they are all carried in great secrecy in a Brown Paper Bag.

I say at first that I will not have time for all of this. Truth to tell I am downhearted and lack inclinashun. But Rosa will not let the matter rest. "You cannot," she cries, "be the only woman in the congregashun who has no luncheon box to auctshun!"

I think long and deep about the matter. There is a qwantity of lilac calico left over from the qwilt, and several pretty patches. I begin to sew. I make the Double Wedding Ring pattern. When a suffishent length is put together I cover my basket with it. When the evening of the auctshun comes, I fill the basket to the brim with the cakes and cookies that *he* fancies most. I go with my children to the school room, and place my *brown paper bag* among fifty or so others. When the people are assembled the paper bags are taken off, and the baskets and boxes lined up upon a trestle-table. Mine looks most *distinctive*.

If James Black does not recognise my message this time, then he is not worthy of my feelings for him!

Oh brave words, Rhoda!

When the moment comes and the bidding begins I am as ankshus and fluttery as any schoolgirl. Suppose he should bid for someone else's basket? I think I could not *bear* it.

When my effort is put-up a silence falls. The bidding starts. It comes from the far side of the room. I recognise the voices of Matthew and Jim. They call for some long time, one against the other. Cheering breaks out among the company as the competishun grows fierce. When the figure called by Jim reaches twenty-five dollars, Matthew cries: "Enough! I can't match that!"

Everybody starts to laughing. There is much good-natured teasing. It is clear to all that the contest was *arranged* between them.

The custom is that the winner of a basket should sit together with the maker of it, and eat the lunch provided. As the young men claim the makers of their prize, I see how many a romance is begun in this way. The winner of my particular prize comes striding towards me. His face is flushed and he is smiling *broadly*. We retire to a secluded corner and sit down together.

He says: "I shall treshur this basket all my life, Rhoda! I recognised your pattern straight away."

He looks deep into my eyes, he takes my hand.

He says: "Will you not share a double wedding ring of gold with me?"

March 1

Captain James Kerr Black has proposed marriage to me, and I have accepted. The date has been set for April first, the ceremony to be held in Green Bay. Elizabeth and Robert are overjoyed. Likewise my three children. As for myself, well, my heart was decided upon Jim these many months past; it just takes a little longer for my mind to follow.

March 4

Elizabeth comes over. She finds me churning in the dairy. She says: "You look pale, Rhoda."

"I had but an hour of sleep last night," say I. "There is much to think over."

My sister looks troubled. "I hope you do not feel that we have manoeuvred you towards this marriage?" Her voice is wistful. "But, oh my dear, it does seem so *right* that you and Jim should be together."

I smile. "I do have my own mind, and usually I know it. But in this case, there are the children to think about." I pause. The heavy actshun of the churn-blades tells me that my butter has at last "come." I lean heavily across the handle.

I say: "This marriage will also mean that I never see Somerset again."

She says: "We are Americans now, likewise our children."

"In his last days," I tell her, "poor George spoke often about England. He had always seemed so American in all his ways of thinking, yet, at the very end, it was Dorset that he yearned for."

"I think," says Elizabeth, "that it is better for us women to keep our minds fixed on hearth and home, and family. No good can come of longing for what we can never have. As for your children and their feelings, you must know that they are devoted to Jim and Matthew."

I nod, finding it difficult to speak the next words. I say at last, "Do you not perhaps think that this remarriage is a little *soon?*"

Elizabeth smiles. "I wondered how long it would take you to get around to that point. You still think like an Englishwoman. This is pioneer land, Rhoda! For practical reasons it does not do to live alone. Why, I have seen a widowed man remarry within *weeks*. Jim's courtship of you has been lengthy by local standards."

"I did not," I point out, "realise at first that I was being courted."

I turn to face her. "What do you suppose that George is thinking of me? I know that he is with Susanna, but it is only eighteen months . . ."

"Did you never talk about the matter?"

"Yes," I say slowly, and even as I speak the memory returns. George, saying in those last, sad days: "Thou hast borne much on my account. I have not deserved thee. Should I ever go under—if thou'rt left alone—remember my words. Seek out a good man to be a husband to thee, and a father to our children."

I straighten my shoulders. I go back to the churn and lift out the butter.

"You are right," I tell my sister. "George would want me to be happy."

March 10

For the first time in many weeks the temperature goes up! Jim says it is above the freezing point. There is a softness in the air and a south wind rising. I am drawn from the house by the sounds of a slow thaw; water trickles everywhere, snow slides and thuds from roofs. I walk alone to the edge of my meadowland and stand for a while beside the fence. The depth of the lying snow grows less even as I watch. If I listen hard, I can hear my clover growing.

Elizabeth comes over, bringing a dress-length of silk she "just happened" to have by her. It is a deep gold colour, and very handsome. "You cannot," she says, "wear any of your old gowns to get married."

She and Rosa begin to cut and stitch.

"Keep it simple," I say, "remember that I am no blushing girl, but a woman of forty-four years!"

March 20

There is much to talk over. Jim comes every evening. He is shy but loving, and tho' the time is short he is set upon a proper courtship of me. He brings me little gifts: a tiny gold-and-amethyst brooch that was his mother's; a handful of pussy-willows. On Sunday afternoon we drive out, just the two of us; the snow is almost gone and there is colour in the

land. We follow the course of the Suamico River to the place where it
runs into the Bay. Jim points out Willer Island and the Tail Point Light-
house. We gaze on the cold green waters of the Bay. A steamship passes,
and I look back, inland, to where winter wheat and rye is showing in the
fields. From this spot I can view the tidy farmsteads of our good friends.
There is the Valentine house, and that of Peter Krause. The Sensiba
place, and that of Al Fraker which runs down I see to the very shoreline.

I say to Jim: "I hadn't realised that Suamico stood so close upon the
Bay."

He says: "How happy are you, Rhoda? Does the sight of a ship set
you hankering for England?"

I choose my words with care. "For twenty years I have moved from
one place to another, and none of them a settled home." I take his hands
in both of mine. "I will always be an Englishwoman. You will have to
bear with me in that."

He grins. "It's no hard thing. That bit of starchiness is what first
drew me to you." He pulls me closer. He murmurs above my head:
"Guess I still can't qwite believe that you agreed to have me."

I gaze up into his face. "I was beginning to fear that you would never
ask."

We fell to laughing, and I marvel at the easy way we have with one
another. "I am happy, Jim," I whisper. He halts my words with a long
kiss. I say at last: "We must go back. There is the milking to be done."

"Ah, yes. There is always *that* confounded chore!" His words are cross
but his mouth is smiling, and this time it is I who seeks the long kiss.

We drive back at last thru' the cold spring twilight and to the sound
of birdsong, what comes, says Jim, from the vesper-sparrows and the
killdeers down in the marshlands. We drive into Suamico, and between
the budding trees we see lamplight shine out from kitchen windows. I
have a sense of peace such as I have never known in all my life.

March 29

Have only now considered how two extra men in our household is bound
to make a difference. Jim and Matthew drive over in a waggon loaded high
with fishing-gear and shotguns, heavy boots and clothes, and trunks filled
with "treashures" which they haul up to my attic-room.

Matthew is a new man since Jim and I became promised. He says it is
the prospekt of a proper home at last that has so cheered him up. By his
own reqwest he is to have the small room what opens off the kitchen. It

is warm in the winter, and he makes it cosy with the help of Rosa. He hands back to me the Double Wedding Ring qwilt.

He says: "This rightly belongs on your bed now, ma'am." He grins. "Well, it surely will in just a few days."

I see that he knows about the hidden meaning. I take it from him, blushing. I say: "It has served its purpose."

March 31

We are to start very early in the morning for Green Bay. Elizabeth and Robert will come with us to be our witness. Jim *insists* that we two bide-over an extra day or two. He has waited, he says, much longer than most men for a "honeymoon holiday." He will make the most of it now! I point out that the Green Bay hotels crawl with bed-bugs. He says that he knows of clean lodgings kept by a decent Canadian couple. I say, but what about my Holsteins? What about Jon?

He grows stern. He says that Matthew will be already moved into the house to oversee things. That Robert and Elizabeth will come across each day. He asks: "Can't you *trust* George and Rosa to be responsible for once? Must you always be checking on them? As for Jon, well they would never see him come to any harm!"

He is right. I bow my head.

So all has now been done that can be done to make our absence easy on the family. A large batch of baking, loaves and pies, cake and pud-dings, stand in the pantry. Jim has cut a qwantity of hay bales, and brought grain and feed to lighten Georgie's labour. Jon has been promised a present from Green Bay. My children are so excited at the prospekt of my absence, that I still wonder if I am *wise* to go! Rosa asks what should they call Captain Black after I am married to him? She and Georgie have talked about this. They can never bear, says she, to call him Papa. I say that Jim and I would not expect this. That they must find for themselves a name that suits them all.

My butter is packed ready for the Green Bay market. If the price is good then the profit should purchase two, maybe three more Holsteins for my herd.

The gold silk gown, stitched by my dear Elizabeth, hangs ready for tomorrow. I shall wear my cameo brooch, and keep my hair dressed in its new style.

Jim has bought *two* wedding rings, one for each of us, so that the meaning of the qwilt shall be fulfilled.

III
RADICAL ROSE

Stories of Struggle and Change

The Dream of
Washing Quilts

Rebecca Cox Jackson

A DREAM. I was washing. I was squatting down, washing three bed quilts and singing as I was awashing. And this same sister came to the south door and said, "What are you adoing here?" "I am awashing." "Ain't you afraid to be here?" "No." "Why, you are in great danger."

I then looked and saw I was in a place walled all around with stone. The place was four square. I was in the center of it. There was no window in it, only one door. That was in the southwest corner, opened in. The south door she stood in, which brought her behind me, rather to my left. My face was east. Under me was a pool of water. This walled place was full of water like a bowl. Nobody could get to me. There was three pieces of boards about one yard in length. They were all one size. On one of them I sat. On the one at my right side sat a tub. In it was two quilts, which I had washed in this pool, though I knowed not I was in such a dangerous place till she spoke. Yet I did not feel to move till I had done my washing. So I sat still singing until I was done.

Then I picked up my tub with my three clean quilts in, put the tub on my head, came out with great ease and went eastward, came into a street ran north and south. I then stopped, turned around to see where I had come from, found I was standing by a gate as though I had come through it, saw a bridge alongside the gate. This bridge was over a stream of water. I could not tell whether I had come through this gate or over the bridge.

While I stood here awonder, I looked up, saw the gate post on the south side had a steeple on it, and on the top of the steeple was a gold ball. As I looked from the top to where I stood, I found a little white cord hanging right by my right hand. I caught hold of it, made a squat, then leaped into the air, placed my right foot on the ball, with my left foot swinging in the air. I was above all earthly things. I saw three cities, one in the east, one in the south, one in the west. These cities were clean and beautiful. Then I leaped down with as great ease as I ascended.

Then I heard this same sister speak behind me. "What are you doing here?" "Why, I have been on that pinnacle." She doubted. I caught hold of the cord and leaned upon it again. This I done three times—I had done it twice before she came. I then went through the gate and along this stream of water until I headed it. This was the same way I had come with my clean quilts in the tub upon my head, but I did not see this water nor this gate nor this bridge until I got into the street that ran north and south. This street which I came in from the washing ran east and west. Now as I returned the same way, it brought me westward, and when I headed this stream, I went south—but when I found myself at that gate, I had no tub nor quilts.

So now I went south. After I got far in the south, I looked up to the heavens, saw three pictures all of one size and one appearance, very majestic, long, and beautiful, of the male order. They were some distance apart. They faced the north. Each one was on a black cloud. And there was three heavy claps of thunder. Each clap came out of each cloud. I found I had traveled a long distance—no house nor shelter near, as far as my eyes could see, and I saw a heavy thunderstorm rising. I wondered what I should do. It was said, "Turn back." I turned, and when I turned in the same road that I came—for I never turned out of the road in all my journey—being turned on my right that is, on my right hand side off the road, east, I saw a beautiful white cottage into which I was told to enter, which I did. And when I found myself in so beautiful a house, sheltered from the storm, I was filled with joy and rejoicing. And it was said to me, "This is yours."

Then I heard this sister holler behind the cottage, "What are you adoing here?" "Why, I live here." "You live here?" "Yes, I live here." "Why, how can you live here? Nobody lives here." "Why, this is my cottage, and I am as happy as a lord." "Why, the sun never rises here." "The sun never rises here?" As I made this reply I advanced to the door which I came in at, which was in the south side of the cottage. (She was on the north side which made her behind the cottage—I only heard her voice.) And when I went out and looked in the west, I saw the fourth picture, like the three I saw in the south—same size, same height in the heavens—and it faced the east and it was on a black cloud. And as I kept repeating, "The sun never rises here? No? Why, yonder she is arising—arising now!" "Well, she has only rose to you."

The sun, while I looked on the faces of the pictures, rose from behind the picture as though it came out of the cloud. And it rose out on the south side of this fourth picture, bearing her course toward these three pictures in the south, out of which came three claps of heavy thunder. The thunder out of the three black clouds behind the three pictures in the south, the sun out of the black cloud behind the fourth picture in the west. Then I waked.

Gospel Quilt

Alice MacGowan

T HE GREAT OAKS in the yard whispered together in full-hearted summer happiness. Several teams were hitched along the fence, men standing near them or sitting about on the roots of the big trees, conversing in a Sabbath undertone. Children ran out and in, one fat, flaxen-haired girl of six leading always. The Mase cabin was in Sunday trim and full of company, for there was preaching at the Brush Arbor church.

Within the big, shady, black-raftered kitched Lavena stood cooking tirelessly. Her face, as delicately oval and purely white as a pearl, was set in pathetic lines this morning; the wide, dark eyes were full of misery, and the big twist of dusky gold hair seemed too heavy for the slender neck to uphold, so that the head drooped as she went about her tasks. Cooking for seventeen on a Sunday was no new thing to Lavena Mase— that was not the trouble.

Feminine voices in shrill tones of admiration and astonishment came to Lavena now across the open porch from the other room, where her mother was in her glory exhibiting to the visitors her gospel quilt. Like the cooking, this, too, was an old story to sixteen-year-old Lavena, and she listened but intermittently.

"Oh, for goodness sake, Mary Ann Martha, do watch out!" she cried suddenly to the flaxen-haired child who was dragging a reluctant cat across the floor by the tail. "Oh—oh! Don't do that-a-way. Old Spotty's mighty apt to turn and claw you."

Mary Ann Martha herself "turned," and promptly. Out of a round, distorted countenance she protruded a red tongue, wagging it about till the need for speech became too pressing, and she withdrew it.

"Won't, neither. Won't never claw me,' she declared, giving the cat a last yank. "I drug her all over the place a-yisteddy an' she never scratched me oncet. Me an' Bill's goi' to hitch her up for a nag and plow with her."

Lavena gave it up, and the cat-hauling went on once more. Keziah Mase's household consisted of her husband, gentle, self-effacing Simrall Mase; his oldest daughter, Lavena; a row of small graves of varying lengths in the neglected graveyard on the hill southward, and finally, Mary Ann Martha, the baby, six years old. Mary Ann Martha and the gospel quilt were the two pursuits, the twin idols of Keziah Mase's days. Toward Mary Ann Martha the mother's heart was as butter. It may have been remembrance of those little graves in the neglected church-yard that broke her rod of office in her hands, when it came to this last of her children. At any rate, the fiat had gone forth early to Simrall and his daughter, "Don't you never lay the weight o' yo' hand on that child." And Mary Ann Martha was notorious all over the Big and Little Turkey Track neighborhoods as "the worst chap the Lord A'mighty ever made and the old davil himself wouldn't have." "Sp'iled rotten," was the mildest comment ever heard in connection with her. And the gospel quilt was as famous in its way as Mary Ann Martha. Keziah had begun it far back in the early days of her marriage, before Lavena was born, when she was beginning to learn that Simrall Mase would never amount to much, and she had indeed, as her parents asserted, "driven her pigs to a poor market." Then it was that there came to her a vision in the night, and she rose up and took bits of quilt pieces and began to fashion a new thing. Other women might have the Rising Sun, the Log Cabin, the Piney-blow, the Basket of Posies; she had conceived and would execute a masterwork in the way of quilts, quite outside the line of these. Keziah lacked entirely that crude art sense which finds its expression in the mountain woman's beautifully pieced quilt; she had within her only a fire which demanded that she excel somewhere, that she make of herself a marked figure by some means. The big square of muslin was bought at some expense of pinching and saving, and she began to set upon it those figures which had occupied her mind, her time and her fingers through many years since. Clumsily done, with no feeling whatever for form, proportion or color, she poured into it a passion of desirous energy which yet produced its effect. The quilt was always at hand to bring out if there was trouble, or if someone needed to be overawed. Lavena could remember occasions on which her mother had dressed herself in her best of a morning—a thing unheard of in that primitive society—and set to work upon the quilt as a sort of disciplinary measure, a showing forth to her family of what she stood for. She had done that the day Cloud Lackland had asked Simrall Mase for his daughter and was refused. Lavena, heavy-eyed, heavy-hearted, hearkened once more to the sounds in the other room, where Ollie Leeper's wife was exclaiming with fervor:

"Laws, Miz Mase, I don't see how you ever did think of all o' them critters!"

"What's this here thing with birds a roostin' on it?" inquired Iley Turrentine incautiously.

"That thar's Jacob's Ladder—don't you see the postes, and the pieces a-goin' acrost?" returned Keziah with dignity. "Lord, the trouble I had with them angels! I don't wonder you took 'em for birds. I had a mind to turn 'em into birds, time and again. I done well on Noey's dove—see, here's it—an' a ark—well, hit ain't no more than a house with a boat un'neath."

She pulled the folds about to get at the period of the deluge.

"Course I see now jest what it was intentioned for," Iley hastened to say. "If I'd looked right good I could 'a' made out the angels goin' up *an'* down. How"—she hesitated, but the resolve to retreive herself overcame all timidity—"how natural them loaves an' fishes does look!"

"That thar's the ark," explained Keziah, putting her finger on the supposed loaf. There was a moment of depressed silence; then Keziah, willing to let bygones be bygones, observed:

"Over here is the whale and Joney." These twin objects were what Iley had taken for the fishes.

"Ye see, I had to make the whale some littler than life," Keziah deprecated. "I sort o' drawed him in, as a body may say, 'kase course I couldn't git him all on my quilt without. I didn't aim to git Joney quite so big, but that thar sprigged percale that he's made outen was so pretty, and the piece I had was just that len'th, an' I hated to throw away what wouldn't be good for anything, an' I'd already got my whale, so I sort o' len'thened the beast's tail with a few stitches. Would you call a whale a beast or a fish?"

"Well, I should sure call anything that could swaller a man a beast," opined one of the old ladies.

"An' yit he's sorter built like a fish," said the other.

"An' he lives in the water," concluded Mrs. Ollie Leeper firmly.

Keziah had not been listening. "Would you"—she began doubt-

fully—"I've got a fine piece o' turkey red calico, an' hit does look power-
ful well on white; I thought o' makin' the Red Sea out of it," she sighed.
"But land! hit'd take me forever to cut out all them children of Isrul; an'
I never *would* get done makin' Egyptians."

Lavena glanced along the line of skillets and pots on her hearth.
Everything was ready to leave. She went slowly, dejectedly toward the
door, crossed the porch and stood leaning in the doorway of that other
room. There was Keziah, flushed with triumph, rapt in the artist's dream
of her artistry, a skilful hand run under the fabric to bring into promi-
nence two figures cut from blue-checked gingham, while the other wom-
en admired and wondered.

"I hain't never had the heart to put it in the frames and quilt it," she
was saying, "kase every time I say I'm done I'm shore to study about
something else to put on it. I'm skeered I might quilt it and bind it, and
then all at oncet ricollect something that jest *ort* to have been on. Thar,
'Liza Ann, them's Adam and Eve—that's what I begun on," she pur-
sued. "That gingham they're cut out'n was a piece o' Laveny's first short
dress.

"Yes, an' I can tell which is Adam and which is Eve, just as easy,"
Mrs. Ollie Leeper said, proud of her perspicacity. "That thar's Eve in the
skirts, whilst Adam's got laigs."

Keziah beamed. She regarded fondly the small archaic figures on the
white domestic background. When one comes to think of it, a domestic
background is fairly proper for Adam and Eve. The mother of mankind
had feet, but it would have taken some one unacquainted with the moral
code of the mountain woman to deduce legs from those feet. Yes, Ollie
Leeper's wife had spoken truly; Eve had skirts and Adam had legs.

"What's that thar, Keziah?" inquired old Mrs. Peavey, putting her
finger on a twisty bit of polka-dotted calico. She asked, not because she
did not know, but for the pleasure of being told. "Looks like that must be
the sarpent."

"Hit air," returned Keziah solemnly.

The Ancient Evil was represented as standing sociably on his tail,
facing the tempted pair.

"My! Don't he look fiesty?" commented the Leeper woman, with
deep admiration. "Watch him jest a-lickin' out his tongue in Eve's face.
Lord," she sighed conventionally, "how prone women air to sin!"

"Women? Huh!" snorted Keziah Mase. "Not nigh so prone as them

men, 'specially such as has lived in the Settlement. Look a-here," turning
the quilt to get at the Tree of Good and Evil. "Look at them thar apples.
Now, Miz Peavey, you can see I made some of them out of red calico and
some out of yaller. Do you-all think I ort to have a few green amongst 'em?
Looks like green apples is mighty sinful and trouble-makin'."

There was a murmur of assent from the two old neighbors, but Ollie
Leeper's wife objected.

"I don't know," she debated as she ran her fingers over a brave attempt at one of the Beasts of Revelation.

"Course you might add a few green ones. Hit shore looks like the
Old Boy is in green apples more than in ripe ones, but ef them that Eve
tempted Adam with had been green—do you reckon he'd 'a'bit?"

The scandal was such an old one that Keziah evidently resented its
revival.

"Well, o' course," she said a bit sharply, "a body cain't gainsay what's
in the Bible; but I've always had my doubts about that thar apple fuss.
Hit's men that prints the good Book, and does about with it—not wom-
en; an' I've always had a feelin' that mo' likely hit was Adam got into
that apple business first."

Again there was silence; nobody wanted to take issue with Keziah
Mase. Finally, as a safe side movement, Mrs. Ollie Leeper exclaimed
impressively:

"Laws, Miz Mase, looks like yo' family ort to be perfectly happy with
that thar quilt in the house. I'm might shore I would be. I tell you, sech a
work as that is worth a woman's while."

Keziah's comely face set itself in hard lines. "There's them that thinks
different," she said, looking directly at Lavena. "There has been folks
come to this house and made game of my gospel quilt—made game of it!"

"The Lord—no!" cried old Mrs. Peavey; and the Leeper woman put
in with unction:

"Well, I'd never forgive 'em this side o' Canaan!"

"I never will," agreed Keziah solemnly. "Them that would make game
of sech is blasphemious. Mebbe it ain't adzactly the Bible, but hit's—"

"Hit's mo' so," asseverated the Leeper woman swiftly. "The Bible is
protected like, but yo' gospel quilt is standin' up alone, as a body may say,
an' you've got to speak for it. No, ef I was you, and anybody made game
of that thar quilt, I never would forgive 'em."

Lavena's delicate face was crimson. "Aint't that something boiling over on the hearth?" she murmured hastily, and fairly turned and ran. She found her father, gentle, nearsighted, kneeling before the fire, stirring one of the pots. Simrall Mase looked up at his girl deprecatingly— he had held the deprecating attitude ever since he married handsome, high-headed Keziah Luster.

"Yo' mammy showin' her quilt?" he inquired rather superfluously. "Looks like it's a great pride and joy to her."

"I wish it was burnt up!" choked Lavena, crouching beside her father and resting against his shoulder for the solace of contact, the feeling of comradeship. He put an arm around her swaying figure to steady her.

"Ye ort not to speak that-a-way," he reproved her. Hit's been the comfort of your mammy's life. She made a pore match when she wedded me, and if it hadn't a-been for that gospel quilt I reckon she'd a-seed nothing but sorrow."

"She didn't," rebelled Lavena; "she made a good match—only you're too say-nothin' to speak up for yourself, Pappy; and now she goes an' interferes with me and Cloud because she says he made fun o' her quilt. Well— he did. He didn't mean any harm. He wasn't fetched up on it like I was."

She rose and went sighingly to the table, preparing to put her dinner on. Cloud Lackland's face came before her as she had seen him last, when he was sent away denied. The handsomest, best-hearted boy in the neighborhood, her playmate of years ago, and now graced by a new interest since he had been working three years in the Settlement, and brought back from it a polish and an air of ease that overshadowed the attractions of the other boys.

The old horse plodded doggedly in a circle. A fat child with a switch in her hand ran perilously close at his heels, yelling automatically. The big log rollers, set up endwise in the center of a bowl, turned slowly, crushing the jade-green stalks between them, while the absinthe-colored juice gathered in the bowl and ran down its small trough to the barrel, whence it was dipped into the great evaporating pan above the steady furnace fire. Everything was sticky and sour-sweet. It was sorghum-making time at the Mase cabin, and Cloud Lackland had come with the sorghum-makers to help. Lavena stood by the furnace with a long-handled ladle and skimmed and skimmed, pouring her skimmings into a hole in the ground beside her. She scarce dared look up from the bubbling surface of the big square pan, as long and broad almost as a wagon-bed, for fear of encountering Cloud's ardent eyes.

"Come here just as bold as cast-iron brass," Keziah muttered in a mixed figure. "Reckon he thinks I'm ashamed of my quilt. I won't do a thing but spread it out on the big bed, where all them men can see it when they go in to they dinner. I reckon his behavior is town ways. A mountain boy'd know better than to come back when a gal's folks have told him 'no' oncet."

Young Cloud, at the furnace, fed the fire. "Lavena," he appealed in an undertone, "don't you aim to never look at me again? I've done found out what it was that made your ma mad. I'm mighty sorry, but she's bound to get over that."

"You don't know ma—and you don't know about the quilt," returned Lavena in the same carefully guarded undertone. She glanced toward the crusher, where the work was going noisily forward, Simrall passing out bundles of cane to old man Pingree, whose sorghum-making outfit it was, Mary Ann Martha redoubling her shouts and caperings at the heels of the horse, the men calling back and forth with much rough banter and loud laughter. "I believe in my soul Ma thinks more o' that quilt than she does of any child she's got—unless it would be the baby."

"Well, that just means that she thinks more of it than she does of you," supplied young Lackland resentfully; "you an' the baby's all they is."

"They ain't no use to talk about it; you just don't understand," Lavena choked, as her mother came hurrying out, looking suspiciously from one young face to the other.

"You go into the house and get the dinner, Veny," she said brusquely. "I'll 'tend to the skimming."

It was Keziah's intention to attend not only to the skimming, but to the case of Cloud Lackland, who did not know his place, and needed a severe setting down. She was sorting phrases in her mind and getting ready to begin, when Mary Ann Martha, who had forsaken the old horse to investigate her mother's activities, fell shrieking into the skimming-hole.

"The good land!" shouted Keziah, flinging her ladle into the pan and reaching down to grab her offspring. "If there's anything you ort not to be in of course you're in it. Now look at you!" she ejaculated as she hauled the fat six-year-old out dripping. "You ain't got another frock to yo' name, an' what am I going to do with you?"

Mary Ann Martha showed a blissful indifference to what might be done with her. She was in that state of sweetened stickiness wherein she was able to lick, with satisfaction, almost any portion of her anatomy or her costume.

"Don't want no other frock," she announced briefly, as she sat down in the dust to begin clearing her hands of skimmings, very like a puppy or kitten.

"Well, I'm a-goin' to put boy clothes on you," declared the mother. "You act as bad as a boy." And she hustled the protesting delinquent away to put her threat into execution.

Five minutes later, burning with wrongs, Mary Ann Martha came stormily forth to rejoin her kind, pent in a tight little jean suit which had belonged to one of the small dead brothers, and from which her solid limbs and fat, tubby body seemed fairly exploding. Humiliated, alienated, and with her hand against every man, she lowered upon them all from under flaxen brows.

Keziah had returned to the skimming and begun upon her campaign against Cloud, but Pingree called him away to work at the crusher.

"You, Ma'y-An'-Marth', " admonished the proprietor of the sorghum outfit, as the small marauder raided the cooling-pans and licked the spoons and testing-sticks as soon as they were laid down, "you got to walk mighty keerful around where I'm at, at least in sawgrum-making time."

Mary Ann Martha held down her head and muttered. She was ashamed of her trousers as only a mountain-born child could be ashamed.

"You let my spoons alone, or I'll fling you plump into the b'ilin'-pan, whar you'll git a-plenty o' sawgrum," Pingree threatened.

"You hear now? The last man I made sawgrum for had ten children when I begun. They set in to pester me an' old Baldy jest like yo' a-doin'; and when I got done, thar was ten kaigs of sawgrum and nary chap on the place. Yes, that's right. Ef thar wasn't a chap bar'lled up in every kaig I turned out, I don't know sargrum."

The unsexed and hostile Mary Ann Martha rolled upon Pingree an eye of mute defiance, and returned to an enterprise which she had set up of laying fresh sorghum stalks side by side, pavement-wise, over the skimming-hole. This latter was not the ordinary small skimming-hole of sorghum-making time, but a sizable excavation dug at some previous period for some now-forgotten purpose. Brush had been thrown into it.

Vines had grown and tangled over the brush, till it was a miniature jungle or bear-pit.

The child finally forsook her work; young Lackland came back to the furnace; Keziah returned to the skimming; the two were practically alone together.

"Cloud," she began sharply, "I got something to say to you that better be said before you go into the house. Maybe you'll think best not to stay after I've spoken my mind."

Lackland's brown cheek reddened, and his clear hazel eyes brightened, yet he kept a good curb on that quick temper of his, determined not to lose any chance of Lavena by getting into a fuss with her mother.

"Yes'm," he said civilly. "I wish you would speak out."

"Mother! Mother!" came Lavena's distressed tones from the house. "Mother! Mary Ann Martha is in here putting molasses all *over* your gospel quilt, and I can't stop her!"

"Good land!" wailed Keziah, straightening up from the bending attitude she had assumed to administer her lecture to Lackland. "Take the spoon, Cloud." She cast the ladle toward him without much care whether handle or bowl went first. "Looks like I have the hardest time of anybody I know!" she ejaculated, starting toward the house.

"You better get here quick, Ma," Lavena urged. "She's just a-wipin' her spoon on 'em."

Keziah set a swift foot in the middle of the sorghum-stalk pavement her youngest had laid over the skimming-pit. The stalks gave. She attempted to recover herself and have back the foot, but her momentum was too great. On she plunged, pitching and rolling, descending by degrees and with ejaculatory whoops among the sticky sweetness, part of which was still uncomfortably warm.

Pingree and Mase were engrossed with the crusher and the horse. Cloud leaped to his feet and ran to Keziah's assistance.

"Oh, land!" she gasped, coming to the surface yellow and sticky of countenance, smudged, smeared, and crowned with a mucilaginous wreath of greenery like a sorghumnal bacchante. "I believe in my soul the little sinner aimed to do this. Just wait till I lay a hand on her—ow!" A rotten branch snapped under her foot, letting her down once more into a squelching pool of skimming.

"Take hold of my hand," admonished Cloud. "No, I don't reckon the baby aimed to make trouble; chaps is always doin' things like this, an' meanin' no harm. There—now I've got you. Here you come!" and with a tremendous scrabbling and scrambling, the woman "came," hurtling from her sweet retreat and spattering molasses all over Lackland. As she gained her feet there sounded another distressful call from the house.

"Oh, Ma! Please come on. She's a doin' your quilt scand'lous—and I daresn't to touch her."

"Ain't," protested the infant, appearing suddenly in the doorway, a "trying spoon" in her hand, over which she was running her tongue with gusto. "I thest give a lickin' of long-sweetnin' to Eads." Thus she named the first of womankind. "Po' old Eads looked so-o-o hungry."

"She's done a heap more'n that," Lavena protested, drawing the offender back to where the cherished quilt lay, as Keziah and Lackland entered.

The woman looked tragically at her handiwork. Long amber tracks traversed it from end to end. Mary Ann Martha's mouth began to work piteously. She had indeed meant so well.

"Give Eads some," she began, in a husky, explanatory voice. "An—th'—ol' snake licked out his tongue, and I must put a teenchy-weenchy bit on it. Nen Adam, he's mad 'cause he don't git none; an'—Mammy," in a burst of tears, "has I ruinated the gospel quilt?" It was the family fetish after all, and to ruin it was the ultimate apostasy.

"Ma—why, Mother! For mercy's sake! What's the matter with you?" exclaimed Lavena, suddenly noting her parent's appearance.

"Nothin'," returned Keziah, with the brevity of a woman who feared to speak lest she weep. "I fell in the skimming-hole. Cloud pulled me out. Honey, go get me—no, I reckon you needn't. This thing'll just about have to go into the tub—and that will shore finish it. Oh, I do think I have the worst trouble!"

And suddenly, before them all, the haughty mandatory Keziah crumpled down into a chair and covered her soiled, smeared countenance with her sticky hands, while a few hard-wrung tears seeped between the knotty, trembling fingers.

"Mother," said Cloud—and nobody noticed that he used the word—"if you'll go and 'tend to the sorghum, and let Lavena look after the dinner, I can clean your quilt so you'd never know a thing had happened to it."

She uncovered one eye and looked up at him dubiously. Was the town boy continuing to make fun of her and her quilt? Cloud put a hand to his pocket.

"I've got a bottle of stuff here that'll take every one of them stains out," he declared eagerly. "I've been working in a place where they do what they call dry-cleaning. Why, we have worse jobs than that 'most every day. I know all the tricks. If one thing don't work on it, another will—and nary one of the things I'll put on will take the color out nor show afterwards. I tell ye, it'll look like new."

"Well, what am I goin' to give you for workin' this here merracle?" inquired Keziah suspiciously. "Looks like the job might take considerable time and labor. What you goin' into it so brash for?" She tried to make her inquiry harsh, repellent; but the voice in which she spoke wobbled pitifully; she did so long to be reassured and helped.

The boy cast one swift, shining look at Lavena. If he dared—but no, the girl shook her head.

"I ain't asking a thing for my work," he returned sturdily. "When a body sees a grand quilt like this'n all ruint, and you a grievin' over it, they' rather help out than not."

"I thought you said it was a fool quilt," Keziah caught him up sternly, though one could read relenting in every line of her face.

"I was mad," explained Lackland sheepishly. "I hadn't never looked at it right good. Hit's the biggest thing, and the finest thing of its kind, anybody ever made, I reckon."

With this comprehensive declaration, he drew forth the bottle from his pocket and demanded cloths, setting to work with energy. Keziah, perforce, hastened back to her skimming. Lavena returned to dinner, casting a glance of timid hope over her shoulder as she went. When, after a time, the older woman stole to the door and saw the fabric emerging, a miraculous restoration, from under the boy's skilled, brown fingers, she went noiselessly through into the kitchen, where Lavena was just spreading the table.

"Go in thar and look at what he's a-doin'," she whispered, almost choked by her emotion. "Speak mighty pleasant to him, Sis. A gal that's had a chance to git a feller like that—and let it slip—may never git another. But you talk good to him. If he says anything that looks like it, you tell him—course that quilt stays with me whilst I live, an' I did allow to be laid away in it; but after what he's done, you tell him I aim to leave the gospel quilt to you when I go."

Excerpt from

Black April

Julia Peterkin

B<small>EFORE</small> <small>DAY</small> was clean Big Sue got up out of bed and went to the front door to look at the weather. The cool air was soft and still, trees and birds were asleep. The earth itself was resting quietly, for the sun tarried late in his bed. The stars had not yet faded from the clear open sky, but Big Sue was full of excitement. Only a few hours more and she must have everything ready at Maum Hannah's for the quilting to commence.

Her own big room was almost large enough for a quilting, but it was better to go to Maum Hannah's. The meeting benches could be brought in from under the house where they stayed, to make seats enough for the company, and Maum Hannah's quilting poles stood always in the corner waiting for work to do. Plenty of pots sat on her hearth and two big ones out in the yard besides. Most of the plantation quiltings were held at Maum Hannah's house, the same as the night prayer-meetings.

The raw rations were all ready to cook. Plenty of rice and corn-meal. White flour and coffee and sugar from the store. She'd pot-roast the ducks, and fry the fish, and make the turtle into a stew. She'd roast the potatoes in the ashes. The corn-pone would bake brown and nice in the big oven on the hearth. With some nice fat white-flour biscuits to eat last with the coffee, she would have enough to fill everybody full.

Breeze must get up and hustle! She called him and he tried to raise up his drowsy head, but sleep had it too heavy for his strength to lift. If she'd only let him take one more little nap! But she shook him soundly by the shoulder. To-day was the day for the quilting. He must get up and dress, and get some fat kindling wood to start a fire under both the big pots in Maum Hannah's yard. He'd have to fetch water for those pots too, and tote all the quilts there, and the sack of newly ginned cotton

April had given her for lining the quilts, besides all the rations that had to be cooked for the quilters to eat at dinner-time.

With a sleepy groan Breeze rose and pulled on his shirt and breeches, then his sluggish feet shambled toward the water-shelf where the tin wash-basin sat beside the water-bucket. Big Sue made him wash his face, no matter how soon or cold the morning was. He might as well do it, and get it over with.

As he reached a heavy hand up for the gourd that hung on a nail beside the water-bucket, his arm lengthened into a lazy stretch, the other arm joined in, and his mouth opened into a wide yawn. Then his fingers dropped wearily on to his head where they began a slow tired scratching.

Big Sue stopped short in her tracks, and the sparkle in her beady black eyes cut him clear through to the quick.

"Looka here, boy! Is you paralyze'? I ain' got time to stop an' lick you, now. But if you don' stir you' stumps, you' hide won' hold out to-night when I git back home. Dat strap yonder is eetchin' to git on you' rind right now! Or would you ruther chaw a pod o' red pepper?"

The long thin strip of leather, hanging limp and black against the white-washed wall not far from the mantel-shelf, looked dumb and harmless enough, but Breeze gave a shiver and jumped wide awake as his eyes followed Big Sue's fat forefinger. That strap could whistle and hiss through the air like a black snake when Big Sue laid its licks home. Its stinging lash could bite deep into tender naked meat. But the string of red pepper pods hanging outside by the front door were pure fire.

He wanted to cry but fear crushed back the misery that seized him, and gulping down a sob he hurried about his tasks. First he hastily swallowed a bite of breakfast, then he took a big armful of folded quilt tops, and holding them tight hurried to Maum Hannah's house with them.

The sun was up, and the morning tide rolled high and shiny in the river. The air was cool, and the wind murmuring on the tree-tops strewed the path with falling leaves. Some of them whirled over as they left the swaying boughs, then lay still wherever they touched the ground, while others flew sidewise, and skipped nimbly over the ground on their stiff brown points.

The sunlight smelled warm, but the day's breath was flavored with things nipped by the frost. The sweet potato leaves were black, the squash vines full of slimy green rags. The light frost on the cabin steps sparkled with tinted radiance as the cool wind, that had all the leaves trembling in a shiver, began to blow a bit warmer and melt it back into dew.

This was the second frost of the fall. One more would bring rain. The day knew it, for in spite of the sun's brave shining, the shadows fell heavy and green under the trees. Those cast by the old cedar stretched across the yard's white sand much blacker and more doleful than the sun-spotted shade cast by the live-oaks.

Maum Hannah's house was very old, and its foundations had weakened, so the solid weight of its short square body leaned to one side. The ridge-pole was warped, the mossy roof sagged down in the middle, and feathery clumps of fern throve along the frazzled edge of the rotted eaves.

Two big black iron washpots in Maum Hannah's yard sat close enough to the house to be handy, but far enough away to kill any spark that might fly from their fires toward the house, trying to set fire to the old shack, tottering with age and all but ready to fall.

Inside Maum Hannah, dressed up in her Sunday clothes, with a fresh white headkerchief binding her head, a wide white apron almost hiding the long full skirt of her black and white checked homespun dress, awaited the guests. She was bending over the fire whose reddish light glowed on her cheerful smile, making it brighter than ever.

"Come in, son. You's a early bird dis mawnin'. You's a strong bird too, to tote sich a heavy load. Put de quilts on de bed in de shed-room, den come eat some breakfast wid me. I can' enjoy eatin' by myse'f, and Emma went last night to Zeda's house, so e wouldn't be in my way to-day."

The bacon broiling on a bed of live coals, and fresh peeled sweet potatoes just drawn out from the ashes where they they had roasted, made a temptation that caused Breeze's mouth to water. But he hesitated. Cousin Big Sue was waiting for him, and he knew better than to cross her this morning.

"If you can' set down, take a tater in you' hand an' eat em long de way home. A tater's good for you. It'll stick to you' ribs."

Breeze took the hot bit from her hand and started to hurry away, but she stopped him, "No, son! Don' grab victuals an' run! Put you' hands in front o' you, so. Pull you' foot an' bow, an' say 'T'ank Gawd!' Dat's de way. You must do so ev'y day if you want Jedus to bless you. All you got comes from Gawd. You mustn' forget to tell Him you's t'ankful."

Most of the cabin doors were closed, but the smoke curling up out of every chimney circled in wreaths overhead. Little clouds of mist floated low over the marsh, where the marsh-hens kept up a noisy cackling. Roosters crowed late. Ant-hills were piled high over the ground. All sure signs of rain, even though no clouds showed in the pale blue sky.

As soon as Breeze's work was done, Big Sue had promised he could go to Zeda's house or to April's, and spend the rest of the day playing with their children, and now there were only a few more lightwood splinters to split. The prospect of such fun ahead must have made him reckless, or else the ax, newly sharpened on the big round grind-stone, had got mean and tricky. Anyway, as Breeze brought it down hard and heavy on the last fat chunk to be split, its keen edge glanced to one side and with as straight an aim as if it had two good eyes, jumped between two of his toes. How it stung! The blood poured out. But Breeze's chief thought was of how Big Sue would scold him. Hopping on a heel across the yard to the door-step he called pitifully for Maum Hannah.

"Great Gawd!" she yelled out when she saw the bloody tracks on the white sand. "What is you done, Breeze? Don' come in dis house an' track up dis floor! Wha' dat ail you' foot?"

She made him lie flat on the ground and hold his foot up high, then taking a healing leaf from a low bush, growing right beside her door, she pressed it over the cut and held it until it stuck, then tied it in place. That was all he needed, but he'd have to keep still to-day. Maybe two or three days.

By ten o'clock Big Sue was outside the yard where Zeda stirred the boiling washpots. Onion-flavored eel-stew scented the air. The stout meeting benches had been brought in from under the house, two for each quilt. The quilting poles leaned in a corner waiting to be used. The older, more settled women came first. Each with her needle, ready to sew. The younger ones straggled in later, with babies, or tiny children, who kept their hands busy. They were all kin, and when they first assembled the room rang with, "How you do, cousin?" "Howdy, Auntie!" "How is you, sister?"

Leah, April's wife, had on somewhat finer clothes than the other women. The bottom of her white apron was edged with a band of wide lace, and she wore a velvet hat with a feather in it over her plaid head-kerchief. But something ailed her speech. The words broke off in her mouth. Her well-greased face looked troubled. Her round eyes sad.

"How you do, daughter?" Maum Hannah asked her kindly. "You look so nice to-day. You got such a pretty hat on! Lawd! Is dem teeth you got in you' mouth? April ought to be proud o' you."

But instead of smiling Leah's face looked ready to cry. "I ain' well, Auntie. My head feels too full all de time. Dese teeth is got me fretted half to death. Dey's got my gums all sore, an' dey rattles when I tries to walk like dey is gwine to jump down my throat. I can' eat wid 'em on to save life. De bottom ones is meaner dan de top ones. I like to missed and swallowed 'em yestiddy."

"How come you wears 'em if dey pesters you so bad?"

"April likes 'em. E say dey becomes me. E paid a lot o' money fo' dem, too. E took me all de way to town on de boat to git 'em. But dey ain' no sati'faction." She sighed deep. "An' de blood keeps all de time rushin' to my head ever since I was salivate."

Maum Hannah listened and sympathized with a doleful, "Oh-oh!" while Leah complained that the worst part was she couldn't enjoy her victuals any more. She'd just as soon have a cup and saucer in her mouth as those teeth. It made no difference what she ate, now, everything tasted all the same.

"Fo' Gawd's sake take 'em off an' rest you' mouth to-day!" Maum Hannah exhorted her. "You may as well pleasure you'self now and den. April ain' gwine see you. Not to-day!"

"Somebody'd tell him an' dat would vex him," Leah bemoaned.

But Maum Hannah took her by the arm and looked straight in her eyes. "Honey," she coaxed, "Gawd ain' gwine bless you if you let April suffer you dis way. You an' April all both is too prideful. Take dem teeth off an' rest you' mouth till dis quiltin' is over. It would fret me if you don't."

Screening her mouth with both hands Leah did rid her gums of the offending teeth, but instead of putting them in her apron pocket she laid them carefully in a safe place on the high mantel-shelf.

The room buzzed with chatter. How would such a great noisy gathering ever get straightened out to work? They were as much alike as guinea fowls in a flock, every head tied up turban-fashion, every skirt covered by an apron.

Big Sue welcomed every one with friendliest greetings, and although her breath was short from excitement, she talked gaily and laughed often.

A sudden hush followed a loud clapping of her hands. The closest attention was paid while she appointed Leah and Zeda captains of the first quilts to be laid out. Zeda stepped forward, with a jaunty toss of her head, and, shrugging a lean shoulder, laughed lightly.

"Big Sue is puttin' sinner 'gainst Christian dis mawnin'!"

Leah tried to laugh, her tubby body, bulky as Big Sue's, shook nervously, as her giggling rippled out of her mouth, but her eyes showed no mirth at all.

"You choose first, Leah. You's de foreman's wife."

Leah chose Big Sue.

"Lawd," Zeda threw her head back with a laugh, "Yunnuh two is so big nobody else wouldn' have room to set on a bench 'side you."

The crowd tittered, but Big Sue looked stern.

"Do, Zeda! You has gall enough to talk about bigness? T'ank Gawd, I'm big all de way round like I is." She cast a wry look toward Zeda, then turned her head and winked at the crowd. But Zeda sucked her teeth brazenly. She was satisfied with her shape. She might not look so nice now, but her bigness would soon be shed. Just give her a month or two longer.

"You ought to be shame, wid grown chillen in you' house, an' a grown gal off yonder to college."

"When I git old as you, Big Sue, den I'll stay slim all de time. Don't you fret." Zeda laughed, and chose Gussie, a skinny, undersized, deaf and dumb woman, whose keen eyes plainly did double duty. When Zeda looked toward her and spoke her name, Gussie pushed through the crowd, smiling and making wordless gurgles of pleasure for the compliment Zeda had paid her by choosing her first of all.

"I take Bina next!" Leah called out.

"Bina's a good one for you' quilt. E's a extra fine Christian."

"You better be prayin' you'se'f, Zeda, " Bina came back.

"Who? Me? Lawd, gal, I does pray." Zeda said it seriously, and her look roved around the room. "Sinners is mighty sca'ce at dis quiltin'. Who kin I choose next?" She searched the group.

"Don' take so long, Zeda," Big Sue chided. "Hurry up an' choose. De day is passin'. You an' Gussie is de only two sinners. You' 'bliged to pick a Christian, now."

"Den I'll take Nookie. E's got swift-movin' fingers."

The choosing went on until eight women were picked for each quilt, four to a side. Then the race began.

The two quilt linings, made out of unbleached homespun, were spread on the clean bare floor, and covered over with a smooth layer of cotton.

"How come you got such nice clean cotton to put in you' quilt?" Zeda inquired with an innocent look across at Big Sue.

When Big Sue paid her no heed, she added brazenly, "De cotton April gi' me fo' my quilt was so trashy and dark I had to whip em wid pine-tops half a day to get de dirt out clean enough to use."

Still Big Sue said nothing.

"You must be stand well wid April." Zeda looked at Big Sue with a smile.

Big Sue raised her shoulders up from doubling over, and in a tart tone blurted out, "You talks too much, Zeda. Shut you' mouth and work."

"Who? Me?" Zeda came back pleasantly. "Great Gawd! I was praisin' de whiteness of de cotton, dat was all."

Two of the patch-work covers that Big Sue had fashioned with such pains, stitch by stitch, square by square, were opened out wide and examined and admired.

"Which one you want, Zeda? You take de first pick."

"Lawd, all two is so nice it's hard to say."

Gussie pointed to the "Snake-fence" design, and Zeda took it, leaving the "Star of Bethlehem" for Leah. Both were placed over a cotton-covered lining on the floor, corner to corner, edge to edge, and basted into place. Next, two quilting poles were laid lengthwise beside each quilt, and tacked on with stout ball thread. The quilts were carefully rolled on the poles, and the pole-ends fastened with strong cords to the side-walls. All was ready for the quilting.

Leah's crew beat fixing the quilt on the poles, but the sewing was the tedious part. The stitches must be small, and in smooth rows that ran side by side. They must also be deep enough to hold the cotton fast between the top and the lining.

Little talking was done at first. Minds, as well as eyes, had to watch the needles. Those not quilting in this race stood around the hearth puffing at their pipes, talking, joking, now and then squealing out with merriment.

"Yunnuh watch dem pots," Big Sue cautioned them. "Make Breeze keep wood on de fire. Mind now."

The quilts were rolled up until the quilting poles met, so the sewing started right in the middle, and as the needles left neat stitches, the poles were rolled farther apart, until both quilts were done to the edges. These were carefully turned in and whipped down, with needles running at full racing speed. Zeda's crew finished a full yard ahead. The sinners won. And how they did crow over the others! Deaf and dumb Gussie did her best to boast, but her words were stifled in dreadful choked noises that were hard to bear.

Big Sue put the wild ducks on to roast. They were fat and tender, and already stuffed full of oyster dressing, the same dressing she fixed for the white folks. She said the oysters came from near the beach where the fresh salt tide made them large and juicy.

What a dinner she had! Big Sue was an openhanded woman, for truth.

Some of the farm-hands stopped by on their way home for the noon hour. Coming inside they stood around the fireplace, grinning, joking and smoking the cigarettes they roled with deft fingers.

Everybody was given a pan and spoon. Zeda and Bina helped Big Sue pass around great dishpans of smoking food, and cups of water sweetened with molasses. For a time nothing was said except the exclamations that praised the dinner. Indeed it might have been a wedding feast but for the lack of cake and wine.

The wild ducks, cooked just to a turn, were served last. Their red blood was barely curdled with heat, yet their outsides were rich and brown. Lips smacked. Spoons clattered. Mouths too full dropped crumbs as they munched.

A grand dinner.

"Take you' time, an' chaw," Big Sue bade the guests kindly. "You got plenty o' time to finish de rest o' de quilts befo' night."

As soon as the edge was taken off their appetites they fell to talking. Big Sue did not sit down to eat at all, so busy was she passing around the pans of hot food, and urging the others to fill themselves full.

As more men came by and stopped, the noise waxed louder, until the uproar of shouting and laughter and light-hearted talk seethed thick. When all were filled with Big Sue's good cheer, they got up and went out into the yard to smoke, to catch a little fresh air, and to wash the grease off their fingers. The pans and spoons and tin-cups were stacked up on the water-shelf out of the way where they'd wait to be washed until night.

The quilting was the work in hand now, and when the room was in order again, and the women rested and refreshed, Big Sue called them in to begin on the next set of quilts.

April went riding by on the sorrel colt, on his way back to the field, and Big Sue called him to come in and eat the duck and hot rice she had put aside specially for him. But he eyed her coolly, rode on and left her frowning.

Zeda laughed, and asked Big Sue if April was a boy to hop around at her heels? Didn't she know April had work to do? Important work. The white people made him plantation foreman because they knew they could trust him to look after their interests. He not only worked himself, but he kept the other hands working too. Leah sat silent, making short weak puffs at her pipe.

Maum Hannah's deep sigh broke into the stillness.

"I ever did love boy-chillen, but dey causes a lot o' sorrow. My mammy used to say ev'y boy-child ought to be killed soon as it's born."

"How'd de world go on if people done dat?" Bina asked.

"I dunno. Gawd kin do a lot o' strange t'ings."

This made them all stop and think again.

The kettle sang as steam rushed out of its spout. The flames made a sputtering sound. The benches creaked as the women bent over and rose with their needles. Bina sat up straight, then stretched.

"If all de mens was dead, you could stay in de chu'ch, enty, Zeda?" Bina slurred the words softly.

Zeda came back, "Don' you fret 'bout me, gal. Jake ain' no more to me dan a dead man."

"Yunnah stop right now! Dat's no-manners talk. Jake's a fine man, if e is my gran. I know, by I raise em. When his mammy died an' left em, Jake an' Bully and April was all three de same as twins in my house." Maum Hannah spoke very gravely. Presently she got up and went into the shed-room. She came back smiling, with a folded quilt on her arm. "Le's look at de old Bible quilt, chillen. It'll do yunnuh good."

She held up one corner and motioned to deaf and dumb Gussie to hold up the other so all the squares could be seen. There were twenty, every one a picture out of the Bible. The first one, next to Gussie's hand, was Adam and Eve and the serpent. Adam's shirt was blue, his pants brown, and his head a small patch of yellow. Eve had on a red head-kerchief, a purple wide-skirted dress; and a tall black serpent stood straight up on the end of its tail.

The next square had two men, one standing up, the other fallen down—Cain and Abel. The red patch under Abel was his blood, spilled on the ground by Cain's sin. Maum Hannah pointed out Noah and the Ark; Moses with the tables of stone; the three Hebrew children; David and Goliath; Joseph and Mary and the little baby Jesus; and last of all, Jesus standing alone by the cross. As Maum Hannah took them one by one, all twenty, she told each marvelous story.

The quilters listened with rapt attention. Breeze almost held his breath for fear of missing a word. Sometimes his blood ran hot with wonder, then cold with fear. Many eyes in the room glistened with tears.

The names of God and Jesus were known to Breeze, but he had never understood before that they were real people who could walk and talk. Maum Hannah told about God's strength and power and wisdom, how He knew right then what she was doing and saying. He could see each stitch that was taken in the quilts, whether it was small and deep and honest, or shallow and careless. He wrote everything down in a great book where He kept account of good and evil. Breeze had never dreamed that such things went on around him all the time.

Yet the quilt was made out of pictures of the very things Maum Hannah told. Nobody could doubt that all she said was the truth. In the charmed silence, her words fell clear and earnest. The present was shut out. Breeze's mind went a-roaming with her, back into the days when the world was new and God walked and talked with the children He had so lately made. As she spoke Breeze shivered over those days that were to come when everybody here would be either in Hell or Heaven. It had to be one or the other. There was no place to stop or to hide when death came and knocked at your door. She pointed to Breeze. That same little boy, there in the chimney corner, with his foot tied up, would have to account for all he did! As well as Breeze could understand, Heaven was in the blue sky straight up above the plantation. God sat there on His throne among the stars, while angels, with harps of gold in their hands, sang His praises all day long. Hell was straight down. Underneath. Deep under the earth. Satan lived there with his great fires for ever and ever a-burning on the bodies of sinners piled high up so they could never crumble.

Maum Hannah herself became so moved by the thought of the sufferings of the poor pitiful sinners in Hell, that her voice broke and tears dimmed her eyes, and she pleaded with them all:

"Pray! Chillen! Pray!

"Do try fo' 'scape Hell if you kin!

"Hell is a heat!

"One awful heat!

"We fire ain' got no time wid em!

"Pray! Chillen! Pray! For Gawd's sake, pray!

"When de wind duh whip you

"An' de sun-hot duh burn you

"An' de rain duh wet you,

"All dem say, Pray! Do try fo' 'scape Hell if you kin!"

On the way home through the dusk Breeze stopped short in his tracks more than once, for terror seized him at the bare rustle of a bird's wing against a dry leaf. When the gray shadow of a rabbit darted across the path and the sight of a glowworm's eye gleamed up from the ground, Big Sue stopped too. And breathing fast with anxiety, cried out:

"Do, Jedus! Lawd! Dat rabbit went leftward. A bad luck t'ing! Put dem t'ings down! Chunk two sticks behind em. Is you see anyt'ing strange, Breeze?"

She sidled up close to him and whispered the question.

Breeze stared hard into the deepening twilight. The black shadows were full of dark dreadful things that pressed close to the ground, creeping slowly, terribly. The tree branches rocked, the leaves whispered sharply, the long gray moss streamed toward them.

"Le's run, Cun Big Sue." Breeze leaped with a quick hop ahead, but her powerful hand clutched his shoulder. "Looka here, boy! I'll kill you to-night if you leave me. No tellin' what kind o' sperits is walkin'. I kin run when I's empty-handed, but loaded down wid all dese t'ings a snail could ketch me! You git behind me on de path."

The black smoke rising out of the chimney made a great serpent that stood on the end of its tail. For a minute Breeze was unable to speak. His heart throbbed with heavy blows, for not only did that snake serpent lean and bend and reach threateningly, but something high and black and shapeless stood in front of Big Sue's cabin, whose whitewashed walls behind it made it look well-nigh as tall as a pine tree. It might be the Devil! Or Death! Or God! He gave a scream and clung to Big Sue as the figure took a step toward them.

"Yunnuh is late!" April's voice boomed out.

"Lawd!" Big Sue fairly shouted. "I was sho' you was a plat-eye. You scard me half to death! Man! I couldn' see no head on you no matter how hard I look. How come you went inside my house with me not home?"

April grunted. "You better be glad! I had a hard time drivin' a bat out o' you' house."

"A bat!" Big Sue shrieked with terror. "How come a bat in my house? A bat is de child of de devil."

April declared the bat had squeaked and grinned and chattered in his face until he mighty nigh got scared himself.

"Lawd! Wha's gwine happen now? A bat inside my house! An' look how de fire's smokin'!"

She hurried Breeze off to bed in the shed-room whose darkness was streaked with wavering firelight that fell through the cracks in the wall. Fear kept him awake until he put his head under the covers and shut out all sight and sound and thought.

He was roused by a knock on the front door. Big Sue made no answer, and another knock made by the knuckles of a strong hand was followed by a loud crying, "Open dis door, I tell you! I know April's right in dere!" This was followed by the thud of a kick, but no answer came from inside. Breeze could not have spoken to save his life, for sheer terror held him crouched under the quilts and his tongue was too weak and dry to move.

Where in God's world was Big Sue? The first of those knocks should have waked her. Sleep never did fasten her eyelids down very tight, yet with all this deafening racket, she stayed dumb. Had she gone off and left Breeze by himself? The voice calling at the door sounded like a woman's voice at first, but now it deepened with hoarse fury and snarled and growled and threatened, calling Big Sue filthy names. Breeze knew then for certain it was some evil thing. His flesh crept loose from his bones. His blood ran cold and weak. He realized Big Sue was not at home. Maybe she was dead, in her bed! The thought was so terrible that in desperation he lifted up his head and yelled:

"Who dat?"

At once the dreadful answer came.

"Who dat say 'who dat'?" Then a silence, for Breeze could utter no other word.

Outside the wind caught at the trees and thrashed their leaves, then came inside to rustle the papers on the cabin's walls, and whisper weird terrible things through the cracks. The thing that had knocked on the door was walking away. Its harsh breathing was hushed into sobs and soft moans that made Breeze's heart sink still deeper with horror.

For a minute every noise in the world lulled. Nothing stirred except the ghastly tremor that shook Breeze's body from his covered-up head to the heels doubled up under his cold hips.

A sudden fearful battering in company with despairing howls, crashed at the door! It would soon break down! There was no time to waste putting on clothes! Hopping up into the cold darkness, Breeze eased the back door open and slipped into the night.

The horrible door-splitting blows went right on. Thank God, somebody was coming. Running, with a torch. Breeze forgot that snakes were walking, and leaped through the bushes over ground that felt unsteady to his flying feet. His heart swelled with joy and relief, for the man hurrying toward the cabin lighting his way with a fat lightwood torch was Uncle Bill. Twice Breeze opened his mouth to call out, but the only sound he could make was a whispered—"Uncle Bill—Uncle Bill!"

Following the torch's light he could see a black woman cutting the door down with an ax. Who in God's name would dare do such a thing? Uncle Bill walked right up to her and shook her soundly by the shoulder.

"What is you a-doin', Leah? Is you gone plumb crazy? Gi' me dat ax!" He jerked the ax from her hands and she began shrieking afresh, and trying to push him back. But she couldn't budge him one inch. Holding her off, with his free hand he made a proper, polite knock, although the door was split and the dim firelight shone through its new-made cracks.

"Dis is me, Bill, Miss Big Sue," he called out, a stern note deepening his voice.

Leah shrilled out harshly. "You better open dis door! You low-down black buzzard hussy! You wait till I gits my hands on you' throat! You won' fool wid my husband no mo' in dis world!"

Fully dressed and quite calm Big Sue appeared. She answered with mild astonishment:

"Why, Leah! How come you makin' all dis fuss? You must want to wake up de whole plantation? You ought to be shamed. I never see such a no-manners 'oman!"

"Whe's April?" Leah howled. "Whe's April, I tell you? Don' you cut no crazy wid me to-night! I'll kill you sho' as you do!"

"Fo' Gawd's sake, Leah! Shut you' mouth! I dunno nuttin' 'bout April. You is too sickenin'! Always runnin' round to somebody's house a-lookin' fo' April!"

"Yes, I look fo' em. You had em here too! See his hat yonder on de floor right now! You fat black devil!" Seizing Big Sue's kerchiefed head with both hands Leah tried to choke her, but Big Sue wrenched herself loose and with a wicked laugh raised one fat leg and gave Leah a kick in the middle of her body that sent her backward with a slam against the wall.

"You'd choke me, would you? I'll tear de meat off you' bones!" Big Sue screamed, but Leah crumpled sidewise and fell flat on the floor, her eyes lifeless, her face stiffened.

Big Sue had roused into fury. She staggered forward and bent over and rained blows with both fists on Leah's silent mouth, until Uncle Bill grappled her around her huge waist and dragged her to the other side of the room.

Big Sue bellowed. "You'd choke me, enty? You blue-gummed pizen-jawed snake! Gawd done right to salivate you an' make you' teeth drop out."

For all the signs of life she gave, Leah may as well have been dead. She lay there on the floor, limp and dumb, even after Uncle Bill took the bucketful of water from the shelf and doused her with it. She didn't even catch her breath. Uncertain what to do, Uncle Bill knelt over her and called her name.

"Leah! Leah! Don't you die here on dis floor. Leah! Open you' eyes. I know good and well you's playin' 'possum."

Except for the fire's crackling and the low chirping of one lone cricket, the stillness of death was in the room.

"Put on you' shirt and pants, Breeze. Run tell April Leah is done faint off. E must come here quick as e kin."

The darkness of the night was terrible as Breeze ran through it toward the Quarters. A cedar limb creaked mournfully as the wind wrung it back and forth. Its crying was like sorrowful calls for aid. Breeze tried to hurry, to make his legs run faster, but they were ready to give way and fall. His feet stumbled, his throat choked until he could scarcely breathe. His brain wheeled and rattled inside his skull. How horrible Death is!

A few stars twinkled bright away up in the sky, but the waving tree-tops made a thick black smoke that covered the yellow moon. High-tide glistened in the darkness, all but ready to turn by now. Leah's soul would go out with it if something wasn't done to help her.

Lord how awful her eyeballs were, rolled back so far in her head! Jesus, have mercy! The thought of them made Breeze senseless with terror. Tears gushed from his own eyes and blinded him.

April was not at home, and Breeze raced back, but already Leah was coming to. She lay on the floor, her fat face, black as tar against the whiteness of the pillow under it now, was set and furrowed. Her toothless jaws moved with mute words, as if she talked with some one the others could not see. She kept fumbling with the red charm-string tied around her neck, as her dull eyes rolled slowly from one face to the other.

Breeze longed to fling himself on the bed and cover up his head, but Big Sue sat storming and panting with fury. Leah ought to be ashamed of herself, running over the country at night trying to bring disgracement on her.

"Whyn't you answer Leah when e knocked?" Uncle Bill asked her.

Big Sue jumped at him angrily. "How'd I know Leah wasn' some robber come to cut my throat? Just 'cause Leah is married to de foreman an' livin' in a bigger house dan my own, an' wearin' finer clothes, dat don' gi' em no right to break down my door wid a' ax! No. Leah ain' no white 'oman even if e do buy medicine out de sto'. No wonder e got salivate. Gawd done right to make dat medicine loosen all Leah's teeth an' prize 'em out so e ain' got none to be a-bitin' people up wid. T'ank Gawd! Bought ones can' bite. I wish all e finger-nails would drop off! E toe-nails too! Leah's a dangerous 'oman. E ain' safe to be loose in dis country. No. Leah'd kill you quick as look at you!"

Everyday Use

Alice Walker

I WILL WAIT FOR HER in the yard that Maggie and I made so clean and wavy yesterday afternoon. A yard like this is more comfortable than most people know. It is not just a yard. It is like an extended living room. When the hard clay is swept clean as a floor and the fine sand around the edges lined with tiny, irregular grooves, anyone can come and sit and look up into the elm tree and wait for the breezes that never come inside the house.

Maggie will be nervous until after her sister goes: she will stand hopelessly in corners, homely and ashamed of the burn scars down her arms and legs, eying her sister with a mixture of envy and awe. She thinks her sister has held life always in the palm of one hand, that "no" is a word the world never learned to say to her.

You've no doubt seen those TV shows where the child who has "made it" is confronted, as a surprise, by her own mother and father, tottering in weakly from backstage. (A pleasant surprise, of course: What would they do if parent and child came on the show only to curse out and insult each other?) On TV mother and child embrace and smile into each other's faces. Sometimes the mother and father weep, the child wraps them in her arms and leans across the table to tell how she would not have made it without their help. I have seen these programs.

Sometimes I dream a dream in which Dee and I are suddenly brought together on a TV program of this sort. Out of a dark and soft-seated limousine I am ushered into a bright room filled with many people. There I meet a smiling, gray, sporty man like Johnny Carson who shakes my hand and tells me what a fine girl I have. Then we are on the stage and Dee is embracing me with tears in her eyes. She pins on my dress a large orchid, even though she has told me once that she thinks orchids are tacky flowers.

In real life I am a large, big-boned woman with rough, man-working hands. In the winter I wear flannel nightgowns to bed and overalls during the day. I can kill and clean a hog as mercilessly as a man. My fat keeps me hot in zero weather. I can work outside all day, breaking ice to get water for washing; I can eat pork liver cooked over the open fire minutes after it comes steaming from the hog. One winter I knocked a bull calf straight in the brain between the eyes with a sledge hammer and had the meat hung up to chill before nightfall. But of course all this does not show on television. I am the way my daughter would want me to be: a hundred pounds lighter, my skin like an uncooked barley pancake. My hair glistens in the hot bright lights. Johnny Carson has much to do to keep up with my quick and witty tongue.

But that is a mistake. I know even before I wake up. Who ever knew a Johnson with a quick tongue? Who can even imagine me looking a strange white man in the eye? It seems to me I have talked to them always with one foot raised in flight, with my head turned in whichever way is farthest from them. Dee, though. She would always look anyone in the eye. Hesitation was no part of her nature.

"How do I look, Mama?" Maggie says, showing just enough of her thin body enveloped in pink skirt and red blouse for me to know she's there, almost hidden by the door.

"Come out into the yard," I say.

Have you ever seen a lame animal, perhaps a dog run over by some careless person rich enough to own a car, sidle up to someone who is ignorant enough to be kind to him? That is the way my Maggie walks. She has been like this, chin on chest, eyes on ground, feet in shuffle, ever since the fire that burned the other house to the ground.

Dee is lighter than Maggie, with nicer hair and a fuller figure. She's a woman now, though sometimes I forget. How long ago was it that the other house burned? Ten, twelve years? Sometimes I can still hear the flames and feel Maggie's arms sticking to me, her hair smoking and her dress falling off her in little black papery flakes. Her eyes seemed stretched open, blazed open by the flames reflected in them. And Dee. I see her standing off under the sweet gum tree she used to dig gum out of; a look of concentration on her face as she watched the last dingy gray board of the house fall in toward the red-hot brick chimney. Why don't you do a dance around the ashes? I'd wanted to ask her. She had hated the house that much.

I used to think she hated Maggie, too. But that was before we raised money, the church and me, to send her to Augusta to school. She used to read to us without pity; forcing words, lies, other folks' habits, whole lives upon us two, sitting trapped and ignorant underneath her voice. She washed us in a river of make-believe, burned us with a lot of knowledge we didn't necessarily need to know. Pressed us to her with the serious way she read, to shove us away at just the moment, like dimwits, we seemed about to understand.

Dee wanted nice things. A yellow organdy dress to wear to her graduation from high school; black pumps to match a green suit she'd made from an old suit somebody gave me. She was determined to stare down any disaster in her efforts. Her eyelids would not flicker for minutes at a time. Often I fought off the temptation to shake her. At sixteen she had a style of her own: and knew what style was.

I never had an education myself. After second grade the school was closed down. Don't ask my why: in 1927 colored asked fewer questions than they do now. Sometimes Maggie reads to me. She stumbles along good-naturedly but can't see well. She knows she is not bright. Like good looks and money, quickness passes her by. She will marry John Thomas (who has mossy teeth in an earnest face) and then I'll be free to sit here and I guess just sing church songs to myself. Although I never was a good singer. Never could carry a tune. I was always better at a man's job. I used to love to milk till I was hooked in the side in '49. Cows are soothing and slow and don't bother you, unless you try to milk them the wrong way.

I have deliberately turned my back on the house. It is three rooms, just like the one that burned, except the roof is tin; they don't make shingle roofs any more. There are no real windows, just some holes cut in the sides, like the portholes in a ship, but not round and not square, with rawhide holding the shutters up on the outside. This house is in a pasture, too, like the other one. No doubt when Dee sees it she will want to tear it down. She wrote me once that no matter where we "choose" to live, she will manage to come see us. But she will never bring her friends. Maggie and I thought about this and Maggie asked me, "Mama, when did Dee ever *have* any friends?"

She had a few. Furtive boys in pink shirts hanging about on washday after school. Nervous girls who never laughed. Impressed with her they worshiped the well-turned phrase, the cute shape, the scalding humor that erupted like bubbles in lye. She read to them.

When she was courting Jimmy T she didn't have much time to pay to us, but turned all her faultfinding power on him. He *flew* to marry a cheap city girl from a family of ignorant flashy people. She hardly had time to recompose herself.

When she comes I will meet—but there they are!

Maggie attempts to make a dash for the house, in her shuffling way, but I stay her with my hand. "Come back here," I say. And she stops and tries to dig a well in the sand with her toe.

It is hard to see them clearly through the strong sun. But even the first glimpse of leg out of the car tells me it is Dee. Her feet were always neat-looking, as if God himself had shaped them with a certain style. From the other side of the car comes a short, stocky man. Hair is all over his head a foot long and hanging from his chin like a kinky mule tail. I hear Maggie suck in her breath. "Uhnnnh," is what it sounds like. Like when you see the wriggling end of a snake just in front of your foot on the road. "Uhnnnh."

Dee next. A dress down to the ground, in this hot weather. A dress so loud it hurts my eyes. There are yellows and oranges enough to throw back the light of the sun. I feel my whole face warming from the heat waves it throws out. Earrings gold, too, and hanging down to her shoulders. Bracelets dangling and making noises when she moves her arm up to shake the folds of the dress out of her armpits. The dress is loose and flows, and as she walks closer, I like it. I hear Maggie go "Uhnnnh" again. It is her sister's hair. It stands straight up like the wool on a sheep. It is black as night and around the edges are two long pigtails that rope about like small lizards disappearing behind her ears.

"Wa-su-zo-Tean-o!" she says, coming on in that gliding way the dress makes her move. The short stocky fellow with the hair to his navel is all grinning and he follows up with "Asalamalakim, my mother and sister!" He moves to hug Maggie but she falls back, right up against the back of my chair. I feel her trembling there and when I look up I see the perspiration falling off her chin.

"Don't get up," says Dee. Since I am stout it takes something of a push. You can see me trying to move a second or two before I make it. She turns, showing white heels through her sandals, and goes back to the car. Out she peeks next with a Polaroid. She stoops down quickly and lines up picture after picture of me sitting there in front of the house with Maggie cowering behind me. She never takes a shot without making sure the house is included. When a cow comes nibbling around the edge of the yard she snaps it and me and Maggie *and* the house. Then she puts the Polaroid in the back seat of the car, and comes up and kisses me on the forehead.

Meanwhile Asalamalakim is going through motions with Maggie's hand. Maggie's hand is as limp as a fish, and probably as cold, despite the sweat, and she keeps trying to pull it back. It looks like Asalamalakim wants to shake hands but wants to do it fancy. Or maybe he don't know how people shake hands. Anyhow, he soon gives up on Maggie.

"Well," I say. "Dee."

"No, Mama," she says. "Not 'Dee,' Wangero Leewanika Kemanjo!"

"What happened to 'Dee'?" I wanted to know.

"She's dead," Wangero said. "I couldn't bear it any longer, being named after the people who oppress me."

"You know as well as me you was named after your aunt Dicie," I said. Dicie is my sister. She named Dee. We called her "Big Dee" after Dee was born.

"But who was *she* named after?" asked Wangero.

"I guess after Grandma Dee," I said.

"And who was she named after?" asked Wangero.

"Her mother," I said, and saw Wangero was getting tired. "That's about as far back as I can trace it," I said. Though, in fact, I probably could have carried it back beyond the Civil War through the branches.

"Well," said Asalamalakim, "there you are."

"Uhnnnh," I heard Maggie say.

"There I was not," I said, "before 'Dicie' cropped up in our family, so why should I try to trace it that far back?"

He just stood there grinning, looking down on me like somebody inspecting a Model A car. Every once in a while he and Wangero sent eye signals over my head.

"How do you pronounce this name?" I asked.

"You don't have to call me by it if you don't want to," said Wangero.

"Why shouldn't I?" I asked. "If that's what you want us to call you, we'll call you."

"I know it might sound awkward at first," said Wangero.

"I'll get used to it," I said. "Ream it out again."

Well, soon we got the name out of the way. Asalamalakim had a name twice as long and three times as hard. After I tripped over it two or three times he told me to just call him Hakim-a-barber. I wanted to ask him was he a barber, but I didn't really think he was, so I didn't ask.

"You must belong to those beef-cattle peoples down the road," I said. They said "Asalamalakim" when they met you, too, but they didn't shake hands. Always too busy: feeding the cattle, fixing the fences, putting up salt-lick shelters, throwing down hay. When the white folks poisoned some of the herd the men stayed up all night with rifles in their hands. I walked a mile and a half just to see the sight.

Hakim-a-barber said, "I accept some of their doctrines, but farming and raising cattle is not my style." (They didn't tell me, and I didn't ask, whether Wangero (Dee) had really gone and married him.)

We sat down to eat and right away he said he didn't eat collards and pork was unclean. Wangero, though, went on through the chitlins and corn bread, the greens and everything else. She talked a blue streak over the sweet potatoes. Everything delighted her. Even the fact that we still used the benches her daddy made for the table when we couldn't affort to buy chairs.

"Oh, Mama!" she cried. Then turned to Hakim-a-barber. "I never knew how lovely these benches are. You can feel the rump prints," she said, running her hands underneath her and along the bench. Then she gave a sigh and her hand closed over Grandma Dee's butter dish. "That's it!" she said. "I knew there was something I wanted to ask you if I could have." She jumped up from the table and went over in the corner where the churn stood, the milk in it clabber by now. She looked at the churn and looked at it.

"This churn top is what I need," she said. "Didn't Uncle Buddy whittle it out of a tree you all used to have?"

"Yes," I said.

"Un huh," she said happily. "And I want the dasher, too."

"Uncle Buddy whittle that, too?" asked the barber.

Dee (Wangero) looked up at me.

"Aunt Dee's first husband whittled the dash," said Maggie so low you almost couldn't hear her. "His name was Henry, but they called him Stash."

"Maggie's brain is like an elephant's," Wangero said, laughing. "I

can use the churn top as a centerpiece for the alcove table," she said,
sliding a plate over the churn, "and I'll think of something artistic to do
with the dasher."

When she finished wrapping the dasher the handle stuck out. I took
it for a moment in my hands. You didn't even have to look close to see
where hands pushing the dasher up and down to make butter had left a
kind of sink in the wood. In fact, there were a lot of small sinks; you
could see where thumbs and fingers had sunk into the wood. It was
beautiful light yellow wood, from a tree that grew in the yard where Big
Dee and Stash had lived.

After dinner Dee (Wangero) went to the trunk at the foot of my bed
and started rifling through it. Maggie hung back in the kitchen over the
dishpan. Out came Wangero with two quilts. They had been pieced by
Grandma Dee and then Big Dee and me had hung them on the quilt
frames on the front porch and quilted them. One was in the Lone Star
pattern. The other was Walk Around the Mountain. In both of them
were scraps of dresses Grandma Dee had worn fifty and more years ago.
Bits and pieces of Grandpa Jarrell's Paisley shirts. And one teeny faded
blue piece, about the size of a penny matchbox, that was from Great
Grandpa Ezra's uniform that he wore in the Civil War.

"Mama," Wangro said sweet as a bird. "Can I have these old quilts?"

I heard something fall in the kitchen, and a minute later the kitchen
door slammed.

"Why don't you take one or two of the others?" I asked. "These old
things was just done by me and Big Dee from some tops your grandma
pieced before she died."

"No," said Wangero. "I don't want those. They are stitched around
the borders by machine."

"That'll make them last better," I said.

"That's not the point," said Wangero. "These are all pieces of
dresses Grandma used to wear. She did all this stitching by hand. Imagine!" She held the quilts securely in her arms, stroking them.

"Some of the pieces, like those lavender ones, come from old clothes
her mother handed down to her," I said, moving up to touch the quilts.
Dee (Wangero) moved back just enough so that I couldn't reach the
quilts. They already belonged to her.

"Imagine!" she breathed again, clutching them closely to her bosom.

"The truth is," I said, "I promised to give them quilts to Maggie, for
when she marries John Thomas."

She gasped like a bee had stung her.

"Maggie can't appreciate these quilts!" she said. "She'd probably be backward enough to put them to everyday use."

"I reckon she would," I said. "God knows I been saving 'em for long enough with nobody using 'em. I hope she will!" I didn't want to bring up how I had offered Dee (Wangero) a quilt when she went away to college. Then she had told they were old-fashioned, out of style.

"But they're *priceless*!" she was saying now, furiously; for she has a temper. "Maggie would put them on the bed and in five years they'd be in rags. Less than that!"

"She can always make some more," I said. "Maggie knows how to quilt."

Dee (Wangero) looked at me with hatred. "You just will not understand. The point is these quilts, *these* quilts!"

"Well," I said, stumped. "What would *you* do with them?"

"Hang them," she said. As if that was the only thing you *could* do with quilts.

Maggie by now was standing in the door. I could almost hear the sound her feet made as they scraped over each other.

"She can have them, Mama," she said, like somebody used to never winning anything, or having anything reserved for her. "I can 'member Grandma Dee without the quilts."

I looked at her hard. She had filled her bottom lip with checkerberry snuff and gave her face a kind of dopey, hangdog look. It was Grandma Dee and Big Dee who taught her how to quilt herself. She stood there with her scarred hands hidden in the folds of her skirt. She looked at her sister with something like fear but she wasn't mad at her. This was Maggie's portion. This was the way she knew God to work.

When I looked at her like that something hit me in the top of my head and ran down to the soles of my feet. Just like when I'm in church and the spirit of God touches me and I get happy and shout. I did something I never done before: hugged Maggie to me, then dragged her on into the room, snatched the quilts out of Miss Wangero's hands and dumped them into Maggie's lap. Maggie just sat there on my bed with her mouth open.

"Take one or two of the others," I said to Dee.

But she turned without a word and went out to Hakim-a-barber.

"You just don't understand," she said, as Maggie and I came out to the car.

"What don't I understand?" I wanted to know.

"Your heritage," she said, And then she turned to Maggie, kissed her, and said, "You ought to try to make something of yourself, too, Maggie. It's really a new day for us. But from the way you and Mama still live you'd never know it."

She put on some sunglasses that hid everything above the tip of her nose and chin.

Maggie smiled; maybe at the sunglasses. But a real smile, not scared. After we watched the car dust settle I asked Maggie to bring me a dip of snuff. And then the two of us sat there just enjoying, until it was time to go in the house and go to bed.

Bible Quilt, circa 1900

Jane Wilson Joyce

HARRIET POWERS
stitched the Scripture
as she saw it.

With the joyful animals
dancing in the dawn
of the newmade world, she put
the independent hog
that ran five hundred miles
from Georgia to Virginia.
Her name was Betts.

With Adam and Eve,
the falling of the Stars
in 1833. With Jonah and Moses,
Cold Thursday
when the bluebirds died,
and a woman froze
praying at her gate,
and a mule's breath
fell to icicles.

Christ crucified,
Mary and Martha weeping.

May 19, 1780
when the sun went off

to darkness
the seven stars
were seen at noon,
the cattle went to bed,
the chickens to roost,
and in that Dark Day
a trumpet sounded.
Everywhere
the unwinking eye
of God, the merciful
hand outspread.

Owing
to the hardness of the times,
Harriet Powers
asked ten dollars for that quilt.

Owing to the hardness of the times,
she took
five.

Handed it over
to Jennie Smith
wrapped in two sacks
like a baby; like a mother,
a slave mother,
Harriet slipped away to visit
her quilt. She was
"only in some measure consoled"
by the white woman's promise of
scraps.

How to Make an American Quilt

Otto Whitney

T HERE IS A South African myth regarding a being called *Sikhamba-nge-nyanga*, which translated means "She-who-walks-by-moonlight." This is what is said of her: *It is man's privilege to gaze upon her.* But when he violates *the customs which protect and nourish her, she returns to nature.* In order to ensure her survival, she must be allowed to walk freely, untouched and unmolested.

A Guyanese story says of black slaves that the only way they can be delivered from "massa's clutch" is to *see the extra brightness of the moon in their lives. The darkness will always be there, but they can use the light of the moon as hope.* The light of the moon. The dancing buffalo gal with the hole in her stocking.

One can survive without liberation but one cannot live without freedom. You know it is essential to find one's freedom.

Here are some things you know:

That the English adopted slavery from the Spanish. Found it useful when the white English were no longer motivated to come to the New World. Some masters were unnecessarily cruel, running their "investments" into the ground (you are appalled to learn that in Brazil and the Caribbean this was considered sound business sense). Squeezing every drop. Other masters were benevolent, treating their slaves with a modicum of kindness. Of course, words like *kindness* and *fairness* lose all meaning in a labor system founded on the purchase of human flesh, based on involuntary bondage. To paraphrase a Famous Writer: A master is a master is a master.

Female slaveholders are called mistresses.

A sewing slave in the antebellum South could be had for $1,800. Anything less would be a steal—worth gloating over with the neighboring slaveholders. You get the idea.

Most slave owners did not have fancy Taras and owned just one or two slaves. This meant a female slave could work in the fields all day, only to fill her nights with mountains of sewing and quilting for the family. A slave was fortunate to be in a household that allowed her specialized work like sewing, exclusively. But a word like *fortunate* tends to lose its meaning in a context such as this.

You personally find the piecing together of the work tedious—arduous and dull. Likewise for cutting the pieces, securing the batting between the back and top work. But you find the designing and creation of the quilt theme exhilarating. As if you are talking beauty with your hands. Make yourself heard in a wild profusion of colors, shapes, themes, and dreams with your fingertips. The tedium of quilt construction some days can make you cry; you long to express yourself. To shout out loud in silk and bits of old scarves.

You know that it was not uncommon during the Depression for a wealthy woman to hire out to a poor woman the drudgery of quilting. And that that same wealthy woman could still enter that quilt in a competition solely under her name—no thank-you or acknowledgment to anyone else.

You hold no stock in the prefab, purchased-pattern quilt. You do not understand the point of stitching without your own heart-involvement. Without your ideas incorporated into the work, it is just an exercise, something to fill the long evening spent without companionship.

More things you know:

That only you can tell your story.

That most abolitionists were women striving for suffrage as well. That a significant number of abolitionists were prejudiced against the Negro they fought to free; it was the institution they considered immoral. So the word *free* begins to lose its meaning in a context such as this.

So little in your life has changed. Despite the civil rights movement. Here is an incident emblematic of that time: Myrlie Evers, the widow of Medgar Evers, wanted to tell President Kennedy, at the funeral of her much-loved husband, that she was devastated; that her husband fought for his country in World War II and came home to be a second-class citizen; that she was furious he had been murdered trying to secure his constitutional rights for himself and his people. But all she said, finally, when Kennedy asked her how she was doing, was *Fine, thank you, Mr. President.* This impresses you; this is something you understand without effort. That the story of your life and history should be so plain, so obvious, yet you will be asked to explain it. You, too, can imagine shrugging your shoulders or registering the same reaction to such an inquiry. This is what it is like with your quilts; you simply design and stitch them. You say nothing more than what you have said with fabric and thread.

Here is a glossary of some of the quilts you have designed:

Stars Like Diamonds: Beauty's hands fill with them, as she cries her disloyal tears. You think that tears of diamonds have no value when shed falsely. Embroider the tears with silver thread that was left over from an evening gown made for the lady of the house.

Winter Wheat: Do not use a repeating pattern but instead fill the pale blue field with thin, pliant stocks that undulate in the cool wind. Use blue denim, cotton, down, and flannel from farmer's clothing to comprise the wheat, earth, and sky. You are both drawn to and repelled by agriculture.

Pomegranate Fish: Dyed natural linen for texture, deep red-purple. Fish that swim in blue water; faceted beads of antique garnets circle your neck. Refracts sunlight, calls to mind your own mother, now gone.

Moving by the Light of the Moon: The moment he wanted you. You did not know him, nor did he know you. Even after, he did not know you. Batik cotton allows for the color of the moonlight through the trees. Indigo silk spans the night sky. We all crave the human embrace. We cannot guard our hearts with vigilance.

The Life Before: Reminder of ancestors. What cannot be told to someone who does not want to listen or does not express curiosity. You feel better when you hold the story patches between your fingers. Use yarn, shredded curtain fabric, yards of amethyst satin.

Forest Leaves: A childhood quilt for your daughter. A great and powerful trunk surrounded by swirling leaves in hues of green: hunter, kelly, verdant, grass, dark-green-almost-black. Bull Connor turned hoses on protesters in Birmingham, with water pressure great enough to tear the bark from a tree, roll a small girl down the main street. Not for your child; not for Marianna. Leaves are appliqué.

Broken Star: Traditional pattern made from print fabric on a field of peach. You wanted to study the stars. They made you feel whole. The quilting pattern is of tiny hawk moons.

Blue Moon: That which is rare and hopeful. Comes along when it is the second full moon within the same month. More indigo. Appliqué a

Spanish fan hovering in the sky. With trails of gold and scarlet, as if flung by a dancer.

Friendship Across Time and Distance: Many colors, dyed cotton, scraps of royal-blue velvet, heart of pink muslin. Understand that friendship arrives from the least likely sources and flourishes in the least likely locations. Understand that someone can know you very well though you have not told her about yourself. The base is from bleached white and amber cloth.

Many Shoes: Also for your daughter. Sarah Grimké said, *May the points of our needles prick the slave owners' conscience*. And a quilted needle book made to look like shoes said, *Trample not on the oppressed*. Your daughter will not be trampled upon. Your daughter will travel distances.

A Profusion of Hearts: Pale red satin; appliqués of wings and wheat fields shine golden across the work. This is a moment of love made for Pauline, Marianna, Glady Joe. Imported Chinese embroidery thread; you did all the work on this quilt alone, beginning to end. The tedious next to the inspired. It never felt like work.

When you embark upon a quilting project, you must decide between traditionally American designs using print fabric and the Amish or Hawaiian style of solid blocks, appliquéd in contrasting colors. You are philosophically drawn to the Hawaiian way, because they believe it is bad luck to appropriate another's design, to tell another's story. Hawaiian women learned quilting from white Christian missionaries. Before the missionaries arrived, the Hawaiians had their own way of making garments, which left no excess material. Nothing with which to make a quilt.

The Hawaiian women shunned the quilting bee as soon as they were proficient in the skill, preferring solitude and secrecy. You know in your own life that the quilt made solely by your hand, beginning to end, is very different than those made at Glady Joe's house. Even down to the length of the stitches.

You should share the work but not the idea behind it. You understand this. But in a small, close circle it is difficult to do this. You trust the Hawaiian notion that to share your personal pattern is to share your soul. To compromise your power.

You also understand the Hawaiian woman's perplexity with the concept of sewing and leaving remnants of excess material as well as her rejection of group quilting. (Another concept introduced by the Christian missionaries.) You comprehend that need for solitude. Or for a handmade garment to use all the cloth with nothing left over.

And it seems to you a good idea to limit your "sharing" with the other women, and expect they should see that, too, with you. Do not share.

Many years ago a visitor to Hawaii bought two quilts, took them home to the mainland, copied their designs, and entered them under her own name in a contest. Which she won.

You are sad for the winner of the contest, because she "borrowed" someone else's story and fashioned it as her own. Sorry because she was rewarded by judges who did not understand that these quilts were not truly her own. The loss of power this entailed on the part of the Hawaiian woman; this loss of her history by having another woman appropriate it, in turn, increasing the second woman's already estimable social strength through stealing these designs. Increasing her own power. On your back. At your expense. You feel it most profoundly.

IV
WHEEL OF MYSTERY
Stories of Mystery and Murder

Rose of Sharon

Jane Wilson Joyce

MY WHOLE LIFE is in that quilt.
All my joys, and all my sorrows
stitched into those little pieces.

When I was proud of the boys,
and when I was downright provoked.
When the girls annoyed me,
and when they warmed my heart.

And John, too.
He was stitched into that quilt,
him and all the years
we were married.
The times I sat there
loving him, hating him,
as I pieced the patches
together.

It took me more than twenty years,
nearly twenty-five, I reckon,
in the evenings, after supper
when the children were all put to bed.

I tremble sometimes
when I remember
what that quilt knows.

Trifles

Susan Glaspell

COUNTY ATTORNEY GEORGE HENDERSON
SHERIFF HENRY PETERS
LEWIS HALE, *a neighboring farmer*
MRS. PETERS
MRS. HALE

The kitchen in the now abandoned farmhouse of JOHN WRIGHT, *a gloomy kitchen, and left without having been put in order—unwashed pans under the sink, a loaf of bread outside the breadbox, a dish towel on the table—other signs of incompleted work. At the rear the outer door opens and the* SHERIFF *comes in followed by the* COUNTY ATTORNEY *and* HALE. *The* SHERIFF *and* HALE *are men in middle life, the* COUNTY ATTORNEY *is a young man; all are much bundled up and go at once to the stove. They are followed by two women—the* SHERIFF's *wife first; she is a slight wiry woman, a thin nervous face.* MRS. HALE *is larger and would ordinarily be called more comfortable looking, but she is disturbed now and looks fearfully about as she enters. The women have come in slowly, and stand close together near the door.*

COUNTY ATTORNEY [*rubbing his hands*]. This feels good. Come up to the fire, ladies.

MRS. PETERS [*after taking a step forward*]. I'm not—cold.

SHERIFF [*unbuttoning his overcoat and stepping away from the stove as if to mark the beginning of official business*]. Now, Mr. Hale, before we move things about, you explain to Mr. Henderson just what you saw when you came here yesterday morning.

COUNTY ATTORNEY. By the way, has anything been moved? Are things just as you left them yesterday?

SHERIFF [*looking about*]. It's just the same. When it dropped below zero
last night I thought I'd better send Frank out this morning to make a
fire for us—no use getting pneumonia with a big case on, but I told
him not to touch anything except the stove—and you know Frank.

COUNTY ATTORNEY. Somebody should have been left here yesterday.

SHERIFF. Oh—yesterday. When I had to send Frank to Morris Center for
that man who went crazy—I want you to know I had my hands full
yesterday, I knew you could get back from Omaha by today and as
long as I went over everything here myself——

COUNTY ATTORNEY. Well, Mr. Hale, tell me what happened when you
came here yesterday morning.

HALE. Harry and I had started to town with a load of potatoes. We came
along the road from my place and as I got here I said, "I'm going to see
if can't get John Wright to go in with me on a party telephone." I
spoke to Wright about it once before and he put me off, saying folks
talked too much anyway, and all he asked was peace and quiet—I
guess you know how much he talked himself; but I thought maybe if I
went to the house and talked about it before his wife, though I said to
Harry that I didn't know as what his wife wanted made much difference to John——

COUNTY ATTORNEY. Let's talk about that later, Mr. Hale. I do want to
talk about that, but tell now just what happened when you got to the
house.

HALE. I didn't hear or see anything; I knocked at the door, and still it
was all quiet inside. I knew they must be up, it was past eight o'clock.
So I knocked again, and I thought I heard somebody say, "Come in."
I wasn't sure, I'm not sure yet, but I opened the door—this door [*indi-
cating the door by which the two women are standing*] and there in that
rocker—[*pointing to it*] sat Mrs. Wright.

[*They all look at the rocker.*]

COUNTY ATTORNEY. What—was she doing?

HALE. She was rockin' back and forth. She had her apron in her hand
and was kind of—pleating it.

COUNTY ATTORNEY. And how did she—look?

HALE. Well, she looked queer.

COUNTY ATTORNEY. How do you mean—queer?

HALE. Well, as if she didn't know what she was going to do next. And
kind of done up.

COUNTY ATTORNEY. How did she seem to feel about your coming?

HALE. Why, I don't think she minded—one way or the other. She didn't pay much attention. I said, "How do, Mrs. Wright, it's cold, ain't it?" And she said, "Is it"—and went on kind of pleating at her apron. Well, I was surprised; she didn't ask me to come up to the stove, or to set down, but just sat there, not even looking at me, so I said, "I want to see John." And then she—laughed. I guess you would call it a laugh. I thought of Harry and the team outside, so I said a little sharp: "Can't I see John?" "No," she says, kind o' dull like. "Ain't he home?" says I. "Yes," says she, "he's home." "Then why can't I see him?" I asked her, out of patience. "'Cause he's dead," says she. "*Dead?*" says I. She just nodded her head, not getting a bit excited, but rockin' back and forth. "Why—where is he?" says I, not knowing what to say. She just pointed upstairs—like that [*himself pointing to the room above*]. I got up, with the idea of going up there. I walked from there to here—then I says, "Why, what did he die of?" "He died of a rope around his neck," says she, and just went on pleatin' at her apron. Well, I went out and called Harry. I thought I might—need help. We went upstairs and there he was lyin'——

COUNTY ATTORNEY. I think I'd rather have you go into that upstairs, where you can point it all out. Just go on now with the rest of the story.

HALE. Well, my first thought was to get that rope off. It looked . . . [*stops, his face twitches*] . . . but Harry, he went up to him, and he said, "No, he's dead all right, and we'd better not touch anything." So we went back down stairs. She was still sitting that same way. "Has anybody been notified?" I asked. "No," says she, unconcerned. "Who did this, Mrs. Wright?" said Harry. He said it businesslike—and she stopped pleatin' of her apron. "I don't know," she says. "You don't *know?*" says Harry. "No," says she. "Weren't you sleepin' in the bed with him?" says Harry. "Yes," says she, "but I was on the inside." "Somebody slipped a rope round his neck and strangled him and you didn't wake up?" says Harry. "I didn't wake up," she said after him. We must 'a looked as if we didn't see how that could be, for after a minute she said, "I sleep sound." Harry was going to ask her more questions but I said maybe we ought to let her tell her story first to the coroner, or the sheriff, so Harry went fast as he could to Rivers' place, where there's a telephone.

COUNTY ATTORNEY. And what did Mrs. Wright do when she knew that you had gone for the coroner?

HALE. She moved from that chair to this one over here [*pointing to a small chair in the corner*] and just sat there with her hands held together and looking down. I got a feeling that I ought to make some conversation, so I said I had come in to see if John wanted to put in a telephone, and at that she started to laugh, and then she stopped and looked at me—scared. [*The* COUNTY ATTORNEY, *who had had his notebook out, makes a note.*] I dunno, maybe it wasn't scared. I wouldn't like to say it was. Soon Harry got back, and then Dr. Lloyd came, and you, Mr. Peters, and so I guess that's all I know that you don't.

COUNTY ATTORNEY [*looking around*]. I guess we'll go upstairs first—and then out to the barn and around there. [*To the* SHERIFF.] You're convinced that there was nothing important here—nothing that would point to any motive.

SHERIFF. Nothing here but kitchen things.

[*The* COUNTY ATTORNEY, *after again looking around the kitchen, opens the door of a cupboard closet. He gets up on a chair and looks on a shelf. Pulls his hand away, sticky.*]

COUNTY ATTORNEY. Here's a nice mess.

[*The women draw nearer.*]

MRS. PETERS [*to the other woman*]. Oh, her fruit; it did freeze. [*To the* COUNTY ATTORNEY.] She worried about that when it turned so cold. She said the fire'd go out and her jars would break.

SHERIFF. Well, can you beat the women! Held for murder and worryin' about her preserves.

COUNTY ATTORNEY. I guess before we're through she may have something more serious than preserves to worry about.

HALE. Well, women are used to worrying over trifles.

[*The two women move a little closer together.*]

COUNTY ATTORNEY [*with the gallantry of a young politician*]. And yet, for all their worries, what would we do without the ladies? [*The women do not unbend. He goes to the sink, takes a dipperful of water from the pail and pouring it into a basin, washes his hands. Starts to wipe them on the roller towel, turns it for a cleaner place.*] Dirty towels! [*Kicks his foot against the pans under the sink.*] Not much of a housekeeper, would you say, ladies?

MRS. HALE [*stiffly*]. There's a great deal of work to be done on a farm.

COUNTY ATTORNEY. To be sure. And yet [*with a little bow to her*] I know
there are some Dickson county farmhouses which do not have such
roller towels.

[*He gives it a pull to expose its full length again.*]

MRS. HALE. Those towels get dirty awful quick. Men's hands aren't always as clean as they might be.

COUNTY ATTORNEY. Ah, loyal to your sex, I see. But you and Mrs.
Wright were neighbors. I suppose you were friends, too.

MRS. HALE [*shaking her head*]. I've not seen much of her of late years.
I've not been in this house—it's more than a year.

COUNTY ATTORNEY. And why was that? You didn't like her?

MRS. HALE. I liked her all well enough. Farmers' wives have their hands
full, Mr. Henderson. And then——

COUNTY ATTORNEY. Yes——?

MRS. HALE [*looking about*]. It never seemed a very cheerful place.

COUNTY ATTORNEY. No—it's not cheerful. I shouldn't say she had the
homemaking instinct.

MRS. HALE. Well, I don't know as Wright had, either.

COUNTY ATTORNEY. You mean that they didn't get on very well?

MRS. HALE. No, I don't mean anything. But I don't think a place'd be
any cheerfuller for John Wright's being in it.

COUNTY ATTORNEY. I'd like to talk more of that a little later. I want to
get the lay of things upstairs now.

[*He goes to the left, where three steps lead to a stair door.*]

SHERIFF. I suppose anything Mrs. Peter does'll be all right. She was to
take in some clothes for her, you know, and a few little things. We left
in such a hurry yesterday.

COUNTY ATTORNEY. Yes, but I would like to see what you take, Mrs.
Peters, and keep an eye out for anything that might be of use to us.

MRS. PETERS. Yes, Mr. Henderson.

[*The women listen to the men's steps on the stairs, then look about the
kitchen.*]

MRS. HALE. I'd hate to have men coming into my kitchen, snooping
around and criticising.

[*She arranges the pans under sink which the* COUNTY ATTORNEY *had
shoved out of place.*]

MRS. PETERS. Of course it's no more than their duty.

MRS. HALE. Duty's all right, but I guess that deputy sheriff that came out to make the fire might have got a little of this on. [*Gives the roller towel a pull.*] Wish I'd thought of that sooner. Seems mean to talk about her for not having things slicked up when she had to come away in such a hurry.

MRS. PETERS [*who has gone to a small table in the left rear corner of the room, and lifted one end of a towel that covers a pan*]. She had bread set.

[*Stands still.*]

MRS. HALE [*eyes fixed on a loaf of bread beside the breadbox, which is on a low shelf at the other side of the room; moves slowly toward it*]. She was going to put this in there. [*Picks up loaf, then abruptly drops it. In a manner of returning to familiar things.*] It's a shame about her fruit. I wonder if it's all gone. [*Gets up on the chair and looks.*] I think there's some here that's all right, Mrs. Peters. Yes—here; [*holding it toward the window*] this is cherries, too. [*Looking again.*] I declare I believe that's the only one. [*Gets down, bottle in her hand. Goes to the sink and wipes it off on the outside.*] She'll feel awful bad after all her hard work in the hot weather. I remember the afternoon I put up my cherries last summer.

[*She puts the bottle on the big kitchen table, center of the room. With a sigh, is about to sit down in the rocking-chair. Before she is seated realizes what chair it is; with a slow look at it, steps back. The chair which she has touched rocks back and forth.*]

MRS. PETERS. Well, I must get those things from the front room closet. [*She goes to the door at the right, but after looking into the other room, steps backs.*] You coming with me, Mrs. Hale? You could help me carry them.

[*They go in the other room; reappear, MRS. PETERS carrying a dress and skirt, MRS. HALE following with a pair of shoes.*]

MRS. PETERS. My, it's cold in there.

[*She puts the clothes on the big table, and hurries to the stove.*]

MRS. HALE [*examining her skirt*]. Wright was close. I think maybe that's why she kept so much to herself. She didn't even belong to the Ladies Aid. I suppose she felt she couldn't do her part, and then you don't enjoy things when you fell shabby. She used to wear pretty clothes and be lively, when she was Minnie Foster, one of the town girls singing in the choir. But that—oh, that was thirty years ago. This all you was to take in?

MRS. PETERS. She said she wanted an apron. Funny thing to want, for there isn't much to get you dirty in jail, goodness knows. But I suppose just to make her feel more natural. She said they was in the top drawer in this cupboard. Yes, here. And then her little shawl that always hung behind the door. [*Opens stair door and looks.*] Yes, here it is.

[*Quickly shuts door leading upstairs.*]

MRS. HALE [*abruptly moving toward her*]. Mrs. Peters?

MRS. PETERS. Yes, Mrs. Hale?

MRS. HALE. Do you think she did it?

MRS. PETERS [*in a frightened voice*]. Oh, I don't know.

MRS. HALE. Well, I don't think she did. Asking for an apron and her little shawl. Worrying about her fruit.

MRS. PETERS [*starts to speak, glances up, where footsteps are heard in the room above; in a low voice*]. Mr. Peters says it looks bad for her. Mr. Henderson is awful sarcastic in a speech and he'll make fun of her sayin' she didn't wake up.

MRS. HALE. Well, I guess John Wright didn't wake when they was slipping that rope under his neck.

MRS. PETERS. No, it's strange. It must have been done awful crafty and still. They say it was such a—funny way to kill a man, rigging it all up like that.

MRS. HALE. That's just what Mr. Hale said. There was a gun in the house. He says that's what he can't understand.

MRS. PETERS. Mr. Henderson said coming out that what was needed for the case was a motive; something to show anger, or—sudden feeling.

MRS. HALE [*who is standing by the table*]. Well, I don't see any signs of anger around here. [*She puts her hand on the dish towel which lies on the table, stands looking down at table, one half of which is clean, the other half messy.*] It's wiped to here. [*Makes a move as if to finish work, then turns and looks at loaf of bread outside the breadbox. Drops towel. In that voice of coming back to familiar things.*] Wonder how they are finding things upstairs. I hope she had it a little more red-up up there. You know, it seems kind of *sneaking*. Locking her up in town and then coming out here and trying to get her own house to turn against her!

MRS. PETERS. But Mrs. Hale, the law is the law.

MRS. HALE. I s'pose 'tis. [*Unbuttoning her coat.*] Better loosen up your things, Mrs. Peters. You won't feel them when you go out.

[MRS. PETERS *takes off her fur tippet, goes to hang it on hook at back of room, stands looking at the under part of the small corner table.*]

MRS. PETERS. She was piecing a quilt.

[*She brings the large sewing basket and they look at the bright pieces.*]

MRS. HALE. It's log cabin pattern. Pretty, isn't it? I wonder if she was goin' to quilt it or just knot it?

[*Footsteps have been heard coming down the stairs. The* SHERIFF *enters followed by* HALE *and the* COUNTY ATTORNEY.]

SHERIFF. They wonder if she was going to quilt it or just knot it!

[*The men laugh; the women look abashed.*]

COUNTY ATTORNEY [*rubbing his hands over the stove*]. Frank's fire didn't do much up there, did it? Well, let's go out to the barn and get that cleared up.

[*The men go outside.*]

MRS. HALE [*resentfully*]. I don't know as there's anything so strange, our takin' up our time with little things while we're waiting for them to get the evidence. [*She sits down at the big table smoothing out a block with decision.*] I don't see as it's anything to laugh about.

MRS. PETERS [*apologetically*]. Of course they've got awful important things on their minds.

[*Pulls up a chair and joins* MRS. HALE *at the table.*]

MRS. HALE [*examining another block*]. Mrs. Peters, look at this one. Here, this is the one she was working on, and look at the sewing! All the rest of it has been so nice and even. And look at this! It's all over the place! Why, it looks as if she didn't know what she was about!

[*After she has said this they look at each other, then start to glance back at the door. After an instant* MRS. HALE *has pulled at a knot and ripped the sewing.*]

MRS. PETERS. Oh, what are you doing, Mrs. Hale?

MRS. HALE [*mildly*]. Just pulling out a stitch or two that's not sewed very good. [*Threading a needle.*] Bad sewing always made me fidgety.

MRS. PETERS [*nervously*]. I don't think we ought to touch things.

MRS. HALE. I'll just finish up this end. [*Suddenly stopping and leaning forward.*] Mrs. Peters?

MRS. PETERS. Yes, Mrs. Hale?

MRS. HALE. What do you suppose she was so nervous about?

MRS. PETERS. Oh—I don't know. I don't know as she was nervous. I sometimes sew awful queer when I'm just tired. [MRS. HALE *starts to say something, looks at* MRS. PETERS, *then goes on sewing.*] Well, I must get these things wrapped up. They may be through sooner than we think. [*Putting apron and other things together.*] I wonder where I can find a piece of paper, and string.

MRS. HALE. In that cupboard, maybe.

MRS. PETERS [*looking in cupboard*]. Why, here's a birdcage. [*Holds it up.*] Did she have a bird, Mrs. Hale?

MRS. HALE. Why, I don't know whether she did or not—I've not been here for so long. There was a man around last year selling canaries cheap, but I don't know as she took one; maybe she did. She used to sing real pretty herself.

MRS. PETERS [*glancing around*]. Seems funny to think of a bird here. But she must have had one, or why would she have a cage? I wonder what happened to it.

MRS. HALE. I s'pose maybe the cat got it.

MRS. PETERS. No, she didn't have a cat. She's got that feeling some people have about cats—being afraid of them. My cat got in her room and she was real upset and asked me to take it out.

MRS. HALE. My sister Bessie was like that. Queer, ain't it?

MRS. PETERS [*examining the cage*]. Why, look at this door. It's broke. One hinge is pulled apart.

MRS. HALE [*looking too*]. Looks as if someone must have been rough with it.

MRS. PETERS. Why, yes.

    [*She brings the cage forward and puts it on the table.*]

MRS. HALE. I wish if they're going to find any evidence they'd be about it. I don't like this place.

MRS. PETERS. But I'm awful glad you came with me, Mrs. Hale. It would be lonesome for me sitting here alone.

MRS. HALE. It would, wouldn't it? [*Dropping her sewing.*] But I tell you what I do wish, Mrs. Peters. I wish I had come over sometimes when *she* was here. I—[*looking around the room*]—wish I had.

MRS. PETERS. But of course you were awful busy, Mrs. Hale—your house and your children.

MRS. HALE. I could've come. I stayed away because it weren't cheerful—and that's why I ought to have come. I—I've never liked this place. Maybe because it's down in a hollow and you don't see the road. I dunno what it is but it's a lonesome place and always was. I wish I had come over to see Minnie Foster sometimes. I can see now——

    [*Shakes her head.*]

MRS. PETERS. Well, you mustn't reproach yourself, Mrs. Hale. Somehow we just don't see how it is with other folks until—something comes up.

MRS. HALE. Not having children makes less work—but it makes a quiet house, and Wright out to work all day, and no company when he did come in. Did you know John Wright, Mrs. Peters?

MRS. PETERS. Not to know him; I've seen him in town. They say he was a good man.

MRS. HALE. Yes—good; he didn't drink, and kept his word as well as most, I guess, and paid his debts. But he was a hard man, Mrs. Peters. Just to pass the time of day with him— [*Shivers.*] Like a raw wind that gets to the bone. [*Pauses, her eye falling on the cage.*] I should think she would 'a wanted a bird. But what do you suppose went with it?

MRS. PETERS. I don't know, unless it got sick and died.
[*She reaches over and swings the broken door, swings it again. Both women watch it.*]

MRS. HALE. You weren't raised round here, were you? [MRS. PETERS *shakes her head.*] You didn't know—her?

MRS. PETERS. Not till they brought her yesterday.

MRS. HALE. She—come to think of it, she was kind of like a bird her-self—real sweet and pretty, but kind of timid and—fluttery. How—she—did—change. [*Silence; then as if struck by a happy thought and re-lieved to get back to every day things.*] Tell you what, Mrs. Peters, why don't you take the quilt in with you? It might take up her mind.

MRS. PETERS. Why, I think that's a real nice idea, Mrs. Hale. There couldn't possibly be any objection to it, could there? Now, just what would I take? I wonder if her patches are in here—and her things.
[*They look in the sewing basket.*]

MRS. HALE. Here's some red. I expect this has got sewing things in it. [*Brings out a fancy box.*] What a pretty box. Looks like something somebody would give you. Maybe her scissors are in here. [*Opens box. Suddenly puts her hand to her nose.*] Why— [MRS. PETERS *bends nearer, then turns her face away.*] There's something wrapped up in this piece of silk.

MRS. PETERS. Why, this isn't her scissors.

MRS. HALE [*lifting the silk*]. Oh, Mrs. Peters—its——
[MRS. PETERS *bends closer.*]

MRS. PETERS. It's the bird.

MRS. HALE [*jumping up*]. But, Mrs. Peters—look at it! Its neck! Look at its neck! It's all—other side *to*.

MRS. PETERS. Somebody—wrung—its—neck.

> [*Their eyes meet. A look of growing comprehension, of horror. Steps are heard outside. MRS. HALE slips box under quilt pieces, and sinks into her chair. Enter SHERIFF and COUNTY ATTORNEY. MRS. PETERS rises.*]

COUNTY ATTORNEY [*as one turning from serious things to little pleasantries*]. Well, ladies, have you decided whether she was going to quilt it or knot it?

MRS. PETERS. We think she was going to—knot it.

COUNTY ATTORNEY. Well, that's interesting, I'm sure. [*Seeing the birdcage.*] Has the bird flown?

MRS. HALE [*putting more quilt pieces over the box*]. We think the—cat got it.

COUNTY ATTORNEY [*preoccupied*]. Is there a cat?

> [MRS. HALE *glances in a quick covert way at* MRS. PETERS.]

MRS. PETERS. Well, not *now*. They're superstitious, you know. They leave.

COUNTY ATTORNEY [*to* SHERIFF PETERS, *continuing an interrupted conversation*]. No sign at all of anyone having come from the outside. Their own rope. Now let's go up again and go over it piece by piece. [*They start upstairs.*] It would have to have been someone who knew just the——

> [MRS. PETERS *sits down. The two women sit there not looking at one another, but as if peering into something and at the same time holding back. When they talk now it is in the manner of feeling their way over strange ground, as if afraid of what they are saying, but as if they can not help saying it.*]

MRS. HALE. She liked the bird. She was going to bury it in that pretty box.

MRS. PETERS [*in a whisper*]. When I was a girl—my kitten—there was a boy took a hatchet, and before my eyes—and before I could get there— [*Covers her face an instant.*] If they hadn't held me back I would have—[*Catches herself, looks upstairs where steps are heard, falters weakly*]—hurt him.

MRS. HALE [*with a slow look around her*]. I wonder how it would seem never to have had any children around. [*Pause.*] No, Wright wouldn't like the bird—a thing that sang. She used to sing. He killed that, too.

MRS. PETERS [*moving uneasily*]. We don't know who killed the bird.

MRS. HALE. I knew John Wright.

Mrs. Peters. It was an awful thing was done in this house that night, Mrs. Hale. Killing a man while he slept, slipping a rope around his neck that choked the life out of him.

Mrs. Hale. His neck. Choked the life out of him.

[*Her hand goes out and rests on the birdcage.*]

Mrs. Peters [*with rising voice*]. We don't know who killed him. We don't know.

Mrs. Hale [*her own feeling not interrupted*]. If there'd been years and years of nothing, then a bird to sing to you, it would be awful—still, after the bird was still.

Mrs. Peters [*something within her speaking*]. I know what stillness is. When we homesteaded in Dakota, and my first baby died—after he was two years old, and me with no other then——

Mrs. Hale [*moving*]. How soon do you suppose they'll be through, looking for the evidence?

Mrs. Peters. I know what stillness is. [*Pulling herself back.*] The law has got to punish crime, Mrs. Hale.

Mrs. Hale [*not as if answering that*]. I wish you'd seen Minnie Foster when she wore a white dress with blue ribbons and stood up there in the choir and sang. [*A look around the room.*] Oh, I *wish* I'd come over here once in a while! That was a crime! That was a crime! Who's going to punish that?

Mrs. Peters [*looking upstairs*]. We mustn't—take on.

Mrs. Hale. I might have known she needed help! I know how things can be—for women. I tell you, it's queer, Mrs. Peters. We live close together and we live far apart. We all go through the same things—it's all just a different kind of the same thing. [*Brushes her eyes; noticing the bottle of fruit, reaches out for it.*] If I was you I wouldn't tell her her fruit was gone. Tell her it *ain't*. Tell her it's all right. Take this in to prove it to her. She—she may never know whether it was broke or not.

Mrs. Peters [*takes the bottle, looks about for something to wrap it in; takes petticoat from the clothes brought from the other room, very nervously begins winding this around the bottle; in a false voice*]. My, it's a good thing the men couldn't hear us. Wouldn't they just laugh! Getting all stirred up over a little thing like a—dead canary. As if that could have anything to do with—with—wouldn't they *laugh*!

[*The men are heard coming down stairs.*]

Mrs. Hale [*under her breath*]. Maybe they would—maybe they wouldn't.

County Attorney. No, Peters, it's all perfectly clear except a reason for doing it. But you know juries when it comes to women. If there was some definite thing. Something to show—something to make a story about—a thing that would connect up with this strange way of doing it——

> [*The women's eyes meet for an instant. Enter* HALE *from outer door.*]

HALE. Well, I've got the team around. Pretty cold out there.

COUNTY ATTORNEY. I'm going to stay here a while by myself. [*To the* SHERIFF.] You can send Frank out for me, can't you? I want to go over everything. I'm not satisfied that we can't do better.

SHERIFF. Do you want to see what Mrs. Peters is going to take in?

> [*The* COUNTY ATTORNEY *goes to the table, picks up the apron, laughs.*]

COUNTY ATTORNEY. Oh, I guess they're not very dangerous things the ladies have picked out. [*Moves a few things about, disturbing the quilt pieces which cover the box. Steps back.*] No, Mrs. Peters doesn't need supervising. For that matter, a sheriff's wife is married to the law. Ever think of it that way, Mrs. Peters?

MRS. PETERS. Not—just that way.

SHERIFF [*chuckling*]. Married to the law. [*Moves toward the other room.*] I just want you to come in here a minute, George. We ought to take a look at these windows.

COUNTY ATTORNEY [*scoffingly*]. Oh, windows!

SHERIFF. We'll be right out, Mr. Hale.

> [HALE *goes outside. The* SHERIFF *follows the* COUNTY ATTORNEY *into the other room. Then* MRS. HALE *rises, hands tight together, looking intensely at* MRS. PETERS, *whose eyes make a slow turn, finally meeting* MRS. HALE's. *A moment* MRS. HALE *holds her, then her own eyes point the way to where the box is concealed. Suddenly* MRS. PETERS *throws back quilt pieces and tries to put the box in the bag she is wearing. It is too big. She opens box, starts to take bird out, cannot touch it, goes to pieces, stands there helpless. Sound of a knob turning in the other room.* MRS. HALE *snatches the box and puts it in the pocket of her big coat. Enter* COUNTY ATTORNEY *and* SHERIFF.]

COUNTY ATTORNEY [*facetiously*]. Well, Henry, at least we found out that she was not going to quilt it. She was going to—what is it you call it, ladies?

MRS. HALE [*her hand against her pocket*]. We call it—knot it, Mr. Henderson.

CURTAIN

Excerpt from

The Hangman's Beautiful Daughter

Sharyn McCrumb

Nora sat down in one of the wing chairs, and pulled a length of quilted cloth out of her sewing basket. "I'm glad for some company, Laura Bruce. I don't get much these days. You don't mind my sewing while we talk, do you? I see better in daylight."

Laura took a sip of her coffee. "Please do. What are you making now?"

Nora Bonesteel looked down at the dark fabric in her lap, and her expression became somber. "It's an old-fashioned quilt. I reckon. I've been working on it for a few weeks now. Something has been troubling me lately. It devils me when I try to sleep, and when I'm awake, it hovers just on the edge of my thoughts, where I can't get a good look at it, but it's a dark shape. I can't quite put my finger on what it is. So I thought I'd start a quilt, and see if occupying my hands would ease my mind. I didn't think about any set pattern; just set to working to see could I find out anything by what I was called on to make. This is what I got."

She held the quilt up by the corners so that Laura could see its design. A three-inch border of black velvet framed the quilt, and against its green background she had embroidered a scene: a wavy swatch of blue fabric suggested a river, placed below rounded rows of dark blue and green satin mountains. The foreground of the picture contained a full-leafed oak tree towering over gray satin crosses and rounded gravestones, surrounded by an unfinished web of black stitchery resembling a wrought-iron fence.

"It's a cemetery," said Laura, staring at the textile landscape. "It's very well done, but . . . what are those things on the bottom hem?"

Along the bottom of the quilt, Nora Bonesteel had tacked six coffin-shaped pieces of black satin. "Caskets. I think they're meant to go in the center of the quilt by and by," said Nora, speaking dispassionately, as if it were someone else's work.

"I've never seen a quilt with that design," said Laura. The design was executed in rich velvet and satin, and the stitchery was flawless, but she found herself reluctant to touch the fabric. "Did the making of it ease your mind?"

"No, but it centers the feeling. When I put that heavy material across my lap to sew on it, it gives me chills."

"What do you think it means?" asked Laura, staring at the white needlepoint crosses in the quilted scene.

"Death, of course," said Nora Bonesteel in the voice she might have used to tell you the name of a wildflower. "But it isn't coming sudden and accidentallike, the way a truck might smash into a car next week. This death got rolling a good while back. Just lately it's been picking up speed."

"Who?" asked Laura. Her thoughts, a litany of *crazy old woman, crazy old woman*, did not drown out her fears.

"I'll know when it hits them."

Excerpt from

The Body in the Kelp

Katherine Hall Page

A<small>ND SO THE AUCTION</small> unfolded, assuming a character distinct from all the other auctions Gardiner and Company had run or the crowd attended. You never knew what was going to happen. The Warhol cookie jars turned out to be wooden lobster pots that had been in the barn. Few lobstermen used them anymore, and as the tourists and dealers bid them up, all the locals resolved to go clean out their sheds.

Pix and Faith were determined to wait until the bitter end for all the real bargains, and at about four o'clock the box lots started. Faith quickly snared one with tools she had noted for three dollars and Pix bought two mystery boxes of china for four dollars each, which upon inspection proved to contain a lovely Wedgewood ironstone teapot, lots of saucers without cups, something that could possibly be a piece of Imari, some Tupperware, and other treasures. Faith grabbed another box, one filled with board games of varying vintages, which she had seen at the viewing. Tom's family was addicted to board games, and she knew they would be happy to have more, especially for a dollar fifty. She bought two more boxes of china on speculation for two dollars each and figured she was done. After the cradle she had successfully bid on an odd lot of plate serving pieces for thirty-five dollars, elegant Victoriana with elaborate scrolls etched on the knife blades and ladles and repoussé flowers on the handles. It had been a productive day.

Just as she and Pix were packing up and getting ready to settle their accounts, the runners brought out another quilt, or actually a quilt top. It had been pieced, but not quilted to the batting and underside. Faith paused to watch as they unfolded it. It was a sampler quilt. Every square was different, connected with lattice stripping. The colors were repeated in each design, strong blues, greens, and touches of the same pink as the granite rocks by the shore.

It was a Maine quilt. Maine colors. And Faith had to have it. She sat down and pulled Pix into her chair.

"A beautiful quilt top here. All it needs is a back, and I'm sure a lot of you ladies out there could put this together in no time. What am I bid? Do I heayre ten dollahs?" Faith raised her card. She was so excited she felt slightly light-headed. There was something about this quilt. It was ridiculous, really. She hadn't the slightest idea how to quilt; it was not one of her accomplishments. In fact any sewing more complicated than buttons or a running stitch went to the tailor and always had. But she'd solve that problem once she had it. And she got it. Apparently there weren't any quilters in the audience and it was hers for forty dollars.

"Faith, it's gorgeous, and I can show you how to quilt. It's not difficult at all," Pix said.

"I think it would be easier if you quilted it, Pix, but as you have seen with the clamming, I'm willing to try anything." And with that they went home to gloat over their finds and bemoan all the ones that got away.

They passed Eric and Jill on the way out. Eric was tight-lipped and Jill was talking to him in a low voice. They stopped and Pix asked if they wanted to come to the cottage for a drink, but Jill said they were going to the mainland to get some dinner and distance. Eric smiled wryly. "Can you believe they actually think the mythical gold is in that weather vane? And how is it supposed to have gotten there? Did Darnell climb up one night and ballast it with doubloons, in which case it would have toppled off the barn long ago? Or maybe he took it down and replaced it with one cast of solid gold and no one ever heard anything about how he got it made? Well, at least we got the wicker porch furniture and some of the bedroom sets. I'm just glad it's over and we can move in."

Pix patted his arm. "Situations like this are always horrible. You should hear some of the stories Sam tells about settling estates."

"Did you get some nice things?" Jill asked as they turned to leave.

"Oh yes, nothing earth-shattering, but you have to go home with something from an auction, especially a historic one like this. Faith got a cradle, a quilt top, and who knows what in the boxes, and I got my usual— china, glass. Sam says we're going to have to have an auction soon."

"Thanks for the invitation, Pix. We'll see you soon," Eric said. "Good-bye, Faith—I haven't forgotten about our gazebo party. You and Pix and whatever husbands are around can come sometime next week."

"That would be lovely, but husbands are not arriving until close to Labor Day, so you'll have to put up with the company of women."

"Never a chore." Eric smiled. His mood seemed to have lifted, and Faith was sure it was not just her imagination that Jill gave them a look filled with gratitude as she said good-bye.

The events of the auction had been unsettling, and Faith found it hard to sleep that night. It had been after six when she finally got back, and she was exhausted. She left the boxes in the barn to go through later and brought the quilt top into the house. It was even more beautiful than she had thought when they had held it up. She spread it on the bed in the spare room. It seemed at home.

After a hasty supper she read to Benjamin and settled him into his crib, then got an Angela Thirkell out of the bookcase and went to bed herself. She must have slept, because when she looked at the clock several hours had passed, but now she felt wide awake. She opened the book again and tried to lose herself in Barsetshire, but the comings and goings of the Brandons did not distract her.

There also seemed to be a lot of comings and goings in the cove and on the shore road opposite the cottage. She remembered that she had heard the same boat and truck noises a week ago Thursday night, because Tom had been lying next to her and thought it might be night fishing. The next day they had seen herring nets, so the fishermen must have been catching a run, then unloading at Prescott's straight into the trucks.

She got up, turned out the light, and went to the window. She couldn't see much, just pinpoints of light and the occasional long sweep of headlights. She didn't hear any talking—just the boat engines and the trucks. Well, it was after two o'clock and they, of all people, would know how voices carried on the water. Still, it surprised her a little that they should be so considerate. From what she had seen at the auction, Sonny Prescott didn't seem like a man who would whisper if he had something to say. If it *was* Sonny out there in the dark, that is.

Benjamin would be up in a few, very few hours. Faith crawled back into her bed, thought wistfully about Tom, and wondered if she would feel better or weird if she piled some pillows in his approximate shape next to her. Weird. She fell asleep.

Faith spent most of Friday in the hammock watching Benjamin chase croquet balls on the lawn. The owners of the cottage maintained a large carefully manicured lawn in the back of the house, bordered on three sides by the meadow filled now with Indian paintbrush, Queen Anne's lace and other wildflowers. The lawn looked a bit odd there, as if someone had spread a piece of felt over the meadow, but it provided a place to sit and play all those games stored in the barn.

She did rouse herself to get lunch, which the two of them ate on the grass. Faith found feeding Benjamin al fresco made life much simpler. Anything he dropped would be picked up by the gulls later. At four o'clock Tom called. They had decided he would call her, since he wasn't as sure of his schedule as she was of hers. No schedule.

It was a case of two people who are very close to each other with not much to say. Or rather a lot to say, but nothing to say of common interest. Faith started to tell him about the Casserole Supper and Bird's entrance and the auction and the trouble between the Prescotts and Roger and Eric, then she realized he didn't really know these people and it all meant nothing to him. Tom started to tell Faith about the difficulty he was having keeping his Ecclesiastes study section on the path; the incipient power struggle between this year's conference chairman and the recently named next year's; and the distracting presence of a certain lady from Minneapolis—distracting of course not to *moi*, Tom protested a bit too much to himself, but some of the other men—when he also realized how boring it all was when you weren't there. Of course, Faith would have been even more bored if she had been there. And so they talked at cross purposes for a while, tried to explain, then Faith said, "Tom, I love you. Is that it? I mean isn't that why you called?"

"In a word, yes. And I love you. And I miss you. You do sound like you're having more fun. And getting better things to eat."

"Think of it as good for the soul, and I'll make it up to you when you get back. The things to eat and especially the fun."

"I hope you're thinking of the same kind of fun I'm thinking of," Tom commented.

"Absolutely, brisk swims in the ocean followed by volleyball and ten-mile hikes. Isn't that what you Fairchilds call 'fun'?" Faith teased.

"Watch out, sweetheart, or I'll hold you to it."

"Oh, Tom, I almost forgot. I had a letter from Hope on Friday. She and Quentin are going to be visiting friends in Bar Harbor and wondered if we wanted company over Labor Day weekend. What do you think?"

"I think I don't want any company but yours, but you know I love your sister dearly, and if there were the slightest chance that our example of connubial bliss would nudge the two of them toward the altar, I'd take it."

"Good. I already said they could come."

"Dammit, Faith! What did you ask me for if you had the whole thing decided?"

"I wanted to hear what you would say and it was what I thought, so there's no problem. Besides, you always like Quentin after the first shock of the new wears off and he forgets he's flawless."

"That's beside the point."

"Are we quarreling?" Faith asked. "I hope not, because it's horrible enough on the phone."

"No, not quarreling. It's just necessary that I occasionally try to cling to what's left of my independence."

"Oh, Tom, this is silly. All right. It was a little high-handed of me." She paused. Tom didn't say anything. "Okay, even very high-handed and I promise faithfully, don't laugh, to consult you first in the future about house guests. And when you see the wonderful box lots I got at the auction, you'll let me do anything I want."

"I do anyway, but promise me that you'll leave at least one box for me to go through myself."

"Better, I'll give you two. I bought four, so that's fair. You can have the tools and one that looks like old games. I thought your family might like them."

"That's terrific, Faith. Now I have to go, honey. A group of us are going to Portsmouth for dinner at The Blue Strawberry."

"Sounds tough, Tom."

"Believe me, Faith, after a week of this food, we deserve it."

"I'm sure you do. Just make sure any legs you encounter under the table belong to it."

After some more of this nonsense, they hung up and Faith went back to the yard. Ben was still napping. Must be all the sea air, she thought. She had noticed that the locals touted it as either invigorating or soporific depending on what the situation called for. Just another one of those charming contradictions that seemed to crop up on Sanpere.

No sooner was she outside than she decided to go in. She felt at loose ends. Pix had invited them for supper, but Faith had wanted to go to bed early after her wakefulness the night before and declined. She sat down at the big rolltop desk by the window facing the cove and got out her recipe notebook to jot down a few ideas. The phone rang. Of course.

"Hello, Pix," she said.

"How did you know it was me?"

"You and Tom are the only people who call me, and Tom just called, so that leaves you, Watson, my good fellow."

"Oh, I see. I called to see if you wanted to change your mind. John Eggleston is bringing over some lobster from his traps—he just has a few in front of his house—and the Fraziers are dropping by. Oh, and Jill is coming, though she wasn't sure when. She's taking inventory or something. Eric went up to some friends on Drake's Island for a couple of days, so she's at loose ends. I asked Roger too, but he's up to his elbows in new glazes, he told me this morning."

"You people seem to exist in a frantic whirl of gaiety here. One party after another. How are we going to settle down to life in Aleford? And think how bored I'll be next time I go home to the City for a visit," Faith said, reflecting on the difference between Pix the hostess as hostage of Aleford and Pix the Perle Mesta of Sanpere. Several times a year she had to give dinner parties for Sam's law partners or clients, and she would start worrying a month before. The night of the dinner something disastrous always occurred. Either with the food—one time she had forgotten to remove the plastic bag with the innards from her roast chicken—or with her person—a zipper stuck halfway up on the dress she was attempting to put on and Faith had to rush over to save her. But on Sanpere Pix thought nothing of inviting large groups on the spur of the moment. If she didn't have enough plates, she switched to paper with casual aplomb.

"I do want to get to bed early, Pix, but I'd like to see the Fraziers and especially your renegade priest again. Could Ben and I come for the aperitif?"

"Of course, and Faith, you'll never guess! The Prescotts took turns watching the weather vane all night until they got some expert down from Orono this morning. And Eric was right. There was no way the gold could have been hidden in it. Too heavy. Anyway, the man didn't mind climbing on the roof, so he went up, poked around, and took scrapings. It's copper through and through. So now it goes in the next auction Gardiner has, and they'll all go to bid against Eric and Roger out of spite and disappointment. Since the weather vane was part of the contents of the house, if it had been gold, it would have been the Prescott clan's. That's a lot of trips to Florida for the winter."

"From everything I hear about her, Matilda would have enjoyed all this," Faith commented.

"Definitely. Fortunately, she liked me—or didn't dislike me, I should say. I used to take her some of my strawberry preserves every once in a while. Oh, and Louise Frazier told me that your quilt top is probably the last one Matilda made. She was piecing one with those colors when Louise visited her just before she died."

"Thanks, Pix. It's nice to know who made it. If she appreciated your delectable jam, she couldn't have been too horrible."

"Oh, she wasn't horrible at all—just lonely and unappreciated, I think. Sam used to enjoy talking with her, sparring really. He thought she should have gone into politics. She was bright and totally honest, and had so much drive. Too much for her family. She liked to be in charge, and when she got old and couldn't be, they were used to keeping their distance."

"I want to hear more about all this, Pix, but Ben's awake. He's starting to hurl things violently out of the crib, always a bad sign, so I'd better go. When do you want us?"

"Around five?"

"Fine. I'll see you soon."

Faith hung up and raced upstairs before one of Benjamin's missiles found the window as a target. Everything was on the floor, and Ben, having taken all his clothes off, was just climbing out of the crib. She carried him into the bathroom and sat him on the potty seat. Unpredictable in all things, he had virtually toilet trained himself. Just as she was culling information from all the experts and getting ready to start, he had announced, "No diapers," and had scarcely looked back. It was big-boy underpants—BBUs, as Tom called them—from here on in.

An hour later Faith was sipping a glass of wine and eating cold mussels and the remoulade sauce she had taught Pix how to make. She was enjoying herself. Samantha was reading to Ben, which she appeared to be able to do for hours on end without going crazy and/or speaking like Mr. Rogers.

John Eggleston was regaling them with tales of the island during Prohibition, which he had heard mostly from his neighbor and good friend, Elwell Sanford.

"Of course Elwell swears he himself wasn't involved in any of this illegal activity, although his constant references to a 'friend of mine' leave me a mite skeptical. Maine was a rum runner's dream, with this convoluted coastline—twenty-seven hundred miles of small coves, harbors, and inlets sandwiched into a four-hundred-mile loaf. And all the islands off shore. People tell me there are still cases buried on the Point, but I haven't heard of anyone finding one recently. Elwell's classic story, which I must admit I have heard up and down the coast, is about one of the Marshalls who was feuding with his neighbor. They were both selling hootch. One stormy night a revenuer came to Amos Marshall's house, desperate for a drink, he said. Well, Amos looked at him. His slicker was weatherbeaten and he needed a shave, but his boots were brand-new; so Amos sent him up the road saying he had taken the pledge himself, but his neighbor could oblige. The neighbor, unfortunately, wasn't so observant."

Everyone laughed, and Pix said, "Maybe you have heard it elsewhere, but I'm sure it started here."

After the laughter died down, Elliot Frazier remarked, "Of course we have the modern-day version with the illegal drug traffic. You're right about the coastline, John—it is virtually impossible to police it, and boats are landing the stuff all the time."

"When I first came to Sanpere in the late sixties, it had just started, or people had just become aware of it, and every newcomer to this island was thought to be either a drug peddler or an undercover agent. They certainly didn't know what to make of me," John said, laughing. "I used to fill in during the summer for a preacher over in Cherryfield, and when that got back to the island, they were even more confused."

"But John," Louise interrupted in her soft, faintly Southern voice, "you were doing so much good work with the teenagers here." She turned to Faith. "There was, and is, a big problem with alcohol on the island, and some drugs. There is really nothing for these kids to do here. John was the one who started the community center."

A different kind of ministry, Faith thought. John Eggleston was certainly a compelling figure, and she could imagine he had quite an effect on kids once he got going. She liked his stories and certainly he was to be admired for whatever he'd done for Sanpere, yet there was still a suggestion of fire and brimstone lurking just behind the pupils of his eyes and the clarion surety of his voice made her uneasy. A man who thinks he is absolutely right in everything he says and does. She had the feeling that if you ever got in his way, he'd roll implacably over you. No turning the other cheek here. Maybe that was why he had left the ministry. Tom wasn't a doormat, but he had a sense of his own limitations, humility in the presence of imponderables. Faith slid in somewhere between the two. She hoped she'd go around, and not over, but knew too that humble was not her best pie.

"Faith, whatever are you thinking about? You have the most peculiar expression on your face—sort of like the two corners of your mouth can't decide whether to go up or down," Pix commented.

"That's about it, Pix. I was thinking about good and evil," Faith replied, not realizing until she said it that that was what she had actually been considering.

There was silence for a moment as they all looked at her. Then Elliot Frazier asked, "Is this in light of the auction? I ask that because the day triggered many thoughts for me, starting with the whole event. Was it good or evil of Matilda to separate things that way? We knew her well, and I am still puzzled that she wanted to have the house dismantled after she died. The things in it were as much a part of the house as the structure itself for her."

"I hadn't connected my thoughts to the auction, but you may be right. I certainly have been restless since yesterday. There seemed to be so much tension, and I don't even know all these people." Faith looked at him with a feeling of respect. An insightful man.

The Fraziers had moved to Sanpere almost forty years ago. They were in their early thirties then, with two small children. Elliot had had a serious heart attack and they had wanted to get away from the stress of life in Washington, where he had built up a thriving accounting firm. At about the same time, Louise had inherited enough money from her family to enable them to buy their lovely old house on Sanpere. Elliot never had another heart attack. He had retired years before from the job he got the first year they were here—postmaster of Sanpere Village. They were the exception to the rule—most people on the island had forgotten the Fraziers weren't born on Sanpere. They moved comfortably among all the groups on the island. Sanpere had few secrets the postmaster and his wife hadn't heard—and kept.

"I think I know why Matilda divided things," Louise offered. "She might have felt slightly guilty about leaving the house to Roger and Eric, but more likely she wanted to get everything cleaned out. Have someone start fresh, which I'm sure she wanted to do herself at times, much as she worshipped those ancestors of hers."

"You could be right," Pix said. "The end of an era."

"Exactly." John closed the gate on the conversation, and Faith realized it was getting late. She resisted their attempts to convince her to stay for dinner and set off through the woods with Benjamin in tow. The path led close to the shore at times, and Faith could glimpse the sunset through the trees. The sun was a fiery-red rubber ball making a straight path across the water, the clouds streaming out along the horizon like purple and scarlet kite tails. Life with Ben was reducing her to kindergarten imagery.

The rocks that sloped down to the water were already in darkness, and on the other side of the cove she could see a few lights at Prescott's lobster pound and the houses to either side. Bird's tiny cabin stood out against the sky. There were no lights on, and Faith wasn't sure Bird even had electricity. She had seen her with the baby on the shore again and this time had received a brief nod and slight smile in answer to her greeting. The baby, who appeared to under a year old, still looked pale, and whether this was from the macrobiotics or lack of sunshine penetrating the sling Bird carried it in Faith didn't know.

The porch light at her own cottage blinked a welcome as she emerged from the woods carrying Benjamin, who had suddenly decided he wanted to be picked up and was now sound asleep.

She had no trouble sleeping that night either. Her last semi-conscious thought was that she had never realized Nature was quite so noisy— crickets, owls, bullfrogs, and always the sea, just close enough so she could make out the faint rhythmical lappings of the waves on the rocks.

The next morning Faith was up virtuously early. If she was a jogger, she'd go jogging, she thought. It was that kind of day. Newborn and sparkling. She packed a lunch in one of the two or three hundred knapsacks hanging from nails in the barn and set off with Benjamin for the beach at the Point. She had her bathing suit on under her shorts and shirt and thought they might even go wading, which would be something to tell Tom when he called next.

By the time they got to the beach, she was worn out. It wasn't that Benjamin didn't keep up. He could match her pace for pace, but he was stubbornly determined to forge his own trails, and it took all her energy and patience to keep him on the track. Now he could roam at will over

the beach and had already found a little stick with which he was furiously digging his way to China or whatever was directly below. Faith
opened the knapsack and spread out a towel next to him. She sat down
and looked at the water. The tide was out and had left a wavy line of
seaweed, shells, odd pieces of wood, rope from traps and buoys, and other
assorted flotsam—bleach bottles, which people cut to use as bailers, a
waterlogged shoe, a sardine tin. The beach itself was arranged in layers.
Farthest from the sea, near the wild roses, sea lavender, and spreading
junipers, the sand was covered with stones and broken shells, pushed up
by the waves. A line of dried, blackened seaweed separated this layer from
the sand that had recently been underwater and still glistened in the sun.
When it dried, it would be soft and almost white. Down near the water's
edge the rocks started again.

One of the big schooners sailed by, and Ben jumped up and down
waving excitedly. "Wanna ride! Wanna ride!" He was actually beginning
to make sense these days, and the next step might be conversation. In a
way it was nice to concentrate on Ben, although a few days would have
more than sufficed. Before he was born, she hadn't realized that there
would be times when husband and child would pull at her from different
directions. Like that poem of Robert Frost's that compared a woman to a
silken tent with "ties of love and thought" binding her to the earth.
They were either holding her up or pulling her down, depending on the
day, or as Frost pointed out, the movement of the wind.

Faith and Ben ate their sandwiches and wandered out to the reced-
ing water. This wasn't a clam flat and there was no mud. Faith held tight
to Benjamin's chubby little paw. He was racing toward the water crying,
"Swim! Swim!" Faith stuck her big toe in and promptly lost all feeling.
She decided her shoes would fit better if she did not get frostbite and
managed to steer Ben away from the beckoning deep, over to the tidal
pools that had been left behind in the warm sun.

"Sweetheart, we'll go look for little fishes and shells in the pools,
okay? We'll swim another day." And in another place, Faith added to
herself.

She helped Ben climb up onto the flat ledges that stretched around
the Point, and they began to explore the endlessly fascinating pools. At
first Ben wanted to jump in or at least stick his hand in right away, but
Faith was able to get him to pause and look first—to see the busy world of
tiny fish darting among the sea anemones and starfish, small crabs making

their way across the mussels and limpets clinging to the pink and orange algae that lined the bottoms of the pools. They went farther away from the beach, carefully avoiding the sharp remains of the sea urchins the gulls had dropped on the rocks and the lacelike barnacles that covered the granite.

"What's that, Ben?" Faith looked up from the life in the pool she had been studying. It looked so arranged, so deliberate, like the pine cones she had found in the woods placed on a mat of gray moss in a star shape with a feather in the middle.

"Wait, honey, I'm coming." She made her way across the flat rock and stood next to Ben, who was crouched and gazing intently at something in a lower pool.

"Man swimming," he said. "Ben wanna swim."

"What man?" Faith started to say before she looked and the question was answered for her.

It was Roger Branett, draped over the rocks and secured with thick ropes of brown kelp. Small waves were systematically covering and uncovering his head, filling his slackly opened mouth with sea water, fanning his long brown hair against the rockweed. His shirt was gone, and the dark kelp stood out against the unnatural whiteness of his bare arms and chest. His eyes were open and staring straight into the sun. Roger wasn't swimming.

Roger was dead.

Pieces to a Quilt

Mari Sandoz

T HE LANG EIGHTY contained not even a shirt-tail patch of level ground. Most of it was a deep gullied cup of gravel and crumbling sandstone, sloping abruptly into a dark pool. Now and then a glimpse of a summer cloud lay on the still surface but its whiteness only accentuated the dark reflections from the ten-foot bank of volcanic ash just above the water line. Even the cress-grown spring didn't bubble but welled up with slow complaint of green water under ice.

Back from the pool, under a solid nose of stone, squatted Lang's old shack weathered to the gray of ashes. A silent little creek slipped past the sagging doorstep and out between sheer sandstone bluffs toward the hay flats north, as though eager to escape the deep pool, the stark canyon walls, and the shack, empty since the man who built it hanged himself there with a silk muffler.

At least it was assumed he hanged himself. Sarah Reimer, schooled in patience with her slow-witted son, asked no questions when he brought home a square of figured silk with a corner cut off. He washed it and ironed it and made blocks for his crazy quilt. It was all right. Somebody was always giving him old silk pieces.

A week later, when the mail carrier mentioned that Lang's newspapers were piling up at the box, Rusty flung his clumsy hands about in a frenzy at the slowness of his tongue.

"I-I-I forgot to tell. Lang died."

The father and two neighbors went over and found that it was so. Lang had died, of hanging, probably with the muffler, as Rusty tried to explain. He had seen the man and, fancying the pretty silk, cut him down. It was August. The sheriff came out that night.

They took Lang outside, burned a little plug tobacco on a stove lid, and looked around, but there wasn't anything, no papers, no letters, not even a trunk, only the name of a New York tailor in his coat, which didn't mean anything. Lang's hands had been small and soft, never touched work. Just another hide-out.

Although Lang had lived in the canyon five years, not even the neighborly Jacob Reimer knew anything about him except that he was graying, never got farther from his place than the mailbox, and always seemed to have money for the groceries the mail-carrier brought out. None of his neighbors had seen him more than once or twice, unless it was Rusty.

"That half-wit ought to be looked after," a suspicious newcomer suggested.

"Aw, Rusty wouldn't hurt a fly," the sheriff defended. "His father's a damned good neighbor; too good to get ahead."

And there it was.

A week after the write-up of the Sad End, as the local paper called it, a woman, a young one, came to the county seat with the clipping. She made a fuss because Lang was already buried. No, she had no idea who he was.

A few days later Sarah Reimer spoke to her husband over Rusty's empty chair.

"He took his quilt blocks away this morning and then came back for that old revolver. I haven't seen anything of him since."

Jacob brushed his thinning hair back decently and looked with friendly blue eyes upon his wife's uneasiness.

"I will see to it," he said.

After supper he went out to smoke his pipe and wait for his son. On the way through Sarah's flowers he picked a golden calendula for the bib of his wash-bleached overalls, as Rusty often did. Then he leaned both tired elbows over the garden gate and looked off into the sunset, into the evening haze over the meandering creek and its soft green clumps of willow. Perhaps he should straighten the bed as he had helped his neighbors do long ago; cut out the willows. But a stream laid out by compass, hurrying away between weed-grown ridges of dirt and sod torn from their place in the earth—no, he preferred the first yellow-green of spring creeping shyly into the willow clumps, long grass dipping into the little stream in midsummer, thin sharp knives of anchor ice around the backwater in the fall.

Sometimes he could not forget the drouth and hail, or that his wife had once been ambitious to have a big house too, and a broad red barn, but she never complained. She had been as ready as he to spend the butter money for those five little Meyers last week. She even sewed all night so they could have dresses to wear to the funeral of their father who started home with too much Short Grass moon aboard and drove off into a canyon. Jacob was glad about the dresses. There should always be something nice to remember about funerals.

By the time his pipe was cold a black speck broke from the bluffs toward the Lang eighty, followed by a grotesque shadow down the long, sun-gilded slope. It was Joseph, Rusty, as the neighbors called him, on flea-bitten, stiff-kneed old Sarry. On her back lurched the top the sun-sensitive Rusty made of two forged rake-teeth fastened to the broken cantle of his old saddle, with canvas across them. Bobbing up and down like a jockey in his short stirrups, canvas flopping and rods rattling, Rusty rode towards his home.

When he saw his father waiting between the hollyhocks, his flat face softened into a broad, short-toothed grin and his eyes flecked with yellow glints. After the old mare was fed and curried he picked up the sack of water cress he brought his mother and walked beside Jacob to the house, the silence of good feeling between them.

Once or twice the father looked past the lamp to his son's thick mat of coarse sorrel curls, his heavy shoulders stooped over the clumsy fingers. It seemed foolish to ask Joseph what he had been doing. Never in his twenty years had his father ever known him to harm a living thing. Even after a day of fasting he was eating very slowly because this unreasonable procedure seemed to please his mother. Because Jacob saw this he was a little ashamed and hid behind talk of his work. Tomorrow he would help the Johnsons, and the next day Ivan Vach.

Rusty went to bed unquestioned.

Not until a year later did the community discover the cave that Lang had dug in the bluffs overlooking his shack and the canyon. The opening was concealed behind a big sandstone boulder with just enough space to slip in at one side. He even had a little fireplace opening into a gully.

Rusty had evidently found it long before. At least that seemed to be where he took his quilt blocks and later the phonograph his father bought at a sale for a quarter, with a stack of French and German records nobody wanted thrown in. Rusty liked them. He pulled out the carved wood front of the machine so he could get his head closer to the sound and kept it going. When his mother's impatience became too evident, he shambled out into the yard with the phonograph in a gunny sack. That was how the cave was discovered. A visiting geologist examining the bank of volcanic ash heard a scratchy but unmistakable rendition of the Jewel Song from Gounod's *Faust* drift thinly down to him. He followed the sound. As his shadow struck the mouth of the cave Rusty sprang up, swinging an old revolver like a club.

"I-I-I thought you was *him*," was all the explanation he would give. The geologist catalogued Rusty at a glance and dismissed the incident. But he was pleased when the youth took him into a deeply washed draw where a ledge of rock with bones on it lay exposed. In return he sent Rusty two records by the mail man, a Tyrolean yodel and a laughing Chaliapin. Rusty liked the yodel best.

News of the cave spread. Lang *had* been hiding out. But when nobody could produce any details, the sightseers soon tired of his cave. Rusty went back to it now, but openly, begging cookies from his mother or potatoes and eggs to roast in the fireplace so he wouldn't have to come home at noon. Several times tough fellows from town came out with bottles. They tried to get him to do things fit only for pigs. When he wouldn't, they wanted him to drink Short Grass moon with them, but it burned his mouth and choked him and that seemed reason enough to refuse it. So he sat away from them, watching under his bushy brows as from behind sandstone boulders. Their kind laughed at him away from the cave. They could go.

When they kept coming back he got a skunk carcass from old Amos, who trapped a little. After they went away the last time he scooped the contaminated sand down the slope, carried in clean dirt, and built a smudge of twisted mint from the creek bank in the fireplace. When the cave was sweet again he listened to the yodel and tried to forget the black mist of things that had been said and done.

After that nobody came to the cave to bother him and from the earliest spring winds until the narrow tongues of grass along the creek were the autumn brown of young beaver, Rusty's old mare, Sarry, spent many days picketed above the bluffs. When the July noon heat made Rusty's head ache, he spent hours on the crazy quilt, arranging and rearranging the blocks a hundred times before he sewed them, taking joy in the feel and the color, although all dark, shiny things were red to him. He never went near the Lang shack, even before people said it was haunted.

Once several squirts from the community brought a Hallowe'en fruit jar of white dynamite. They went home pretty well scratched up and muddy, as though their departure had been a hasty one. After that Rusty had the canyon to himself, he and the cat, Bidge.

That was his own name for her, as the cat was his own. His mother, tired of the constant mewing of hungry kittens underfoot, told Rusty to take the old gray and white tabby out and drown her.

"B-b-but she don't like water. She swim out," he argued, trying very hard to manage his tongue well for his mother.

"Of course," Sarah Reimer agreed. "Get the old clothesline hanging on the post and tie a rock to her neck."

Rusty scratched his head, exposing his short teeth in a doubtful smile. "Please do as I tell you."

Rusty got his equipment on old Sarry, and with Bidge mewing across the saddle before him, the clothesline snaking along behind him like an Indian's picket rope, he disappeared toward Lang canyon. The mother watched him out of sight and then returned to her churning.

The next morning the cat was crying outside the screen door.

"I just knew it would be like that. Now take her out and tie a rock to her tight so she won't come back. Maybe I had better do it myself."

Rusty pulled at the lobe of his ear and grunted. The cat didn't return. After that he tied her up in a web of clothesline in the cave every time he left.

In corn-plowing time Rusty usually helped. Wearing a watersoaked red handkerchief under his rush hat, the corners flopping about his face, he wielded a hoe against the weeds in the rows. He didn't like it and when the heat dances shimmered before his eyes and the sweat trickled down his broad shoulder blades, he loitered along, wondering if he was certain enough which were sunflowers and which corn. But only until his father came by with the walking cultivator, his round shoulders furry with dust, his horny hands reaching out to pull the weeds the shovels missed. Then Rusty's head felt better. He could tell the difference between weeds and corn quite clearly, and after supper he could have music.

One evening as he plodded down towards his cave, the window in the Lang shack suddenly glowed as from a lamp. Rusty looked toward the moon, standing big and full on the horizon, but it was not that, for the canyon was a deep cup of shadow.

He wanted music but he couldn't have drunks in his cave, so he sprawled out on a sandy cliff, the cat across his chest, and looked into the face of the moon. It had dark spots like black canyons. Perhaps throwing pebbles at the shack might scare them away down there. But it was too much bother, after hoeing.

Sometime after the moon rose high enough to light the sandstone bluffs to a blue-white, Rusty realized there was a splashing in the little pond. He dumped the cat away and, sneaking down the gully, squatted on a knee of rock overlooking the water. A girl swam the moon-gilded pond as smoothly as an otter, then turned and, flailing her white arms upon the water, made a crystal and silver showering all about her. At the far side she climbed out upon a bit of rock, her wet body gleaming like pale silk. Folding her palms together she cut the air and water, disappearing as completely into the still pond as though she had never been. Rusty hugged his knees and watched her come up, shake moonlit drops and weeds flying from her streaming hair, and stretch out upon a bit of sand, breathing in soft little gasps almost lost under the mournful complaint of the spring.

Suddenly far up the slope the deserted cat mewed and came bounding to Rusty, arching her back against him. The girl heard but she did not retreat from the watching figure hunched dark on the rock.

"Who are you—spying on me?"

When there was no answer, she picked up something, a dark garment that shimmered like the moon on black water, slipped it about her and approached the youth with the green eyes of the cat beside him.

"Who are you and what do you want here?"

Still Rusty gave her no answer, staring instead at the lounging robe tied with a long, loose bow.

"P-p-pretty ribbon, red ribbon," he said, as though to himself, reaching out a finger for an end.

"Oh," The girl was relieved. Then she smiled coyly, running the end through her fingers. "Do you like it?"

"P-p-pretty," he said again, rubbing his thick hands together.

"Have you a knife? I'll give you one."

But he had no knife, as his shaking head indicated, and so she deftly twisted one tie about her to hold the robe and ripped the other off. Rusty took the ribbon from her hand, making a little sucking noise between his teeth.

"I-I-I show you my quilt—"

"Quilt, did you say *quilt?*"

His head waggled up and down as he stroked his rough thumb over the silk.

The girl snapped a casual finger at the cat and asked if they lived near. Rusty pointed off towards the north. The woman nodded a little and strolled away to the shack. A long time after she was gone the two plodded up the steep incline. "Pretty ribbon, red ribbon," he told the cat, speaking easily enough now that there was no one but Bidge.

After he had been in bed an hour, his mind a vague pattern of moonlight on the dark robe of a girl, he remembered that he still had his shoes and pants on. Growling like a dog disturbed at his rest, he pulled them off. At last he slept.

After that he watched the woman almost as much as he listened to the phonograph. A few times he perched on the bank outside her doorstep, delighted with the sheen of her dress, the play of her spiked heels. At first she moved in a cloud of annoyance, perhaps even of fear, but later she got so she waved to him, tried to dawdle away a little time talking. One evening she approached very close to him with a letter.

"Will you take this to the post office and tell no one where you got it?" she asked.

Rusty shook his head, remembering a blur of faces there that laughed at him.

"The mailbox then?"

Yes, he could do that, bobbing his head vigorously in delight. When she tried to give him a quarter he growled and made a grab at her dress.

"S-s-scraps!"

Scraps? What did he want with them? Didn't he get enough to eat?

Scraps! He insisted upon scraps, fingering the material of her skirt. When she still did not understand he brought a canvas-rolled bundle from his cave and spread his crazy quilt over her lap, clinging to a corner all the while.

"P-p-pretty," he said.

"Gorgeous!"

Rusty regarded the strange word dubiously, turning it over in his mind as he might a stick of chewing gum from a stranger, afraid it was a joke.

"But I didn't make the dress. There are no scraps," the girl said, and dragged him back to the matter of the mailbox. He rushed off and was back in half an hour, motionless, watching her swim from the knee of rock, now and then rubbing fat blue sparks from the cat.

But the idyllic isolation of Lang's canyon couldn't last. A woman, particularly a strange young woman living in the shack where the man had hanged himself, was a welcome diversion, even in the busy haying season. When the first investigator reported that she was slim as a movie actress and had hair like a brass washboard, there was an epidemic of grouse hunting over that way. Women with straying men suddenly developed a taste for water cress. But the shack door remained closed to all of them. At the post office and at sales there were conjectures. Perhaps a constable might go over to find out who she was. Still, as no heirs ever appeared for the place, there wasn't much to do. The mail carrier admitted that he brought her out, left groceries for her every week at Lang's old box. She got no mail and gave him no name.

Then somebody saw Rusty sitting on a hump of rock, watching the house, the gray and white cat at his side.

"I'll talk to him," Jacob Reimer told his wife and she had to be content.

After supper Rusty seemed eager to escape but his father motioned him to stay. "Want to help me catch sparrows tonight?"

Rusty's short upper lip drew back in a grin. He liked catching sparrows if his father held the lantern and let him run along the stringers and reach into the nests and nooks until his pockets were full. But it was only a game, for he could never bear to see the little birds killed, and after counting them, stroking the quivering backs, feeling the pounding of their little hearts against his palm, he let them go, one after another, until all were lost in the darkness. Then he liked to lie back in the hay, his arms under his head, while his father talked of his own boyhood, and his three brothers.

"B-b-brothers," Rusty would say, almost as though his impediment of speech were all that made him different. "Brothers fine."

Then his father always looked away into the darkness. There could never be any others, but Jacob was thankful. Almost he had lost everything—the son and the mother.

"Bedtime, son," he would say, very gently. But tonight there was more. "You aren't bothering the woman on the Lang place?" he asked.

Rusty moved his head in the hay. "S-s-she give me ribbon, red ribbon," he said after a time.

So? Then it was good. And now to bed.

The next evening a dark cloud leaned out of the west and sent low rumbles of thunder before it as Rusty started old Sarry towards the Lang eighty. The mother looked after him.

"It is good," the father said. "She gave him a ribbon—red, he calls it."

The mother was not entirely satisfied. "What does she want here—such a woman?"

Her husband looked up from his paper. "It cannot mean anything to us and to Joseph."

At the cave Bidge, neglected for two days, her pan of water almost dry, rubbed against Rusty with loud purrs. He pulled her ears and stretched out on the sand to watch the woman. She came from the spring with a pail, stopped, looked all about as she always did lately, and then disappeared into the house to make the window full of light.

In the west the thunder cloud was sending a long arm around behind them and the lightning brightened. A car roared along the mail road. Rusty looked for the shafts of light against the clouds as it climbed Peeler's hill, but there were none.

Just when he first saw the man creeping through the dusk towards the shack Rusty could not tell. It was as though he clotted from the gloom across the creek, taking form as he circled the house. He sneaked to the window, then to the door, as a cat stalks a bird. Silently Rusty slipped down a draw and flattened himself against the shack.

Inside there was a little cry, not loud, but like that of a young badger he caught once. There were words, quick, fending ones from the woman, slow, hard ones like stones dropping into deep water from the man. A stirring in his mind troubled Rusty, a memory almost tangible. Then he had it. It was the *man*. And after he left, Lang had been dead.

Rusty's lips curled back from his teeth. He threw a handful of sand over head and loped up the steep incline to the cave. Gripping the old revolver by the barrel like a club of stone he charged down the slope. From the window he saw the woman was not yet hanging. She had the table between them, but the man clutched her wrist and ran a taunting hand up her arm while she flinched like a wild horse that would paw a man down when the moment came.

In the doorway Rusty blinked once from the glare of light, took aim and brought the gun down upon the bald spot at the man's crown. He swayed, half-turning, and slumped into the shadow of the table.

"Well," the woman said with a little laugh as she rubbed her wrist. "You killed him. Now we better get him out, bury him."

Rusty looked from her to the floor, his eyes blurring. He wiped at them with thick fingers. They cleared a little and, dropping the revolver with a clatter, he vanished into the darkness. At his heels ran a faint patter of rain.

For a moment the woman hesitated, but when the man stirred, groaned, she grasped the revolver and with flat lips she brought the butt down into his temple. It gave like ice-crusted mud.

Before she could straighten up, Rusty was back with the clothesline. Not looking at her at all he dragged the man away to the pond, tied him close to a big rock, and rolled both into the water. There was a deep *plunk* but the lap of the far ripples was lost in the increasing patter of rain.

Rusty wiped the sweat from his face and, trying to remember something, went back into the shack. Before his approaching bulk the woman once more took refuge behind the table. Rusty stopped in the doorway, eyes blinking and searching the floor.

"G-g-g-give me the shooter," he demanded, his voice suddenly harsh.

For a moment she faced him, then slowly she laid the gun on the table. Rusty took it, wiped the skin and blood from the butt on his overalls, and went through the door.

"Where—where are you going?" she asked, in new fear.

But the doorway was empty.

In the cave Rusty sat on a rock for a long time, his hand making rhythmic poppings of sparks from the back of Bidge. Now and then sheet lightning set the hunched figure into bright relief against the deep blackness behind him. The rain quickened.

Somewhere west a car started up; the lights cut the clouds in a half circle. As the roar died away Rusty had a queer prickling of fear along his arms. Once more he plunged down the slope to the shack. The lamp burned in an empty room. The woman was gone; everything was gone except the dark robe, folded on the table, as though for someone. Rusty lifted it. The folds swept downward, gleaming like moonlight on dark water.

V
OLD MAID'S RAMBLE

Stories of Age and Wisdom

An Honest Soul

Mary Eleanor Wilkins Freeman

"T HAR'S MIS' BLISS'S PIECES in the brown kaliker bag, an' thar's Mis' Bennet's pieces in the bed-tickin' bag," said she, surveying complacently the two bags leaning against her kitchen-wall. "I'll get a dollar for both of them quilts, an' thar'll be two dollars. I've got a dollar an' sixty-three cents on hand now, an' thar's plenty of meal an' merlasses, an' some salt fish an' pertaters in the house. I'll get along middlin' well, I reckon. Thar ain't no call fer me to worry. I'll red up the house a leetle now, an' then I'll begin on Mis' Bliss's pieces."

The *house* was an infinitesimal affair, containing only two rooms besides the tiny lean-to which served as wood-shed. It stood far enough back from the road for a pretentious mansion, and there was one curious feature about it—not a door nor window was there in front, only a blank, unbroken wall. Strangers passing by used to stare wonderingly at it sometimes, but it was explained easily enough. Old Simeon Patch, years ago, when the longing for a home of his own had grown strong in his heart, and he had only a few hundred dollars saved from his hard earnings to invest in one, had wisely done the best he could with what he had.

Not much remained to spend on the house after the spacious lot was paid for, so he resolved to build as much house as he could with his money, and complete it when better days should come.

This tiny edifice was in reality simply the L of a goodly two-story house which had existed only in the fond and faithful fancies of Simeon Patch and his wife. That blank front wall was designed to be joined to the projected main building; so, of course, there was no need of doors or windows. Simeon Patch came of a hard-working, honest race, whose pride it had been to keep out of debt, and he was a true child of his ancestors. Not a dollar would he spend that was not in his hand; a mortgaged house was his horror. So he paid cash for every blade of grass on his lot of land, and every nail in his bit of a house, and settled down patiently in it until he should grub together enough more to buy a few additional boards and shingles, and pay the money down.

That time never came: he died in the course of a few years, after a lingering illness, and only had enough saved to pay his doctor's bill and funeral expenses, and leave his wife and daughter entirely without debt, in their little fragment of a house on the big, sorry lot of land.

There they had lived, mother and daughter, earning and saving in various little, petty ways, keeping their heads sturdily above water, and holding the dreaded mortgage off the house for many years. Then the mother died, and the daughter, Martha Patch, took up the little homely struggle alone. She was over seventy now—a small, slender old woman, as straight as a rail, with sharp black eyes, and a quick toss of her head when she spoke. She did odd housewifely jobs for the neighbors, wove rag-carpets, pieced bed-quilts, braided rugs, etc., and contrived to supply all her simple wants.

This evening, after she had finished putting her house to rights, she fell to investigating the contents of the bags which two of the neighbors had brought in the night before, with orders for quilts, much to her delight.

"Mis' Bliss has got proper handsome pieces," said she—"proper handsome; they'll make a good-lookin' quilt. Mis' Bennet's is good too, but they ain't quite ekal to Mis' Bliss's. I reckon some of 'em's old."

She began spreading some of the largest, prettiest pieces on her white-scoured table. "Thar," said she, gazing at one admiringly, "that jest takes my eye; them leetle pink roses is pretty, an' no mistake. I reckon that's French caliker. Thar's some big pieces too. Lor', what bag did I take 'em out on! It must hev been Mis' Bliss's. I mustn't git 'em mixed."

She cut out some squares, and sat down by the window in a low wooden rocking-chair to sew. This window did not have a very pleasant outlook. The house was situated so far back from the road that it commanded only a rear view of the adjoining one. It was a great cross to Martha Patch. She was one of those women who like to see everything that is going on outside, and who often have excuse enough in the fact that so little is going on with them.

"It's a great divarsion," she used to say, in her snapping way, which was more nervous than ill-natured, bobbing her head violently at the same time—"a very great divarsion to see Mr. Peters's cows goin' in an' out of the barn day arter day; an' that's about all I do see—never git a sight of the folks goin' to meetin' nor nothin'."

The lack of a front window was a continual source of grief to her.

"When the minister's prayin' for the widders an' orphans he'd better make mention of one more," said she, once, "an' that's women without front winders."

She and her mother had planned to save money enough to have one some day, but they had never been able to bring it about. A window commanding a view of the street and the passers-by would have been a great source of comfort to the poor old woman, sitting and sewing as she did day in and day out. As it was, she seized eagerly upon the few objects of interest which did come within her vision, and made much of them. There were some children who, on their way from school, could make a short cut through her yard and reach home quicker. She watched for them every day, and if they did not appear quite as soon as usual she would grow uneasy, and eye the clock, and mutter to herself, "I wonder where them Mosely children can be?" When they came she watched their progress with sharp attention, and thought them over for an hour afterwards. Not a bird which passed her window escaped her notice. This innocent old gossip fed her mind upon their small domestic affairs in lieu of larger ones. To-day she often paused between her stitches to gaze absorbedly at a yellow-bird vibrating nervously round the branches of a young tree opposite. It was early spring, and the branches were all of a light-green foam.

"That's the same yaller-bird I saw yesterday, I do b'lieve," said she. "I reckon he's goin' to build a nest in that ellum."

Lately she had been watching the progress of the grass gradually springing up all over the yard. One spot where it grew much greener than elsewhere her mind dwelt upon curiously.

"I can't make out," she said to a neighbor, "whether that 'ere spot is greener than the rest because the sun shines brightly thar, or because somethin's buried thar."

She toiled steadily on the patchwork quilts. At the end of a fortnight they were nearly completed. She hurried on the last one morning, thinking she would carry them both to their owners that afternoon and get her pay. She did not stop for any dinner.

Spreading them out for one last look before rolling them up in bundles, she caught her breath hastily.

"What hev I done?" said she. "Massy sakes! I hevn't gone an' put Mis' Bliss's caliker with the leetle pink roses on't in Mis' Bennet's quilt? I hev, jest as sure as preachin'! What shell I do?"

The poor old soul stood staring at the quilts in pitiful dismay. "A hull fortni't's work," she muttered. "What shell I do? Them pink roses is the prettiest caliker in the hull lot. Mis' Bliss will be mad if they air in Mis' Bennet's quilt. She won't say nothin', an' she'll pay me, but she'll feel it inside, an' it won't be doin' the squar' thing by her. No; if I'm goin' to airn money I'll airn it."

Martha Patch gave her head a jerk. The spirit which animated her father when he went to housekeeping in a piece of a house without any front window blazed up within her. She made herself a cup of tea, then sat deliberately down by the window to rip the quilts to pieces. It had to be done pretty thoroughly on account of her admiration for the pink calico, and the quality of it—if figured in nearly every square. "I wish I hed a front winder to set to while I'm doin' on't," said she; but she patiently plied her scissors till dusk, only stopping for a short survey of the Mosely children. After days of steady work the pieces were put together again, this time the pink-rose calico in Mrs. Bliss's quilt. Martha Patch rolled the quilts up with a sigh of relief and a sense of virtuous triumph.

"I'll sort over the pieces that's left in the bags," said she, "then I'll take 'em over an' git my pay. I'm gittin' pretty short of vittles."

She began pulling the pieces out of the bed-ticking bag, laying them on her lap and smoothing them out, preparatory to doing them up in a neat, tight roll to take home—she was very methodical about everything she did. Suddenly she turned pale, and stared wildly at a tiny scrap of calico which she had just fished out of the bag.

"Massy sakes!" she cried; "it ain't, is it?" She clutched Mrs. Bliss's quilt from the table and laid the bit of calico beside the pink-rose squares.

"It's jest the same thing," she groaned, "an' it came out on Mis' Bennet's bag. Dear me suz! dear me suz!"

She dropped helplessly into her chair by the window, still holding the quilt and the telltale scrap of calico, and gazed out in a bewildered sort of way. Her poor old eyes looked dim and weak with tears.

"Thar's the Mosely children comin'," she said; "happy little gals, laughin' an' hollerin', goin' home to their mother to git a good dinner. Me a-settin' here's a lesson they ain't larned in their books yit; hope to goodness they never will; hope they won't ever hev to piece quilts fur a livin', without any front winder to set to. Thar's a dandelion blown out on that green spot. Reckon thar *is* somethin' buried thar. Lordy massy! *hev* I got to rip them two quilts to pieces agin an' sew 'em over?"

Finally she resolved to carry a bit of the pink-rose calico over to Mrs. Bennet's and find out, without betraying the dilemma she was in, if it were really hers.

Her poor old knees fairly shook under her when she entered Mrs. Bennet's sitting-room.

"Why, yes, Martha, it's mine," said Mrs. Bennet, in response to her agitated question. "Hattie had a dress like it, don't you remember? There was a lot of new pieces left, and I thought they would work into a quilt nice. But, for pity's sake, Martha, what is the matter? You look just as white as a sheet. You ain't sick, are you?"

"No," said Martha, with a feeble toss of her head, to keep up the deception; "I ain't sick, only kinder all gone with the warm weather. I reckon I'll hev to fix me up some thoroughwort tea. Thoroughwort's a great strengthener."

"I would," said Mrs. Bennet, sympathizingly; "and don't you work too hard on that quilt; I ain't in a bit of a hurry for it. I sha'n't want it before next winter anyway. I only thought I'd like to have it pieced and ready."

"I reckon I can't get it done afore another fortni't," said Martha, trembling.

"I don't care if you don't get it done for the next three months. Don't go yet, Martha; you ain't rested a minute, and it's a pretty long walk. Don't you want a bit of something before you go? Have a piece of cake? You look real faint."

"No, thanky," said Martha, and departed in spite of all friendly entreaties to tarry. Mrs. Bennet watched her moving slowly down the road, still holding the little pink calico rag in her brown, withered fingers.

"Martha Patch is failing; she ain't near so straight as she was," remarked Mrs. Bennet. "She looks real bent over to-day."

The little wiry springiness was, indeed, gone from her gait as she crept slowly along the sweet country road, and there was a helpless droop in her thin, narrow shoulders. It was a beautiful spring day; the fruit-trees were all in blossom. There were more orchards than houses on the way, and more blooming trees to pass than people.

Martha looked up at the white branches as she passed under them. "I kin smell the apple-blows," said she, "but somehow the goodness is all gone out on 'em. I'd jest as soon smell cabbage. Oh, dear me suz, kin I ever do them quilts over agin?"

When she got home, however, she rallied a little. There was a nervous force about this old woman which was not easily overcome even by an accumulation of misfortunes. She might bend a good deal, but she was almost sure to spring back again. She took off her hood and shawl, and straightened herself up. "Thar's no use puttin' it off; it's got to be done. I'll hev them quilts right ef it kills me!"

She tied on a purple calico apron and sat down at the window again, with a quilt and the scissors. Out came the pink roses. There she sat through the long afternoon, cutting the stitches which she had so laboriously put in—a little defiant old figure, its head, with a flat black lace cap on it, bobbing up and down in time with its hands. There were some purple bows on the cap, and they fluttered; quite a little wind blew in at the window.

The eight-day clock on the mantel ticked peacefully. It was a queer old timepiece, which had belonged to her grandmother Patch. A painting of a quaint female, with puffed hair and a bunch of roses, adorned the front of it, under the dial-plate. It was flanked on either side by tall, green vases.

There was a dull colored rag-carpet of Martha's own manufacture on the floor of the room. Some wooden chairs stood around stiffly; an old, yellow map of Massachusetts and a portrait of George Washington hung on the walls. There was not a speck of dust anywhere, nor any disorder. Neatness was one of the comforts of Martha's life. Putting and keeping things in order was one of the interests which enlivened her dullness and made the world attractive to her.

The poor soul sat at the window, bending over the quilt, until dusk, and she sat there, bending over the quilt until dusk, many a day after.

It is a hard question to decide, whether there were any real merit in such finely strained honesty, or whether it were merely a case of morbid conscientiousness. Perhaps the old woman, inheriting very likely her father's scruples, had had them so intensified by age and childishness that they had become a little off the bias of reason.

Be that as it may, she thought it was the right course for her to make the quilts over, and, thinking so, it was all that she could do. She could never have been satisfied otherwise. It took her a considerable while longer to finish the quilts again, and this time she began to suffer from other causes than mere fatigue. Her stock of provisions commenced to run low, and her money was gone. At last she had nothing but a few potatoes in the house to eat. She contrived to dig some dandelion greens once or twice; these with the potatoes were all her diet. There was really no necessity for such a state of things; she was surrounded by kindly well-to-do people, who would have gone without themselves rather than let her suffer. But she had always been very reticent about her needs, and felt great pride about accepting anything for which she did not pay.

But she struggled along until the quilts were done, and no one knew. She set the last stitch quite late one evening; then she spread the quilts out and surveyed them. "Thar they air now, all right," said she; "the pink roses is in Mis' Bennet's, an' I ain't cheated nobody out on their caliker, an' I've airned my money. I'll take 'em hum in the mornin', an' then I'll buy somethin' to eat. I begin to feel a dreadful sinkin' at my stummuck."

She locked up the house carefully—she always felt a great responsibility when she had people's work on hand—and went to bed.

Next morning she woke up so faint and dizzy that she hardly knew herself. She crawled out into the kitchen, and sank down on the floor. She could not move another step.

"Lor sakes!" she moaned, "I reckon I'm 'bout done to!"

The quilts lay near her on the table; she stared up at them with feeble complacency. "Ef I'm goin' to die, I'm glad I got them quilts done right fust. Massy, how sinkin' I do feel! I wish I had a cup of tea."

There she lay, and the beautiful spring morning wore on. The sun shone in at the window, and moved nearer and nearer, until finally she lay in a sunbeam, a poor, shrivelled little old woman, whose resolute spirit had nearly been her death, in her scant nightgown and ruffled cap, a little shawl falling from her shoulders. She did not feel ill, only absolutely too weak and helpless to move. Her mind was just as active as ever, and her black eyes peered sharply out of her pinched face. She kept making efforts to rise, but she could not stir.

"Lor sakes!" she snapped out at length, "how long *hev* I got to lay here? I'm mad!"

She saw some dust on the black paint of a chair which stood in the sun, and she eyed that distressfully.

"Jest look at that dust on the runs of that cheer!" she muttered. "What if anybody come in! I wonder if I can't reach it!"

The chair was near her, and she managed to stretch out her limp old hand and rub the dust off the rounds. Then she let it sink down, panting.

"I wonder ef I *ain't* goin' to die," she gasped. "I wonder ef I'm prepared. I never took nothin' that shouldn't belong to me that I knows on. Oh, dear me suz, I wish somebody would come!"

When her strained ears did catch the sound of footsteps outside, a sudden resolve sprang up in her heart.

"I won't let on to nobody how I've made them quilts over, an' how I hevn't had enough to eat—I won't."

When the door was tried she called out feebly, "Who is thar?"

The voice of Mrs. Peters, her next-door neighbor, came back in response: "It's me. What's the matter, Marthy?"

"I'm kinder used up; don't know how you'll git in; I can't git to the door to unlock it to save my life."

"Can't I get in at the window?"

"Mebbe you kin."

Mrs. Peters was a long-limbed, spare woman, and she got in through the window with considerable ease, it being quite low from the ground.

She turned pale when she saw Martha lying on the floor. "Why, Marthy, what is the matter? How long have you been laying there?"

"Ever since I got up. I was kinder dizzy, an' hed a dreadful sinkin' feelin'. It ain't much, I reckon. Ef I could hev a cup of tea it would set me right up. Thar's a spoonful left in the pantry. Ef you jest put a few kindlin's in the stove, Mis' Peters, an' set in the kettle an' made me a cup, I could git up, I know. I've got to go an' kerry them quilts hum to Mis' Bliss an' Mis' Bennet."

"I don't believe but what you've got all tired out over the quilts. You've been working too hard."

"No, I 'ain't, Mis' Peters; it's nothin' but play piecin' quilts. All I mind is not havin' a front winder to set to while I'm doin' on't."

Mrs. Peters was a quiet, sensible woman of few words; she insisted upon carrying Martha into the bedroom and putting her comfortably to bed. It was easily done; she was muscular, and the old woman a very light weight. Then she went into the pantry. She was beginning to suspect the state of affairs, and her suspicions were strengthened when she saw the bare shelves. She started the fire, put on the tea-kettle, and then slipped across the yard to her own house for further reinforcements.

Pretty soon Martha was drinking her cup of tea and eating her toast and a dropped egg. She had taken the food with some reluctance, half starved as she was. Finally she gave in—the sight of it was too much for her. "Well, I will borry it, Mis' Peters," said she; "an' I'll pay you jest as soon as I kin git up."

After she had eaten she felt stronger. Mrs. Peters had hard work to keep her quiet until afternoon; then she would get up and carry the quilts home. The two ladies were profuse in praises. Martha, proud and smiling. Mrs. Bennet noticed the pink roses at once. "How pretty that calico did work in," she remarked.

"Yes," assented Martha, between an inclination to chuckle and to cry.

"Ef I ain't thankful I did them quilts over," thought she, creeping slowly homeward, her hard-earned two dollars knotted into a corner of her handkerchief for security.

About sunset Mrs. Peters came in again. "Marthy," she said, after a while, "Sam says he's out of work just now, and he'll cut through a front window for you. He's got some old sash and glass that's been laying round in the barn ever since I can remember. It'll be a real charity for you to take it off his hands, and he'll like to do it. Sam's as uneasy as a fish out of water when he hasn't got any work."

Martha eyed her suspiciously. "Thanky; but I don't want nothin' done that I can't pay for," said she, with a stiff toss of her head.

"It would be pay enough, just letting Sam do it, Marthy; but, if you really feel set about it, I've got some sheets that need turning. You can do them some time this summer, and that will pay us for all it's worth."

The black eyes looked at her sharply. "Air you sure?"

"Yes; it's fully as much as it's worth," said Mrs. Peters. "I'm most afraid it's more. There's four sheets, and putting in a window is nothing more than putting in a patch—the old stuff ain't worth anything."

When Martha fully realized that she was going to have a front window, and that her pride might suffer it to be given to her and yet receive no insult, she was as delighted as a child.

"Lor sakes!" said she, "jest to think that I shall have a front winder to set to! I wish mother could ha' lived to see it. Mebbe you kinder wonder at it, Mis' Peters—you've allers had front winders; but you haven't any idea what a great thing it seems to me. It kinder makes me feel younger. Thar's the Mosely children; they're 'bout all I've ever seen pass *this* winder, Mis' Peters. Jest see that green spot out thar; it's been greener than the rest of the yard all the spring, an' now thar's lots of dandelions blowed out on it, an' some clover. I b'lieve the sun shines more on it, somehow. Law me, to think I'm going to hev a front winder!"

"Sarah was in this afternoon," said Mrs. Peters, further (Sarah was her married daughter), "and she says she wants some braided rugs right away. She'll send the rags over by Willie to-morrow."

"You don't say so! Well I'll be glad to do it; an' thar's one thing 'bout it, Mis' Peters—mebbe you'll think it queer for me to say so, but I'm kinder thankful it's rugs she wants. I'm kinder sick of bed-quilts somehow."

Aunt Jane of Kentucky

Eliza Calvert Hall

T HEY WERE a bizarre mass of color on the sweet spring landscape, those patchwork quilts, swaying in a long line under the elms and maples. The old orchard made a blossoming background for them, and farther off on the horizon rose the beauty of fresh verdure and purple mist on those low hills, or "knobs," that are to the heart of the Kentuckian as the Alps to the Swiss or the sea to the sailor.

I opened the gate softly and paused for a moment between the blossoming lilacs that grew on each side of the path. The fragrance of the white and the purple blooms was like a resurrection-call over the graves of many a dead spring; and as I stood, shaken with thoughts as the flowers are with the winds, Aunt Jane came around from the back of the house, her black silk cape fluttering from her shoulders, and a calico sunbonnet hiding her features in its cavernous depth. She walked briskly to the clothes-line and began patting and smoothing the quilts where the breeze had disarranged them.

"Aunt Jane," I called out, "are you having a fair all by yourself?"

She turned quickly, pushing back the sunbonnet from her eyes.

"Why, child," she said, with a happy laugh, "you come pretty nigh skeerin' me. No, I ain't havin' any fair; I'm jest givin' my quilts their spring airin'. Twice a year I put 'em out in the sun and wind; and this mornin' the air smelt so sweet, I thought it was a good chance to freshen 'em up for the summer. It's about time to take 'em in now."

She began to fold the quilts and lay them over her arm, and I did the same. Back and forth we went from the clothes-line to the house, and from the house to the clothes-line, until the quilts were safely housed from the coming dewfall and piled on every available chair in the front room. I looked at them in sheer amazement. There seemed to be every pattern that the ingenuity of woman could devise and the industry of woman put together,—"four-patches," "nine-patches," "log-cabins," "wild-goose chases," "rising suns," hexagons, diamonds, and only Aunt Jane knows what else. As for color, a Sandwich Islander would have danced with joy at the sight of those reds, purples, yellows, and greens.

"Did you really make all these quilts, Aunt Jane?" I asked wonderingly.

Aunt Jane's eyes sparkled with pride.

"Every stitch of 'em, child," she said, "except the quiltin'. The neighbors used to come in and help some with that. I've heard folks say that piecin' quilts was nothin' but a waste o' time, but that ain't always so. They used to say that Sarah Jane Mitchell would set down right after breakfast and piece till it was time to git dinner, and then set and piece till she had to git supper, and then piece by candle-light till she fell asleep in her cheer.

"I ricollect goin' over there one day, and Sarah Jane was gittin' dinner in a big hurry, for Sam had to go to town with some cattle, and there was a big basket o' quilt pieces in the middle o' the kitchen floor, and the house lookin' like a pigpen, and the children runnin' around half naked. And Sam he laughed, and says he, 'Aunt Jane, if we could wear quilts and eat quilts we'd be the richest people in the country.' Sam was the best-natured man that ever was, or he couldn't 'a' put up with Sarah Jane's shiftless ways. Hannah Crawford said she sent Sarah Jane a bundle o' caliker once by Sam, and Sam always declared he lost it. But Uncle Jim Matthews said he was ridin' along the road jest behind Sam, and he saw Sam throw it into the creek jest as he got on the bridge. I never blamed Sam a bit if he did.

"But there never was any time wasted on my quilts, child. I can look at every one of 'em with a clear conscience. I did my work faithful; and then, when I might 'a' set and held my hands, I'd make a block or two o' patchwork, and before long I'd have enough to put together in a quilt. I went to piecin' as soon as I was old enough to hold a needle and a piece o' cloth, and one o' the first things I can remember was settin' on the back door-step sewin' my quilt pieces, and mother praisin' my stitches. Nowadays folks don't have to sew unless they want to, but when I was a child there warn't any sewin'-machines, and it was about as needful for folks to know how to sew as it was for 'em to know how to eat; and every child that was well raised could hem and run and backstitch and gether and overhand by the time she was nine years old. Why, I'd pieced four quilts by the time I was nineteen years old, and when me and Abram set up housekeepin' I had bedclothes enough for three beds.

"I've had a heap o' comfort all my life makin' quilts, and now in my old age I wouldn't take a fortune for 'em. Set down here, child, where you can see out o' the winder and smell the lilacs, and we'll look at 'em all. You see, some folks has albums to put folks' pictures in to remember 'em by, and some folks has a book and writes down the things that happen every day so they won't forget 'em; but, honey, these quilts is my albums and my di'ries, and whenever the weather's bad and I can't git out to see folks, I jest spread out my quilts and look at 'em and study over 'em, and it's jest like goin' back fifty or sixty years and livin' my life over agin.

"There ain't nothin' like a piece o' caliker for bringin' back old times, child, unless it's a flower or a bunch o' thyme or a piece o' pennyroy'l—anything that smells sweet. Why, I can go out yonder in the yard and gether a bunch o' that purple lilac and jest shut my eyes and see faces I ain't seen for fifty years, and somethin' goes through me like a flash o' lightnin', and it seems like I'm young agin jest for that minute."

Aunt Jane's hands were stroking lovingly a "nine-patch" that resembled the coat of many colors.

"Now this quilt, honey," she said, "I made out o' the pieces o' my children's clothes, their little dresses and waists and aprons. Some of 'em's dead, and some of 'em's grown and married and a long way off from me, further off than the ones that's dead, I sometimes think. But when I set down and look at this quilt and think over the pieces, it seems like they all come back, and I can see 'em cryin' and laughin' and callin' me jest like they used to do before they grew up to men and women, and before there was any little graves o' mine out in the old buryin'-ground over yonder."

Wonderful imagination of motherhood that can bring childhood back from the dust of the grave and banish the wrinkles and gray hairs of age with no other talisman than a scrap of faded calico!

The old woman's hands were moving tremulously over the surface of the quilt as if they touched the golden curls of the little dream children who had vanished from her hearth so many years ago. But there were no tears either in her eyes or in her voice. I had long noticed that Aunt Jane always smiled when she spoke of the people whom the world calls "dead," or the things it calls "lost" or "past." These words seemed to have for her higher and tenderer meanings than are placed on them by the sorrowful heart of humanity.

But the moments were passing, and one could not dwell too long on any quilt, however well beloved. Aunt Jane rose briskly, folded up the one that lay across her knees, and whisked out another from the huge pile in an old splint-bottomed chair.

"Here's a piece o' one o' Sally Ann's purple caliker dresses. Sally Ann always thought a heap o' purple caliker. Here's one o' Milly Amos' ginghams—that pink-and-white one. And that piece o' white with the rosebuds in it, that's Miss Penelope's. She give it to me the summer before she died. Bless her soul! That dress jest matched her face exactly. Somehow her and her clothes always looked alike, and her voice matched her face, too. One o' the things I'm lookin' forward to, child, is seein' Miss Penelope agin and hearin' her sing. Voices and faces is alike; there's some that you can't remember, and there's some you can't forgit. I've seen a heap o' people and heard a heap o' voices, but Miss Penelope's face was different from all the rest, and so was her voice. Why, if she said 'Good mornin'' to you, you'd hear that 'Good mornin' all day, and her singin'—I know there never was anything like it in this world. My grandchildren all laugh at me for thinkin' so much o' Miss Penelope's singin', but then they never heard her, and I have: that's the difference. My grandchild Henrietta was down here three or four years ago, and says she, 'Grandma, don't you want to go up to Louisville with me and hear Patti sing?' And says I, 'Patty who, child?' Says I, 'If it was to hear Miss Penelope sing, I'd carry these old bones o' mine clear from here to New York. But there ain't anybody else I want to hear sing bad enough to go up to Louisville or anywhere else. And some o' these days,' says I, '*I'm goin' to hear Miss Penelope sing.*'"

Aunt Jane laughed blithely, and it was impossible not to laugh with her.

"Honey," she said in the next breath, lowering her voice and laying her finger on the rosebud piece, "honey, there's one thing I can't git over. Here's a piece o' Miss Penelope's dress, but *where's Miss Penelope*? Ain't it strange that a piece o' caliker'll outlast you and me? Don't it look like folks ought 'o hold on to their bodies as long as other folks holds on to a piece o' the dresses they used to wear?"

Questions as old as the human heart and its human grief! Here is the glove, but where is the hand it held but yesterday? Here the jewel that she wore, but where is she?

> "Where is the Pompadour now?
> *This* was the Pompadour's fan!"

Strange that such things as gloves, jewels, fans, and dresses can outlast a woman's form.

"Behold! I show you a mystery"—the mystery of mortality. And an eery feeling came over me as I entered into the old woman's mood and thought of the strong, vital bodies that had clothed themselves in those fabrics of purple and pink and white, and that now were dust and ashes lying in sad, neglected graves on farm and lonely roadside. There lay the quilt on our knees, and the gay scraps of calico seemed to mock us with their vivid colors. Aunt Jane's cheerful voice called me back from the tombs.

"Here's a piece o' one o' my dresses," she said; "brown ground with a red ring in it. Abram picked it out. And here's another one, that light yeller ground with the vine runnin' through it. I never had so many caliker dresses that I didn't want one more, for in my day folks used to think a caliker dress was good enough to wear anywhere. Abram knew my failin', and two or three times a year he'd bring me a dress when he come from town. And the dresses he'd pick out always suited me better'n the ones I picked.

"I ricollect I finished this quilt the summer before Mary Frances was born, and Sally Ann and Milly Amos and Maria Petty come over and give me a lift on the quiltin'. Here's Milly's work, here's Sally Ann's, and here's Maria's."

I looked, but my inexperienced eye could see no difference in the handiwork of the three women. Aunt Jane saw my look of incredulity.

"Now, child," she said, earnestly, "you think I'm foolin' you, but, la! there's jest as much difference in folks' sewin' as there is in their hand-writin'. Milly made a fine stitch, but she couldn't keep on the line to save her life; Maria never could make a reg'lar stitch, some'd be long and some short, and Sally Ann's was reg'lar, but all of 'em coarse. I can see 'em now stoopin' over the quiltin' frames—Milly talkin' as hard as she sewed, Sally Ann throwin' in a word now and then, and Marie never openin' her mouth except to ask for the thread or the chalk. I ricollect they come over after dinner, and we got the quilt out o' the frames long before sundown, and the next day I begun bindin' it, and I got the premium on it that year at the Fair.

"I hardly ever showed a quilt at the Fair that I didn't take the premium, but here's one quilt that Sarah Jane Mitchell beat me on."

And Aunt Jane dragged out a ponderous, red-lined affair, the very antithesis of the silken, down-filled comfortable that rests so lightly on the couch of the modern dame.

"It makes me laugh jest to think o' that time, and how happy Sarah

Jane was. It was way back yonder in the fifties. I ricollect we had a
mighty fine Fair that year. The crops was all fine that season, and such
apples and pears and grapes you never did see. The Floral Hall was full o'
things, and the whole county turned out to go to the Fair. Abram and
me got there the first day bright and early, and we was walkin' around
the amp'itheater and lookin' at the townfolks and the sights, and we met
Sally Ann. She stopped us, and says she, 'Sarah Jane Mitchell's got a
quilt in the Floral Hall in competition with yours and Milly Amos'.' Says
I, 'Is that all the competition there is?' And Sally Ann says, 'All that
amounts to anything. There's one more, but it's about as bad a piece o'
sewin' as Sarah Jane's, and that looks like it'd hardly hold together till
the Fair's over. And,' says she, 'I don't believe there'll be any more. It
looks like this was an off year on that particular kind o' quilt. I didn't get
mine done,' says she, 'and neither did Maria Petty, and maybe it's a good
thing after all.'

"Well, I saw in a minute what Sally Ann was aimin' at. And I says to
Abram, 'Abram, haven't you got somethin' to do with app'intin' the
judges for the women's things?' And he says, 'Yes.' And I says, 'Well, you
see to it that Sally Ann gits app'inted to help judge the caliker quilts.'
And bless your soul, Abram got me and Sally Ann both app'inted. The
other judge was Mis' Doctor Brigham, one o' the town ladies. We told
her all about what we wanted to do, and she jest laughed and says, 'Well,
if that ain't the kindest, nicest thing! Of course we'll do it.'

"Seein' that I had a quilt there, I hadn't a bit o' business bein' a judge;
but the first thing I did was to fold my quilt up and hide it under Maria
Petty's big worsted quilt, and then we pinned the blue ribbon on Sarah
Jane's and the red on Milly's. I'd fixed it all up with Milly, and she was jest
as willin' as I was for Sarah Jane to have the premium. There was jest one
thing I was afraid of: Milly was a good-hearted woman, but she never had
much control over her tongue. And I says to her, says I: 'Milly, it's mighty
good of you to give up your chance for the premium, but if Sarah Jane ever
finds it out, that'll spoil everything. For,' says I, 'there ain't any kindness
in doin' a person a favor and then tellin' everybody about it.' And Milly
laughed, and says she: 'I know what you mean, Aunt Jane. It's mighty hard
for me to keep from tellin' everything I know and some things I don't
know, but,' says she, 'I'm never goin' to tell this, even to Sam.' And she
kept her word, too. Every once in a while she'd come up to me and
whisper, 'I ain't told it yet, Aunt Jane,' jest to see me laugh.

"As soon as the doors was open, after we'd all got through judgin' and puttin' on the ribbons, Milly went and hunted Sarah Jane up and told her that her quilt had the blue ribbon. They said the pore thing like to 'a' fainted for joy. She turned right white, and had to lean up against the post for a while before she could git to the Floral Hall. I never shall forgit her face. It was worth a dozen premiums to me, and Milly, too. She jest stood lookin' at that quilt and the blue ribbon on it, and her eyes was full o' tears and her lips quiverin', and then she started off and brought the children in to look at 'Mammy's quilt.' She met Sam on the way out, and says she: 'Sam, what do you reckon? My quilt took the premium.' And I believe in my soul Sam was as much pleased as Sarah Jane. He came saunterin' up, tryin' to look unconcerned, but anybody could see he was mighty well satisfied. It does a husband and wife a heap o' good to be proud of each other, and I reckon that was the first time Sam ever had cause to be proud o' pore Sarah Jane all the rest o' her life jest on account o' that premium. Me and Sally Ann helped her pick it out. She had her choice betwixt a butter-dish and a cup, and she took the cup. Folks used to laugh and say that that cup was the only thing in Sarah Jane's house that was kept clean and bright, and if it hadn't 'a' been solid silver, she'd 'a' wore it all out rubbin' it up. Sarah Jane died o' pneumonia about three or four years after that, and the folks that nursed her said she wouldn't take a drink o' water or a dose o' medicine out o' any cup but that. There's some folks, child, that don't have to do anything but walk along and hold out their hands, and the premiums jest naturally fall into 'em; and there's others that work and strive the best they know how, and nothin' ever seems to come to 'em; and I reckon nobody but the Lord and Sarah Jane knows how much happiness she got out o' that cup. I'm thankful she had that much pleasure before she died."

There was a quilt hanging over the foot of the bed that had about it a certain air of distinction. It was a solid mass of patchwork, composed of squares, parallelograms, and hexagons. The squares were of dark gray and red-brown, the hexagons were white, the parallelograms black and light gray. I felt sure that it had a history that set it apart from its ordinary fellows.

"Where did you get the pattern, Aunt Jane?" I asked. "I never saw anything like it."

The old lady's eyes sparkled, and she laughed with pure pleasure.

"That's what everybody says," she exclaimed, jumping up and spread-

ing the favored quilt over two laden chairs, where its merits became more
apparent and striking. "There ain't another quilt like this in the State o'
Kentucky, or the world, for that matter. My granddaughter Henrietta,
Mary Frances' youngest child, brought me this pattern *from Europe*."

She spoke the words as one might say, "from Paradise," or "from
Olympus," or "from the Lost Atlantis." "Europe" was evidently a name
to conjure with, a country of mystery and romance unspeakable. I had
seen many things from many lands beyond the sea, but a quilt pattern
from Europe! Here at last was something new under the sun. In what
shop of London or Paris were quilt patterns kept on sale for the American tourist?

"You see," said Aunt Jane, "Henrietta married a mighty rich man,
and jest as good as he's rich, too, and they went to Europe on their bridal
trip. When she come home she brought me the prettiest shawl you ever
saw. She made me stand up and shut my eyes, and she put it on my
shoulders and made me look in the lookin'-glass, and then she says, 'I
brought you a new quilt pattern, too, grandma, and I want you to piece
one quilt by it and leave it to me when you die.' And then she told me
about goin' to a town over yonder they call Florence, and how she went
into a big church that was built hundreds o' years before I was born. And
she said the floor was made o' little pieces o' colored stone, all laid
together in a pattern, and they called it mosaic. And says I, 'Honey, has
it got anything to do with Moses and his law?' You know the Command-
ments was called the Mosaic Law, and was all on tables o' stone. And
Henrietta jest laughed, and says she: 'No, grandma; I don't believe it
has. But,' says she, 'the minute I stepped on that pavement I thought
about you, and I drew this pattern off on a piece o' paper and brought it
all the way to Kentucky for you to make a quilt by.' Henrietta bought the
worsted for me, for she said it had to be jest the colors o' that pavement
over yonder, and I made it that very winter."

Aunt Jane was regarding the quilt with worshipful eyes, and it really
was an effective combination of color and form.

"Many a time while I was piecin' that," she said, "I thought about
the man that laid the pavement in that old church, and wondered what
his name was, and how he looked, and what he'd think if he knew there
was a old woman down here in Kentucky usin' his patterns to make a
bedquilt."

It was indeed a far cry from the Florentine artisan of centuries ago to this humble worker in calico and worsted, but between the two stretched a cord of sympathy that made them one—the eternal aspiration after beauty.

"Honey," said Aunt Jane, suddenly, "did I ever show you my premiums?"

And then, with pleasant excitement in her manner, she arose, fumbled in her deep pocket for an ancient bunch of keys, and unlocked a cupboard on one side of the fireplace. One by one she drew them out, unrolled the soft yellow tissue-paper that enfolded them, and ranged them in a stately line on the old cherry center-table—nineteen sterling silver cups and goblets. "Abram took some of 'em on his fine stock, and I took some of 'em on my quilts and salt-risin' bread and cakes," she said, impressively.

To the artist his medals, to the soldier his cross of the Legion of Honor, and to Aunt Jane her silver cups! All the triumph of a humble life was symbolized in these shining things. They were simple and genuine as the days in which they were made. A few of them boasted a beaded edge or a golden lining, but no engraving or embossing marred their silver purity. On the bottom of each was the stamp: "John B. Akin, Danville, Ky." There they stood,

"Filled to the brim with precious memories,"—

memories of the time when she and Abram had worked together in field or garden or home, and the County Fair brought to all a yearly opportunity to stand on the height of achievement and know somewhat the taste of Fame's enchanted cup.

"There's one for every child and every grandchild," she said, quietly, as she began wrapping them in the silky paper, and storing them carefully away in the cupboard, there to rest until the day when children and grandchildren would claim their own, and the treasures of the dead would come forth from the darkness to stand as heirlooms on fashionable sideboards and damask-covered tables.

"Did you ever think, child" she said, presently, "how much piecin' a quilt's like livin' a life? And as for sermons, why, they ain't no better sermon to me than a patchwork quilt, and the doctrines is right there a heap plainer'n they are in the catechism. Many a time I've set and listened to Parson Page preachin' about predestination and free-will, and I've said to myself, 'Well, I ain't never been through Centre College up at Danville, but if I could jest git up in the pulpit with one of my quilts, I could make it a heap plainer to folks than parson's makin' it with all his big words.' You see, you start out with jest so much caliker, you don't go to the store and pick it out and buy it, but the neighbors will give you a piece here and a piece there, and you'll have a piece left every time you cut out a dress, and you take jest what happens to come. And that's like predestination. But when it comes to the cuttin' out, why, you're free to choose your own pattern. You can give the same kind o' pieces to two persons, and one'll make a 'nine-patch' and one'll make a 'wild-goose chase,' and there'll be two quilts made out o' the same kind o' pieces, and jest as different as they can be. And that is jest the way with livin'. The Lord sends us the pieces, but we can cut 'em out and put 'em together pretty much to suit ourselves, and there's a heap more in the cuttin' out and the sewin' than there is in the caliker. The same sort o' things comes into all lives, jest as the Apostle says, 'There hath no trouble taken you but is common to all men.'

"The same trouble'll come into two people's lives, and one'll take it and make one thing out of it, and the other'll make somethin' entirely different. There was Mary Harris and Mandy Crawford. They both lost their husbands the same year; and Mandy set down and cried and worried and wondered what on earth she was goin' to do, and the farm went to wrack and the children turned out bad, and she had to live with her son-in-law in her old age. But Mary, she got up and went to work, and made everybody about her work, too; and she managed the farm better'n it ever had been managed before, and the boys all come up steady, hard-workin' men, and there wasn't a woman in the county better fixed up than Mary Harris. Things is predestined to come to us, honey, but we're jest as free as air to make what we please out of 'em. And when it comes to puttin' the pieces together, there's another time when we're free. You don't trust to luck for the caliker to put your quilt together with; you go to the store and pick it out yourself, any color you like. There's folks that always looks on the bright side and makes the best of everything, and that's like puttin' your quilt together with blue or pink or white or some other pretty color; and there's folks that never see anything but the dark side, and always lookin' for trouble, and treasurin' it up after they git it, and they're puttin' their lives together with black, jest like you would put a quilt together with some dark, ugly color. You can spoil the prettiest quilt pieces that ever was made jest by puttin' 'em together with the wrong color, and the best sort o' life is miserable if you don't look at things right and think about 'em right.

"Then there's another thing. I've seen folks piece and piece, but when it come to puttin' the blocks together and quiltin' and linin' it, they'd give out; and that's like folks that do a little here and a little there, but their lives ain't of much use after all, any more'n a lot o' loose pieces o' patchwork. And then while you're livin' your life, it looks pretty much like a jumble o' quilt pieces before they're put together; but when you git through with it, or pretty nigh through, as I am now, you'll see the use and the purpose of everything in it. Everything'll be in its right place jest like the squares in this 'four-patch,' and one piece may be pretty and another one ugly, but it all looks right when you see it finished and joined together."

Did I say that every pattern was represented? No, there was one notable omission. Not a single "crazy quilt" was there in the collection. I called Aunt Jane's attention to this lack.

"Child," she said, "I used to say there wasn't anything I couldn't do if I made up my mind to it. But I hadn't seen a 'crazy quilt' then. The first one I ever seen was up at Danville at Mary Frances', and Henrietta says, 'Now, grandma, you've got to make a crazy quilt; you've made every other sort that ever was heard of.' And she brought me the pieces and showed me how to baste 'em on the square, and said she'd work the fancy stitches around 'em for me. Well, I set there all the mornin' tryin' to fix up that square, and the more I tried, the uglier and crookeder the thing looked. And finally I says: 'Here, child, take your pieces. If I was to make this the way you want me to, they'd be a crazy quilt and a crazy woman, too.'"

Aunt Jane was laying the folded quilts in neat piles here and there about the room. There was a look of unspeakable satisfaction on her face—the look of the creator who sees his completed work and pronounces it good.

"I've been a hard worker all my life," she said, seating herself and folding her hands restfully, "but 'most all my work has been the kind that 'perishes with the usin',' as the Bible says. That's the discouragin' thing about a woman's work. Milly Amos used to say that if a woman was to see all the dishes that she had to wash before she died, piled up before her in one pile, she'd lie down and die right then and there. I've always had the name o' bein' a good housekeeper, but when I'm dead and gone there ain't anybody goin' to think o' the floors I've swept, and the tables I've scrubbed, and the old clothes I've patched, and the stockin's I've darned. Abram might 'a' remembered it, but he ain't here. But when one o' my grandchildren or great-grandchildren sees one o' these quilts, they'll think about Aunt Jane, and, wherever I am then, I'll know I ain't forgotten.

"I reckon everybody wants to leave somethin' behind that'll last after they're dead and gone. It don't look like it's worth while to live unless you can do that. The Bible says folks 'rest from their labors, and their works do follow them,' but that ain't so. They go, and maybe they do rest, but their works stay right here, unless they're the sort that don't outlast the usin'. Now, some folks has money to build monuments with—great, tall, marble pillars, with angels on top of 'em, like you see in Cave Hill and them big city buryin'-grounds. And some folks can build churches and schools and hospitals to keep folks in mind of 'em, but all the work I've got to leave behind me is jest these quilts, and sometimes, when I'm settin' here, workin' with my caliker and gingham pieces, I'll finish off a block, and I laugh and say to myself, 'Well, here's another stone for the monument.'

"I reckon you think, child, that a caliker or a worsted quilt is a curious sort of a monument—'bout as perishable as the sweepin' and scrubbin' and mendin'. But if folks values things rightly, and knows how to take care of 'em, there ain't many things that'll last longer'n a quilt. Why, I've got a blue and white counterpane that my mother's mother spun and wove, and there ain't a sign o' givin' out in it yet. I'm goin' to will that to my granddaughter that lives in Danville, Mary Frances' oldest child. She was down here last summer, and I was lookin' over my things and packin' 'em away, and she happened to see that counterpane, and says she, 'Grandma, I want you to will me that.' And says I: 'What do you want with that old thing, honey? You know you wouldn't sleep under such a counterpane as that.' And says she, 'No, but I'd hang it up over my parlor door for a—"

"Portière?" I suggested, as Aunt Jane hesitated for the unaccustomed word.

"That's it, child. Somehow I can't ricollect these new-fangled words, any more'n I can understand these new-fangled ways. Who'd ever 'a' thought that folks'd go to stringin' up bed-coverin's in their doors? And says I to Janie, 'You can hang your great-grandmother's counterpane up in your parlor door if you want to, but,' says I, 'don't you ever make a door-curtain out o' one o' my quilts.' But la! the way things turn around, if I was to come back fifty years from now, like as not I'd find 'em usin' my quilts for window-curtains or door-mats."

We both laughed, and there rose in my mind a picture of a twentieth-century house decorated with Aunt Jane's "nine-patches" and "rising suns." How could the dear old woman know that the same esthetic sense that had drawn from their obscurity the white and blue counterpanes of colonial days would forever protect her loved quilts from such a desecration as she feared? As she lifted a pair of quilts from a chair near by, I caught sight of a pure white spread in striking contrast with the many-hued patchwork.

"Where did you get that Marseilles spread, Aunt Jane?" I asked, pointing to it. Aunt Jane lifted it and laid it on my lap without a word. Evidently she thought that here was something that could speak for itself. It was two layers of snowy cotton cloth thinly lined with cotton, and elaborately quilted into a perfect imitation of a Marseilles counterpane. The pattern was a tracery of roses, buds, and leaves, very much conventionalized, but still recognizable for the things they were. The stitches were fairylike, and altogether it might have covered the bed of a queen.

"I made every stitch o' that spread the year before me and Abram was married," she said. "I put it on my bed when we went to house-keepin'; it was on the bed when Abram died, and when I die I want 'em to cover me with it." There was a life-history in the simple words. I thought of Desdemona and her bridal sheets, and I did not offer to help Aunt Jane as she folded this quilt.

"I reckon you think," she resumed presently, "that I'm a mean, stingy old creetur not to give Janie the counterpane now, instead o' hoardin' it up, and all these quilts too, and keepin' folks waitin' for 'em till I die. But, honey, it ain't all selfishness. I'd give away my best dress or my best bonnet or an acre o' ground to anybody that needed 'em more'n I did; but these quilts— Why, it looks like my whole life was sewed up in 'em, and I ain't goin' to part with 'em while life lasts."

There was a ring of passionate eagerness in the old voice, and she fell to putting away her treasures as if the suggestion of losing them had made her fearful of their safety.

I looked again at the heap of quilts. An hour ago they had been patchwork, and nothing more. But now! The old woman's words had wrought a transformation in the homely mass of calico and silk and worsted. Patchwork? Ah, no! It was memory, imagination, history, biography, joy, sorrow, philosophy, religion, romance, realism, life, love, and death; and over all, like a halo, the love of the artist for his work and the soul's longing for earthly immortality.

No wonder the wrinkled fingers smoothed them as reverently as we handle the garments of the dead.

The Bedquilt

Dorothy Canfield

O F ALL THE Elwell family Aunt Mehetabel was certainly the most unimportant member. It was in the old-time New England days, when an unmarried woman was an old maid at twenty, at forty was everyone's servant, and at sixty had gone through so much discipline that she could need no more in the next world. Aunt Mehetabel was sixty-eight.

She had never for a moment known the pleasure of being important to anyone. Not that she was useless in her brother's family; she was expected, as a matter of course, to take upon herself the most tedious and uninteresting part of the household labors. On Mondays she accepted as her share the washing of the men's shirts, heavy with sweat and stiff with dirt from the fields and from their own hard-working bodies. Tuesdays she never dreamed of being allowed to iron anything pretty or even interesting, like the baby's white dresses or the fancy aprons of her young lady nieces. She stood all day pressing out a monotonous succession of dish-cloths and towels and sheets.

In preserving-time she was allowed to have none of the pleasant responsibility of deciding when the fruit had cooked long enough, nor did she share in the little excitement of pouring the sweet-smelling stuff into the stone jars. She sat in a corner with the children and stoned cherries incessantly, or hulled strawberries until her fingers were dyed red.

The Elwells were not consciously unkind to their aunt, they were even in a vague way fond of her; but she was so insignificant a figure in their lives that she was almost invisible to them. Aunt Mehetabel did not resent this treatment; she took it quite as unconsciously as they gave it. It was to be expected when one was an old-maid dependent in a busy family. She gathered what crumbs of comfort she could from their occasional careless kindnesses and tried to hide the hurt which even yet pierced her at her brother's rough joking. In the winter when they all sat before the big hearth, roasted apples, drank mulled cider, and teased the girls about their beaux and the boys about their sweethearts, she shrank into a dusky corner with her knitting, happy if the evening passed without her brother saying, with a crude sarcasm, "Ask your Aunt Mehetabel about the beaux that used to come a-sparkin' her!" or, "Mehetabel, how was't when you was in love with Abel Cummings?" As a matter of fact, she had been the same at twenty as at sixty, a mouselike little creature, too shy for anyone to notice, or to raise her eyes for a moment and wish for a life of her own.

Her sister-in-law, a big hearty housewife, who ruled indoors with as autocratic a sway as did her husband on the farm, was rather kind in an absent, offhand way to the shrunken little old woman, and it was through her that Mehetabel was able to enjoy the one pleasure of her life. Even as a girl she had been clever with her needle in the way of patching bedquilts. More than that she could never learn to do. The garments which she made for herself were lamentable affairs, and she was humbly grateful for any help in the bewildering business of putting them together. But in patchwork she enjoyed a tepid importance. She could really do that as well as anyone else. During years of devotion to this one art she had accumulated a considerable store of quilting patterns. Sometimes the neighbors would send over and ask "Miss Mehetabel" for the loan of her sheaf-of-wheat design, or the double-star pattern. It was with an agreeable flutter at being able to help someone that she went to the dresser, in her bare little room under the eaves, and drew out from her crowded portfolio the pattern desired.

She never knew how her great idea came to her. Sometimes she thought she must have dreamed it, sometimes she even wondered reverently, in the phraseology of the weekly prayer-meeting, if it had not been "sent" to her. She never admitted to herself that she could have thought of it without other help. It was too great, too ambitious, too lofty a project for her humble mind to have conceived. Even when she finished drawing the design with her own fingers, she gazed at it incredulously, not daring to believe that it could indeed be her handiwork. At first it seemed to her only like a lovely but unreal dream. For a long time she did not once think of putting an actual quilt together following that pattern, even though she herself had invented it. It was not that she feared the prodigious effort that would be needed to get those tiny, oddly shaped pieces of bright-colored material sewed together with the perfection of fine workmanship needed. No, she thought zestfully and eagerly of such endless effort, her heart uplifted by her vision of the mosaic-beauty of the whole creation as she saw it, when she shut her eyes to dream of it—that complicated, splendidly difficult pattern—good enough for the angels in heaven to quilt.

But as she dreamed, her nimble old fingers reached out longingly to turn her dream into reality. She began to think adventurously of trying it out—it would perhaps not be too selfish to make one square—just one unit of her design to see how it would look. She dared do nothing in the household where she was a dependent, without asking permission. With a heart full of hope and fear thumping furiously against her old ribs, she approached the mistress of the house on churning-day, knowing with the innocent guile of a child that the country woman was apt to be in a good temper while working over the fragrant butter in the cool cellar.

Sophia listened absently to her sister-in-law's halting petition. "Why, yes, Mehetabel," she said, leaning far down into the huge churn for the last golden morsels—"why, yes, start another quilt if you want to. I've got a lot of pieces from the spring sewing that will work in real good." Mehetabel tried honestly to make her see that this would be no common quilt, but her limited vocabulary and her emotion stood between her and expression. At last Sophia said, with a kindly impatience: "Oh, there! Don't bother me. I never could keep track of your quiltin' patterns, anyhow. I don't care what pattern you go by."

Mehetabel rushed back up the steep attic stairs to her room, and in a joyful agitation began preparations for the work of her life. Her very first stitches showed her that it was even better than she hoped. By some heaven-sent inspiration she had invented a pattern beyond which no patchwork quilt could go.

She had but little time during the daylight hours filled with the incessant household drudgery. After dark she did not dare to sit up late at night lest she burn too much candle. It was weeks before the little square began to show the pattern. Then Mehetabel was in a fever to finish it. She was too conscientious to shirk even the smallest part of her share of the housework, but she rushed through it now so fast that she was panting as she climbed the stairs to her little room.

Every time she opened the door, no matter what weather hung outside the one small window, she always saw the little room flooded with sunshine. She smiled to herself as she bent over the innumerable scraps of cotton cloth on her work table. Already—to her—they were ranged in orderly, complex, mosaic-beauty.

Finally she could wait no longer, and one evening ventured to bring her work down beside the fire where the family sat, hoping that good fortune would give her a place near the tallow candles on the mantelpiece. She had reached the last corner of that first square and her needle flew in and out, in and out, with nervous speed. To her relief no one noticed her. By bedtime she had only a few more stitches to add.

As she stood up with the others, the square fell from her trembling old hands and fluttered to the table. Sophia glanced at it carelessly. "Is that the new quilt you said you wanted to start?" she asked, yawning. "Looks like a real pretty pattern. Let's see it."

Up to that moment Mehetabel had labored in the purest spirit of selfless adoration of an ideal. The emotional shock given her by Sophia's cry of admiration as she held the work towards the candle to examine it, was as much astonishment as joy to Mehetabel.

"Land's sakes!" cried her sister-in-law. "Why, Mehetabel Elwell, where did you git that pattern?"

"I made it up," said Mehetabel. She spoke quietly but she was trembling.

"No!" exclaimed Sophia. "Did you! Why, I never seen such a pattern in my life. Girls, come here and see what your Aunt Mehetabel is doing."

The three tall daughters turned back reluctantly from the stairs. "I never could seem to take much interest in patchwork quilts," said one. Already the old-time skill born of early pioneer privation and the craving for beauty, had gone out of style.

"No, nor I neither!" answered Sophia. "But a stone image would take an interest in this pattern. Honest, Mehetabel, did you really think of it yourself?" She held it up closer to her eyes and went on, "And how under the sun and stars did you ever git your courage up to start in a-making it? Land! Look at all those tiny squinchy little seams! Why, the wrong side ain't a thing *but* seams! Yet the good side's just like a picture, so smooth you'd think 'twas woven that way. Only nobody could."

The girls looked at it right side, wrong side, and echoed their mother's exclamations. Mr. Elwell himself came over to see what they were discussing. "Well, I declare!" he said, looking at his sister with eyes more approving than she could ever remember. "I don't know a thing about patchwork quilts, but to my eye that beats old Mis' Andrew's quilt that got the blue ribbon so many times at the County Fair."

As she lay that night in her narrow hard bed, too proud, too excited to sleep, Mehetabel's heart swelled and tears of joy ran down from her old eyes.

The next day her sister-in-law astonished her by taking the huge pan of potatoes out of her lap and setting one of the younger children to peeling them. "Don't you want to go on with that quiltin' pattern?" she said. "I'd kind o' like to see how you're goin' to make the grapevine design come out on the corner."

For the first time in her life the dependent old maid contradicted her powerful sister-in-law. Quickly and jealously she said, "It's not a grape-vine. It's a sort of curlicue I made up."

"Well, it's nice looking anyhow," said Sophia pacifyingly. "I never could have made it up."

By the end of the summer the family interest had risen so high that Mehetabel was given for herself a little round table in the sitting room, for *her*, where she could keep her pieces and use odd minutes for her work. She almost wept over such kindness and resolved firmly not to take advantage of it. She went on faithfully with her monotonous house-work, not neglecting a corner. But the atmosphere of her world was changed. Now things had a meaning. Through the longest task of wash-ing milk-pans, there rose a rainbow of promise. She took her place by the little table and put the thimble on her knotted, hard finger with the solemnity of a priestess performing a rite.

She was even able to bear with some degree of dignity the honor of having the minister and the minister's wife comment admiringly on her great project. The family felt quite proud of Aunt Mehetabel as Minister Bowman had said it was work as fine as any he had ever seen, "and he didn't know but finer!" The remark was repeated verbatim to the neigh-bors in the following weeks when they dropped in and examined in a perverse Vermontish silence some astonishingly difficult tour de force which Mehetabel had just finished.

The Elwells especially plumed themselves on the slow progress of the quilt. "Mehetabel has been to work on that corner for six weeks, come

Tuesday, and she ain't half done yet," they explained to visitors. They fell out of the way of always expecting her to be the one to run on errands, even for the children. "Don't bother your Aunt Mehetabel," Sophia would call. "Can't you see she's got to a ticklish place on the quilt?" The old woman sat straighter in her chair, held up her head. She was a part of the world at last. She joined in the conversation and her remarks were listened to. The children were even told to mind her when she asked them to do some service for her, although this she ventured to do but seldom.

One day some people from the next town, total strangers, drove up to the Elwell house and asked if they could inspect the wonderful quilt which they had heard about even down in their end of the valley. After that, Mehetabel's quilt came little by little to be one of the local sights. No visitor in town, whether he knew the Elwells or not, went away without having been to look at it. To make her presentable to strangers, the Elwells saw to it that their aunt was better dressed than she had ever been before. One of the girls made her a pretty little cap to wear on her thin white hair.

A year went by and a quarter of the quilt was finished. A second year passed and half was done. The third year Mehetabel had pneumonia and lay ill for weeks and weeks, horrified by the idea that she might die before her work was completed. A fourth year and one could really see the grandeur of the whole design. In September of the fifth year, the entire family gathered around her to watch eagerly, as Mehetabel quilted the last stitches. The girls held it up by the four corners and they all looked at it in hushed silence.

Then Mr. Elwell cried as one speaking with authority, "By ginger! That's goin' to the County Fair!"

Mehetabel blushed a deep red. She had thought of this herself, but never would have spoken aloud of it.

"Yes indeed!" cried the family. One of the boys was dispatched to the house of a neighbor who was Chairman of the Fair Committee for their village. He came back beaming, "Of course he'll take it. Like's not it may git a prize, he says. But he's got to have it right off because all the things from our town are going tomorrow morning."

Even in her pride Mehetabel felt a pang as the bulky package was carried out of the house. As the days went on she felt lost. For years it had been her one thought. The little round stand had been heaped with litter of bright-colored scraps. Now it was desolately bare. One of the neighbors who took the long journey to the Fair reported when he came back that the quilt was hung in a good place in a glass case in "Agricultural Hall." But that meant little to Mehetabel's ignorance of everything outside her brother's home. She drooped. The family noticed it. One day Sophia said kindly, "You feel sort o' lost without the quilt, don't you, Mehetabel?"

"They took it away so quick!" she said wistfully. "I hadn't hardly had one good look at it myself."

The Fair was to last a fortnight. At the beginning of the second week Mr. Elwell asked his sister how early she could get up in the morning.

"I dunno. Why?" she asked.

"Well, Thomas Ralston has got to drive to West Oldton to see a lawyer. That's four miles beyond the Fair. He says if you can git up so's to leave here at four in the morning he'll drive you to the Fair, leave you there for the day, and bring you back again at night." Mehetabel's face turned very white. Her eyes filled with tears. It was as though someone had offered her a ride in a golden chariot up to the gates of heaven. "Why, you can't *mean* it!" she cried wildly. Her brother laughed. He could not meet her eyes. Even to his easy-going unimaginative indifference to his sister this was a revelation of the narrowness of her life in his home. "Oh, 'tain't so much—just to go to the Fair," he told her in some confusion, and then "Yes, sure I mean it. Go git your things ready, for it's tomorrow morning he wants to start."

A trembling, excited old woman stared all that night at the rafters. She who had never been more than six miles from home—it was to her like going into another world. She who had never seen anything more exciting than a church supper was to see the County Fair. She had never dreamed of doing it. She could not at all imagine what it would be like.

The next morning all the family rose early to see her off. Perhaps her brother had not been the only one to be shocked by her happiness. As she tried to eat her breakfast they called out conflicting advice to her about what to see. Her brother said not to miss inspecting the stock, her nieces said the fancywork was the only thing worth looking at, Sophia told her to be sure to look at the display of preserves. Her nephews asked her to bring home an account of the trotting races.

The buggy drove up to the door, and she was helped in. The family ran to and fro with blankets, woolen tippet, a hot soapstone from the kitchen range. Her wraps were tucked about her. They all stood together and waved goodby as she drove out of the yard. She waved back, but she scarcely saw them. On her return home that evening she was ashy pale, and so stiff that her brother had to lift her out bodily. But her lips were set in a blissful smile. They crowded around her with questions until Sophia pushed them all aside. She told them Aunt Mehetabel was too tired to speak until she had had her supper. The young people held their tongues while she drank her tea, and absent-mindedly ate a scrap of toast with an egg. Then the old woman was helped into an easy chair before the fire. They gathered about her, eager for news of the great world, and Sophia said, "Now, come Mehetabel, tell us all about it!"

Mehetabel drew a long breath. "It was just perfect!" she said. "Finer even than I thought. They've got it hanging up in the very middle of a sort o' closet made of glass, and one of the lower corners is ripped and turned back so's to show the seams on the wrong side."

"What?" asked Sophia, a little blankly.

"Why, the quilt!" said Mehetabel in surprise. "There are a whole lot of other ones in that room, but not one that can hold a candle to it, if I do say it who shouldn't. I heard lots of people say the same thing. You ought to have heard what the women said about that corner, Sophia. They said—well, I'd be ashamed to *tell* you what they said. I declare if I wouldn't!"

Mr. Elwell asked, "What did you think of that big ox we've heard so much about?"

"I didn't look at the stock," returned his sister indifferently. She turned to one of her nieces. "That set of pieces you gave me, Maria, from your red waist, come out just lovely! I heard one woman say you could 'most smell the red roses."

"How did Jed Burgess' bay horse place in the mile trot?" asked Thomas.

"I didn't see the races."

"How about the preserves?" asked Sophia.

"I didn't see the preserves," said Mehetabel calmly.

Seeing that they were gazing at her with astonished faces she went on, to give them a reasonable explanation, "You see I went right to the room where the quilt was, and then I didn't want to leave it. It had been so long since I'd seen it. I had to look at it first real good myself, and then I looked at the others to see if there was any that could come up to it. Then the people begun comin' in and I got so interested in hearin' what they had to say I couldn't think of goin' anywheres else. I ate my lunch right there too, and I'm glad as can be I did, too; for what do you think?"—she gazed about her with kindling eyes. "While I stood there with a sandwich in one hand, didn't the head of the hull concern come in and open the glass door and pin a big bow of blue ribbon right in the middle of the quilt with a label on it, 'First Prize.'"

There was a stir of proud congratulation. Then Sophia returned to questioning, "Didn't you go to see anything else?"

"Why, no," said Mehetabel. "Only the quilt. Why should I?"

She fell into a reverie. As if it hung again before her eyes she saw the glory that shone around the creation of her hand and brain. She longed to make her listeners share the golden vision with her. She struggled for words. She fumbled blindly for unknown superlatives. "I tell you it looked like—" she began, and paused.

Vague recollections of hymnbook phrases came into her mind. They were the only kind of poetic expression she knew. But they were dismissed as being sacrilegious to use for something in real life. Also as not being nearly striking enough.

Finally, "I tell you it looked real *good*," she assured them and sat staring into the fire, on her tired old face the supreme content of an artist who has realized his ideal.

Love Life

Bobbie Ann Mason

Opal LOLLS in her recliner, wearing the Coors cap her niece Jenny brought her from Colorado. She fumbles for the remote-control paddle and fires a button. Her swollen knuckles hurt. On TV, a boy is dancing in the street. Some other boys dressed in black are banging guitars and drums. This is her favorite program. It is always on, night or day. The show is songs, with accompanying stories. It's the music channel. Opal never cared for stories—she detests those soap operas her friends watch—but these fascinate her. The colors and the costumes change and flow with the music, erratically, the way her mind does these days. Now the TV is playing a song in which all the boys are long-haired cops chasing a dangerous woman in a tweed cap and a checked shirt. The woman's picture is in all their billfolds. They chase her through a cold-storage room filled with sides of beef. She hops on a motorcycle, and they set up a roadblock, but she jumps it with her motorcycle. Finally, she slips onto a train and glides away from them, waving a smiling goodbye.

On the table beside Opal is a Kleenex box, her glasses case, a glass of Coke with ice, and a cut-glass decanter of clear liquid that could be just water for the plants. Opal pours some of the liquid into the Coke and sips slowly. It tastes like peppermint candy, and it feels soothing. Her fingers tingle. She feels happy. Now that she is retired, she doesn't have to sneak into the teachers' lounge for a little swig from the jar in her pocketbook. She still dreams of algebra problems, complicated quadratic equations with shifting values and no solutions. Now kids are using algebra to program computers. The kids in the TV stories remind her of her students at Hopewell High. Old age could have a grandeur about it, she thinks now as the music surges through her, if only it weren't so scary.

But she doesn't feel lonely, especially now that her sister Alice's girl,

Jenny, has moved back here, to Kentucky. Jenny seems so confident, the way she sprawls on the couch, with that backpack she carries everywhere. Alice was always so delicate and feminine, but Jenny is enough like Opal to be her own daughter. She has Opal's light, thin hair, her large shoulders and big bones and long legs. Jenny even has a way of laughing that reminds Opal of her own laughter, the boisterous scoff she always saved for certain company but never allowed herself in school. Now and then Jenny lets loose one of those laughs and Opal is pleased. It occurs to her that Jenny, who is already past thirty, has left behind a trail of men, like that girl in the song. Jenny has lived with a couple of men, here and there. Opal can't keep track of all of the men Jenny has mentioned. They have names like John and Skip and Michael. She's not in a hurry to get married, she says. She says she is going to buy a house trailer and live in the woods like a hermit. She's full of ideas, and she exaggerates. She uses the words "gorgeous," "adorable," and "wonderful" interchangeably and persistently.

Last night, Jenny was here, with her latest boyfriend, Randy Newcomb. Opal remembers when he sat in the back row in her geometry class. He was an ordinary kid, not especially smart, and often late with his lessons. Now he has a real-estate agency and drives a Cadillac. Jenny kissed him in front of Opal and told him he was gorgeous. She said the placemats were gorgeous, too.

Jenny was asking to see those old quilts again. "Why do you hide away your nice things, Aunt Opal?" she said. Opal doesn't think they're that nice, and she doesn't want to have to look at them all the time. Opal showed Jenny and Randy Newcomb the double-wedding-ring quilt, the star quilt, and some of the crazy quilts, but she wouldn't show them the craziest one—the burial quilt, the one Jenny kept asking about. Did Jenny come back home just to hunt up that old rag? The thought makes Opal shudder.

The doorbell rings. Opal has to rearrange her comforter and magazines in order to get up. Her joints are stiff. She leaves the TV blaring a song she knows, with balloons and bombs in it.

At the door is Velma Shaw, who lives in the duplex next to Opal. She has just come home from her job at Shop World. "Have you gone out of you mind, Opal?" cries Velma. She has on a plum-colored print blouse and a plum skirt and a little green scarf with a gold pin holding it down. Velma shouts, "You can hear that racket clear across the street!"

"Rock and roll is never too loud," says Opal. This is a line from a song she has heard.

Opal releases one of her saved-up laughs, and Velma backs away. Velma is still trying to be sexy, in those little color-coordinated outfits she wears, but it is hopeless, Opal thinks with a smile. She closes the door and scoots back to her recliner.

Opal is Jenny's favorite aunt. Jenny likes the way Opal ties her hair in a ponytail with a ribbon. She wears muumuus and socks. She is tall and only a little thick in the middle. She told Jenny that middle-age spread was caused by the ribs expanding and that it doesn't matter what you eat. Opal kids around about "old Arthur"—her arthritis, visiting her on damp days.

Jenny has been in town six months. She works at the courthouse, typing records—marriages, divorces, deaths, drunk-driving convictions. Frequently, the same names are on more than one list. Before she returned to Kentucky, Jenny was waitressing in Denver, but she was growing restless again, and the idea of going home seized her. Her old rebellion against small-town conventions gave way to curiosity.

In the South, the shimmer of the heat seems to distort everything, like old glass with impurities in it. During her first two days there, she saw two people with artificial legs, a blind man, a man with hooks for hands, and a man without an arm. It seemed unreal. In a parking lot, a pit bull terrier in a Camaro attacked her from behind the closed window. He barked viciously, his nose stabbing the window. She stood in the parking lot, letting the pit bull attack, imagining herself in an arena, with a crowd watching. The South makes her nervous. Randy Newcomb told her she had just been away too long. "We're not as countrified down here now as people think," he said.

Jenny has been going with Randy for three months. The first night she went out with him, he took her to a fancy place that served shrimp flown in from New Orleans, and then to a little bar over in Hopkinsville. They went with Kathy Steers, a friend from work, and Kathy's husband, Bob. Kathy and Bob weren't getting along and they carped at each other all evening. In the bar, an attractive, cheerful woman sang requests for tips, and her companion, a blind man, played the guitar. When she sang, she looked straight at him, singing to him, smiling at him reassuringly. In the background, men played pool with their girl-

friends, and Jenny noticed the sharp creases in the men's jeans and imagined the women ironing them. When she mentioned it, Kathy said she
took Bob's jeans to the laundromat to use the machine there that puts
knifelike creases in them. The men in the bar had two kinds of women
with them: innocent-looking women with pastel skirts and careful hair-
dos, and hard-looking women without makeup, in T-shirts and jeans.
Jenny imagined that each type could be either a girlfriend or a wife. She
felt odd. She was neither type. The singer sang "Happy Birthday" to a
popular regular named Will Ed, and after the set she danced with him,
while the jukebox took over. She had a limp, as though one leg were
shorter than the other. The leg was stiff under her jeans, and when the
woman danced Jenny could see that the leg was not real.

"There, but for the grace of God, go I," Randy whispered to Jenny. He
squeezed her hand, and his heavy turquoise ring dug into her knuckle.

"Those quilts would bring a good price at an estate auction," Randy says
to Jenny as they leave her aunt's one evening and head for his real-estate
office. They are in his burgundy Cadillac. "One of those star quilts used
to bring twenty-five dollars. Now it might run three hundred."

"My aunt doesn't think they're worth anything. She hides all her
nice stuff, like she's ashamed of it. She's got beautiful dresser scarves and
starched doilies she made years ago. But she's getting a little weird. All
she does is watch MTV."

"I think she misses the kids," Randy says. Then he bursts out laughing. "She used to put the fear of God in all her students! I never will
forget the time she told me to stop watching so much television and read
some books. It was like an order from God Almighty. I didn't dare not do
what she said. I read *Crime and Punishment*. I never would have read it if
she hadn't shamed me into it. But I appreciated that. I don't even remember what *Crime and Punishment* was about, except there was an ax
murderer in it."

"That was basically it," Jenny says. "He got caught. Crime and
punishment—just like any old TV show."

Randy touches some controls on the dashboard and Waylon Jen-
nings starts singing. The sound system is remarkable. Everything Randy
owns is quality. He has been looking for some land for Jenny to buy—a
couple of acres of woods—but so far nothing on his listings has met with
his approval. He is concerned about zoning and power lines and fron-

tage. All Jenny wants is a remote place where she can have a dog and grow some tomatoes. She knows that what she really needs is a better car, but she doesn't want to go anywhere.

Later, at Randy's office, Jenny studies the photos of houses on display, while he talks on the telephone to someone about dividing up a sixty-acre farm into farmettes. His photograph is on several certificates on the wall. He has a full, well-fed face in the pictures, but he is thinner now and looks better. He has a boyish, endearing smile, like Dennis Quaid, Jenny's favorite actor. She likes Randy's smile. It seems so innocent, as though he would do anything in the world for someone he cared about. He doesn't really want to sell her any land. He says he is afraid she will get raped if she lives alone in the woods.

"I'm impressed," she says when he slams down the telephone. She points to his new regional award for the fastest-growing agency of the year.

"Isn't that something? Three branch offices in a territory this size—I can't complain. There's a lot of turnover in real estate now. People are never satisfied. You know that? That's the truth about human nature." He laughs. "That's the secret of my success."

"It's been two years since Barbara divorced me," he says later, on the way to Jenny's apartment. "I can't say it hasn't been fun being free, but my kids are in college, and it's like starting over. I'm ready for a new life. The business has been so great, I couldn't really ask for more, but I've been thinking—Don't laugh, please, but what I was thinking was if you want to share it with me, I'll treat you good. I swear."

At a stoplight, he paws at her hand. On one corner is the Pepsi bottling plant, and across from it is the Broad Street House, a restaurant with an old-fashioned statue of a jockey out front. People are painting the black faces on those little statues white now, but this one has been painted bright green all over. Jenny can't keep from laughing at it.

"I wasn't laughing at you—honest!" she says apologetically. "That statue always cracks me up."

"You don't have to give me an answer now."

"I don't know what to say."

"I can get us a real good deal on a house," he says. "I can get any house I've got listed. I can even get us a farmette, if you want trees so bad. You won't have to spend your money on a piece of land."

"I'll have to think about it." Randy scares her. She likes him, but there is something strange about his energy and optimism. Everyone around her seems to be bursting at the seams, like that pit bull terrier.

"I'll let you think on it," he says, pulling up to her apartment. "Life has been good to me. Business is good, and my kids didn't turn out to be dope fiends. That's about all you can hope for in this day and time."

Jenny is having lunch with Kathy Steers at the Broad Street House. The iced tea is mixed with white grape juice. It took Jenny a long time to identify the flavor, and the Broad Street House won't admit it's grape juice. Their iced tea is supposed to have a mystique about it, probably because they can't sell drinks in this dry county. In the daylight, the statue out front is the color of the Jolly Green Giant.

People confide in Jenny, but Jenny doesn't always tell things back. It's an unfair exchange, though it often goes unnoticed. She is curious, eager to hear other people's stories, and she asks more questions than is appropriate. Kathy's life is a tangle of deceptions. Kathy stayed with her husband, Bob, because he had opened his own body shop and she didn't want him to start out a new business with a rocky marriage, but she acknowledges now it was a mistake.

"What about Jimmy and Willette?" Jenny asks. Jimmy and Willette are the other characters in Kathy's story.

"That mess went on for months. When you started work at the office, remember how nervous I was? I thought I was getting an ulcer." Kathy lights a cigarette and blows at the wall. "You see, I didn't know what Bob and Willette were up to, and they didn't know about me and Jimmy. That went on for two years before you came. And when it started to come apart—I mean, we had *hell*! I'd say things to Jimmy and then it would get back to Bob because Jimmy would tell Willette. It was an unreal circle. I was pregnant with Jason and you get real sensitive then. I thought Bob was screwing around on me, but it never dawned on me it was with Willette."

The fat waitress says, "Is everything all right?"

Kathy says, "No, but it's not your fault. Do you know what I'm going to do?" she asks Jenny.

"No, what?"

"I'm taking Jason and moving in with my sister. She has a sort of apartment upstairs. Bob can do what he wants to with the house. I've waited too long to do this, but it's time. My sister keeps the baby anyway, so why shouldn't I just live there?"

She puffs the cigarette again and levels her eyes at Jenny. "You know what I admire about you? You're so independent. You said what you think. When you started work at the office, I said to myself, 'I wish I could be like that.' I could tell you had been around. You've inspired me. That's how come I decided to move out."

Jenny plays with the lemon slice in the saucer holding her iced-tea glass. She picks a seed out of it. She can't bring herself to confide in Kathy about Randy Newcomb's offer. For some reason, she is embarrassed by it.

"I haven't spoken to Willette since September third," says Kathy.

Kathy keeps talking, and Jenny listens, suspicious of her interest in Kathy's problems. She notices how Kathy is enjoying herself. Kathy is looking forward to leaving her husband the same way she must have enjoyed her fling with Jimmy, the way she is enjoying not speaking to Willette.

"Let's go out and get drunk tonight," Kathy says cheerfully. "Let's celebrate my decision."

"I can't. I'm going to see my aunt this evening. I have to take her some booze. She gives me money to buy her vodka and peppermint schnapps, and she tells me not to stop at the same liquor store too often. She says she doesn't want me to get a reputation for drinking! I have to go all the way to Hopkinsville to get it."

"Your aunt tickles me. She's a pistol."

The waitress clears away the dishes and slaps down dessert menus. They order chocolate pecan pie, the day's special.

"You know the worst part of this whole deal?" Kathy says. "It's the years it takes to get smart. But I'm going to make up for lost time. You can bet on that. And there's not a thing Bob can do about it."

Opal's house has a veranda. Jenny thinks that verandas seem to imply a history of some sort—people in rocking chairs telling stories. But Opal doesn't tell any stories. It is exasperating, because Jenny wants to know about her aunt's past love life, but Opal won't reveal her secrets. They sit on the veranda and observe each other. They smile, and now and then roar with laughter over something ridiculous. In the bedroom, where she snoops after using the bathroom, Jenny notices the layers of old wallpaper in the closet, peeling back and spilling crumbs of gaudy ancient flower prints onto Opal's muumuus.

Downstairs, Opal asks, "Do you want some cake, Jenny?"

"Of course. I'm crazy about your cake, Aunt Opal."

"I didn't beat the egg whites long enough. Old Arthur's visiting again." Opal flexes her fingers and smiles. "That sounds like the curse. Girls used to say they had the curse. Or they had a visitor." She looks down at her knuckles shyly. "Nowadays, of course, they just say what they mean."

The cake is delicious—an old-fashioned lemon chiffon made from scratch. Jenny's cooking ranges from English-muffin mini-pizzas to brownie mixes. After gorging on the cake, Jenny blurts out, "Aunt Opal, aren't you sorry you never got married? Tell the truth, now."

Opal laughs. "I was talking to Ella Mae Smith the other day—she's a retired geography teacher?—and she said, 'I've got twelve great-great-grandchildren, and when we get together I say, "Law me, look what I started!"'" Opal mimics Ella Mae Smith, giving her a mindless, chirpy tone of voice. "Why, I'd have to use quadratic equations to count up all the people that woman has caused," she goes on. "All with a streak of her petty narrow-mindedness in them. I don't call that a contribution to the world." Opal laughs and sips from her glass of schnapps. "What about you, Jenny? Are you ever going to get married?"

"Marriage is outdated. I don't know anybody who's married and happy."

Opal names three schoolteachers she has known who have been married for decades.

"But are they really happy?"

"Oh, foot, Jenny! What you're saying is why are *you* not married and why are *you* not happy. What's wrong with little Randy Newcomb? Isn't that funny? I always think of him as little Randy."

"Show me those quilts again, Aunt Opal."

"I'll show you the crazies but not the one you keep after me about."

"O.K., show me the crazies."

Upstairs, her aunt lays crazy quilts on the bed. They are bright-colored patches of soft velvet and plaids and prints stitched together with silky embroidery. Several pieces have initials embroidered on them. The haphazard shapes make Jenny imagine odd, twisted lives represented in these quilts.

She says, "Mom gave me a quilt once, but I didn't appreciate the value of it and I washed it until it fell apart."

"I'll give you one of these crazies when you stop moving around," Opal says. "You couldn't fit it in that backpack of yours." She polishes her glasses thoughtfully. "Do you know what those quilts mean to me?"

"No, what?"

"A lot of desperate old women ruining their eyes. Do you know what I think I'll do?"

"No, what?"

"I think I'll take up aerobic dancing. Or maybe I'll learn to ride a motorcycle. I try to be modern."

"You're funny, Aunt Opal. You're hilarious."

"Am I gorgeous, too?"

"Adorable," says Jenny.

After her niece leaves, Opal hums a tune and dances a stiff little jig. She nestles among her books and punches her remote-control paddle. Years ago, she was allowed to paddle students who misbehaved. She used a wooden paddle from a butter churn, with holes drilled in it. The holes made a satisfying sting. On TV, a 1950s convertible is out of gas. This is one of her favorites. It has an adorable couple in it. The girl is wearing bobby socks and saddle oxfords, and the boy has on a basketball jacket. They look the way children looked before the hippie element took over. But the boy begins growing cat whiskers and big cat ears, and then his face gets furry and leathery, while the girl screams bloody murder. Opal sips some peppermint and watches his face change. The red and gold of his basketball jacket are the Hopewell school colors. He chases the girl. Now he has grown long claws.

The boy is dancing energetically with a bunch of ghouls who have escaped from their coffins. Then Vincent Price starts talking in the background. The girl is very frightened. The ghouls are so old and ugly. That's how kids see us, Opal thinks. She loves this story. She even loves the credits—scary music by Elmer Bernstein. This is a story with a meaning. It suggests all the feelings of terror and horror that must be hidden inside young people. And inside, deep down, there really are monsters. An old person waits, a nearly dead body that can still dance.

Opal pours another drink. She feels relaxed, her joints loose like a dancer's now.

Jenny is so nosy. Her questions are so blunt. Did Opal ever have a crush on a student? Only once or twice. She was in her twenties then, and it seemed scandalous. Nothing happened—just daydreams. When she was thirty, she had another attachment to a boy, and it seemed all right then, but it was worse again at thirty-five, when another pretty boy stayed after class to talk. After that, she kept her distance.

But Opal is not wholly without experience. There have been men, over the years, though nothing like the casual affairs Jenny has had. Opal remembers a certain motel room in Nashville. She was only forty. The man drove a gray Chrysler Imperial. When she was telling about him to a friend, who was sworn to secrecy, she called him "Imperial," in a joking way. She went with him because she knew he would take her somewhere, in such a fine car, and they would sleep together. She always remembered how clean and empty the room was, how devoid of history and association. In the mirror, she saw a scared woman with a pasty face and a shrimpy little man who needed a shave. In the morning he went out somewhere and brought back coffee and orange juice. They had bought some doughnuts at the new doughnut shop in town before they left. While he was out, she made up the bed and put her things in her bag, to make it as neat as if she had never been there. She was fully dressed when he returned, with her garter belt and stockings on, and when they finished the doughnuts she cleaned up all the paper and the cups and wiped the crumbs from the table by the bed. He said, "Come with me and I'll take you to Idaho." "Why Idaho?" she wanted to know, but his answer was vague. Idaho sounded cold, and she didn't want to tell him how she disliked his scratchy whiskers and the hard, powdery doughnuts. It seemed unkind of her, but if he had been nicer-looking, without such a demanding dark beard, she might have gone with him to Idaho in that shining Imperial. She hadn't even given him a chance, she thought later. She had been so scared. If anyone from school had seen her at that motel, she could have lost her job. "I need a woman," he had said. "A woman like you."

On a hot Saturday afternoon, with rain threatening, Jenny sits under a tent on a folding chair while Randy auctions off four hundred acres of woods on Lake Barkley. He had a road bulldozed into the property, and he divided it up into lots. The lakefront lots are going for as much as two thousand an acre, and the others are bringing up to a thousand. Randy has several assistants with him, and there is even a concession stand, offering hot dogs and cold drinks.

In the middle of the auction, they wait for a thundershower to pass. Sitting in her folding chair under a canopy reminds Jenny of graveside services. As soon as the rain slacks up, the auction continues. In his cowboy hat and blue blazer, Randy struts around with a microphone as proudly as a banty rooster. With his folksy chatter, he knows exactly how to work the crowd. "Y'all get yourselves a cold drink and relax now and just imagine the fishing you'll do in this dreamland. This land is good for vacation, second home, investment—heck, you can just park here in your camper and live. It's going to be paradise when that marina gets built on the lake there and we get some lots cleared."

The four-hundred-acre tract looks like a wilderness. Jenny loves the way the sun splashes on the water after the rain, and the way it comes through the trees, hitting the flickering leaves like lights on a disco ball. A marina here seems farfetched. She could pitch a tent here until she could afford to buy a used trailer. She could swim at dawn, the way she did on a camping trip out West, long ago. All of a sudden, she finds herself bidding on a lot. The bidding passes four hundred, and she sails on, bidding against a man from Missouri who tells the people around him that he's looking for a place to retire.

"Sold to the young lady with the backpack," Randy says when she bids six hundred. He gives her a crestfallen look, and she feels embarrassed.

As she waits for Randy to wind up his business after the auction, Jenny locates her acre from the map of the plots of land. It is along a gravel road and marked off with stakes tied with hot-pink survey tape. It is a small section of the woods—her block on the quilt, she thinks. These are her trees. The vines and underbrush are thick and spotted with raindrops. She notices a windfall leaning on a maple, like a lover dying in its arms. Maples are strong, she thinks, but she feels like getting an ax and chopping that windfall down, to save the maple. In the distance, the whining of a speedboat cuts into the day.

They meet afterward at Randy's van, his mobile real-estate office, with a little shingled roof raised in the center to look rustic. It looks like an outhouse on wheels. A painted message on the side says, "REALITY IS REAL ESTATE." As Randy plows through the mud on the new road, Jenny apologizes. Buying the lot was like laughing at the statue at the wrong moment—something he would take the wrong way, an insult to his attentions.

"I can't reach you," he says. "You say you want to live out in the wilderness and grow your own vegetables, but you act like you're somewhere in outer space. You can't grow vegetables in outer space. You can't even grow them in the woods unless you clear some ground."

"I'm looking for a place to land."

"What do I have to do to get through to you?"

"I don't know. I need more time."

He turns onto the highway, patterned with muddy tire tracks from the cars at the auction. "I said I'd wait, so I guess I'll have to," he says, flashing his Dennis Quaid smile. "You take as long as you want to, then. I learned my lesson with Barbara. You've got to be understanding with the women. That's the key to a successful relationship." Frowning, he slams his hand on the steering wheel. "That's what they tell me, anyhow."

Jenny is having coffee with Opal. She arrived unexpectedly. It's very early. She looks as though she has been up all night.

"Please show me your quilts," Jenny says. "I don't mean your crazy quilts. I want to see that special quilt. Mom said it had the family tree."

Opal spills coffee in her saucer. "What is wrong with young people today?" she asks.

"I want to know why it's called a burial quilt," Jenny says. "Are you planning to be buried in it?"

Opal wishes she had a shot of peppermint in her coffee. It sounds like a delicious idea. She starts toward the den with the coffee cup rattling in its saucer, and she splatters drops on the rug. Never mind it now, she thinks, turning back.

"It's just a family history," she says.

"Why's it called a burial quilt?" Jenny asks.

Jenny's face is pale. She has blue pouches under her eyes and blue eye shadow on her eyelids.

"See that closet in the hall?" Opal says. "Get a chair and we'll get the quilt down."

Jenny stands on a kitchen chair and removes the quilt from beneath several others. It's wrapped in blue plastic and Jenny hugs it closely as she steps down with it.

They spread it out on the couch, and the blue plastic floats off somewhere. Jenny looks like someone in love as she gazes at the quilt. "It's gorgeous," she murmurs. "How beautiful."

"Shoot!" says Opal. "It's ugly as homemade sin."

Jenny runs her fingers over the rough textures of the quilt. The quilt is dark and somber. The backing is a heavy gray gabardine, and the nine-inch-square blocks are pieced of smaller blocks of varying shades of gray and brown and black. They are wools, apparently made from men's winter suits. On each block is an appliquéd off-white tombstone—a comical shape, like Casper the ghost. Each tombstone has a name and date on it.

Jenny recognizes some of the names. Myrtle Williams. Voris Williams. Thelma Lee Freeman. The oldest gravestone is "Eulalee Freeman 1857-1900." The shape of the quilt is irregular, a rectangle with a clumsy foot sticking out from one corner. The quilt is knotted with yarn, and the edging is open, for more blocks to be added.

"Eulalee's daughter started it," says Opal. "But that thing has been carried through this family like a plague. Did you ever see such horrible old dark colors? I pieced on it some when I was younger, but it was too depressing. I think some of the kinfolks must have died without a square, so there may be several to catch up on."

"I'll do it," says Jenny. "I could learn to quilt."

"Traditionally, the quilt stops when the family name stops," Opal says. "And since my parents didn't have a boy, that was the end of the Freeman line on this particular branch of the tree. So the last old maids finish the quilt." She lets out a wild cackle. "Theoretically, a quilt like this could keep going till doomsday."

"Do you care if I have this quilt?" asks Jenny.

"What would you do with it? It's too ugly to put on a bed and too morbid to work on."

"I think it's kind of neat," says Jenny. She strokes the rough tweed. Already it is starting to decay, and it has moth holes. Jenny feels tears start to drip down her face.

"Don't you go putting my name on that thing," her aunt says.

Jenny has taken the quilt to her apartment. She explained that she is going to study the family tree, or that she is going to finish the quilt. If she's smart, Opal thinks, she will let Randy Newcomb auction it off. The way Jenny took it, cramming it into the blue plastic, was like snatching something that was free. Opal feels relieved, as though she has pushed the burden of that ratty old quilt onto her niece. All those miserable, cranky women, straining their eyes, stitching on those dark scraps of material.

For a long time, Jenny wouldn't tell why she was crying, and when she started to tell, Opal was uncomfortable, afraid she'd be required to tell something comparable of her own, but as she listened she found herself caught up in Jenny's story. Jenny said it was a man. That was always the case, Opal thought. It was five years earlier. A man Jenny knew in a place by the sea. Opal imagined seagulls, pretty sand. There were no palm trees. It was up North. The young man worked with Jenny in a restaurant with glass walls facing the ocean. They waited on tables and collected enough tips to take a trip together near the end of the summer. Jenny made it sound like an idyllic time, waiting on tables by the sea. She started crying again when she told about the trip, but the trip sounded nice. Opal listened hungrily, imagining the young man, thinking that he would have had handsome, smooth cheeks, and hair that fell attractively over his forehead. He would have had good manners, being a waiter. Jenny and the man, whose name was Jim, flew to Denver, Colorado, and they rented a car and drove around out West. They visited the Grand Canyon and Yellowstone and other places Opal had heard about. They grilled salmon on the beach, on another ocean. They camped out in the redwoods, trees so big they hid the sky. Jenny described all these scenes, and the man sounded like a good man. His brother had died in Vietnam and he felt guilty that he had been the one spared, because his brother was a swimmer and could have gone to the Olympics. Jim wasn't athletic. He had a bad knee and hammertoes. He slept fitfully in the tent, and Jenny said soothing things to him, and she cared about him, but by the time they had curved northward and over to Yellowstone the trip was becoming unpleasant. The romance wore off. She loved him, but she couldn't deal with his needs. One of the last nights they spent together, it rained all night long. He told her not to touch the tent material, because somehow the pressure of a finger on the nylon would make it start to leak at that spot. Lying there in the rain, Jenny couldn't resist touching a spot where water was collecting in a little sag in the top of the tent. The drip started then, and it grew worse, until they got so wet they had to get in the car. Not long afterward, when they ran short of money, they parted. Jenny got a job in Denver. She never saw him again.

Opal listened eagerly to the details about grilling the fish together, about the zip-together sleeping bags and setting up the tent and washing themselves in the cold stream. But when Jenny brought the story up to the present, Opal was not prepared. She felt she had been dunked in the cold water and left gasping. Jenny said she had heard a couple of times through a mutual friend that Jim had spent some time in Mexico. And then, she said, this week she had begun thinking about him, because of

all the trees at the lake, and she had an overwhelming desire to see him
again. She had been unfair, she knew now. She telephoned the friend,
who had worked with them in the restaurant by the sea. He hadn't
known where to locate her, he said, and so he couldn't tell her that Jim
had been killed in Colorado over a year ago. His four-wheel-drive had
plunged off a mountain curve.

"I feel some trick has been played on me. It seems so unreal." Jenny
tugged at the old quilt, and her eyes darkened. "I was in Colorado, and I
didn't even know he was there. If I still knew him, I would know how to
mourn, but now I don't know how. And it was over a year ago. So I don't
know what to feel."

"Don't look back, hon," Opal said, hugging her niece closely. But
she was shaking, and Jenny shook with her.

Opal makes herself a snack, thinking it will pick up her strength. She is
very tired. On the tray, she places an apple and a paring knife and some
milk and cookies. She touches the remote-control button, and the picture blossoms. She was wise to buy a large TV, the one listed as the best
in the consumer magazine. The color needs a little adjustment, though.
She eases up the volume and starts peeling the apple. She has a little
bump on one knuckle. In the old days, people would take the family
Bible and bust a cyst like that with it. Just slam it hard.

On the screen, a Scoutmaster is telling a story to some Boy Scouts
around a campfire. The campfire is only a fireplace, with electric logs.
Opal loses track of time, and the songs flow together. A woman is lying
on her stomach on a car hood in a desert full of gas pumps. TV sets
crash. Smoke emerges from an eyeball. A page of sky turns like a page in
a book. Then, at a desk in a classroom, a cocky blond kid with a pack of
cigarettes rolled in the sleeve of his T-shirt is singing about a sexy girl
with a tattoo on her back who is sitting on a commode and smoking a
cigarette. In the classroom, all the kids are gyrating and snapping their
fingers to wild music. The teacher at the blackboard with her white hair
in a bun looks disapproving, but the kids in the class don't know what's
on her mind. The teacher is thinking about how, when the bell rings,
she will hit the road to Nashville.

About the Authors

TIMOTHY SHAY ARTHUR. 1809–1885.   Arthur gave up his career as a watchmaker as the success of his writing for *Godey's Lady's Book* led him to found several similar magazines, including *Arthur's Home Magazine* in 1854. He wrote novels and stories against gambling and advocated reforms to eliminate the domestic violence associated with alcohol abuse. His best-known story is *Ten Nights in a Barroom and What I Saw There* (1854), about a drunkard who destroys his family.

DOROTHY CANFIELD. 1875–1958.   Later known as Dorothy Canfield Fisher. Though born in Kansas, she lived most of her writing life in Vermont. Her stories, novels, and nonfiction pieces focus mainly on New England, offering astute interpretations of American life. Her novels include *The Brimming Cup* (1921), *The Home-Maker* (1924), *The Deepening Stream* (1930), and *Seasoned Timber* (1939). Published in 1953, *Vermont Tradition: The Biography of an Outlook on Life* is considered her best nonfiction work.

MARY ELEANOR WILKINS FREEMAN. 1852–1930.   A native of New England, Freeman moved to New Jersey after her marriage to Dr. Charles M. Freeman in 1902. Her most memorable tales record the life she observed in Massachusetts and Vermont. A short story writer as well as a novelist, she is best known for her collection *The New England Nun and Other Stories* (1891) and her novel *Pembroke* (1894). She also wrote children's stories, poems, and a play about the Salem witch trials, *Giles Corey, Yeoman* (1893).

SUSAN GLASPELL. 1876–1948.   A playwright and novelist, Glaspell, along with her husband George Cook, founded the Provincetown Players to provide an alternative to the commercialism of Broadway. They encouraged new playwrights, like Eugene O'Neill, and produced material that challenged the popular theater of the day. Her own plays and novels celebrated women who violated the norms of society. Her play *Alison's House* (1930) won the Pulitzer Prize for its fictionalized account of the life of Emily Dickinson.

ELIZA CALVERT HALL. Pseudonym for Eliza Caroline (Calvert) Obenchain. 1856–1935. She was an author and suffragist who published poems, stories, and essays about her native western Kentucky which appeared in many popular magazines before the First World War.

MARIETTA HOLLEY. 1836–1926. Known as "Samantha Allen" and "Josiah Allen's Wife," Holley was a successful humorist from upstate New York who used her stories and essays to advocate temperance and women's suffrage. Her Samantha series includes *Samantha at the Centennial* (1877), *Samantha at Saratoga* (1887), and *Samantha at the World's Fair* (1893). In 1914, she published *Josiah Allen on Women's Rights*.

REBECCA COX JACKSON. 1795–1871. Born of free Black parents in Philadelphia, Rebecca Cox lived with her brother until her marriage to Samuel Jackson. All three were deeply involved in the Bethel African Methodist Episcopal Church. She earned her living as a dressmaker. After a spiritual conversion in 1830, as she later described it, she learned to read and write but was denied any place of power in the male-controlled churches. Leaving her husband, she joined the Shaker community at Watervliet, New York, along with a close woman companion, Rebecca Perot. She established a Shaker settlement in Philadelphia in the 1870s which survived until 1908.

PAULETTE JILES. 1943–. Born in the Missouri Ozarks, Jiles migrated to Canada in 1969. She has written award-winning poetry, experimental fiction, and radio programs. She describes herself as a "Third Force Feminist," trusting to "quiet feminism" instead of theoretical and political positioning to achieve her goals. Her poetry includes *Waterloo Express* (1973); *Celestial Navigation* (1984), which won three major Canadian awards; and *The Jesse James Poems* (1988).

JANE WILSON JOYCE. 1947–. A Classics teacher at Centre College in Danville, Kentucky, Joyce has translated Lucan's *Pharsalia* and recently published *Beyond the Blue Mountains*, a long narrative poem.

BOBBIE ANN MASON. 1940–.   Born near Mayfield, Kentucky, Mason now lives in Pennsylvania. Her first collection of stories, *Shiloh, and Other Stories* (1982), and her novel *In Country* (1985) are among her best known works, capturing the tension as rural Kentucky undergoes urbanization. *Spence + Lila* (1988) is a story of a woman's fight with breast cancer and *Love Life* (1989) continues her exploration of a culture experiencing the confusing effects of shopping malls, MTV, and mass media.

ALICE MACGOWAN.   No biographical record remains for this writer, whose story was published in the magazine *Ladies World* in 1909.

SHARYN MCCRUMB. 1948–.   An award-winning Appalachian writer, McCrumb lives in Virginia and teaches at Virginia Tech. Her works include *If Ever I Return, Pretty Peggy-O* (1990), *Bimbos of the Death Sun* (1988), and many others. She has won both the Edgar and the Agatha awards for her satirical mystery fiction and is becoming well-known for her serious and literary novels as well.

ROBIN MORGAN. 1941–.   Born in Florida, Morgan grew up in Mount Vernon, New York. Since the publication of her highly influential book *Sisterhood is Powerful: An Anthology of Writings from the Women's Liberation Movement* in 1970, Morgan has continued to write poetry and pursue feminist goals.

JOYCE CAROL OATES. 1938–.   A major American literary figure, Oates is known for her short stories, novels, poems, and nonfiction. A prolific writer, she has produced at least one volume a year since 1965 and has won numerous awards, including the National Book Award and the O'Henry Award. Her fiction incorporates elements of the gothic romance to examine American violence and employs historical and political themes as well. Her works include *them* (1969), *Where Are You Going, Where Have You Been?* (1974), *Bellefleur* (1980), and *Bloodsmoor Romance* (1983), which focus on women's roles. Her more recent titles are *On Boxing* (1987), *American Appetites* (1989), and *Black Water* (1992).

MARGE PIERCY. 1936–.   A poet, novelist, and essayist, Piercy has published extensively since the 1960s, when her political commitment to the anti-Vietnam movement and the women's movement informed her work. Of further interest is *Parti Colored Blocks for a Quilt* (1982).

ADRIENNE RICH. 1929–.   Born in Baltimore, Maryland, Rich was educated at Radcliffe College and later taught at The City College of New
York and Douglass College. Married for seventeen years, she left her
husband in 1970 to redefine herself and her work as lesbian feminist.
Among the best known and most influential of modern feminist poets,
her works include *A Change of World* (1951), *Diving Into the Wreck*
(1973), *The Dream of a Common Language* (1978), and *A Wild Patience
Has Taken Me This Far* (1981).

MARI [SUSETTE] SANDOZ. 1901–1966.   A novelist and historical writer
born in Nebraska of Swiss emigrant parents, Sandoz is best know for her
nonfiction narrative about Native Americans including *Crazy Horse*
(1942) and *Cheyenne Autumn* (1953). She wrote on Sioux history in *The
Battle of Little Bighorn* (1966) and *A Pictographic History of the Oglala
Sioux* (1967). Her fiction includes *Slogum House* (1937), *Capital City*
(1939), and *Miss Morissa* (1955).

JULIA PETERKIN. 1880–1961.   A novelist and short story writer from South
Carolina, Peterkin became a specialist in the language of the Gullahs from
her home state and further south. *Scarlet Sister Mary* (1928), for which she
won the Pulitzer Prize, was dramatized with an all-white cast headed by
Ethel Barrymore, who performed in blackface. Her other works include
Green Thursday (1924); *Bright Skin* (1932); *Roll, Jordan, Roll* (1933), a
collection of photographs for which she wrote the text; and *Plantation
Christmas* (1934).

HARRIET BEECHER STOWE. 1811–1896.   A writer of novels, stories, domestic manuals, and reform tracts, Stowe came from a Calvinist background
and became an active abolitionist with her best-selling novel *Uncle Tom's
Cabin* (1851–52). Her later works include *The Pearl of Orr's Island* (1862),
Oldtown Folks (1868), *Poganuc People* (1878), and *Pink and White Tyranny*
(1871).

ALICE WALKER. 1944–.   Born in Georgia and living today in California,
Walker is best known for her novel *The Color Purple* (1982), but she is also
a poet, essayist, short story writer, and editor. Active in the Civil Rights
Movement, Walker is also famous for her ground-breaking work as a black
feminist literary critic. Her works include the novels *Meridian* (1976) and

The Temple of My Familiar (1989), and *In Search of Our Mothers' Gardens* (1983), her collection of womanist prose that includes the title piece in which she refers to the Harriet Powers gospel quilt.

Patricia Wendorf. 1928–.   A contemporary British writer, Wendorf based her novel *Double Wedding Ring* on the history of her own family's migration from Somerset to the United States in the nineteenth century.

Otto Whitney. 1955–.   A graduate of the University of California at Irvine, Whitney currently lives in San Francisco. *How To Make an American Quilt* is her first novel.

Sources and
Permissions

Annette [pseud. for Harriet Farley or Rebecca C. Thomson]. "The Patchwork Quilt." *The Lowell Offering* 5 (1845): 201-3.

Anonymous. *Aunt Jerusha's Quilting Party*. Boston: Walter H. Baker Company, 1901.

Arthur, T.S. "The Quilting Party." *Godey's Lady's Book*, September 1849, p. 10.

Canfield, Dorothy. "The Bedquilt." From Dorothy Canfield Fisher, *Hillsboro People*, New York: Henry Holt and Company, 1927. Reprinted in *A Harvest of Stories from Half a Century of Writing*. New York: Harcourt, Brace, and World, 1947.

Freeman, Mary Eleanor Wilkins. "An Honest Soul." From *A Humble Romance and Other Stories*. New York: Harper, 1885.

———. "A Quilting Bee in Our Village." From *The People of Our Neighborhood*. New York: Doubleday, 1898.

Glaspell, Susan. *Trifles*. Copyright © 1916 by Susan Glaspell. Copyright © renewed 1951 by Walter H. Baker Company. This edition is published by arrangement with Baker's Plays, 100 Chauncy Street, Boston, Massachusetts 02111.

Hall, Eliza Calvert [pseud. for Eliza Caroline Obenchain]. *Aunt Jane of Kentucky*. 1898. Reprint: Boston: Little, Brown, 1908.

Holley, Marietta. "Miss Jones' Quilting." From *Miss Jones' Quilting by Josiah Allen's Wife, And Other Stories*. New York: Butler Brothers, 1887.

Jackson, Rebecca Cox. "The Dream of Washing Quilts" [1848]. From *Gifts of Power: The Writings of Rebecca Jackson (1795-1871), Black Visionary, Shaker Eldress*, ed. Jean McMahon Humez. Amherst: University of Massachusetts Press, 1981.

Jiles, Paulette. "My Grandmother's Quilt." From *Song to the Rising Sun: A Collection*. Copyright © 1989. Reprinted by permission of Polestar Book Publishers, Winlaw, British Columbia.

Joyce, Jane Wilson. "Whitework, or Bride's Quilt," "Bible Quilt, circa 1900," and "Rose of Sharon." From *The Quilt Poems*, New Market, Tennessee: Mill

Springs Press, 1984. Reprinted from *Quilt Pieces* by permission of Gnomon Press, Frankfort, Kentucky.

Mason, Bobbie Ann. "Love Life." From *Love Life*. Copyright © 1988 by Bobbie Ann Mason. Reprinted by permission of HarperCollins Publishers.

MacGowan, Alice. "Gospel Quilt." *Ladies' World*, September 1909.

McCrumb, Sharyn. Excerpt from *The Hangman's Beautiful Daughter*. Copyright © 1992 by Sharyn McCrumb. Reprinted by permission of Charles Scribner's Sons, an imprint of Macmillan Publishing Company.

Morgan, Robin. "Quilts." From *Upstairs in the Garden: Poems Selected and New, 1968-1988*. Copyright © 1990 by Robin Morgan. Reprinted by permission of W.W. Norton & Company, Inc.

Oates, Joyce Carol. "Celestial Timepiece." From *Invisible Woman: New and Selected Poems, 1970-1982*. Ottawa: Ontario Review Press, 1982. Reprinted by permission of Joyce Carol Oates.

Page, Katherine Hall. Excerpt from *The Body in the Kelp*. Copyright © 1990 by Katherine Hall Page. Reprinted by permission of St. Martin's Press, Inc., New York, NY.

Peterkin, Julia. Excerpt from *Black April*. Copyright © 1927 by Macmillan Publishing Company. Reprinted by permission of Macmillan Publishing Company.

Piercy, Marge. "Looking at Quilts." From *Circles on the Water*. Copyright © 1982 by Marge Piercy. Reprinted by permission of Alfred A. Knopf, Inc.

Rich, Adrienne. Excerpt from "Natural Resources." Reprinted from *The Fact of a Doorframe: Poems Selected and New, 1950-1984*. Copyright © 1984 by Adrienne Rich. Reprinted by permission of W.W. Norton & Company, Inc.

Sandoz, Mari. "Pieces of a Quilt." From *Hostiles and Friendlies*. Copyright © 1932 by Mari Sandoz. Reprint: Lincoln: University of Nebraska Press, 1959. Reprinted by permission of McIntosh and Otis, Inc.

Stowe, Harriet Beecher. *The Minister's Wooing*. 1859. Reprint: Hartford: Stowe-Day Foundation, 1990.

Walker, Alice. "Everyday Use." From *In Love and Trouble: Stories of Black Women*. Copyright © 1973 by Alice Walker. Reprinted by permission of Harcourt Brace and Company.

Wendorf, Patricia. Excerpt from *Double Wedding Ring*. Copyright © 1989 by Patricia Wendorf. Reprinted by permission of Hamish Hamilton, Ltd.

Whitney, Otto. Excerpt from *How to Make an American Quilt*. Copyright © 1991 by Otto Whitney. Reprinted by permission of Villard Books, a division of Random House, Inc.

Suggestions for Further Reading

Bell-Scott, Patricia, et al. *Double Stitch: Black Women Write about Mothers and Daughters*. New York: HarperCollins, 1991.

Callahan, Nancy. *The Freedom Quilting Bee*. Tuscaloosa: Univ. of Alabama Press, 1987.

Cooper, Patricia, and Norma Bradley Allen. *The Quilters: Women and Domestic Art*. New York: Doubleday, 1987.

Cozart, Dorothy. "Women and Their Quilts as Portrayed by Some American Authors." *Uncoverings* 2 (1981): 19-33.

Dublin, Thomas. *Women at Work: The Transformation of Work and Community in Lowell, Massachusetts, 1826-1860*. New York: Columbia Univ. Press, 1979.

Ferrero, Pat, et al. *Hearts and Hands: The Influence of Women and Quilts on American Society*. San Francisco: Quilt Digest Press, 1987.

A one-hour companion film, "Hearts and Hands," produced and directed by Pat Ferrero, is available from Ferrero Films, 371 Twenty-ninth Street, San Francisco, CA 94131.

Hedges, Elaine. "The Needle or the Pen: The Literary Rediscovery of Women's Textile Work." In *Tradition and the Talents of Women*, ed. Florence Howe. Urbana: Univ. of Illinois Press, 1991.

Holstein, Jonathan, and John Finley. *Kentucky Quilts, 1800-1900*. Louisville: Kentucky Quilt Project, 1982.

Hyde, Elisabeth. *Her Native Colors*. New York: Dell, 1986.

Lipsett, Linda Otto. *Pieced from Ellen's Quilt: Ellen Spaulding Reed's Letters and Story*. Dayton, Ohio: Halstead and Meadows, 1991.

Mainardi, Patricia. *Quilts: The Great American Art*. San Pedro, California: Miles and Weir, 1978.

Roach, Susan. "The Kinship Quilt: An Ethnographic Semiotic Analysis of a Quilting Bee." In *Women's Folklore, Women's Culture*, ed. Rosan A. Jordan and Susan J. Kalcik. Philadelphia: Univ. of Pennsylvania Press, 1985.

Schilmoeller, Kathryn J. "The Role of Quilts in Children's Literature." *Uncoverings* 6 (1985): 71-84. Contains an excellent bibliography.

Showalter, Elaine. *Sister's Choice: Tradition and Change in American Women's Writing*. Oxford: Clarendon Press, 1991.

Taylor, Phoebe Atwood. *The Crimson Patch*. 1936. Reprint. Woodstock, Vermont: Foul Play Press/Countryman Press, 1986.